The **Palace** of the **Moon**

Janet Kellough

To Gill
Best Wishes

The Palace of the Moon

First published 2004
This edition published 2017

ISBN 978-0-9937200-2-4 (pbk) 978-0-9937200-3-1 (epub)

www.janetkellough.com

CHAPTER ONE

As usual, Cara heard Vera before she saw her. She craned past the row of people who had lined up to pay their last respects, but poor Vera always did tend to disappear in a crowd and Cara accepted the condolences of half a dozen people she didn't know before the diminutive figure finally toddled into view. Today her chatter came as a relief. Vera Dunlop did not tiptoe around the issue of death; she looked it straight in the eye and talked it into surrender.

"Your mother looks so natural", she said, "just like she's gone to sleep for a little while. I'm glad they put her in that dress, I remember when she bought it. It was last year, in September, when they had that sale on at Grayson's. Green always was her colour, you know. I said to her, 'Edna', I says, ' you might better buy that dress right now. You won't do better."

Cara had been a little dismayed when she was told that her mother had left instructions for an open casket and an afternoon of visitation. One by one the friends, relatives and neighbours lined up to take a last look, to say farewell to Edna Collins, Edna Charles that was. They all shook Cara's hand or kissed her cheek. Then they filed past the coffin, commenting, reminiscing.

"She always was such a looker, such a looker", Vera said, shaking her head. "Beautiful hair, beautiful eyes. My, my, the stories I could tell you. We were best friends we were, when we were young girls. And then again later. I don't know what we'd have done without each other. I don't know what I'm going to do without her now, when you get right down to it."

Cara's mother had found the lump under her arm while getting dressed a year earlier. She had not done anything about it for too long, and by the time she had, the cancer had spread too far. Vera sat with Cara while they waited for the end, watching as Edna's life slipped away, listening while the hospital's shiny machines measured out her final days with clocklike pings and beeps. She had been grateful for Vera's chatter then as well, and she had taken comfort in her presence, as, apparently, had her mother. Cara could think of no friend from her own childhood who would be willing or wanted at her deathbed.

She had left Mickey with Cass. There were only a couple of weeks of school left and she hadn't known how long she would be home. Odd that she still thought of it as "home" when she had lived in the city for so many years, but home it still was, although time had made many changes. Gone were the stately, overhanging maples she remembered along the approach from the west. The road had long ago been widened into four lanes, funnelling summer traffic into a congestion of supermarkets, mini-malls and take-it-out, eat-it-in-your-car fast food places. Lately she had been surprised by the number of studios, art galleries and antique stores that had opened, supported, she supposed by the tourists. Drawn by the rolling banks of sand that fringed the western shore of the island, they left hard currency in exchange for their sunburns and poison ivy; cold cash and brittle plastic traded for one-of-a-kind crafts and pale watercolours. Summer on the island was a bedlam of traffic jams and confusion; city drivers unfamiliar with country ways, bikini-clad girls parading down Main Street drawing scorn and outrage, parks overrun with escapees from high-rise hells.

In the fall the island would settle itself. Then it seemed to shudder and draw its rocky shores in around its central plateau, cocooning the tiny lakes and stony pastures. Slowly the chocolate bar wrappers and pop cans would be gathered up from along the roadsides, the trailer parks and campsites would close for the season and the slow and rhythmic beat of card parties and community dinners would coax the locals out of summer hiding.

Mickey adored the island, but under the circumstances it hadn't seemed appropriate to bring him. She was sure the funeral would only have confused him and there were too many details to sort out, arrangements, decisions, preparations. No time to take a seven year old to the beach, no time to drive the narrow, winding back roads and lanes, no time to deal with his questions. This way explanations could be kept brief, at arm's length, and he was spared the untidy and embarrassing details of his grandmother's final days.

Her mother's friends had rallied round during her illness; Mrs. Rensall, who had always envied her mother's soft voice, sat at Edna's bedside and read to her three afternoons a week. Mrs. Jackson, who wished she could look as well in her clothes, came once a week with nail files and polish and carefully manicured Edna's yellow and misshapen nails. Mrs. Fletcher sent over cupcakes and tarts to tempt the appetite of the invalid; never mind that Edna's meals now consisted of glucose and saline injected drop by drop into her veins. Cara gave the pastries to the nurses, or took them down the hall to other patients. There was no point in taking them home. The neighbourhood ladies, anxious to help and sure that food was the best comfort of all, left casseroles and pies on her doorstep every day. Most of these went into the freezer.

Dear, sweet Rhonda Davis, now Rhonda White, whose mother had been the Collins' housekeeper for so many years, came to the hospital every evening and helped with bathing and dressing, carefully brushing what was left of Edna's lustrous hair and arranging it in as stylish a manner as she could.

"Mrs. Len was always so fussy about her looks, "Rhonda explained. "I can't bear the thought of her not looking as good as she could."

At the funeral these same friends and neighbours filled the room, smelling of talcum powder and peppermints, patting her arm and recalling some small incident in which her mother had figured largely. The memories would feed each other, one anecdote jumpstarting another, the details of long-forgotten stories filled in, pieces added and subtracted until a distilled and acceptable consensus was reached.

Cara was past responding in any meaningful way to them, numb, not from grief, but from the exhausting ritual of saying goodbye to the dead. Her feet hurt and her back ached from standing so long. She had long since confused names, transposed faces and forgotten introductions, relying on what she hoped was a wan smile and a murmur of thanks.

Maybe that's what it's all about, she thought. Maybe that's why we have these barbaric rites. You get so brain dead from the repetition that you can't feel anything. But no, she wasn't brain dead. Heart dead maybe. Feeling nothing. No mourning, no grief. Not even later when the minister intoned the words of comfort to the congregation. He was young, and new to the community and confessed quite frankly that he had difficulty placing Edna Collins. No surprise, her mother hadn't been much of a churchgoer in spite of her upbringing. The minister had relied on scripture readings and a tinny recording of Amazing Grace to complete the service. Cara barely heard his words. She was distracted by the smell of furniture polish, the competing fragrances of assorted bouquets of flowers, and the peculiar and unmistakeable smell of people crowded together in a room.

They crowded at the graveside, too, huddling together in spite of the warm June sunshine, as if the proximity of life could protect them from death. Too young, they thought. Gone so fast. Could have been one of us. Didn't hang on tight enough, or long enough. So sad. Ashes to ashes, intoned the minister, dust to dust. Cara would liked to have had orange daylilies to throw on top of the coffin, but it was not yet their time. Instead, she found a clump of dark purple iris in the back corner of the garden, a relic of some long-ago planting. Her mother had always preferred the old-fashioned colours, but today they looked forlorn against the pale oak of the casket as it was lowered into the ground.

Afterwards, the mourners had nearly all returned to the house where Cara served them coffee, tea and sherry along with the cakes and cookies and squares she had taken out of the freezer to thaw. Bless them, she thought, they're eating their own food. None of them seemed to notice, or at least they were too polite to comment if they did.

Vera took over as hostess. She poured innumerable cups of tea and passed innumerable plates of desserts, commenting and conversing the whole time.

"Try these dear," she would say. "They're Hannah's famous walnut-date squares. Aren't they scrumptious? Let me get you another cup of tea. Or would you prefer coffee? I can never drink coffee this late in the afternoon, I'd be up all night and grumpy with poor Mac all day tomorrow. Cream? Sugar? Just let me go fill up that tray of tarts..."

They all came up to speak to Cara, but she had little to say to any of them. She had been gone too long, and had not come back often enough to be current with their lives. There were too many gaps in her knowledge, and she felt awkward about asking them to fill in the details they thought she already knew. Her Uncle Jack and Aunt Margaret hovered nearby, trying to ease things for her, but even they were strangers. She was grateful for their concern, but she realized it was Vera, really, who managed to make everyone feel welcome.

"Why, this is a party!" Cara thought to herself as the level of noise in the living room rose. Although she had no clear idea who most of these people were, it was evident that they all knew each other. They stood in little clumps, balancing tea cups and sandwiches, conducting business, telling jokes and exchanging pleasantries. In an odd way she was comforted by the hubbub. So different from her father's unexpected funeral, when she had found no solace in the throngs of people who had come to pay their respects. She had been young, then, and shocked at how easily the etiquette of death had dictated the form of her mourning.

Mac and Vera stayed afterwards, along with Jack and Margaret, to help clean up. Mac cleared the living room of dirty dishes while Cara and Vera packed the leftover food to return to the freezer. Margaret washed sinkful after sinkful of teacups while Jack dried. He was awkward and Cara joked with him."I can see Aunt Margaret's not a liberated woman," she said. "You obviously have never been near a tea towel before in your life."

"Now, that's the truth," Margaret smiled. "He's pretty spoiled."

"Aw, but I've been spoiled by the best," he said, smiling at his wife. Cara felt a twitch of envy. Jack and Margaret had been married for decades, and still had eyes only for each other.

While they worked Vera nattered on about the funeral, about who had sent which flowers, who hadn't bothered to wear a hat to the service. Cara found herself, at last, longing for silence.

They must have understood this, or else it showed in her face, because they began their motions to leave after the last teacup was washed and put away. Just as she was at the door Vera turned to Cara, "Now, if you need anything, you call me. That's what we're here for, me and Mac, to help you out."

Mac nodded his agreement. And then Vera had put her arms around Cara's shoulders, which was about as high as she could reach, and hugged.

Cara hugged back, suddenly fierce. How could she ever have managed without this small woman?

The next day Cara stood on the sidewalk looking at the old house with an appraising eye. It had once been spruce and neat, with a new coat of paint every other year. Now the paint was peeling and the shutters hung crookedly. Her mother's garden was overgrown; the sword-like foliage of the daylilies had spread everywhere, and where the lilies had failed to gain a hold, mint and weeds opportunistically filled in.

Her mother's lawyer had advised her to get an estimate on the value of the house and so she had called the first realtor she found in the phone book. She was surprised, and a little startled when the agent turned out to be Peter Melbourne. She had gone to high school with Peter. She thought he had settled into babying his father's herd of Holsteins long since.

"Not much money in farming anymore", he said by way of explanation. "My oldest boy can handle most of the chores, so I do this on the side." They walked around the house together, Peter making ticks against a list on his clipboard. "If you'll show me where the basement is, I'll have a look at the furnace and the electrical service." They climbed the steps to the front door, the company door.

She showed Peter the door to the basement, feeling for the light switch which was just a little too far inside , so that she had to lean out over the steps to reach it.

"The furnace is pretty old, a typical energy hog from the fifties," he shouted up at her. "That will bring the price down some."

He emerged from the basement and walked quickly through the house. "The kitchen's not too bad," he said when they had completed their tour, "although someone will want to gut it and put in oak cupboards and new appliances. It was state of the art forty years ago, but it's pretty dated now. The house needs a new roof and a paint job, but it's sound." Cara nodded. He wasn't telling her anything she didn't already know.

He fiddled with his appraisal sheet. "Unfortunately, most people don't want a house this big. Too hard to heat. A lot of people are moving down from the city and using places like this for bed and breakfast, though. The finished coach house is an asset, of course. I'd put the house at $175,000. You could sell the coach house separately I suppose, and that could be as much as another $50,000. The lot's worth at least half that."

"Okay," Cara said. "Will you let the lawyer know?" He nodded and she walked him back down the steps and to his car. She would probably sell everything. She had no use for it, except as a sort of summer home maybe, but how could she afford that? On the other hand, she wondered how it would feel to see strangers in the house, some other little girl occupying the sunny front bedroom that had always been hers. Would they cut down the old trees in the back yard, put in a swimming pool, paint the trim a different colour, do things that would change it irrevocably from her home to some forbidden and unfamiliar house that could be viewed forevermore only from the curbside?

She tried to look at the property from the viewpoint of a prospective buyer. The ivy needed to be cut back. She could certainly do that. A coat of paint on the steps was well within her capability. She wandered through the house, making mental note of a hundred small things that needed doing. She supposed she should start going through closets and drawers cleaning out her mother's personal items first. She should have started it long ago, she knew, they had all known that Edna was dying, but it would have seemed too much like hurrying it along to start packing before she had actually gone.

She climbed the stairs, counting the steps in twos, her talisman against bad luck since she was five years old. The smaller bedrooms at the back were neat, untouched, as they had been since Bernice Davis, defeated by arthritis, had moved to a nursing home on the outskirts of town. Cara's old bedroom was at the front, and across the hall from it, her mother's room. It had not been tidied since her final departure. The bed was unmade, her hairbrushes lying on the floor. Bernice would have been appalled at the disorder, but Cara suspected her mother wouldn't have cared.

I must pick out something of mother's to give to Vera, she thought, something personal to remember her by. Her silver hairbrushes maybe, or was that too intimate an item, with dead hairs still stuck in the bristles? She opened a dresser drawer of neatly stacked sweaters, mothballed and wrapped in plastic. Christmas and birthday presents, rarely used, but carefully packed away. She pulled two from the drawer and shook them out of the plastic. Too small, not her style anyway, they'd have to go the used clothing shop or the church rummage sale. She emptied the drawer, intending to go to the basement later to find a box for them. The next drawer she opened contained underwear; too personal for her to deal with just yet. Maybe the closet would be easier. It was filled with dresses and hat boxes. Cara was surprised. Her mother always wore a hat on the few occasions she went to church, she had never got out of the habit, but she never wore one at any other time. She had been too vain about her hair, her glorious thick hair, with its own waves and curls. She'd never cover it up with a hat if she didn't have to. What do people do with hats nowadays anyway, she wondered, other than toques and woolly hats for winter. She couldn't give Vera a hat.

"I was your mother's best friend, you know," Vera had said, patting her hand as they sat in the pastel hospital room.

"I know. She always spoke of you with great affection."

"We weren't always you know. At one time we were at odds. But we got over it." She sighed. "I'll miss her so much. We're all going now."

This was an old story, this tale of some conflict between the two. Cara had never quite understood, they would never make it clear what they had argued over, but went off into gales of laughter whenever it was mentioned. She tried to think of her mother the way other people must have seen her. Beautiful hair, she had always had beautiful hair, and lovely eyes. She guessed that at one time she must have had an attractive figure, but passing years had blurred the memory of this, and all she could recall now was a slight stoop and the sag of maturity.

She tried to pull down the top box from the closet shelf, but it was too heavy for her to balance, and three other boxes toppled down with it, their contents spilling onto the carpeted floor. Two nondescript brown hats and a parcel of old letters and postcards. She picked one up. It was from Niagara Falls, showing the inevitable Maid of the Mist in a daring flirt with the cascade of water and spray at the bottom of Horseshoe Falls. She flipped it over to read,

"You're still the best model I ever had. Meet me at the
Palace of the Moon at 9 on Thursday. I'll wait for an hour.
Love, Sacha. XXX."

She had no idea who Sacha was or what the message meant. She had never heard her mother speak of anyone called Sacha. And why was he sending her mother his love? Suddenly the room was too full of Edna's presence; her scent lingered on the clothing in the closet, Cara imagined that her imprint was still on the rumpled sheets of the bed. She went out of the room and closed the door.

I'll start in the attic, she thought. Start at the top and work my way down. Maybe by the time I get to mother's room, I'll be able to deal with it.

Access to the attic was by a steep and narrow set of stairs leading from the hall closet. She left the door open to let some fresh air up; the attic was stuffy and surprisingly hot. Her mother's outmoded dresses hung from a rack near the top of the stairs. Cara had played dress-up in this attic when she was a little girl, donning elegant hats and high heels while she pretended to be a movie star, or a secretary or a wife. These had been mostly solitary games, except for Mud, who never minded when she dressed him up too. His wild hazel eyes and fluffy ginger eyebrows would peer out at her from under a toque or baby hat, trusting, but slightly puzzled. He never knew what the joke was, only that he was part of it, and if Cara was playing it, then everything was all right.

She needed boxes and bags to pack all this stuff in. She made a mental note to check with the grocery stores. Uncle Jack might have something down at the store, too, although the boxes would be too big, refrigerator and sofa size.

The big box of Christmas decorations sat over to the left. They're mine, now, I guess, Cara thought, but what am I going to do with them? At home they had always had a gigantic spruce that required myriad strings of lights and many brightly-coloured ornaments. The tree she and Mickey had was artificial and packed away neatly in a box in her sole closet.

A rack by the window held plastic-wrapped suits and jackets. They had been her father's, elegant grey pinstripes and comfortable looking tweeds. Her father had always known how to dress well, she reflected, had always worn his clothes as though they were skin. She pulled a jacket off the rack and tried it on. It was a near fit; she was almost as tall as her father had been. The jacket was old, probably from the fifties judging by the style, with narrow lapels and patches on the elbows. The sleeves were a little too long. She rolled them up and grabbed a felt fedora from the rack, perching it forward on her head, over her eyes. Very funky. She giggled. There was a full-length mirror over in the corner, near the window and she stood in front of it, turning this way and that, trying the hat at various angles.

"You dirty rat." She grimaced into the mirror. James Cagney. Or was it Edward G. Robinson? Somebody from the old movies. She thrust her hands into the jacket pockets. There was a hole in one, the right, where her father had always thrown loose change, punishing the fabric until it gave way. She pulled out the pocket lining, to see how big the hole was. There was something underneath, stuck between the jacket and the lining. A key, on the end of a small keychain with a rose on it. It looked like a door key to Cara, but for what door she had no idea. An extra key for the house? An old key from the boat? Shrugging, she shoved it into her own pocket. There was a collection of unidentified keys in one of the kitchen drawers, along with bits of string and garbage bag ties. She supposed she should try all these keys in the house locks before she threw them away.

She needed boxes. You'd think there would be boxes in an attic. Over in the far corner, near the front of the house where the light from the naked bulb barely reached, there was a stack of them. I just hope they aren't full of stuff, she thought, but they were heavy and here the roof sloped at an odd angle, making it difficult for her to manoeuvre. She tried to pull them away from the corner, out to the centre of the floor, but the cardboard had weakened with age and moisture and the flaps pulled away in her hands. She had to stoop and carry them out, one by one. "Glass bottles" she read on the side of one of them. Canning jars, left over from the days when Bernice preserved everything she could lay her hands on, proudly stacking jar after jar and bottle after bottle of peaches, plums, strawberries, raspberries and pears, awash in sticky syrup, awaiting reappearance in pies and pastries in the dead of winter. These should have been put in the cellar, she thought. Why are they up here? She pulled them over closer to the stairs, so they would be easier to take down later. She'd give them to Rhonda.

There was something in behind the boxes, too, a stretched canvas with its face to the wall. It was covered in dirt, tethered to the slope of the ceiling with thick ropes of grimy cobwebs. Cara pulled it to the centre of the room, sneezing from the dust. She propped it against the boxes of bottles, under the electric light. Whatever it was, it was both unfinished and unframed. She could see the outline of a figure, but it was rudimentary and poorly drawn, the proportions off and the perspective wrong. Green paint had been splashed across the bottom, but she was at a loss as to what it was supposed to be.

She tried to remember if her mother had ever painted, and wondered if this represented an early attempt in oils gone sadly awry, but as far as she knew she was the only artist in the family. Her mother had been a reader and a gardener. Her father had always had a wonderful eye and sense of colour and proportion, but he would have found painting far too passive and inactive a pastime. Besides, she was sure that even his beginning efforts would have been better than this.

Shrugging, she put it over by the stairs. First item in what promised to be a gigantic trash heap. For crying out loud, she thought, did my mother never throw anything away?

CHAPTER TWO

Vera stood impatiently in the park. Damn him, damn him, damn him, she thought. He was already fifteen minutes late and she had ruined her last pair of good stockings climbing out of her bedroom window and across the porch roof. She felt vulnerable and exposed, even though she tried to stay in the shadows of the looming maple trees. It was such a small town, surely someone who knew her would drive by at any moment and see her. There would be comments, probably tomorrow at church, and her mother would smile politely and nod, saving her wrath and questions for when they got home. She shivered. After a day of oppressive heat, the breeze was finally turning cool. She must remember to tell Len not to call her house; usually she was the one who ran and answered the phone, but there was always the chance that her mother might get there first.

Finally she heard the purr of a heavy car and he pulled to a stop in front of her, a bottle of rye cradled in his lap and two strangers in the back seat.

"Vera, baby." He hauled her into the passenger seat and kissed her, then waved his hand at the pair in the back. "This is Francine and Joe. Francine and Joe, this is Vera."

The tough-looking blonde nodded at her. Joe grunted and held up his flask in a wordless salute.

"I thought we were going to be alone tonight, Len." Vera was peevish from the long wait, and she didn't like the looks of Francine, or Joe either.

"We are, baby, we are. We're just giving these guys a ride out, okay?" He sped off, spraying gravel behind him. Vera grabbed the door handle as they careened around a corner and roared along Lake Street.

She tensed. "Are we going Ridge Road?" she asked.

"Yeah, it's a nice drive." Len looked over at her and grinned, a lazy lopsided grin. "It's the scenic route."

Ridge Road was a winding, gravelled byway that snaked along the top of a sandy ridge, full of tortuous blind corners. It made her nervous at the best of times. This evening was not starting out well at all, she thought, not the romantic pas de deux she had imagined when Len had said he was taking her dancing at The Palace of the Moon. She had never been there, it had the reputation of being a racy dancehall, her mother would never have agreed to let her go. She figured, from the name, that it should be very elegant.

Len took the turn onto the Ridge at fifty. Vera screamed.

Len frowned. "Will you relax?"

"I can't when you go so fast. It scares me."

"Don't worry. I've got it under control ." He reached over and stroked her hair. "Can't you move a little closer?"

Vera didn't really want to let go of the door handle, but she gulped and scooched across the seat. Len drove with one arm around her, nuzzling her neck, one eye on the road.

"That's better."

"Why were you so late tonight?" she asked. "I was waiting in the park a long time before you got there."

"We had to pick Francine up. She wasn't quite ready, so we hung around for a while."

Vera was annoyed. She was pretty sure they wouldn't have bothered waiting for her if she hadn't been at the park at the agreed time. Len took another corner too fast, and she grabbed his arm. He chose to misinterpret her clutch and moved his hand from her shoulder to her knee. A horn sounded behind them.

"All right, there's Bob!" He returned his attention to the car. "Hang on guys." He downshifted and stomped on the gas.

"Len!" Vera yelled, "Stop! What are you doing?" She retreated across the seat to the comfort of the door handle.

"Just having a little competition. Don't worry, I can take him."

Francine laughed in the back seat, "Go, Len, go."

Len laughed too and swigged on his rye, just as they headed into one of the blind corners.

"Here hang on to this." He threw the bottle at Vera and hit the horn, honking insistently as they rounded the corner on two wheels. She made a grab for it and managed to catch it, but not before a lot of rye whiskey slopped over the top and down the front of her dress.

She was very scared. "What are you doing?" she shouted at Len. "You're going to get us killed, or arrested or something and you've got rye all over my dress! And will you slow down going around these corners?"

"Relax, will ya. I honked the horn. Anybody coming the other way will know enough to get off the road. Why do you think they're called horn trips?"

Vera indignantly turned to the two in the back seat, hoping for support, but they were oblivious to their peril. Francine's blouse was mostly undone, showing vast expanses of white breast in the moonlight. Joe's hand had disappeared underneath her skirt. She gulped and clutched the door handle even harder. Len braked slightly, blared the horn again and ignored the stop sign as they pulled onto the main highway. The other car pulled even with them, and the two cars raced side by side down the road. Vera closed her eyes and prayed that nothing was coming the other way. The driver kept pace with the Buick for half a mile when a pickup pulled out from a side road ahead of them. There was the sound of squealing brakes and the other car slid across the road, coming to a rest on the shoulder facing the other way.

"Well, that'll show him," said Len. He didn't slow down a bit as they belted around a hairpin turn.

Vera stared straight ahead, unwilling to look at him, or at the two in the back seat, or at the ditches and trees and fences speeding by. She would like to have asked him to turn the car around and take her home, but the ride out had been wild enough and she didn't think she could deal with the return trip so soon. The car sped past dunes now, the lovely white sand dunes where Vera and her family often came for picnics and swimming. Blown in by westerly winds and piled up against the shore, the shifting sands guarded the shoreline, a bulwark between the shallow bay and the inland lake that lay further to the east. They seemed sinister, somehow, at night.

Len screeched to a halt at the end of a level area that was full of cars.

"Pull yourself together back there, Francine," he said, "the bus just arrived." Vera slammed the car door open and stood stonily with her back turned as Francine climbed out of the car to adjust her buttons and stockings.

"Joe. Come on Joe." Francine reached inside and shook her date. "Oh damn, he's passed out already."

"What did you do to him, Francine?"

"It wasn't me, it was the rye."

"That's not what I've heard," Len sidled up to her and stroked her bottom, "I've heard you can kill a man." Francine giggled.

He grabbed Vera's arm, then pushed them both in the direction of the path. "I'll meet you two on the beach. There's a fella over there I want to talk to." He strode away before she could protest. She realized she was still holding the bottle of rye. She threw it behind a parked car, then crashed off into the bushes, leaving Francine standing alone in the sandy lot.

She couldn't see anything. The moon was nothing but a thin silver crescent, casting almost no light, and she kept snagging her dress and stockings on the thin bushes that struggled to grow in the fine white sand. She wanted to take off her shoes, but wondered about poison ivy and decided against it. The sand was treacherous, the dunes full of roots buried just below the surface, waiting to snag her feet. She was just cresting the top when her heels sank down and caught and she tumbled down the hill of sand, rolling over and over, hairpins flying. She was at the beach.

The soft sand cushioned her fall, but she lay for a moment to catch her breath, the peculiar fishy smell of the lake invading her nostrils as she gasped. The poplar trees chattered and clacked, providing a counterpoint to the steady rhythm of waves hitting the shore. Off in the distance she could hear faint strains of dance music, punctuated by the occasional burst of raucous laughter. Sitting up, she took her shoes off and wondered what she should do next. She decided she didn't care whether she found Len or not, but then she remembered that she had no way home without him.

Finally, she got up and walked towards the water, stumbling over driftwood and sliding in the sand. The moon cast strange shadows, reflecting oddly from the rippling surface of the lake. She dipped a handkerchief in the water and tried to scrub away the sandy particles that clung to the rye stain on her dress.

"Vera?"

She jumped. "Who is it?"

"Who do you think it is?" It was Len. "I told you I'd meet you on the beach."

"Go away."

"Oh come on. You're not pissed off at me, are you?"

"What do you think? You almost got us killed!"

"I did not. I had everything under control!"

"And then you took off and left me, and I couldn't see anything, and then I tripped and fell down a sand dune, and... and..." To her disgust, she started to cry, like she always did when she was really angry.

"There, there, baby, it's all right. Len's here to look after you." He took her in his arms, patting her back.

"I don't want you to look after me. You can hardly look after yourself!" She tried to pull away, but he held her, stroking her hair, rocking her gently and making soothing sounds.

She felt herself calming down, didn't particularly want to and fought it for a while, then gave in and let herself be comforted. Len, sensing his advantage, kissed her lightly, then more insistently. His hand was sneaking lower and lower when she finally pulled herself away.

"Don't. I don't want to feel like I'm just another Francine."

"What's wrong with Francine?"

"Did you see what she was letting Joe do in the back seat of the car?"

He seemed unconcerned. "She was just being friendly, that's all."

"Friendly? You call that just friendly?" She felt herself getting upset again, and walked away, towards the lake. Len moved too fast. She wasn't ready to deal with this yet, accustomed as she was to polite, well-scrubbed boys who picked her up in their fathers' cars and shyly held her hand at church dances. She had been so flattered when he had asked her to dance that night at the Rickarton. She had gone with Gerald Gorman, a nice boy who had been admonished to have her home by eleven and who politely brought her cokes between dances. She wasn't sure who Len had been there with; he seemed to spend most of the evening wandering out to the parking lot with a glass of coke and returning with it fuller than when he'd left.

She knew who he was. He had a reputation among the girls for being dangerous. She could see why, he was so good-looking. He'd asked her to dance, not once but three times. Gerald sat by grumpily, unsure how to reclaim his date. Vera knew she was a good dancer and had melted into the arms of this tall boy without a second thought. She had been even more flattered, and a little alarmed when he called her house the next day to ask her out. Gerald was soon forgotten. She knew that she wasn't the sort of girl that boys like Len usually went out with. She guessed that he thought she was. After all, there she'd been, at a dance hall, and had willingly dumped her date to dance with him.

The notion of a date with Len Collins had been exhilarating at first, but as Saturday drew near, she began to get nervous. What if he pushed the stakes too high, too fast? An older man was how she thought of him. Older men had older expectations. She hadn't told anyone about him, she didn't dare. Not even her best friend Edna.

Sighing, she walked towards the water's edge, looking out over the lake as if it held an answer for her. She was cold, the wind was blowing in a cool dampness. As she looked out over the dark water, she could see a hazy glow of light far off in the south.

Len walked up beside her. "What'd you do with the bottle, honey?" he asked.

"What?"

"What did you do with the bottle of rye?"

"It broke when you went around a corner too fast," she lied.

"Oh great," he said glumly. "Now I'll have to find some inside. Unless Francine or Joe has some more."

"Where are they anyway? Don't you think we should go and look for Francine?" She felt suddenly that there might be safety in numbers.

"Don't worry," he said. "Francine can look after herself."

"You bet Francine can look after herself," said a disembodied voice. "Hi, guys." Francine emerged from behind a dune, shoes in hand. She walked over to them.

"Where's Joe?" Vera asked, because she felt she was supposed to. She didn't really care.

"Still passed out in the car."

"Aw geez," Len said, " He didn't puke did he? I just had the upholstery cleaned."

"Should we go and check on him?" Vera asked.

Francine shrugged. "He'll be all right as soon as he comes to. We'll be able to tell. He'll start hollering." She lifted her skirt and pulled a mickey from her garter.

"Is that all you brought? A mickey?" Len was disgusted. "That's not gonna last all night."

"Well, why didn't you bring your own then?"

"I did. Vera broke it", he said. I'm gonna go see if anybody inside has any." He stomped off down the beach.

Francine sat down on a piece of driftwood, patted her hair, took a long pull on her bottle, then held it out to Vera. "Here honey, want a swig?"

"No thank you," Vera said stiffly.

"Aw come on, you haven't had anything to drink all night."

"I'm all right thanks."

"Come on. It won't hurt you any. If you're gonna keep up with Len all night, you better have a little gasoline in the tank."

"I really don't care for it, thank you."

"What's the matter?" Francine was just drunk enough to be a little belligerent. "You too good to drink with me?"

"Oh, no it's not that," Vera said hastily.

"Little Miss Goody Two Shoes is too good to drink with an old broad like Francine O'Brien, is that it?"

"No... I.... oh well...," Vera didn't want to offend her. She was after all, female, and possibly the only ally she had tonight. "All right... give it here." She took a mighty gulp and choked, spilling most of it down her already bedraggled dress.

"Hey, hey, don't waste it." Francine grabbed the bottle back.

"How can you drink that stuff? It tastes like lighter fluid."

"It's an acquired taste." She took another comfortable pull and smiled. "And I intend to acquire a lot more of it before the night is over."

Vera didn't know what to make of this woman, who drank straight gin and casually let men undo her blouse. She wasn't sure she wanted to sit on the beach with her. Anything could happen. "Let's go inside," she said hopefully.

Francine waved her away. "There's lots of time yet. The dance is only just getting started. They'll go on all night."

"Oh, I hope not!" Vera knew for sure she was in over her head now.

"What's the matter?", Francine asked, taking another swig. "Don't you like to dance?"

"Oh, it's not that." Vera fiddled with the bodice of her dress, worrying the stain that had spread across the front, " It's just that... um....I was really hoping not to be out too late tonight."

The older woman looked at her shrewdly, " Oh, I see. Mummy doesn't know we're out tonight huh?"

Vera nodded. She felt the relief of confession, as if the weight of her secret had been transferred to other shoulders, shoulders that could be counted on to rearrange the evening so that everything would be all right.

Francine grimaced. "I wondered why we had to pick you up in the park.

So, does Mummy know we're hanging around with big bad Len Collins?"

"Well... no. You'll help me, won't you?" She was certain now that such a worldly woman would realize her predicament and come to her aid.

"Help you what?"

"Help me get Len to take me home."

She snorted and Vera's certainty vanished. "Tell you what honey. Have another drink, then you won't worry about it so much."

Sighing, she took the bottle. She didn't choke quite so badly this time.

"Here we go, girls!" Len had had a successful quest for liquor and was carrying a twenty-sixer of whiskey. "We're in business."

She ran up to him. "Can we go in now Len?"

"Go in?" He looked puzzled. "The night is young. What do you want to go in for?"

"You said we were going to go dancing."

"We will, darlin', we will. Yo, Francine, want some rye?"

"I'm sticking with gin," Francine said," Until its gone, anyway. Then I'll have some rye."

"Suit yourself, but there may not be much left by the time we're finished with it."

Vera suddenly realized that the combination of liquor and adrenalin was having an unwelcome effect on her bladder. She craned around, looking for an outhouse or a sign indicating washrooms but couldn't see anything that looked promising. She couldn't go in the bushes. From the time she was a small child she had had difficulty with squatting down under a tree the way most of her friends could. Besides, she would have to struggle with stockings and a panty girdle. But she had to do something, and soon.

"Francine?"

"Yeah, hon?"

"Where's the little girls' room?" She felt as if she would burst soon.

Francine looked amused. "I don't know where the little girls go, " she said, "but us big girls go over behind that dune over there." Vera sighed and trudged off through the sand.

Francine sprawled on the driftwood and watched Len. He stood by the water until Vera was well out of sight, then sauntered over and sat down, casually slinging his arm over her shoulders.

"So, how you doing, sweetheart?"

"Go away." She removed his arm.

"What's the matter?"

"You know what the matter is."

Len groaned. "Oh God, Francine, don't pull that 'You know what the matter is' line. You know I can't handle that women's stuff."

"Women's stuff?" Francine was huffy. "Just in case you hadn't noticed, I'm a woman, so I guess you better get used my women's stuff, huh?"

Len put his arm back. "Yeah, I noticed your woman stuff all right."

"Stop it! You know damn well what I'm talking about."

Len sighed. "Vera?"

"Yeah, Vera. Len, what on earth are you doing with that baby? She's got no business being out here."

"She's not a baby. She's eighteen. She's legal."

"And still wet behind the ears. Look, her mother doesn't even know she's out tonight."

"Oh shit."

"Don't swear, there's a lady present."

Len stroked her shoulder and chuckled. "You may be a woman, Francine, but you're no lady."

"I should slap your face for that, " she said woozily.

"It's a compliment. You're too snuggly to be a lady." He pressed his advantage and stroked her breast.

"Stop it!"

"Say that again and I just might."

"Stop it," she giggled.

"Do you really mean it?" He kissed her and switched his attack to her thigh, achieving greater heights with each stroke.

Francine groaned, then pushed him away. "Dammit, Len, why did you stick me with Joe tonight if that's what you want?"

Len grinned. "You know how I feel about you Francine!"

"So what's with Miss Clinging Vine? You're always doing this to me Len. Every time there's a pretty new face around, you ignore me until they figure out what you're really all about, then you expect me to welcome you back like nothing happened."

"You know how it is, Francine. I may sample a little here and there, but I always come back to you."

"Yeah, just like a bad penny. But you're going to get yourself into trouble one of these days, you know that, don't you?"

He just grinned again and renewed his attack, slipping his hand inside her blouse and kissing her neck.

It had been very dark behind the dune and Vera was concentrating on adjusting her girdle, and not stepping on anything horrible and not getting lost, so she didn't see Len and Francine until she was about ten feet away, when the moon emerged from behind a cloud and lit their embrace. She was so stunned that momentarily she couldn't even react. When she did, her protest emerged in one loud word of outrage.

"Len!"

Len took another couple of nibbles on Francine's neck and removed his hand from inside her blouse, but kept his arm around her.

"Oh, hi, Vera."

"What are you doing?" Vera could hear her voice getting high and hysterical and wanted to stop it, but couldn't.

Len shrugged. "Nothing. Francine and I are just having a friendly drink together."

"Yeah, right. It looked pretty friendly all right."

"Well, Francine and I are old friends."

Vera was confused. She felt that she was the injured party, but Len was acting like she was being unreasonable. She stood, speechless, not knowing what she was supposed to do. This was outside her experience and there didn't seem to be any of the usual ground rules in operation. Finally, she decided to retreat.

"I'm going in." She turned and marched off in what she hoped was the general direction of the dancehall.

Len finally moved. He caught up with her and grabbed her wrist. "What's bugging you? Where are you going?"

Vera turned to him furiously. "You're supposed to be here with *me*, Len. I turn my back for five minutes and you're kissing someone else. My mother was right."

"About what?"

"She says you're nothing but a womanizer, and a playboy and... and... a *bounder*." Vera's mother was from England and sometimes used odd words.

Len looked puzzled. "A bounder? What the hell's a bounder?"

"YOU! You're a bounder. Now go away and leave me alone."

He let her go, then turned back to Francine, who was calmly doing up her buttons. "Uh.. listen," he said, "Can you just wait out here for about ten minutes? Give me a little time to calm her down?"

"It's too cold."

"You'll be all right. You've got plenty of padding." He strode off after Vera.

"Her mother's right," Francine yelled after him. "You are a bounder." She hunkered down on the driftwood and returned to her bottle of gin.

The Palace of the Moon was a ramshackle, clapboard hall perched precariously on a dune, one side propped up with long cedar poles. A makeshift board walk led to the front entrance where the fifteen year old nephew of the bandleader took the fifty cent admission. Smoke and noise hit Len like a shot of adrenalin when he walked in. Everyone knew him here and he waved or spoke to a dozen people as he waded through the crowd, looking for Vera.

"Hey, Len, drive much?" hollered the man at the hot dog counter. "Your friend was here looking for you."

"Oh, yeah? When?"

"Five minutes ago. He seemed a little steamed. Told him you'd been here all night, and left just before he walked in."

Waving his thanks, he continued his tour of the polished dance floor. He found Vera in a corner by the bandstand, trying to get the rest of the sand off her dress. He walked up to her, grabbed her hand, and tried to pull her out onto the floor. She pulled away and said something to him, but he couldn't hear what it was, the band was too loud. He made a grab for her hand again.

The Mell-o-Tones were just finishing a number when the bandleader's voice broke over the final chords. "That's it for a few minutes ladies and gentlemen, we're going to take a short break now, but don't go away, we'll be back in about ten."

"Oh great." Len rolled his eyes.

"Go away." Vera pushed him.

"I thought you wanted to dance?"

"Not any more."

"Oh, for crying out loud."

"I want to go home."

"We just got here."

Vera looked around her. "I thought The Palace of the Moon was supposed to be romantic. This isn't romantic. It's just a shabby old shack."

He looked around. "What's wrong with it? It's got a nice dance floor."

"We could have gone to Rickarton Castle. They have a marble dance floor at Rickarton Castle, you know. We could have gone there."

"It costs two dollars and fifty cents to get in at The Rick!"

"So what?" She added cheapness to her mental list of Len's evident shortcomings. "I'd probably have had to pay my own way in there as well."

"It's only fifty cents," he pointed out.

"It's the principle of thing," she said firmly. "A girl shouldn't have to pay her own way into a dancehall. I've never felt so cheap in my life."

"Look if you're that upset about it, I'll give you the lousy fifty cents!"

"And you could have reserved a table for us. This isn't exactly a high-toned evening here, Len." She knew there was no such thing as a reserved table at a place like The Palace of the Moon, but she didn't care. She was on the offensive for once and it felt good.

"Look", he said calmly. "I'll go find Francine and we'll go to the Rickarton, okay?"

"I don't want to. I don't want to drive with you anymore." she tried to match his tone.

"Why not?"

"You almost killed us on the way out here."

"I did not!" he protested. "I had everything under control."

"You're supposed to drive *around* the corners, not *straight through*," she pointed out.

"I honked the horn! It was a *horn trip*, Vera!"

"And you should have pulled over when that other car went in the ditch." She was getting better at this.

"He didn't expect us to pull over for crying out loud. That's not how the game is played."

"I want to go home."

"Oh, cripes."

Vera turned her back to him and folded her arms. She scanned the crowded hall, wondering if there was someone there she knew, someone who could take her home if she couldn't get Len to. A familiar figure was leaning up against the snack bar, munching a hot dog.

"Oh my God!"

"What now?" Len was standing with his hands in his pockets, kicking at the floor with one foot.

"Hide me." She mashed herself against him, burying her face in his jacket.

"Why?"

"That's my uncle over there!"

"Where?" Len turned to scan the crowd.

"Don't look!" Vera grabbed his face and hauled it back around.

"Wait a minute, wait a minute, it doesn't matter if he sees *me*." He looked around again. "Where is he?"

Vera hid her face with her hands. "Over there by the bar."

A stout man in a pin-stiped suit lounged against the bar, his hand absently stroking the backside of a blowzy looking brunette. "And is that your aunt with him?" Len asked.

Vera looked over his shoulder carefully.

"No. It isn't," she said with a puzzled tone.

He started to laugh and patted her shoulder. "Well I wouldn't worry, darlin', I don't think you have to bother too much about your uncle. I doubt he'll ever mention that either of you were here."

It took her a few minutes to figure it out, but in the end, she had to admit that Len was right - Uncle Harry could probably be counted on not to say a word as long as she didn't either.

Len was still patting her shoulder. "Look, if you want we'll leave and go to Tobe's."

"I'm not driving all the way to Tobe's Gardens with you. You almost killed me tonight! Just take me home, will you Len?"

He sighed. "Sure, baby," he said, "I'll take you home, don't worry. If that's what you want to do we'll do it. Only...."

"Only what?" He was hedging and she knew it meant trouble.

"Only... we have to go and find Francine first okay?"

"Why?"

"Well she came with us," he pointed out, "we can't just leave her stranded here."

"I'm sure Francine is perfectly capable of finding another ride home." Vera said coldly.

"But it's the principle of the thing. She came with me, so I feel I have a moral obligation to see her home safely. You can't just leave a lady stranded."

Vera snorted. "If you want my opinion, Len, Francine is no lady."

"Vera! I'm shocked. How could you say such a thing about a friend of mine?"

"I'm sorry, Len, Francine is loud and coarse and she's *old*. What are you doing with an old woman like that? And you were kissing her! I find that really disgusting."

"I wouldn't have to kiss her if you'd let me kiss you," he wheedled.

"Oh...ick! I don't want to kiss you after her!"

He sighed again. "Okay, okay, but we still have to find her. You go check the ladies' washroom, then meet me outside. Okay?"

Vera disappeared in the direction of the washrooms just as Francine entered the dance hall. Len hustled over to her.

"Can you make yourself scarce for about an hour?" he hissed at her.

"What?" Francine was outraged. "I've been sitting outside in the cold for a half an hour so I wouldn't be in your way. Now you want me to get lost again? You really are a shit, Len."

"Look, just hide yourself for a minute until I can get Vera back outside, okay?"

"Oh, you're going in for the kill are you? And when she won't go for it and kicks you in the balls, I suppose you're going to come hobbling to me for an icepack right?" She glared at him. "Okay, I'll keep out of sight for a few minutes. But this is the last time, do you hear? The last time I'm going along with this crap!"

"Thanks Francine," he patted her fanny, "you're a dear."

She glared again and went off to find the band.

Vera emerged from the Ladies'.

"She's not in there."

"She must still be outside." He grabbed her arm and they headed for the door.

The clouds had rolled by and thin moonlight shone eerily off the water. Waves shimmered in a silver undulation as they slapped against the shore. Francine's empty bottle of gin glinted beside the driftwood.

Len kicked it. "Hmmm, she must have found a friend."

"Great, so what do we do now, sit here and wait for her?"

"Look, I know you're upset. We'll wait ten minutes and if she doesn't show, I'll take you home. Okay?"

Vera searched his face. She didn't trust him.

"I promise." He looked solemn and serious.

"Okay." She knew when she said it she would regret it later. She walked to the water's edge and stood looking out over the lake. The strange glow in the south had intensified.

"What's that light?" she asked.

"Oh, it's probably Rochester." He stood beside her, his hands in his pockets.

"You can't see Rochester from here!"

"Honest! On certain nights you can see the lights. Some sort of reflection of the moon on the water or something. And in the wintertime, all sorts of things get reflected because of the ice, like boats and buildings and things, except usually they're upside down. Happens sometimes when its cloudy too. Or so they say."

"You're pulling my leg, aren't you?"

"I'm just telling you what I heard. There are a lot of strange stories out here."

"Did you ever go looking for the buried treasure?"

"What that old business about the French sea captain and his gold?" Len laughed. "Heck, people have been trying to find that for years. I figure its just a story."

"My uncle went looking one time, but he never found it."

"There's supposed to be a map you know."

"Really?"

"Oh yeah." He moved a little closer to her. " I don't expect it would help much."

"Why not?" Vera sat on the piece of driftwood. He sat beside her.

"The dunes shift so much, all the landmarks are probably covered up by now. And the Outlet river has changed course umpteen times over the years. That gold could be anywhere."

"Still, it would be fun to look for buried treasure, wouldn't it?"

He put his arm around her. "Nah, I already found my treasure right here."

"Oh Len." She didn't know if it was the moonlight or the sound of the waves lapping, but suddenly she wasn't nearly as mad at him as she had been. He kissed her neck and she let him. Encouraged he moved to her lips, exploring her mouth with his tongue.

"We could go and look for buried treasure if you want," he said after a while.

"When?"

He stroked her hair. "Tonight."

"We'd never find anything in the dark!"

"Well, let's go look anyway."

Vera knew what he was suggesting and wasn't sure what to do. Len had behaved badly tonight and she wasn't sure she would ever forgive him, but now that she was finally alone with him, she was unwilling to cede ground to Francine again. The ten minutes he had allotted was long since up, but she no longer wanted to go home. She wanted to go on sitting with him on this piece of driftwood by the shore. She wanted to go on kissing him. He was so charming when he wanted to be and so handsome and sitting here in the moonlight was so romantic, it was just like a scene in a book, with herself cast as the romantic heroinc. Len made an ideal hero, too, or at least he did when she could get his attention. She had been out of her depth all evening, a child looking in on the land of the grown-ups, but now she felt beautiful and desirable and terribly mature, and suddenly she wanted to be forever done with childish things.

She stroked his face gently."Where do you suppose we should start looking?"

He smiled a slow, crooked smile and gently took her by the hand. "Probably over in the trees behind that dune," he said pulling her along.

"Oh" she thought as they sank down in the sand. "The band's started playing again. That's "Stardust".

CHAPTER THREE

The more she looked, the more junk Cara found. Tucked away in odd corners, forgotten closets and under stairs, there were broken tools, discarded linens and outmoded coats. Long forgotten boxes revealed hats that hadn't been worn in thirty years, boots that had split at the soles, orphaned mittens and matted scarves. Stacks of magazines teetered in the basement, rows of books were piled up under the bed. Several of these were from the local library, and Cara wondered if she would have to pay a fine when she took them back.

Her father's desk was full of notes, letters, invitations, and ticket stubs. In one of the drawers she found the program from her first ballet recital, when she had proudly worn a pink tutu and stunned the audience with her virtuoso performance. Or, at least, that was what her father had claimed, when he scooped her up backstage after her triumphant exit from the finale. She couldn't recall where her mother had been, although she was sure she had been there. It was always her father she remembered on those occasions.

Mickey would only ever remember his mother on the sidelines; there was no one else to cheer for him. She wondered sometimes if he felt the difference, if he secretly needed or wanted two parents in his audience, but then most of his schoolmates had only a mother or a father; some had a step-parent; some of them had a series of them. She couldn't have imagined Randy at Parents' Night anyway. Or at a little boy's soccer game. Or helping with homework or doctoring an ear infection or shouldering any of the unexpected obligations that came with a child.

Randy had been a musician. In Cara's opinion he played a decent blues guitar, but he was never able to get along with anybody long enough to achieve the kind of success he was sure he deserved. She had met him on her thirtieth birthday, at a party given by her friend Cass, who owned the trendy shop that had first used Cara's artwork.

"Do you know everybody, Care?" Cass had asked. "Hmmm....nope, you don't. This is my mother. Mom, this is the famous Cara."

Cara hadn't known she was famous, but smiled at the small, plump woman, a wrenish version of her flamboyant daughter.

"And, this is Nathan Carter. Nathan has asked me out, I'll have you know. Way to go, Nathan, do you realize what a lucky man you are?"

Nathan grinned and shook his head.

"And this is Randy Bowen. Randy, Cara Collins."

"Hey Cara." That was as far as the introductions went. Someone else arrived and Cass flitted off to take coats and replenish dips.

Cara really didn't know anyone at the party, so she leaned against the wall beside Randy. He was taller than she was, a welcome surprise in a world that seemed to be populated by an extraordinary percentage of short men. Cara had always refused to downplay her height, in fact she emphasized it by wearing heels and platform shoes, but Randy still had an inch or so on her. There was something very familiar about him, but she hadn't been able to put her finger on it at the time. Parties were always so full of odds and ends of people, it was sometimes hard to get a read on any one of them. She would have liked a drink, but there was a crush in the kitchen, so she stuck her hands in her jeans pockets and leaned. Randy noticed.

"Want a swig?" he asked, handing her the bottle of Blue he was holding.

Cara gulped a mouthful and handed it back. "Just like high school. Pass the bottle."

He laughed. "Oh, I know who you are now. You're the party girl. Every high school has one."

"Guilty as charged. I got over it though."

"Yeah? Gee that's too bad."

She shrugged. "Everybody's got to grow up sooner or later."

"So what did you grow up to be?" he asked as she took the bottle back and gulped again.

"Artist."

"Watercolours on rocks? Little children with big eyes? Elvis on black velvet?"

"Commercial. I do Cass's catalogue."

He looked surprised. "Really? Your stuff is neat. And here I had you pegged for one of these girls who go to Art College on a whole lot of artistic temperament and half a tank of talent."

Oh, no, she thought, you're not getting away with that one. "So what are you doing with your particular half tank?" she asked.

"Musician."

" Oh. Guitar lessons for thirteen year olds who only want to learn the riffs?"

"Ouch. Tongue in her head this girl has. No, I'm lead guitarist for Markwell Marston's back-up band. And I do studio work on the side."

Cara had actually heard of Markwell Marston, a fact that seemed to inch her up another notch in Randy's estimation. Not that she cared, particularly. But he was pretty good-looking. She'd see what happened.

He lit a cigarette and exhaled wearily. "God, this country. It's so damned hard for anybody with talent. Nobody ever wants to pay what anything is worth."

She didn’t answer him. She considered that she was paid quite well for what she did, more, in fact, than she privately thought her stuff was worth. Randy looked at her speculatively through the smoke. "Are you real hooked in to this scene? Some friends of mine are playing down the street. Wanna go?"

“Sure.” She might just as well. It was a typical Cass party, too many people who didn't know each other crowded into too small a space.

Randy's friends were playing R&B in a bar that was every bit as crowded, noisy and smoky as the party had been, but at least Cara could get her own drink. Randy sat in on most of one set, and she had to admit he was pretty good. She also had to admit she liked bar scenes. She didn't have to talk to anybody; the music was always too loud.

In retrospect, she secretly blamed noisy bars for the ensuing shambles. If only they had talked more, she thought, she'd never have let things go as far as they did. But then, she wouldn't have had Mickey, would she?

She began sifting through piles of paper, trying to make some sense of the mass of things her mother had left behind. There seemed to be no coherent order to anything that Cara could see, no reason for keeping most of the stuff she found. She had expected to find legal documents, deeds, account books. It had originally been her father’s den and she remembered him working in it often, but there was nothing of his that she could see. The filing cabinet was full of old Christmas paper and gardening magazines. The lawyers must have taken it all away, she thought.

One of Bernice’s cookbooks had been shoved into the bottom-most desk of the drawer and inside she found a brown and acid-eaten certificate. "Senior Matriculation" it read in looped, Italianate letters. Underneath, in plainer type was her mother's name, Edna Charles, "With Honours" added underneath. Funny to think of her mother as a school girl, sitting in class, sweating over essays and homework. She and Vera together, side by side at their desks passing notes and making eyes at the boys.

Cara had not attended her own high school graduation. There had been no point, really. She had barely scraped through her academic subjects, the only area she excelled in had been art class where a grey and decaying teacher had discovered Cara's eye for colour and proportion. Mr. Winston had taught for some thirty years. The earnest and painful efforts of his pupils had left him, for the most part, phlegmatic, and Cara had been surprised when he appeared enthusiastic over her work.

Her first assignment in Grade 10 had been a nature scene, in egg tempura. She noted that the other girls were painfully crafting meadow scenes of pastel wildflowers or charming, babbling streams, one featuring a small misshapen mouse under an equally misshapen toadstool. Repelled, she mixed her palette with colours as dark as she could make them and splashed them onto the paper.

It was a lake scene, from the perspective of a boat in the middle of it. Across the lower right hand corner the prow slashed across the page. The rest was black and angry sky or black and angry water, the two warring with each other in tempestuous collision. To the left, directly in the boat's path, was a protruding rock, one that without doubt was capable of punching a large, fatal hole in the boat's hull. She was quite happy by the time she finished. Her picture had a brooding quality that at the same time captured a promise of impending chaos.

Winston awarded her a B+ and asked her to stay after class.

"This scene you've painted," he said to her. "Is it something you've seen, or something you've imagined?"

Cara was surprised at the question, so surprised that she actually thought about it for a few moments in an attempt to answer truthfully instead of giving a glib, automatic reply. She had not ever been out on the lake in the kind of weather the picture showed, certainly, but she had heard her father describe it.

"I haven't seen it, but I imagined it from something I was told."

"Ahhh."

Cara didn't know what "aaah" meant, but from then on Winston showed infinite patience with her, instructing her in techniques that were far beyond the rest of the class. She was one of those students who affirm a teacher's decision to teach. A talent.

The other girls noticed and teased her unmercifully.

"Teachers pet!"

"Teacher's got a crush on Cara!"

"Cara's got a crush on the teeeeecher!"

She ignored them all, fascinated by what Winston could show her, by what was locked up inside her head, and by what was required to get it to flow from her mind onto the paper. She knew then that she wanted to be an artist.

She realized now that she didn't know whether or not her mother had ever wanted to be anything.

Edna was just leaving the church by the side door, the Sunday School door, her arms full of crayoned pictures of The Sermon on the Mount. She had difficulty with the latch, but finally the heavy oak door with the sticky lock agreed to close and she set off briskly down the sidewalk. She needed to hurry. It was their Sunday to have the Minister and his Wife for dinner and her mother would be awaiting her help in the kitchen.

She was just rounding the corner when a gust of wind caught the topmost paper and whirled it into the air. She grabbed for it, but the wind lifted it just out of her reach. She shifted her load to the crook of her other arm and chased the wayward piece out into the street, not noticing the large car that came speeding around the corner until it was almost too late. When, at the last moment, she realized that a very large and very black Buick was about to run her over, she instinctively threw herself backward out of the way, landing hard on the outstretched palm of her right hand and laddering her stockings on the gravel.

The Buick screeched to a halt. The driver threw open the door and leapt out.

"Holy Jeez, are you okay? You ran right in front of me!"

Edna shifted her weight and examined her hand. The palm was scraped and full of bits of gravel, blood welling up through the torn skin. Oh great, she thought, I have to write an exam tomorrow and this hand is going to be sore as the dickens.

"Are you okay? You didn't hit your head or anything, did you?"

Finally, she looked up at him.

"You ran right out in front of me. I nearly ran you down."

"Sorry. The wind blew a paper away and I was trying to catch it. I guess I wasn't paying much attention." She knew this person. Len Collins. He was notorious. Several years older than Edna, he was the object of fascination and speculation on the part of all her friends. Len always had a car, always had a girl on his arm, and nearly always had a bottle in an inside pocket. Where he got the money that he also always seemed to have, nobody knew for sure, although the rumour was that he was a bootlegger, an honoured profession learned at his father's knee.

"Here, I'll help you up" he said, extending his hand to her.

"No thank you. I just need to sit here for a minute to catch my breath."

"Well, here, let me pick up these papers for you, anyway." He scurried around, piling the scattered crayon drawings beside her. "Miss Charles, Junior Class", he read from the top of one."Where were you going Miss Charles? I'll give you a ride."

"No, thank you. I'm fine", she said. "This was entirely my fault. I wasn't paying attention. Please, just go about your business. I'll be okay."

But he didn't go away. He sat on the curb beside her. "Well, that's true", he said, "It was your fault."

Edna felt a little put out. She was only trying to be gracious. After all, he had been going way too fast, he could share a little of the responsiblity.

"But I must admit," he continued, "I feel funny about leaving a beautiful woman just sitting by the side of the road."

He grinned at her, his lean brown face splitting, his eyes sizing her up.

"Would you please just go?" Edna had been brought up to be polite, no matter what.

"No."

"Mr. Collins, please."

"Oh, so you know who I am?" His grin was even wider.

"Everyone knows who you are. Now will you please leave? I'm fine."

"At least let me help you up." He stood and reached out to take her hand, and just as he was pulling her up, Rev. Henderson's car came out of the manse driveway and around the corner. Two heads swivelled to peer through the glass at her, two sets of disapproving stares, two tongues that would go wagging to her mother in a very short while, before she had a chance to get home herself to quell the gossip.

She stared after the car. "Well, thanks a lot. I'm in trouble now." She pushed past him, almost knocking him down.

He followed her. "What, in trouble just for talking to me?"

"Yes."

"My God, I'm not that bad. Don't tell me people can get in trouble just for talking to me."

"Yes, they can and they will, now go away!"

He pushed his fedora to the back of his head and started to laugh as she strode down the sidewalk.

"Hey, Miss Charles!"

She blushed furiously and kept walking.

"Hey, Miss Charles, can I give you a call sometime?"

She kept walking, past the Miller children playing in their front yard, past the twitching lace curtains at the Hutchings, past old Mrs. Lewis pottering in her flowerbed, not saying a word, wishing she could go and hide under one of the bushes until she was old and died.

He just stood on the sidewalk, laughing at her retreat.

She knew as soon as she walked into the kitchen that the Hendersons were already there and that they had already broadcast their news. She could tell from the set of her mother's shoulders as she took the pot roast from the oven, and the way she slammed down the oven mitts.

"Go and wash your hands and take this in", she hissed. "I have no time to deal with you now!"

"But..."

"No, buts, just do as I say."

Her mother's eyes snapped as she furiously mashed the potatoes.

Oh well, at least there won't be any lumps today, Edna thought.

Reverend Henderson glared at her as she took the roast into the dining room. Her father was hunched at one end of the table, the minister's wife at his right. Mrs. Rev. Henderson looked at her smugly, her duty to God and the family done. Her brother Billy smirked.

"Oh, almighty God," Rev. Henderson intoned as they all sat with heads bowed, "thank you for the bounty you have set before us today..."

God didn't set it, Edna thought rebelliously. Father bought it, mother cooked it and I brought it in.

"...and thank you for the gifts you bring us every day, especially the gift of our children," Edna tensed, waiting, "...especially those of our young people who are on the brink of adulthood, may you keep them safe and from harm and set their feet firmly on thy holy path. Amen."

She knew she was in deep trouble then. She pushed her slice of pot roast around on the plate and arranged the peas in a pattern in the gravy. Her mother kept the Hendersons entertained with a painfully detailed description of the last meeting of the Ladies' Aid. Her father, as usual, nodded politely at the correct intervals, but she knew he was off in his own world somewhere. She never knew what he thought about while he was there, but when conversation required a response, he would come to, blinking and disoriented for a moment, smile slightly and reply, then sink back into that inner place he preferred.

"What?" She had been asked a question, but she had missed it.

"Could you pass the potatoes down to Billy, please?" her mother said sharply. "And stop playing with your food."

Billy giggled and stuck his tongue out at her when his mother wasn't looking. Her older brother Jack poked him under the table and smiled at her sympathetically.

"I wasn't talking to him, he was talking to me", Edna pointed out later in the kitchen.

"How could you, how could you", her mother hissed. "How could you be seen in public talking to that Len Collins. You know what his reputation is."

"What was I supposed to do? I kept telling him to go away."

"Well, what was he doing talking to you in the first place? Where did you meet him? He must know you from somewhere!"

"He doesn't. I told you, he nearly hit me with his car! I've never talked to him before in my life!"

"Oh, so you admit you were talking to him." As usual her mother could twist things around so that Edna was in the wrong.

"No. I don't know. Oh, for Pete's sake."

Her mother's eyes grew narrow and hard. "I don't ever want to hear that you have had anything to do with him again, do you hear me? "

"Well, what am I supposed to do? Pick a different car? I'll be sure and check next time to see who it is first before I let them run me over."

"Watch that smart mouth of yours, Edna. You're supposed to not have anything to do with the likes of Len Collins. That's what you're supposed to do."

"And if I'm just standing there and he comes up and starts to talk and won't go away when I ask him to, what am I supposed to do then? Pick up a rock and bash him over the head? Maybe I should carry a knife or a gun, what do you think?"

Her mother's face was a deep red. "I will not have this impertinence, do you hear me? I have made myself clear, and as long as you live under my roof, you'll follow my rules. Do you understand?"

Edna shrugged. As usual, everything she did in her mother's eyes was wrong, and no amount of logic would ever make it right. She dried the dishes without another word, but put them away with as much rattling and crashing as she dared. She was about to go to her room to study when her mother stopped her.

"Go sit in the parlour. Your father wants a word with you."

Although Hetty Charles made a great pretence of deferring to her husband, she was the disciplinarian of the family and made most of the decisions. "Don't upset your father" was a constant refrain in the Charles household, although, from what Edna could see, it was mostly her mother who got upset. The only time her father reacted at all was when he deemed it an appropriate response to her mother's rantings. "Your father wants a word with you" was Hetty's way of signalling that she wasn't finished yet, but required her husband's complicity in her pronouncements. Bert Charles would passively acquiesce to whatever his wife wanted and they would all pretend that the decree was his.

"Um....he said," setting himself uncomfortably in a stiff armchair as Edna went into the parlour. Hetty bustled in behind her, with her glasses and a piece of paper. "Your mother wanted me to have a little talk with you."

Edna decided she wasn't going to make it easy for him.

"Yes, father." She arranged an expectant, and she hoped, irritating look on her face.

"What your father means to say," Hetty interrupted, "is that you graduate from high school in a couple of weeks and we need to talk about what happens after that." Edna was surprised. She had expected another lecture on the evils of Len Collins, not a chat about her career expectations. She had told them at Christmas that she wanted to go to Teachers' College. Her mother had been dubious at the time, her father embarrassed. She picked at the brown upholstery of the parlour sofa waiting for her parents to continue. The looped nap of the fabric made Edna think of thousands of tiny nooses. Outside she could hear Jack and Bill arguing over possession of the catcher's mitt they had jointly received for Christmas.

Her father cleared his throat. "It's just that, well, I just can't seem to see my way clear to sending you on. The room and the board in Toronto and all that. And of course, we couldn't let you stay just anyplace. It would have to be a good boarding house. But the store just hasn't been doing too well, lately, you know." He shook his head sadly. "Bad times, bad times all around."

The rest of the world seemed to be in the middle of a boom, she thought, but Charles and Sons Fine Furniture lingered perpetually on the brink of bankruptcy.

"So, your father and I talked it over," Hetty carried on for him. "We decided that if you could work for a while, and then maybe later on, next year, we could manage it. Dr. Pierson, the optometrist, was telling me the other day that his receptionist wants to retire and he's looking for someone to replace her. You could save some of your wages and that would help too."

Edna refused to give her mother the satisfaction of a response. Hetty mistook her silence for assent.

"Now, it won't be that hard, you see. I've got it all figured out." She smoothed the paper and adjusted her glasses. "By the time you take off room and board, you should still be able to save quite a lot." She waved the paper under Edna's nose. "It shouldn't be more than a year or two, you see, even when you take into account that you would have to have buy some clothing suitable for business."

"Room and board?" Edna said. "What are you talking about?"

"Why, it's only fair dear, if you're working, that you pay us room and board. After all, we're feeding you and providing a roof over your head."

Both her heart and her hopes sank. She knew what happened to girls who worked "for a while". They either married as fast as they could or hung on to their jobs grimly, hoping against hope that something better would come along. She had an image of herself at forty, still filing and doing accounts for the optometrist, living still with her parents, paying them for the privilege of doing most of the housework and looking after them as they got older, becoming more and more desperate every year, clinging to an out of date hair style and relying frantically on rouge to maintain an air of youthful gaiety; of Monday evening bridge parties with other, similarly rouged middle-aged women; of good works on Sunday at the church; of a creeping, disapproving judgment on the behaviour of young people.

"If I have to pay room and board anyway, why don't I just get my own place?" she asked.

Her mother was horrified. "Oh, no , that would never do. Why, what would people say? You living on your own? They'd think something was wrong. You'd be taken advantage of, you have no idea of what's out there, just waiting to prey on young girls. Besides, I need your help here. The boys are no use, no use at all."

So that was that, Edna thought. My money gone, my time used up and my life decided.

Her father tried to soften it for her. "It's just temporary", he said, patting her hand. "Just until we're through this little bad patch. After all, Charles and Sons has been in business for over fifty years."

Charles and Sons had limped along for a good forty-five of the fifty,

Edna knew. She wasn't going to hold her breath.

"Fine," she said, rising. "I'm going to my room to study. I have an English exam tomorrow, but why I'm even bothering to write it, I'll never know." She flounced out of the room.

Bert Charles sat back in his easy chair, relieved that the conversation was at an end.

"Well," he said slowly, "that didn't go too badly."

Hetty wasn't so sure. Her daughter had given in far too easily.

Vera sat beside her in the exam room. English was Edna's favourite subject, but today she found it difficult to concentrate. She just didn't feel like discussing the "Oh What a Rogue and Peasant Slave Am I" soliloquy in no more than three paragraphs and kept stealing sidelong glances at her friend labouring over the paper, writing, erasing and writing again. Vera was not nearly as good a student as Edna.

Usually she and Vera walked to school together. Edna's mother liked it that way, after the girls had grown too old to have their mothers walking them.

"You never know who's lurking out there waiting to prey on young girls", was Hetty's refrain. "You two stay together and don't ever talk to strangers." She never specified the term "prey", or who exactly it was who would be lurking. The girls had no idea what she was talking about. They imagined some grey, faceless wraith-like creature that lived in bushes and trees, and especially in old, abandoned buildings, because that was where they were always warned to stay away from.

Hetty Charles was always mildly disapproving of Vera, implying that her family was not quite on a par with the Charles', who after all, were "old family". Vera's father was a bricklayer. It was the peculiar snobbery found in those who had been lucky and married up; Hetty came from a family of small farmers and fishermen, and she had set her sights on the Charles boy in high school, relentlessly monopolizing him into marriage. It hadn't really been all that hard; Edna's father, even then, had merely floated down the easiest path available. Vera was Edna's best friend and she ignored her mother's barbs.

After school and on weekends the girls had always played in the woods behind Edna's father's store, although they suspected, quite correctly, that Hetty would never approve. The wood was little more than scrubland, although there were tall trees at the back of it. The town had been built around the head of a bay, the stores and office buildings climbing drunkenly up the hill from the harbour. When Edna's grandfather purchased a large lot for his furniture store at the turn of the century, there had still been the odd working farm at the edge of town and one of these had included the land behind his new store. Too steep for ploughing, it had been used for pasture, but over the years the sale of commercial lots along the street had cut the land off, the yard around Charles Furniture providing the only easy access. Eventually the empty land was abandoned. The trees crept back into the fields, claiming them first with red cedar and prickly ash, then oak and hickory saplings.

It was a fine place to play; Vera and Edna were Loyalist settlers one time, cowboys the next, whooping and swooping through the trees with makeshift rifles and axes fashioned from branches. Brave pioneers, outcasts from revolution, they conquered the wilderness with nothing more than grit and determination, settled the west from the back of a conestoga wagon. Vera always wanted to be the mother or the cook or the saloon girl. Edna let her. It seemed to her that these roles were too passive, and she was happy to take the lead in fashioning a log cabin or fighting off the perfidious, attacking Indians.

They went to the woods as often as they could, walking past the imposing facade of Charles Furniture and down the broad laneway along its side. Edna had no fear that her father would notice them and tell her mother. He seldom noticed anything.

Slipping down the path and through the underbrush, the two girls were dimly cognizant of a sudden and somehow awe-inspiring transition. Prickly ash and dogwood guarded the way from the casual intruder, but Edna and Vera pushed past these, unaware of the scratches on their arms they would have to explain away later. As they walked deeper into the woods, the trees grew thicker, young hickory and poplar and sometimes even white oak interspersed amongst the cedars. Running through the centre of the wood was a small stream, marshy at its edges. Here they found frogs and bright iridescent green snakes, which slithered away in alarm at their approach. Trilliums grew profusely under the trees and they obeyed the prohibition against picking them. The woodland at times erupted in glory. In what was left of the meadows, a living watercolour was painted in hues of blue phlox, purple vetch and Queen Anne's Lace, along with the burnished yellow of goldenrod. The woods had its own smell, too, the rich organic mustiness of decomposing leaves and steaming stagnant water. In town, black squirrels dominated the treetops, but here small brown chipmunks scurried everywhere, their cheeks stuffed with treasures.

The girls always headed straight for the middle of the woods, where they had built a fort out of old rail fences and discarded boards. They were constantly rebuilding it, because the older children constantly discovered it and ripped it down, gleefully destroying for the sake of destruction. The vandals never bothered the girls themselves. They thought, because of the proximity, that Edna's father owned the woods, and she, therefore, had proprietorial rights over it. Instead they launched craven sneak attacks.

Several times Vera and Edna found strange tokens left behind from other incursions; empty beer bottles, odd shrivelled-up rubber tubes and once, a pair of girl's panties, with the legend "Tuesday" on them. They debated trying to find the owner.

"She'll be looking for them, don't you think?" Edna said. "After all, they're obviously part of a set. She'll have all the other days of the week, except for that one."

Vera wasn't so sure. "How did they get here?" she wanted to know. "How can you leave your underpants behind and not notice?"

In the end, they opted to hook them on the end of a stick and leave them on a bush a little way away from their fort. They would be out of sight that way, but if the girl came looking, still findable. Over the summer, the thin nylon panties faded from the rain and disintegrated from the sun. By September there were only a few pink tatters left.

As they grew older, their games changed, and grew more sedate. By the time they were twelve, they no longer whooped through the woods. The fort was no longer a fort, but a miniature and rustic house, which must be cleaned and tidied and fussed over. They invented boyfriends and speculated about husbands.

"I'll never marry anyone who isn't rich", Vera announced. "I may fall in love with a poor but honest man, but I would never marry him. I would just have to languish." Languish was a word they had discovered in books. Vera's mother was a voracious reader of gothic novels and the girls stole them away into the woods to pore over and pounce on details. It seemed to Vera that languishing for love was a terribly romantic and wonderful thing to do.

Edna was less concerned with the material."I would marry the poor man anyway, and work hard to make a happy home", she said. "I don't care how rich the man is, I won't marry him if I don't love him."

But they both agreed that the best thing was to have both, preferably in England or Scotland where, according to the novels they read, there seemed to be a surfeit of stately old castles and homes inhabited by brooding and available heirs. There would be trials and tribulations, of course, but they both knew they were plucky, and could be counted upon to face peril with courage, whether it was supernatural, or merely a disgruntled and dangerous younger brother.

They taught themselves to dance back by the fort in the woods. Vera's mother had a vast selection of 78's, which they played on the phonograph over and over until they knew them by heart. Along with tinny renditions of "White Cliffs of Dover" and "Over There" there were several discs of dance music. They sang the tunes in a breathless monotone while they waltzed and tangoed and cha-cha-ed through the clearing, with the help of an instructional manual from the library.

"One, two, three, one two three," they would chant as they danced back and forth across the meadow, trying the easy steps first, but quickly mastering the more complicated ones. They imagined themselves in long, flowing ball gowns of velvet or satin, their grace and elegance on the dance floor sure to catch the eye of any errant prince.

Later, when they had real boyfriends, or almost-boyfriends or even potential boyfriends, the woods made a convenient place to discuss them, out of the hearing of adults, who could be counted on to find some black mark against the boy, some reason for disapproval, some remark that would reduce him from Prince Charming to just another grubby, awkward adolescent.

They planned their careers. There were not many options open to them; teaching or nursing seemed to be what girls did. Neither of them was attracted to nursing, too many icky things to clean up, they decided. Of course the payoff was greater - a handsome young doctor might fall in love with them, but in the end they vowed to go through Teacher's College together and spend their lives improving the minds of small, sweet children who would bring them apples and Valentines and go on to become successful, at which point they would give all the credit to the wonderful public school teachers who had been their inspiration. At least, that's what they would do until they settled down and married, producing a passel of their own small sweet children who would adore their mothers and be the best of friends and support each other, just like in "Little Women" and "The Five Little Peppers." They plotted their lives, planning to move along in lock-step forever.

Lately, though, they had not gone often to their woods. It seemed to Edna that Vera was distracted. Sometimes she wasn't ready when Edna called at her house on the way to school; sometimes Edna arrived to discover that Vera had already left. She had no idea why this was so. She meant to ask her, but Vera left right after the exam to go home and help her mother.

She didn't see her again until the next week, at graduation, but couldn't talk to her then. They were herded to the front of the hall, where chairs had been reserved for them, in strict alphabetical order. Vera Matlin was far down the row. Edna waited for her name to be called, smoothing the soft fabric of the black gown they had given her to wear. She felt ridiculous in a mortarboard and the tassel kept falling forward into her eyes. The smell of old sweat permeated the air; the school auditorium was also the gymnasium, used for both assemblies and basketball. At least the net has been swung up out of the way, she thought, otherwise the boys would be tipping their diplomas through the hoop. Chairs scraped along the wooden floor as other students shifted in their seats, coughing occasionally and fanning themselves with rolled up programs. The heat was oppressive.

Graduation had been something she and Vera had dreamed about for years, as a mark of maturity and a signal that they were, at last, moving into adulthood. It was the portal through which they had to pass to take up their new and exciting lives. How disappointing to discover that the country on the other side was both less interesting and more proscribed than this one. Suddenly graduation didn't seem quite so important.

At least her name was called relatively soon. Edna felt sorry for Hannah Young, who would have to wait in her chair until the end.

She walked out onto the stage when they called "Edna Charles". The principal smiled and shook her hand and announced that she had won the English prize. Edna had to work hard to give him a reciprocal smile. Afterwards they posed for a graduating class picture, the girls in the front row, except for Hannah, who rivalled the boys in height.

She had promised to go to the class picnic afterwards with Charlie Cashen. He had had a crush on her for the last year and had haunted the hallway around her locker, waiting passively for the opportunity to carry her books. She often found him seated beside her in class; it could have been co-incidence, many teachers arranged their classrooms alphabetically, but Edna didn't think so.

She was faintly irritated by the attention. She had not had a lot of time for boyfriends. She and Vera were generally inseparable and most times they insisted on double dates. She also knew she had a reputation as a "brain" who always got good marks. Boys who overlooked that and asked her out were often puzzled by her habit of making bad puns and nonsense jokes that left them struggling to understand, and by the fact that she tended to be bored by their conversations. She would often chase a random thought through her head while they prattled on about football or hockey, not realizing until the middle of their stories that she wasn't listening.

The picnic was at the Outlet Beach, where all school picnics were held. The girls picked their way across the dunes trying to appear ladylike. The boys were boisterous, tripping each other and making raucous remarks. Mr. Elroy, the supervising teacher, finally marshalled them into order and marched them to the water, where the girls spread blankets and organized food while the boys splashed in the shallows. Off in the distance they could see The Palace of the Moon.

"Have you ever been there?" Vera suddenly asked Hannah, who was sharing their blanket.

Hannah looked shocked. "Of course not. My mother would kill me. There's all sorts of things that go on there."

What sorts of "things", Edna wondered. Drinking? She knew that. Dancing? Of course, that was the primary purpose of the place. But what else? Things that their mothers didn't want them to know about, obviously.

She suddenly realized how hot she was. She and Vera had put their bathing suits on under their clothes before they left the school, to spare themselves the embarrassment of having to go off behind a bush to change. They took off their slacks and sleeveless shirts to the accompaniment of wolf whistles from the boys and strode towards the water.

Hannah decided then that she wasn't swimming that day. Faintly annoyed, she watched Edna walk into the water. Always a pretty girl, in a bathing suit she transcended into spectacular. Slim, but with a hint of cozy roundness, a swelling bosom that wanted to spill out over the top of her suit. At six feet tall, Hannah had barely a curve anywhere. Even the petite Vera had a larger bosom than she did.

Edna waded in until the water reached her knees. In June the lake was always cold. Later on in the season, the little bay would become soupy and weedy, but now it was frigid. She hesitated for a few moments, hoping she would get used to the temperature. She could feel her legs going numb. Nothing for it, she thought, and plunged. The cold sliced through her like a razor. She swam under water for a few strokes, opening her eyes to look at the sandy bottom distorted by the sunlight shining through the prismatic water. There was the odd smooth stone embedded in the sand, but little else. When she surfaced, the water was up to her shoulders. She had trouble finding her feet. Too cold, she thought, but I'll bake in the sun and come in again later. She stroked back towards shore, standing only when she reached the shallows, where Vera still hovered, shaking and shivering.

Charlie was waiting at their blanket, wolfing down an egg salad sandwich and watching her as though she were dessert. She dripped water on him, deliberately.

"Your hair is going to be ruined now", Hannah pointed out.

Edna smiled. "Nah, it'll be okay. It just all curls up again as soon as it dries."

Hannah looked put out.

"Wanna go for a walk?" Charlie asked.

Edna shrugged. She didn't really, or at least not with Charlie, but he was her official date. They wandered down the beach, not talking, and when they were out of sight of the others, he shyly grabbed her hand. Edna knew he was probably supposed to, but it annoyed her.

"Let's climb up over the hill", she suggested. He had to let her hand go then, so they could balance in the loose sand. They trudged their way across the top of the dune, avoiding the poison ivy that grew everywhere.

And then, in a shallow depression in the sand, he made his move, grabbing her by the shoulders and kissing her, nearly knocking her backwards in his zeal. She dug her feet in and stood her ground. Their teeth clashed. One of his hands slid down her back while the other groped for her chest.

"Charlie, don't!"

"Aw, come on. You know how I feel about you. I'm crazy about you."

"I don't want to do this."

He groaned. "Aw, just a little. Come on."

"No."

Charlie was big, and well-muscled from the many chores he did on his father's farm. He held her tighter with his right arm while his left stroked her breast.

"No!" Edna planted her feet as well as she could in the sand and pushed as hard as she could manage. Charlie, focused on the swell of Edna's bosom, was taken by surprise and lost his footing. He fell, nearly taking her down with him, but at the last moment he let go of her and she regained her balance.

"I said 'no'"

"Aw come on." Charlie's face was hurt and bewildered, then angry. "You strut up and down the beach showing off in that bathing suit, what do you expect a guy to do?"

Strut? Edna didn't think she strutted. She hadn't thought about anything but going for a swim.

"You really are an ice princess, aren't you?" he sneered.

"What do you mean, an ice princess?" But Edna knew what he meant.

"You just never let anybody get close to you, do you, Miss Brain? All you do is drive men crazy with that body of yours, but you won't deliver, even when somebody does manage to get past Vera."

Edna looked at Charlie lying in the sand. A bit of egg salad clung to a corner of his mouth. His hair was full of sand. He was already turning red from the sun and had a raw, meaty look to him.

"I'd rather be an ice princess than a lobster", she said, and walked off.

"What?" Charlie didn't know what she was talking about, but then, he never had.

Edna started work the following week. Dr. Pierson had a busy practice and the tasks of answering the telephone, making appointments and recording payments at first filled her day, leaving her exhausted and drained by the end of it. Slowly she settled into a routine and the work seemed less chaotic and too quickly, boring. At night, after Dr. Pierson had left, Edna tidied up the last of the files and put them away in the cabinet, locking them in carefully. Her employer was very emphatic about office routine. Put the files away, sweep the office floor, tidy up the magazines, turn out the lights and lock the door carefully. As if anyone would break into an optometrist's office, Edna thought. Steal all that vital information. What prominent businessman in town is nearsighted? Which gay socialite has an astigmatism? That's the stuff of blackmail, isn't it? She massaged the back of her neck, grown stiff from bending over the accounts. She'd need glasses soon herself, if this kept up. She wondered if she should stop at the drug store and get a pop after she made the day's deposits. She certainly didn't feel like going home. Not that it was much of a home these days.

Within a week of starting work, she had challenged all the chores her mother expected her to do.

"After all, I'm working all day plus paying room and board. Maybe you should start treating me like a real boarder instead of expecting me to do all the housework," she had pointed out.

"You want to be a boarder, fine I'll treat you like a boarder", her mother had replied.

Hetty Charles had been as good as her word. From then on, Edna's breakfast porridge was lumpy, the roasts were burnt, her bed linen was never changed, and her mother complained every time she set foot in the house. Whenever she tried to read, Hetty would knock on the door to ask if she were going to be there for dinner.

Where else would I go? she thought resentfully.

Edna in turn left shoes and boots all over the front hall and took food to her room. It attracted mice, just like her mother had always warned her, but it was worth the aggravation.

Hetty politely asked if she could refrain from leaving her personal items in the bathroom. "With young boys in the house," she explained, "You can't be too careful."

Edna refused to go to church on Sunday and left the tap running at the kitchen sink.

Hetty put Edna's new white cotton blouse with the French lace collar into the wash with a pair of red combinations and ironed long creases into the back of her skirts.

Edna bought a radio and turned it on full blast every evening until her mother banged on her door and asked her to turn it down so they could get some sleep.

She was informed that guests were not allowed in her room, but that the front parlour was available for callers at reasonable hours.

Edna invited Vera over. She would loved to have had a gentleman caller, but couldn't think of anybody she felt like making that much conversation with. She hadn't spoken to Charlie since the picnic. Vera had found summer employment at one of the local factories, her days spent with her hands immersed in ice cold vegetables and fruits, picking out bruised and scabbed rejects. Later she would peel tomatoes, her pretty hands picking up a stain of red that would take weeks to disappear.

"It's only temporary, of course," she told Edna. "In the fall I suppose I'll have to look for something over the winter."

Vera wasn't going to Teacher's College either; her marks had never been quite good enough, and the final blow to her dreams had been delivered last November, when her father had suffered a massive and debilitating stroke. Vera was needed at home, not only for her paycheque, but to help her mother with the backbreaking and neverending task of tending to the speechless and broken hulk that lay in the little bedroom off the kitchen.

They had had little chance to talk over the last few weeks. Vera sometimes had to work overtime and on weekends, her hours dictated by the weather and the state of the crops. Now they sat stiffly in the uncomfortable brown chairs while Hetty flapped in and out of the parlour, manufacturing chores and little tasks that demanded her immediate attention.

"My work is never done, you know. Sorry to interrupt, but I simply must have this room clean before next Sunday."

Vera rolled her eyes, and waited until Edna's mother took a mat outside to shake off the front porch. "Has Charlie called you since the picnic?"

Edna shook her head. She'd told Vera about Charlie's pass and the look on his face when she'd called him a lobster.

"Haven't heard a word. Can't say I'm sorry."

They giggled as Edna's mother flounced back into the room.

"Will you girls be much longer in here?", she asked. "I was thinking of taking up the carpet and sweeping the floor."

"Perhaps I could come and visit you tomorrow", Edna said.

"I have to work," Vera said ruefully. "Maybe next week some time." Edna's mother went in search of a broom. "I need to talk to you about something."

But Hetty returned, triumphant with a broom and dustpan. Vera gathered up her things to go. "Call me," she said. "Sometime when we can talk."

Edna sighed and saw her to the door, then went to her room to read, leaving her mother in undisputed possession of the parlour.

CHAPTER FOUR

The lights were turned out, the office door slammed to and locked, and Edna was just pulling on her gloves when he stepped out of the shadows.

"Good evening." It was Len Collins, wearing, as usual, a fedora and a wide smile.

"Go away."

"Why? Why should I go away Edna Charles?"

"Because I don't want to be seen with you. You have a terrible reputation."

"I do?" He pretended to be shocked. "I didn't know that. What an awful thing to find out."

Edna turned on him. "Oh, don't be so silly. You know perfectly well that there isn't a respectable girl in this town who would be caught dead talking to you."

"You're talking to me, aren't you? Somebody catch you dead?"

"Oh, no you don't. You don't get away with that one, Buster. You started this, now I'm finishing it." She marched off. She was headed in entirely the wrong direction, of course, but she could always backtrack later. She could hear him laughing as she left. Their paths had crossed once or twice before, always unexpectedly. Once, she had been sitting in the park on her lunch hour, feeding the squirrels, when he came strolling down the path, his hands in his pockets.

"Oh, hello," he said when he saw her. "It's Edna, isn't it? How's your hand?"

"Perfectly healed, thank you," she replied coolly.

"Let's see." Before she knew what he was doing, he grabbed her left hand and was inspecting it closely.

"It was the other hand," she pointed out.

"Oh." He made a grab for her right hand, but she pulled it away. "Well, I'm glad to see there were no lasting ill effects. It would be a shame if I'd scarred you for life."

"No harm done. Now, if you'll excuse me, I have to get back to work." She stood and brushed the crumbs off her lap.

"I'll walk you back."

"No thank you, I'm perfectly capable of finding my own way back to the office."

"Oh well, that's all right then," he said airily. "I'm supposed to be meeting somebody here anyway."

She mustered as much dignity as she could and walked away. It was only later, in the middle of the afternoon, when it occurred to her to wonder how he had found out her first name.

She'd told Vera about Len nearly running her down in front of the church. She thought Vera would find it amusing, especially in light of the enormous argument that had ensued because of the incident. To her surprise, Vera reacted with alarm.

"Len Collins?" she said. "No wonder your mother was upset. He's notorious."

"What? For running people down?"

But Vera was serious, she realized. "Just stay away from him," she said. "He's nothing but trouble. Trust me."

Edna looked at her friend curiously. "You've gone out with him, haven't you? Why didn't you tell me?"

"It was just a couple of times. We went dancing, that's all. There was nothing to tell. He's a jerk."

Edna was a little hurt. Up until then, she and Vera had shared everything. She decided not to mention to Vera that she'd seen Len in the park. She also didn't mention that she'd run into him again in front of her father's store one day. Like Vera, she really didn't have anything to tell did she? It was nothing but a chance encounter, such as might happen any day in so small a town. A nod, a "Good Morning" and both of them went on their ways.

She crossed the street and went into Fletcher's Drug Store. Maybe by the time she had a cold drink, he'd have got the message and gone on his way. She settled herself in one of the back booths and was deliberating between a strawberry soda and a vanilla milkshake when he came in, and without a by your leave, sat across from her.

"Two chocolate malteds, please Francine", he called to the blowsy blonde who worked behind the counter of the soda fountain.

"I hope both of those malteds are for yourself", Edna said stiffly.

"Nope. One's for you."

"No thank you", Edna said. "I'd prefer a strawberry soda."

"Nah, you look like a chocolate malted girl to me." He pushed his hat to the back of his head and smiled. "I like chocolate malted girls."

"Why, Mr. Collins, you can have any girl you want. So why don't you just find yourself a chocolate malted girl and leave us strawberry sodas to ourselves."

He chuckled. "I'd heard you had a tongue in your head."

"From whom?" She was careful to use the grammatically correct "whom". She felt it put him in his place.

"Oh, now let me see." He deliberated for a moment. "Whom have I been talking to? I talked to whom at home last week, whom can hum you know, but only when there's ham."

Edna giggled. She didn't mean to, not out loud, but it was the sort of silly wordplay she loved.

"If whom hums for ham, who hums for him?" she countered.

"Why everybody knows that", he said. "For whom the ham hums. It hums for he."

Edna tried very, very hard not to laugh, but her chuckle grew into a chortle and finally exploded in a guffaw.

Len grinned. He had a lovely roguish look when he grinned. "That's the first time I've ever heard you laugh," he said.

"That's awful. That's the worst piece of nonsense I've ever heard."

"Oh, surely not the worst."

"Pretty close."

"So, can I buy you a chocolate malted since we have now established that you are indeed a chocolate malted girl?"

"I'm not sure we've established that."

"Sure we have. You laughed."

In any event, the chocolate malteds were ready. The blonde waitress dumped them onto the table grumpily.

"Why thank you Francine." He smiled up at her.

She glared.

Len shrugged.

Edna busied herself with the malted, sucking the rich sweetness through a double straw. Between sips, she stole glances at Len.

How old was he? she wondered. He must have finished high school before she'd even started. She couldn't ever remember seeing him in the halls. That would make him at least twenty-three. Maybe even twenty-five. He had always run with a loose crowd, she knew. When the rumour went around that a girl was "getting out of hand", nine times out of ten, Len's name was mentioned, along with booze and fast cars. He was certainly attractive. She could understand why girls would be anxious to go out with him. Even slumped in the booth, he looked graceful, all of a piece. No awkward movements or moments.

He drank quickly and when he reached the bottom continued to suck, making a harsh and noisy slurping sound.

"Don't", she said.

"Why?"

"It's not polite."

"Well, I'm not very polite."

"I noticed."

He slurped again, his eyes smiling at her over the top of the glass, daring her to try and stop him. She declined to comment again.

"How long have you been working for Doc Pierson?" he asked, shoving his glass to the edge of the table.

"Just since the end of June, after graduation."

"And how is it, working for the Doc?"

She shrugged. "Okay, I guess, it's not really what I wanted to do, but it's okay for now."

She expected him to ask what it was she did want to do, but he didn't.

"So how old are you? Eighteen?"

"Nearly nineteen," she said. "and how old are you, since we're getting personal?"

He laughed. "Old enough to know better."

"I've heard that."

"Oh? Where did you hear that?"

"From one of my friends."

"Is this friend only yours, or do we have an acquaintance in common?"

"Vera Matlin. Apparently you went out with her a couple of times."

He hesitated. "Aw yes, dear little Vera. Nice girl, but not really my type."

"What is your type?"

"Why, you know that," he said slowly. "I like chocolate malted girls."

He walked her home. They stopped in front of the gate.

"May I see you again Miss Charles?" he asked, with a slight bow of the head.

Edna hesitated. Her mother would have a fit, and that alone would make it worth doing, but she decided that she wouldn't mind seeing him again anyway. She had never before met a boy she found so entertaining. No, not a boy. A man. Best to keep that in mind. She studied the oil mark in the sidewalk and listened to the cicadas who were still buzzing in the late afternoon heat.

Finally she looked up at him. "Perhaps our paths may cross again sometime, Mr. Collins. I get off work at five tomorrow."

"Chocolate malted for two?"

"I may feel like a strawberry soda tomorrow."

"I doubt that." There was that grin again. He tipped his hat and walked away, whistling, hands in his pockets.

Her mother was waiting for her in the front hall.

"What are you doing?" she said. "What on earth are you doing with that awful boy?"

"He walked me home from work, mother", Edna said coolly. "He wanted to make sure I got home safely. He was a perfect gentleman, and said that he would be happy to walk me home every evening after work." Her statement had the effect she was hoping for.

"You can't be serious." Hetty was red in the face, longing to explode into a volley of threats and ultimatums, but only too aware of Edna's new independence. "Don't you realize how this will upset your father?" she said, playing what she thought was a trump card.

"If father would like to discuss it with me, I'd be perfectly happy to do so. Right now I'm tired and I think I'll retire to my room." She climbed the stairs, trying to control her shaky knees. Her mother was still a formidable opponent and Edna's rebellion was too new to come easily, but she felt she had acquitted herself well.

But Hetty followed.

"Edna, I really cannot allow this. This is a respectable family, and I will not have you bringing someone like that into my house."

"Don't worry", Edna said over her shoulder. "If he comes calling we'll be sure to use the front parlour."

Hetty sputtered. "That's Len Collins! Len Collins! You know what he's like. He's no good. Everybody knows what he's like."

"I don't, mother. I've only just met him. No doubt I'll find out what he's like in due time."

She carried on up the stairs, and as she rounded the landing had the satisfaction of seeing her mother, for once, speechless.

He was there again the next evening, and again they sat in Fletcher's and drank chocolate malteds. Two days went by after that with no sign of him. Edna was a little disappointed, but not particularly disturbed. You didn't have to spend much time with Len to realize why girls found him so attractive and mothers felt he was so dangerous. He had a quirky sense of humour that was only a thin overlay for a smoky sensuality, and Edna knew that she was probably no match for it. She couldn't for the life of her figure out why he was bothering with her at all, but she did enjoy his company, and the effect on her mother was priceless.

Besides Vera, she knew that several of her high school classmates had gone out with him a few times, the girls whose reputations were none too good anyway. She supposed they must have met him at one of the dancehalls, or when they were out drinking in cars. No one girl ever seemed to hold his attention for more than a few dates, and Edna had once overheard wild weeping in the washroom at school.

"We w-w-w-went out three times," Marsha Lampman sobbed to her best friend, "and then he just never c-c-c-alled again. Oh God, I think I'm going to die!"

Edna had no intention of dying, over Len or anybody else for that matter. If he wanted to see her, he knew where to find her. In the meantime, she wasn't going to worry about it. She wondered where Vera had met him, and where they had gone dancing. She wasn't his type, he had said, and she could see that. Vera was very pretty, in an pixie-ish sort of way, but she waged a constant battle against the creeping fat that tended to settle with distressing sullenness around her hips. She chattered too, and she didn't think Len was a chatterer. She'd always liked double dating with Vera; any awkwardness was covered by her prattle about hair, about clothes, about the latest movie, or about their classmates. But at times, even Edna found it irritating. A man like Len would soon find it a major annoyance.

He turned up the next evening, but offered no explanation as to where he had been.

"It's too hot to be inside," he said. "Let's go walk down by the harbour." He had a brown paper bag with him.

They strolled along Main Street to a little park that overlooked the bay. As always, there was a breeze blowing in, and Edna held her face up to it to cool off. The late afternoon sun turned the surface of the harbour into a glistening pool of sparkling light, near blinding in its intensity.

They sat a little way down the bank, over the rise where they wouldn't be seen from the street.

Len reached into the bag. "Sorry, I don't have any chocolate malteds in here. Want a beer?" He opened the bottle and handed it to her before she could reply. She was suddenly uneasy. Was this the come-on? A couple of malteds and a bottle of beer and she was supposed to fall into his arms? She took a tentative sip from the bottle. She had never tasted beer before, or any other alcohol for that matter. It was strictly forbidden in her mother's Baptist household. She watched Len warily.

"Sorry, I didn't think to bring a glass." He drank deeply, then grimaced. "It was cold when I bought it. Hope you like warm beer."

"This is okay." She took another small sip. It wasn't bad. Slightly bitter, but with a pleasant, almost spicy taste.

They sat in silence for a few minutes, watching the boats in the harbour as they bobbed on their moorings, their brightly coloured hulls contrasting with the blue of the water. Len stretched out beside her, propped up on one elbow.

"Sometime I'll take you out on my boat if you like," he said.

"I didn't realize you had a boat."

"Oh yes," he said. "I kept up my father's fishing licence. I go out occasionally. Occasionally I catch something."

She suddenly remembered the rumours about Len and knew he wasn't talking about fish.

"Are you a bootlegger?" she asked.

"No," he said. "I'm a businessman. Supply and demand, that's the rule of the marketplace, isn't it? You demand, I supply. So what can I supply you with Edna Charles? Another beer?"

She had barely drunk any of the first. "No thanks. I'd never make it back up the hill."

He started to talk about the boat then. He told her how his father had taken him out on the lake when he was only ten and taught him how to read the skies for storms, and how to take soundings from the lakebottom.

"He could tell just by what he brought up from the bottom where he was. Even in the thickest fog. Most people don't realize how dangerous the lake can be; part of the problem is that your compass doesn't always work out there. Nobody knows why, they just know you can't trust it. And when the visibility is poor, your chances of running into a shoal are pretty high. Some sailors listen for the fog horns, and can tell where they are by the sound each of them makes."

Edna was fascinated. This was heady stuff compared to the conversations she had previously had with boys. Most of her dates had been tongue-tied and awkward and when encouraged, could talk only about the hockey game they'd played last weekend, or when their fathers planned to plant the beans.

"What happened to your father?" she asked. She had heard something about Harold Collins, she was sure, an accident or something, but she wanted to hear about it from Len. She wanted to keep him talking, to know more, to find out who he was.

But he just shrugged. "He died." He rose, brushing grass and twigs from his trousers. "Come on, I'll walk you home." He held his hand out to help her up.

She knew it was time to go. It was getting late and her mother would be wondering where she was, but it was the first time Len had offered any sort of personal information, and she was disappointed when he so abruptly shut her out.

By the time they got to her front gate, she was desperate. The beer seemed to have gone straight through her and her bladder was bursting. She bid a hasty goodnight and ran into the house.

She saw him three or four times a week after that. He would always meet her just as she was locking up, then they would walk in the park, sitting on the bench in the sunlight, or drink malteds, always chocolate, at Fletcher's. She found his company charming and they talked for hours, but he never made a move to push things any further than that.

She began to think there was something wrong with her. Where was the dashing, dangerous man who swept so many girls off their feet? He was always so polite with her, so well mannered, nothing but a perfect gentleman. Chocolate malteds and the occasional beer didn't gel with the Len Collins she had been warned about. Not that she wanted anything more to happen, mind you, but her mother was convinced it already had, and it would have been nice to have something to flaunt. She knew that he had seldom courted the same girl for more than a few dates. She had already broken the longevity record, apparently, and yet he hadn't even attempted to hold her hand.

She puzzled over it throughout the rest of August and into the sultry September, with its constant threat of fierce thunderstorms. When the days turned steamy, she had begun rolling her hair into a large bun at the back of her head, but it always escaped its pins and crinkled into a mass of tendrils around her face. The band under her bra was constantly wet with sweat. Her stockings made her legs itch. The tiny office was unbearably close, the waiting room permeated with the smell of perspiring clientele. By the end of each day, she was sodden and exhausted and ready to scream with boredom.

Len always looked cool. He seldom wore a tie anyway, but in the worst of the heat he left several buttons of his white shirt undone and rolled the sleeves up past his elbows.

"You look like something the cat dragged in", he said to her one afternoon.

"What? You mean I look like a dead mouse?" She was sweaty and cross.

He chuckled. "Pretty much. Do you really want to get a chocolate malted or would you rather go somewhere cool?"

"Like where?"

"How about we take a cruise out to the beach? At least there'll be a breeze."

She hesitated. It was one thing to sit in Fletcher's Drug Store or go for a walk through the middle of town. It was quite another to go off in his car with him. In spite of the fact that she wanted to move things a little further along, Edna also wanted to retain control of where they moved to.

He noticed her hesitation. "Oh for crying out loud, I know I'm a well-known seducer of women, but the way you look right now, I'd have to be desperate."

She decided to take offence. "Well, never mind then, I'll just go home, if I don't meet your standards."

"Oh, come on. You're tired, you're hot and you're grouchy and I'm not surprised, locked up all day in that stuffy little office. Let's go blow the cobwebs out and then I'll like you better." He grabbed her hand and played with her fingers. "I promise I'll be good."

A part of her wanted him to be anything but. Besides, her only other option was to go home to her hot little house and read in her hot little bedroom until suppertime.

"I'm sorry," she said. "I am grouchy. So let's go cheer up."

Even though she was well aware of his reckless driving habits, the speed with which he took the corners alarmed her. It's no wonder he nearly ran me down, she thought, but she didn't comment since she had a suspicion that he was, in fact, attempting to drive carefully on her account. The

Buick's engine purred as the car ate up the miles to the beach. They pulled off the road at a spot where Edna had seldom been. Families usually picnicked near the river, where it spilled out into the bay from the small inland lake behind the dunes.

He slipped off his shoes and socks and threw them in the back of the car.

"Why don't you take your shoes and stockings off too? he suggested. "They'll end up full of sand if you don't."

He was right, but Edna was unsure how to accomplish it gracefully. Taking her stockings off meant hitching up her skirt and unhooking them from her garter belt. Leaving them on meant being uncomfortable and carting home small piles of sand, which would collect on her bedroom floor when she undressed.

"Turn your back."

He grinned and turned.

Quickly she unhooked, watching him the whole time. I hope no one drives by, she thought. She rolled the stockings down and threw them and her shoes on the floor of the front seat. Lord only knows how she would ever get them back on again before she went home, but she'd figure that out later.

"Okay."

He was still grinning as they climbed the dune bank. They hesitated for a moment at the top, lifting their faces to the sultry breeze from the lake.

"Last one to the water's a skunk," she suddenly shouted and flew down the dune, stopping only when she was ankle deep in the water.

He was at a disadvantage, of course, since he was taken by surprise and had to stop at the water's edge to roll up his pantlegs. She splashed him lightly water as he bent over.

"Two can play at that game you know."

"You wouldn't."

"Why wouldn't I?"

"Because you're a gentleman."

"Am I? I wonder."

Edna wondered too, so she started wading down the shore. She expected him to start splashing her back at any moment, but instead he quickly caught up with her, grabbing her by the arm. He scooped up a palmful of water and gently dribbled it over her face. She closed her eyes as the cool and slightly fishy smelling liquid rolled down her cheeks. He scooped again and again and let it run over her forehead, her eyes, her nose and her throat, the rivulets coursing over her face, soothing and cooling her. It was the most sensuous thing she had ever experienced.

"There. That's better. You're not red now."

She opened her eyes then. He still had her by the arm and she expected him to try and kiss her. She wanted him to try and kiss her, but instead he let go and waded off. She followed.

"Have you ever been out on the lake?" he asked. He'd obviously forgotten that he'd promised to take her.

"In a fishing boat?"

"In any kind of boat. Way out in the middle where there's nothing but you and the water and the wind."

"No. I haven't."

"I'll take you sometime. You'll like it out there. You have a wild streak."

A wild streak? She didn't think so, although her mother might be tempted to agree with him. She had always been a good girl, as far as she could tell. Good marks, good manners. "I do not!" she protested.

"Oh, yes you do. I can tell. That's why I'll take you out on the lake."

They walked on through the shallows in a comfortable silence. He made no attempt to kiss her or even to hold her hand, which again left her disappointed but at the same time, mildly relieved. What did he want from her? She couldn't read him at all. On the way home, she was once again aware that he was holding back, fighting the car's urge to accelerate down the straight sections of the road. When they reached her gate he turned to her.

"I have to go away for a few days, so I won't be around." It was the first time he had given her any warning that he would be absent.

"Did you think I would miss you?"

He grinned. "I have faint hopes. I should be back Saturday. Can I give you a call? We'll go out on the boat if it's a nice day."

Edna knew that if her mother answered the phone she would never get the message. It would be better if she called him, but girls didn't do that, did they?

"Just don't say who it is, okay? Just ask to speak to me."

"My, my I am a pariah, aren't I?"

"It's your own fault."

"Okay, I'll ask for you especially. What was your name again?"

She stuck her tongue out at him and only then remembered that she hadn't put her stockings back on. Quickly she scooped them off the floor and shoved them in her handbag. With any luck at all, she could get upstairs before her mother noticed.

But she had no luck at all.

Her mother was waiting in the front hall, huffing, outrage etching her face. "Where have you been? You've missed supper."

"I was out."

"With that man."

"Mr. Collins was kind enough to take me for a drive, yes."

"*Mister* Collins will take you for more than that! And where on earth are your stockings? What have you been doing, Edna? You know better than to go off in cars with men. I raised you better than that!"

"We went to the beach for crying out loud. It was hot."

"What else did you take off besides your stockings, young lady?"

All the cooling effect of the beach had dissipated. Edna felt sweaty and hot and claustrophobic. The smell of fried pork still hung in the air, cloying and heavy. Bill and Jack hung over the rail of the landing above her, anxious to overhear the argument, but from a safe distance. She could hear the floor creaking as they shifted their weight. The late afternoon sun illuminated the dingy hall, highlighting the stain on the wallpaper where the rain came through at the corner. She could scarcely breathe.

"I didn't take anything else off, thank you very much, mother. Mr. Collins was a perfect gentleman, not that it's any of your business. If I decide to take off all my clothes and roll around in the sand with Len Collins or Jack the Ripper or anybody else I care to, then I'll do it, and I'll do it without consulting you."

She knew she had gone too far then.

Her mother's face turned an alarming shade of deep red. Edna was suddenly dismayed and wondered about her mother's blood pressure. But then Hetty found her voice.

"As long as you're living in this house, your behaviour is my business", she snapped. "I told you I didn't appreciate you hanging around with that crook, and you've completely ignored my wishes."

Crook? Edna had heard Len called all kinds of things, but never a crook. What kind of crook could he be? Her hands were shaking. She closed her eyes for a moment to try and collect her thoughts, but the images that floated into her head were all of middle-aged women with outdated hairstyles and too much rouge. She couldn't back down now. She took a deep breath and plunged.

"I would just like to remind you that I pay you for my room and board", she said calmly. "You are no longer responsible for my upkeep and therefore no longer responsible for my behaviour. I'll see whom I like." She wasn't sure that was grammatically correct, but, as always, it sounded good.

She expected an explosion. She expected shouting. She expected her mother to clutch her chest and fall to the floor or to throw something or to hit her. To call for her father. To chase her brothers away from the landing. She expected everything and anything but what actually happened.

"Get out." It was said quietly, flatly.

"What?"

"Get out. Get your things and leave. I run a respectable household here and I won't have your kind under my roof." Hetty turned and stamped down the hall to the kitchen, slamming the door.

Billy hooted from the landing. "You're in trouble now!"

"Oh, Edna." Jack said, shaking his head.

Edna ignored them as she went upstairs to pack her suitcase.

Had Vera not been at work, and had Vera's mother not been busy trying to turn her moribund husband over so he wouldn't get bedsores, things might have turned out very differently. But the canning factory was in the middle of the first big run of tomatoes and Vera was asked to stay late and peel. Mrs. Matlin was back in the little bedroom off the kitchen, where she couldn't see down the hallway to the front door. She had the radio blaring. It kept her company during the long hours when Vera was at work, now that there was no conversation to be had from Vera's father.

Edna rang the front doorbell for a full five minutes. She wondered where everybody was. Mr. Matlin was never left alone, not even for a few minutes. She tried the door. It was locked, a precaution Vera's mother had taken to now that there was no able-bodied man in the house. Edna supposed she could go around to the back and try the door there, but the back of the Matlin house was in visual range of her mother's kitchen, and she wasn't sure whether or not she would be watching. Better to make a dignified retreat down the street than to be seen hovering around, standing pathetically on the back stoop of an empty house.

She was dragging her heavy suitcase around the corner when Len's car pulled up beside her.

"Where you going?" he called out the window.

"Back to the office. Guess I'm sleeping on the waiting room floor."

"What happened?" He still hadn't got out of the car. He could at least offer me a ride, Edna thought.

"Had a fight with my folks and they threw me out."

"Why don't you go to the hotel?"

The only hotel in town was above the local beer parlour, not a place where any woman would stay, much less an unmarried one. "Oh, that's good thinking", she said, exasperated. "I'll just barricade the door with my suitcase. That should keep the drunks out." She had no money for a hotel anyway. By the time she paid for room and board every week, there was only enough left to make a payment on the clothes she'd needed for work.

"Hmm". Len rubbed his chin absently while he considered her plight. He had recently shaved, she could she, the slight stubble that had been on his face that afternoon had been pared away. "Haven't you got a friend you could stay with?"

"She's not home."

“Haven’t you got more than one friend?”

She didn’t. Not really. Not someone she count on like Vera. Except that Vera wasn’t there now that she needed her. “No,” she said shortly.

"Oh well, hop in, we'll think of something."

She opened the back door and hefted the case onto the seat. It was all she could do to push its bulk in far enough to close the door again.

"You could help, you know," she said to him.

He shook his head. "Oh no, not me. I don't want anybody to see me putting your suitcase in the back seat of my car. Why they'd jump to all sorts of conclusions."

She slid into the front seat, slamming the door as hard as she could. Slamming a door was the most dramatic thing she could think of doing right then.

"Where are we going?" she asked as he put the car in gear.

"My place."

"Oh, my God. Stop the car!"

"Why?" he asked, but he pulled over to the curb again anyway.

"I can't go there. I can't go home with you. It'll be all over town that I was there. Talk about jumping to conclusions."

"Well", he said, rubbing his chin again. "I don't see that you have too many other options. You can't sleep in Doc Pierson's office. You can't check into a hotel. You don't have a friend you can stay with. It seems to me you're between a rock and a hard place. Now, here I am, offering my hospitality to a stray waif. I'd think you'd be grateful."

Edna burst into tears.

"This argument was about you, you know", she stormed. "I stood up for you."

"Did you? Did you really?" He smiled. "Wow. You must like me."

"Shut up and drive."

Len lived about five miles out of town, down a long lane obscured by trees. From the outside, the house looked like a shack, unpainted trim, scraggly shrubs and a broken picket fence around the front dooryard. He pulled the car into the garage, which was filled with a jumble of tools, garbage cans, rolls of wire and garden implements.

He hustled around the front end of the car and opened the door for Edna, then grabbed the suitcase and easily lifted it out of the back seat.

"Welcome to my humble abode", he said, "it's this way."

A door led into the kitchen. Bits of rope and empty whiskey bottles stood on the counter amid dirty dishes and boxes of nails. Edna looked around, dismayed.

He noticed the look on her face. "Don't worry, the rest of the house is a little tidier. Come on, I'll give you a tour."

She followed him down the hall. A door on the right opened to a small room with an old iron bedstead, a small painted dresser, and a chair. Then the bathroom, and across one side of the house, a bigger bedroom. Len merely opened the door so she could have a quick peek. Along the front of the house was a large living room with a picture window.

"Why don't you go hang your dresses up, and I'll put the kettle on for tea," he said. "You'd probably like a cup of tea, wouldn't you?"

Edna nodded.

He left her standing in the hall. She could hear him whistling in the kitchen.

She wasn't sure where she was supposed to put her things, but finally opted for the little bedroom. She hung her dresses in the closet, but left the rest of her belongings in the suitcase. Idly, she picked up the silver brush and mirror that lay on top of the dresser. The handles were carefully polished, and the silver filigree around the mirror's face gleamed. On the wall above the dresser hung a small watercolour painting of a pond, surrounded with wild iris and pink phlox.

Len appeared in the doorway. "Tea's steeping."

"What a pretty painting", Edna remarked.

"It was my mother's. Come and sit down."

He led her to the living room. Two brown leather chesterfields stood face to face, with a huge coffee table in the middle. There was no other furniture in the room. One large painting, an abstract, hung over the fireplace. The walls were painted a creamy colour and thick broadloom covered the floor.

"I don't like a lot of clutter", he said.

"Except in the kitchen, I suppose," but she compared this room with her mother's parlour, with its Victorian bric-a-brac and busy Axminster rug. She decided she didn't like a lot of clutter either.

"The important thing about this room is that you can be comfortable. I'll just go pour the tea. Take your shoes off and curl up on a chesterfield. That's what it's for."

Edna did as she was told, her still un-stockinged feet luxuriating in the feel of the carpet. Len brought her tea in a thick mug, the steamy liquid laced with sugar and a faint, rich taste she couldn't identify.

"I threw in a tot of rum", he said. "I figured you could use it."

She almost choked. Beer was one thing, spirits something else again.

"It's all right", he said. "It's just a dollop. The perfect thing for someone who's had a shock."

She felt clumsy and unsophisticated, but when she took a small tentative sip of the tea, she discovered that she quite liked the taste. Len sat politely on the other sofa.

"Well", he said, "what are we going to do with you?"

"Are you a crook?" she asked. "My mother says you're a crook."

He laughed. "Oh that's what they all say. Was that your mother's only objection to me?"

She felt like a stammering twelve year old, but she went on anyway.

"No. She thinks you're a womanizer."

"Well, now that's pretty true. I do like women, I admit that." She was startled to hear him actually say it.

"You know," he said by way of explanation, "there are so many of them out there who are so pretty, why shouldn't I enjoy their company? And I do like a clever woman, but what's wrong with that? Most of the men I know either hate women or are scared of them. They marry them, partly for the company, partly for the sex and partly because it's expected of them, but they don't really like them the way I do."

Edna thought about it for a minute and decided he was probably right. In her limited experience, most men really were scared of women. Take her father for instance. She could never remember a real conversation between her mother and her father. Most of the time they shared the house because it was convenient, domestic duties divvied up as appropriate. As for their sex life, although there must have been one sometime since they had three children, she preferred not to think about it.

He went on. "I like the way women look, I like the way they smell, I like talking to them, and most of all I like making love to them."

She jumped and spilled her tea in her lap. Len sprang forward with his handkerchief to mop it up.

"I'm being honest with you, you know. I figure I at least owe you that." He looked up at her and grinned.

"Why do you think you owe me anything?"

"Well, I do seem to be the cause of an awful lot of trouble for you."

"That's true." She sighed. "And more to come, I'm afraid."

He finished mopping and moved back to the other sofa. Edna had been sure he was going to sit beside her.

"Yes, well, as I said, I do have a well-deserved reputation as a womanizer. And you are in kind of a pickle. I don't think anybody is going to believe that you stayed the night out here and nothing happened."

Edna flushed. No, they wouldn't, she thought. And then she realized what he'd said. Nothing? Nothing was going to happen? She had no intention of going to bed with him, but she had been looking forward to fighting him off a little.

"On the other hand," he went on, " I've noticed that you can pretty much do whatever you want around here, as long as you make up for it later. If, for example, we were to get married, I expect no one would ever remember that you had spent an unchaperoned evening with me before the wedding, now would they?"

That was true, she admitted to herself. She knew any number of girls who had done it before they were married and had gone to the altar with an uninvited guest under the wedding dress. Wait a minute, what had he said?

She really must try and pay more attention. "Did you say married?"

"Yes." He knelt before her on one knee, in the classic position of the beseeching lover. "Will you marry me Edna Charles?"

"Oh, don't be so silly". She reached out with one bare foot and pushed him backwards.

"Gadzooks, I am undone", he cried, clutching his chest. "My heart has been impaled forever by my one true love." Edna giggled. "Please, tell me, dear love, tell me that your answer is not no!"

Edna got tangled in the negatives. "What?" she said.

He rolled over on his side and propped his head up on his elbow. "Why don't we get married?"

"I don't even know you very well."

"You'll like me."

"I don't know that."

He got up and sat beside her, took her hand and began absently stroking it.

"We could have a pretty nice life, you and me. I know I've been having a wild old time of it up until now, but I think it's time I settled down a little. I've got plans, things I want to do with my life. It would be nice to have somebody to do it with. Somebody like you."

Edna thought of her parents and their stifling house on Elm Street. She thought of the endless filing at the optometrist's office and how little money she had been able to save. She thought of the receding dream of Teachers' College and the endless arguments and recriminations that were sure to follow this night.

She looked at Len, at his hazel eyes, his tanned face. It was a stranger's face still. She knew almost nothing about this man who sat beside her, proposing the outlandish. But what were her alternatives? She could leave town, she supposed, leave her suffocating mother and her mindless job and her soon-to-be-damaged reputation. But what then? Another hot stifling little room in a shabby boarding house? Another mindless job filing or typing or answering the phone? Factory work, with her hands turning rough and stained like Vera's? What would be different from the way she lived now?

She didn't love this man, not by any stretch of the imagination. She didn't know him well enough, but she knew she liked him. Her mother had always accused her of being impulsive, of not thinking of anyone but herself. She knew this wasn't true; she had tried to play the game by the rules. She had studied hard and got good marks, but it hadn't got her a career. She had never been forward with boys, and as a result they had seldom asked her out. She had always gone to church and done her homework and kept her room clean and washed behind her ears and she couldn't see one single thing it had ever gained her. Marry Len Collins?

Wild, woolly Len Collins? Well, why not? Maybe it was high time to be impulsive, to do the unthinkable, to set the world on its ear. Besides, his offer was better than anything else she could see on the horizon.

"Okay", she said.

"Okay, yes?"

"Okay, yes."

His hand moved to her cheek and stroked it gently. It traced the slope of her nose, then the outline of her lips. Very gently, he leaned forward and kissed her.

He smelled of rum and cigarettes and car leather.

She pulled away. "Well, what do we do now?" she asked nervously. She was afraid she knew the answer.

"You've had a long, exhausting day", he said "I'll run you a bath, and bring you another cup of tea, okay? It'll relax you."

He pulled her into the bathroom behind him and turned on the taps. She sat on the toilet while the tub filled. While the water ran, he disappeared into the kitchen, returning a few moments later with another mugful of tea, heavily laced with the sweet, dark rum. He set it down on the edge of the bath and turned the taps off.

"Come here." He pulled her up and slowly, like one would do with a tired child, unbuttoned her dress and pulled it over her head. Edna was frozen, mute, and it was only when he started to pull up her slip that, with a great shuddering gasp, she cried "No!" and pushed him out of the room, locking the door firmly behind him.

She was already in the bath when she realized there was no soap in the dish. She got out, dripping water on the floor and looked in the medicine cabinet, into a jumble of razor blades, shaving soap and aspirin bottles. Nothing there. She opened the cupboard beside the sink. To her astonishment, there were several bars of fragrant soap with exotic names. "Jasmine Nights" she read, and "Evening Interlude". Not at all like the plain old Ivory soap they used at home. There were containers of bath salts, a huge loofah sponge and a strange apparatus with a bag and a hose which she examined and, stumped as to its purpose, put back. She emptied a packet of bath salts into the water, grabbed a bar of Jasmine Nights and climbed in.

She lay there for a moment, then reached for a washcloth. Oh, she thought. I don't have to hurry. At home, there was always someone waiting outside the door who needed to get in. She knew Len was waiting, but figured, under the circumstances, he could just darned well wait.

She looked at her body, slightly distorted in the water. What would he think when he saw the rest of her? She appraised her breasts. Not huge, but ample and very round. Not really small, either, but didn't men like large breasts? What would it feel like when he touched them? When they were married, he would be touching them a lot, she was pretty sure of that. She looked at her legs. They were pretty good, long, a nice shape. She and Vera had compared legs, Vera sighing because hers were so short, and Edna hated to admit it but it was true, kind of thick at the ankles. She had a nice bottom, though. So do I, Edna thought, my bottom's pretty good.

Married. Married to Len Collins. He was good-looking enough. There was certainly nothing repulsive about him. All the other girls seemed to think he was drop-dead gorgeous from what she heard. Tall, slim, but with a sinewy quality about him. Hard, compact muscles. What will it be like to be with him?

She tried to imagine it. She pictured herself in a long, white nightgown, with many ruffles and a lot of lace, lying languorously on a bed with a mound of pillows around her. Enter Len, who takes her in his arms and kisses her passionately and then.....and then what? Undoes the top button of her nightgown. And then the next button of her night gown. And then she undoes his top button. Oh, this is going way too slow, she thought. Okay, he takes his shirt off. And then we crawl under the satin sheets. Oh, wait a minute, he still has his pants on doesn't he? Okay, he stands up and takes his pants off, oh yeah, and his shoes and socks and he crawls under the covers in his underwear. She thought of the rows and rows of men's shorts she had hung out on the line on washdays. Her father's, her brothers'. They were kind of squalid looking when they just hung there, limp and sodden, dripping onto the ground.

Let's just skip the preliminaries, she thought. All right, we're under the covers and he takes me in his arms and then slowly lifts my night gown. She knew men lifted nightgowns. She'd read it in one of the racier novels that she and Vera had giggled over when the town librarian wasn't looking. And then we dissolve in passion, she thought. But what does that mean, exactly? She knew that her private areas and the man's private areas linked together and then you were both swept away by desire, but she had a hard time imagining it ever happening to her. She'd be too embarrassed at letting anyone touch her there.

She gave up. She'd just have to figure it out when she got there. At least Len had plenty of experience, or at least that's what everybody said. She thought of him touching the private areas of the girls he had taken out before her and shuddered. They obviously had plenty of experience too. I'm going to look like an idiot, she thought. I wish some of the other girls had talked to me. It would be nice to be able to talk to someone who had actually done it and could fill her in on the details. Mothers were supposed to do that, but she couldn't ever see her mother telling her what she needed to know. When Edna was thirteen and experienced her first monthly period, her mother had simply handed her a booklet and a box of cotton wadding. The many books she read were no help either. They stopped at the bedroom door, or made veiled references to the man "having his way." What way? she thought. Why can't they be more explicit?

She got out of the bath and dried herself off with the thick terrycloth towel. There was a full-length mirror on the back of the door. She stopped and stood in front of it. Slowly, her hand moved to the area between her legs. The hair there was much coarser than the hair on her head. She stroked it, then moved past it, still stroking. Oh, she thought, if he did that, it would be nice. She felt a wetness on her hand. Oh no, not her period, it wasn't time. She was dismayed, but when she lifted her hand there was none of the bright-red blood she expected, just a clear mucousy smear. Oh dear, was this supposed to happen? Puzzled, a little embarrassed, she wrapped herself in one of the large towels hanging from the door. Unable to ignore the routine instilled in her by her mother, she carefully washed out the bath tub and set the soap in the wire holder so it would dry.

Well, she thought, that's that. I wish I'd thought to get my dressing gown before I took a bath. Maybe, I can just tiptoe down the hall and at least get my nightgown on.

He heard the bathroom door open and was in the hall before she could get further than a few steps.

"Come here", he said and held out his hand.

She went to him. He folded her in his arms. He started to sway with her and to her surprise, she realized they were dancing, waltzing slowly to some strange song in Len's head. Slowly and around she followed, relaxing into the rhythm of the unknown waltz. He kissed her gently and then, without saying a word, he unwrapped her from the folds of the towel and let it fall to the floor.

Oh dear, she thought, that will get mildew if it lies there.

"Ahh". An almost inaudible exhalation. Still holding her by the hand, he turned her around in a full circle.

"Oh, my, but you are beautiful", he said.

He pulled her against him and kissed her hard then. Edna tried to kiss back, but things moved far too fast for her, Len's tongue sliding into her mouth, tasting, biting, sucking. Edna couldn't breathe. He scooped her into his arms and carried her into the big bedroom, staggering slightly as he hefted her onto the bed. Edna giggled.

"I'm sorry", she said. Then, unable to control it any longer, she began to laugh. "Boy, that was romantic."

He looked a little put out for a moment, and she wondered if she had done something unforgivable, but then he started to laugh too.

"Oh, God, you're wonderful", he said, nuzzling her. "We're going to have so much fun."

She undid his shirt and removed it, kissing the smooth brown chest while she took it off. Soon he was as naked as she. She forgot to notice how he got his shoes and socks off. His underwear posed no problem because he wasn't wearing any. He took his time with her, stroking and kissing.

Oh my God, Edna thought, this is incredible. It's no wonder mothers don't want us to find out about this. We'd be doing it everywhere, with everyone. She stroked him back, exploring his body with growing boldness.

And yet, in spite of the fact that she wanted Len Collins, in spite of the fact that she was oh, so ready for him, in spite of the fact that he was careful to be gentle, when he entered her, she was not swept away by passion as she expected.

It hurt.

CHAPTER FIVE

In the middle of the night she woke up and looked at the alarm clock. One a.m. Oh good, I don't have to get up for a while, she thought. She fell asleep again, not hearing the sound of the car as it pulled out of the garage.

Len wasn't there when she woke again at six with a pounding headache. She felt sticky and sore and bruised, although there were no marks that she could see. She was embarrassed at first when she realized she was naked, but then she decided it was no big deal. Not in comparison with what had happened the previous night, anyway. So that was it, she thought. The mysterious "it". The first part of it had certainly been nice, but she wasn't so sure about the rest of it. She had heard somewhere, God knew where, that it always hurt the first time, but that after that it was all right. She hoped so anyway, because she was fairly certain that she would be doing "it" with Len on a regular basis. Maybe she would get used to it.

She grabbed a bathrobe off the clothes-littered floor and padded to the bathroom, then down the hall to the little bedroom to get her clothes. She felt better after she got dressed. Not knowing what else to do, she wandered back to the bedroom. The sheets were tangled and spilled onto the floor. When she gathered them up so she could make the bed, she realized that the sheets and pillowcases smelled like Len. A little of the aftershave he wore, a little sweat, a little mustiness she couldn't identify, a touch of cigar. She liked the smell, she decided. Well, that's a relief, she thought. Imagine being married to someone you didn't like the smell of.

Married. Soon she would be married to Len Collins. Sharing a house, this house. Sharing a bed. Every night. Did married people do it every night, she wondered. Did married people share everything? When did you ever get a chance to be by yourself when you didn't have your own room? As the only girl in the Charles household, Edna was privileged to have the tiny back bedroom to herself. She wondered where her mother went when she wanted to be alone. Was that why she spent so much time in the kitchen? Was that why she had made the kitchen such an unwelcome place, a place of chores and tasks and frosty disapproval, so that they would all stay out of it and leave her alone?

She wandered into Len's kitchen. A cup of tea would be nice, she thought. She set the kettle on the stove to boil and wondered where he was. It would have been nice if he had been there when she woke up. She could use a little reassurance. She hoped she hadn't done anything wrong or embarrassing or downright laughable the night before. Maybe she been a disappointment, maybe he had had second thoughts about his ludicrous proposal and was even now trying to manufacture an excuse to back out. It had taken him long enough to get their romance off the ground, after all. Maybe he just didn't find her attractive and had taken her to his bed out of a sense of chivalry. It seemed out of character, but she knew so little about him, really, that she had no basis on which to form a judgment. She didn't know what to think.

She did know that his kitchen was a mess. By the time he walked in the door with a bag of groceries, Edna had washed most of the dishes and was just starting on the pots and pans. He smiled when he saw her, up to her elbows in sudsy, greasy water.

"Don't bother with that right now. Bacon and eggs coming up. Oh good, you've got the kettle on."

He whistled through his teeth while he let the water out of the sink and scoured an iron frying pan under the tap. "I must say it's nice to see what you look like in the morning", he said. "Not every bridegroom gets to have an advance look at what he's going to face every day for the rest of his life."

"So do I pass muster?" she asked.

"Flying colours, Eddie, flying colours."

She sat at the tiny kitchen table, playing with the salt and pepper shakers while he bustled around the kitchen, boiling water, throwing rashers of bacon into the cast iron frying pan, cracking eggs expertly with one hand.

"Are you going into town anytime soon?" It was already seven, if she didn't hurry she was going to be late.

"Oh, by and by. What do you need to go into town for?"

"I have to go to work."

"Oh I don't think so", he said over his shoulder. "I think you just resigned. The eye doc will have to find somebody else."

"But I can't just leave him flat. He has to have time to find a replacement." Edna didn't like her job, but she did feel an obligation to give notice.

"I think the filing will wait for someone else. It's not like the world will grind to a halt if you're not there to do it. Besides, I want you here when I get back."

"Back from where?" She was dismayed. He had only just returned and now he was talking of leaving again.

"Back from talking to your father of course." He looked around and smiled at her. "If I'm going to marry you, I really ought to go tell your folks that I intend to keep their little girl in the manner to which she's accustomed. And a whole lot better besides." He seemed unconcerned, as if he were talking of going to pick up his mail, or to buy a newspaper or a quart of milk.

"Listen, Len", she said slowly. "It really is awfully sweet of you to offer to marry me, but you don't have to, you know. I was just in a panic and I wasn't thinking. You really don't have to go through with this."

He turned and looked at her. She had never realized how cold hazel eyes could get. Funny, she thought, it's blue eyes that are always described as cold.

"Sweetness has nothing to do with it," he said harshly." And you're not welching. Last night you said you'd marry me and I intend to hold you to it."

He turned back to the frying bacon, flipping it in the pan.

"But you don't even know me. Why me, anyway? From what I understand you can have any girl you want."

He slid the bacon and fried eggs onto a plate and set it in front of her, then slouched in the kitchen chair opposite her. "Why do I want to marry you?" he considered. "Hmmm. Because you're presentable, you're well-mannered, your family is respectable and you're the sort of woman I need as a wife. Your mother may be an old battleaxe, but she brought you up right."

Edna looked back at him bleakly. "You know, I had always imagined that a marriage proposal would have some mention of love. Silly me." She grabbed a fork and stabbed at her eggs.

"Why, darlin', you know I love you." He poured himself a cup of tea, lit a cigarette and leered at her. "I thought I proved that last night."

Unexpectedly, Edna wanted to cry. I'm tired, she thought, in a strange place with a strange man. Too much to absorb all at once. She finished her breakfast in silence, while Len watched her eat. She stood up and put the dishes in the sink.

"I'll finish the kitchen," she offered.

"Aw, don't bother", he said. "Have a nice long, hot bath and I'll be back soon." He picked his jacket from the back of the chair, slung it over his shoulder and left.

She wandered into the bathroom and looked at herself in the mirror. She looked tired and worn and her hair tumbled down her shoulders in an untidy mess. Don't know what he sees in me, she thought.

He was jaunty. "Ready to go?" he asked.

"Go where? What happened?" She was dying to find out what her mother, via her father, had said, her reaction to this latest astounding turn of events. She was pretty sure this would be the coup de grace, after all what could her mother do or say at this point, but even so she didn't underestimate Hetty. If there was a way she could throw a monkey-wrench into Edna's works, she would.

"Wanna go shopping?", Len said. "Let's go to Kingston."

The Buick roared along the road, taking the corners too fast, passing other cars with abandon. Edna clung to the armrest. They drove in silence until they got to the ferry. There were only two other cars, already on board, and they were waved through, the ramp closing behind them. Just as well, Edna thought. She couldn't imagine Len having the patience to wait while the ferry chugged its way across the bay from the other side.

The deckhand grinned at them as he walked by. He thinks I'm just another of Len's girlfriends, Edna thought. Just wait until he hears. It was slowly dawning on her that it was really going to happen. She was going to be married.

They slowly chugged away from the shore. Len got out, then came around to her side and opened the door. "Let's stand and look over the rail like tourists", he said.

The ferry crossed a narrow reach that interrupted the highway on its way to Kingston. Behind them, the massive grey of the old stone mill nestled into the side of the cliff and from the middle of the reach they could see the tiny village that perched precariously above it. In the still of the morning, the scene had a fairytale quality to it, an enchanted place that would lay sleeping peacefully until the giant awoke and brought it to life.

They leaned over the rail and watched the shoreline slip away from them. "My dad always said there was a cave with gold buried in it somewhere up on that cliff", Len said.

Edna hadn't ever heard this. "Whose gold was it?"

"Oh, around here it's always some French sea captain, isn't it? I don't know what it is about those French sea captains. They always seemed to be sailing around the lake with chests full of gold and silver and then losing them somehow. You'd think they'd smarten up after a while and just leave the valuables at home."

"The story I heard was about the Indian maiden who was separated from her one true love," said Edna leaning with her back against the rail. "She was about to marry another and her tribe lit huge bonfires on the top of the cliff in celebration of the wedding feast. Her lover saw them just in time to return and claim his bride."

He turned to her then. "Well, I didn't have to light any bonfires or dig for buried gold this morning. I explained the facts to your father and he gave me his blessing quite readily."

Edna didn't believe it could have been that easy. "And what did my mother say?"

"Your mother was a trifle cool with me, I'll admit that." He kissed the tip of her nose. "She did, however, seem to be quite eager to get you off her hands. What have you been doing to upset her so much?"

"Seeing you." She felt a little disappointed that there hadn't more of a fuss. She had vaguely imagined a large and noisy argument, her mother beating Len around the head and shoulders with an umbrella or a rolling pin or something. She wanted a blow by blow account. She wanted to know what Len had said to them. Did he mention anything about love? Did he tell her father that he was madly in love with her, couldn't live without her, would turn over a new leaf and be a dutiful son-in-law for the rest of his days? She didn't think so somehow.

"They both seemed relieved that they weren't expected to pay for the wedding," he went on. "Of course, I did ask them for a dowry."

"What?"

He laughed, and kissed her again, a loud smack on the lips this time. "Everything's fine. I stopped and picked up a marriage license. We can get hitched on Thursday."

"Thursday. So soon?"

"Yeah, that's okay isn't it? Why wait? Can you round up somebody to stand up with you by Thursday?"

There was only one choice. Vera. "What about my parents?" she asked.

"Oh, they'll be there with their best faces on. It will only take a few minutes. I thought you might have some friend you'd like there."

Like every girl, Edna had dreamed of her wedding, but she had always pictured herself in a long white gown with four or five bridesmaids, and maybe a little flower girl. It would take place in the church she had attended with her parents since she was a baby, her father leading her, smiling, down the aisle, her mother dabbing at her eyes. She sighed. Nothing else about her life seemed to be turning out the way she expected it, why should her wedding be any different? She turned to look back at the cliff top, the sunlight sparkling off the spire of the little church that anchored the village. No little churches for her.

"Anyway," he said, "since we're leaving on our honeymoon so soon, I thought we'd better get you a trousseau today."

"But I don't have any money for a trousseau."

He laughed. " Sorry babe. I'm not hanging around with no shabby bride. "We're getting you a trousseau, Rousseau."

"In case we go to a soir-ee, Charlie." She smiled at him, closed her eyes and let the wind blow through her hair. What will happen will happen, she thought. She could no more alter the course of events than she could alter the course of the ferry.

The highway picked up where it had left off on the other side of the reach. Originally no more than a cart track along the shore, it had never lost its meandering and unhurried quality, in spite of modern improvements like paving. Century old houses guarded the road, dowagers who turned up their noses and looked down disapprovingly at the riffraff that now paraded in front of them.

They sped along the road and into Kingston, following Princess Street into the main part of the city. Len pulled up in front of Searling's. Edna had only ever looked in the windows of Searling's.

"We'll see what they've got here", he said as he helped her out of the car, "I really ought to take you to Montreal some time , but this will do for starters. And no looking at price tags. If you like something, try it on."

The first floor was dedicated to day wear. The polished sales lady peered over her spectacles at Edna's flowered cotton dress and directed them to the mark-down rack at the rear of the store. Len paid no attention to her, walking instead directly to a display near the front.

"How about this one", he said, pulling out a froth of white.

"White's so impractical", Edna objected. "You only wear it once and then you have to wash it."

"I like it. It'll make you look virginal."

"And I won't be able to wear it until next summer."

"Oh, okay. How about these?" He went along to the latest arrivals and picked out three dresses that Edna thought were astoundingly sophisticated. "Go try them on."

She had never seen anything so fine. The dresses fit her perfectly across the shoulders and fell from her waist in a beautiful flow to her knees. Len bought all three while she was still in the changeroom. The saleslady's attitude improved noticeably when she saw the wad of cash he pulled out of his pocket to pay for them.

The second floor had coats and hats.

"Try on some hats." Len said. Edna picked up a small froth of felt and veil. She perched it on top of her head, looking at herself in the mirror from several angles.

"I don't think so", she said.

"Those hats really suit women with shorter hair", the saleslady said. "Perhaps if madam had her hair done first...."

"No", Len said. "Madam doesn't want to have her hair done. Madam's hair is beautiful the way it is." The saleslady sniffed and walked away.

They settled on a large-brimmed hat that made Edna look at least twenty-five. Shoes were next, to match the dresses they had bought.

She noticed a sign that said "Lingerie - Fourth Floor". When Len asked the elevator operator to go up, she looked at him quizzically. Surely he wasn't going to help her buy underwear? He just grinned that crazy, lopsided grin at her and whistled through his teeth.

And oh, what underwear! She was embarrassed at his male presence in this world of lacy garter belts and beribboned brassieres, but he didn't seem at all uncomfortable. Left to herself, she would have picked sensible cotton, but Len swooped down on black satin panties, low-cut bras, silk stockings.

She looked at lovely white nightgowns, buttoned high on the neck, with lace and ruffles, just like the one she had imagined herself wearing on her wedding night, but Len insisted on slinky satin in dark, rich hues, nightgowns Edna could not imagine anyone actually sleeping in. I guess they're not for sleeping, she thought.

Over lunch, she protested at the amount of money he had spent.

"Oh, for God's sake, you've spent most of your life counting nickels and dimes, it's about time you learned how much fun it is to throw money around," he said. "Besides, I expect my wife to be well-dressed, especially on our honeymoon. The way you look is a reflection on me. Think of it as a business investment," he went on. "After all, what would you think of the Prime Minister if the Prime Minister's wife slouched around in an old housedress?"

"You planning on being Prime Minister?"

"Of course."

"I can't believe you went with me to buy underwear. Would a Prime Minister do that?"

"I told you I like women. Their clothes are a lot more fun than men's. Especially when I get to remove them." He wiggled his eyebrows at her in a bad imitation of Groucho Marx.

"Idiot." Still, she was pleased. If this was what her marriage was going to be like, she could certainly get used to it pretty fast. Besides, he was right. Neither her school clothes nor the business suits she had bought for work were appropriate for a honeymoon. She was just surprised that it had occurred to him.

They roared back home the same way they had come. He does everything in such a hurry, Edna thought, he doesn't give you time to think. When they pulled into the driveway, she was struck by the decrepit appearance of the house.

"Why don't you fix up the outside?" she asked. The inside is nice."

"Until now, I haven't wanted anyone to know how well I'm really doing", he said. "Besides, it makes it harder to see the house from the road. Don't worry, that'll change now."

They unpacked the boxes and bags, Edna shaking the clothes out in delight. Len sat at the end of the sofa watching her and blowing smoke rings. At around eight o'clock he got up.

"You'd better get on the phone and get your Thursday girlfriend lined up", he said. "I wasn't kidding last night. I really do have some business to take care of. I won't go out of town just now, but I do have some things to see to. I'll be back later, okay?" He kissed her quickly, grabbed his jacket and left.

She was dismayed. She had expected they would spend the evening together, trying on her new clothes and talking about their new life, now that everything was settled. She had expected that they would laugh together, maybe cuddle a little on the couch, that Len would kiss her like he had kissed her last night only longer and more, and then he would lead her to the fourposter in the big bedroom. Sighing, she picked up the phone and dialed Vera's number.

Vera was tired, grumpy and profoundly worried. She had spent the day peeling tomatoes, carefully removing the thin outer skin that had been loosened by hot water, the still-warm juice flowing down her hands and arms, staining them a dull and dirty red. She had started work at seven that morning, and worked through until six, side by side with farmers' wives and the women from the army camp who jumped at the chance to supplement their husband's meagre pay. Vera found their conversation tedious; the farm wives talked about children and recipes, the army wives about childbirth and men. This last topic frequently veered to the coarse, and she was embarrassed by their talk. They were all half in love with the foreman, who remained oblivious to their ogling and ribald remarks, or at least he seemed to.

Not so poor Mac Dunlop, whose job it was to take the crates of canned tomatoes and stack them on the truckbed that would take them to the warehouse. Mac had been in several of her classes at school, and Vera had been a little taken aback when she started work and discovered he was there too. She knew he had a crush on her, but had never overcome his shyness enough to go further than to nod at her as they walked down the hall.

Mac was big, at least six feet tall, with large hammy hands and broad shoulders. Strong as an ox, he had no difficulty with the heavy crates. The army wives speculated as to what other parts of him were like an ox, and he blushed as red as the tomatoes he carried every time he was near enough to hear one of their comments.

Vera felt sorry for him; he was as out of place as she, and sometimes she would drink a pop with him at break or lunch, but not often, because that only fuelled the fires and made their comments bolder.

Lately she had had no time for poor Mac. As soon as breaks were called, she scurried to the washroom hopefully, only to emerge a few minutes later, downcast.

She was late. Very late. Usually her body functioned with clock-like precision, but there had been no sign for the last two months. For the last week, she had felt a pressure in her abdomen and a need to go to the bathroom frequently, something that had sometimes happened to her just before a period, but so far no welcome flow had appeared.

Why do they call it the curse? she wondered. At this point it would be no curse, but a blessing. She knew, deep down, what the problem was, and she knew that sooner or later she was going to have to come to terms with it. But how?

There was no question in her mind who was responsible; there had been only one. One she wasn't even sure she liked, and who, apparently, didn't like her. He hadn't called again after that night at The Palace of the Moon and she had been devastated, lying on her bed weeping late into the night. Her mother had been right all along, she thought, men were after only one thing, and if you gave it to them, you'd regret it for the rest of your life. Still, at some point she supposed she'd have to discuss it with him, he was going to have to shoulder some of the blame, but she dreaded the interview. She wondered what he would do. If he had been any of the other boys she had gone out with, she could have counted on him to do the right thing, to make an honest woman of her, to legitimize the situation. But he wasn't any of the other boys. She would have to call him, she guessed, since he hadn't called her. She'd do it soon. Some day when she wasn't so tired.

There had been more work waiting for her when she finally got home from the factory. Her father was taking up more and more of her mother's time and most of the household tasks were now left to Vera.

"I think we're out of butter and milk," her mother called from the back bedroom. "Can you run down to the store?"

She sighed and pulled a couple of dollar bills out of the jar on top of the refrigerator. She'd go to Buchanan's, it was the closest.

As usual, there was a cluster of people by the counter, telling jokes, gossiping, passing the time of day. She ignored them and headed for the back of the store, where the long refrigerated cases held dairy products and cold meats.

"I wouldn't mind running off with her myself," she heard over the whirring of the fans and the buzz of the compressors.

"You'd run off with anybody who'd have you...." Raucous laughter.

"Len has really done it now..."

"....wonder Bert Charles don't take a horsewhip to him..."

".....Norah Lewis saw them getting into the car...."

They fell silent as she approached the counter and paid for her bottle of milk and half-pound of butter, but the chatter resumed as she let the wooden door slam, setting its bell tinkling.

She had no time to think about what she'd overheard. There was still a mound of soiled linen to be washed, supper to be cooked and the dishes to clear up. She had been working such long hours that she'd got behind in all the housework. She was bone-weary and her head nodded over her after-dinner tea.

"Have you talked to Edna lately?" her mother asked.

Vera shook her head. It had been at least a week since she'd had time to do anything but work and sleep.

"I heard something from old Mrs. Lewis today, but I can hardly believe it. She says Edna has run off with Len Collins. I told her she was nothing but an old gossip, but she says she saw Edna getting into Len's car with a suitcase last night."

The telephone rang before Vera could reply. It was Edna.

"Edna? Oh, Edna what have you done?" Vera wailed when she realized who it was. "That old busybody Mrs. Lewis is telling everybody you've gone off with Len Collins."

Edna was irritated. "I got thrown out of the house and I couldn't get anybody to answer at your place! What did you want me to do? Sleep in a ditch?"

"You mean it's true? God, you should hear what they're saying around town!"

She was curious. "What are they saying?"

"They're saying it's a wonder your father doesn't take a gun and shoot Len. They're saying that it's a crying shame what Len Collins has done to a nice girl like you! They're saying he's gone just a little too far this time."

"He's asked me to marry him. On Thursday. Do you suppose that'll be respectable enough for them?" She had a sudden desire to call the whole thing off, to remain the wild and ruined girl her neighbours and relatives imagined her to be. It was kind of exciting to be ruined.

"You believed him?" Vera wailed. "You actually believed him when he said he'd marry you?"

"We went to Kingston today and bought a lot of clothes for the honeymoon. I've seen the license. We have an appointment at the court house. I think it's really going to happen. Listen, Vera, I'd like you to stand up with me."

"What?"

"I want you at my wedding. I know we've grown apart a little since we both started work, but you're my best friend!"

"Don't ask me to do this."

"Please, Vera, I need you!"

"Oh, God!" Vera's voice, like her heart, was hollow.

"Vera, what's wrong with you? Are you afraid of what people might say? I didn't think you were like that!"

"It's not that", she said, her voice choking. "It's not that at all.....oh God....yes, Edna I'll be there. I'll stand up with you."

She hung up and surprised her mother by bursting into tears.

Vera stood with her nervously, worrying the little knot of wildflowers she carried into a limp and unidentifiable mass, bits of stem and leaves collecting on the front of her dress. Len had seemed unsurprised when Edna told him her choice of bridesmaid. "Oh that's right," he said, "I forgot. You only have one friend. Well, we'll just have to put up with the chatty Miss Matlin, won't we?"

Her parents arrived and without a word sat stiffly and unmoved in the first row of hard wooden chairs that were set across the room.

She had dithered over what she should wear. She had tried on all her new clothes, the clothes that Len had bought her, but none of them seemed appropriate. She finally decided on the plain grey suit that had been her church clothes in another life, with a corsage of tiny mums she had picked from the ruined garden behind Len's house.

She had spent a pleasant afternoon in the little garden. In the two days before the wedding, Len had hardly been around. They would lie in bed until quite late in the morning, but after that he quickly left, pleading "business". He took her out for dinner both nights, then back to the house to make love to her. But again he drove off sometime after she fell asleep, not returning until almost dawn. She wondered how he managed to stay so alert with so little sleep.

During the day, she had pottered around, mostly outside, pulling away quackgrass and maple seedlings. Someone had planted the garden with care, she noted, mostly in perennials and flowering shrubs. It was the dead season of the year, when little bloomed except mums and asters, but she could see that there would be a progression of flowers starting in the spring, beginning with narcissus and tulips and working the palette through lilacs, hydrangea and burning bush. Untended lilies had spread across the lawn in an exuberant march, claiming territory that nothing else could survive in.

Len said that his mother had liked to garden, it was probably hers. Probably? Edna thought. You mean he didn't even notice? You don't plant a garden like that overnight, and it must have been beautiful. How could you not notice?

She was being asked to say something. She looked at the yellow hands of the Justice of the Peace, then up into his disapproving face.

"Will you, Edna Elizabeth Charles take this man to be your lawfully wedded husband?" he repeated.

"I will", she whispered. Oh God, here she was at her own wedding, and all she could think of were daylilies. And then Len was putting a ring on her finger and the Justice of the Peace pronounced them bound together forever. She wondered where the ring had come from. It looked old and was a little too big.

Her wedding was over with in a matter of moments, it seemed. She and Vera signed some papers, then Len and someone called Joe, whom Edna had never met before. Her father signed papers as well. She had no idea what it all meant, except that evidently everything was now legal.

They all shook hands, and then she and Len climbed into the Buick and drove off. Her mother had not spoken a word to her. Vera hugged her, then stood forlornly on the sidewalk as they left. Edna watched her in the rear view mirror as long as she could, until she disappeared into a tiny, lumpish dot.

They drove north, over the bridge and through Belleville. There was a noticeable change in the landscape as they headed towards Highway #7, the soft, rolling hills of the south giving way suddenly to upthrusts of bare, pinkish granite. The leaves here had already turned in a spectacular splash of colour, the countryside a blur of scarlet and yellow. Len chattered about each village and town they drove through, demonstrating a breadth of knowledge about the area that impressed her.

She was just beginning to wonder if he had arranged to spend their honeymoon camping and forgotten to tell her when they turned off the highway and after another half hour's drive down a narrow county road, pulled through a pair of massive granite gates.

Beside a lake stood a magnificent three storey lodge with verandas and towers and balconies spilling off it in frivolous random. On every veranda and porch, and out on the expanse of lawn, wooden adirondack chairs were arranged in cozy groupings. She was enchanted.

"The summer crowd has thinned out", Len said. "So we shouldn't be bothered too much."

He signed the register "Mr. and Mrs. Len Collins" and it was only then that the fact of her marriage hit home. I should have practiced signing my name, she thought, like we used to do in public school. Edna Collins. Mrs. Len Collins. What if someone calls me Mrs. Collins and I don't answer? she thought. There were a lot of practicalities to marriage she hadn't considered before.

She stood at the window while the bellboy showed Len the bathroom and light switches. Their room had a spectacular view of the long narrow lake in front of the hotel. It was still dotted here and there with fishermen, unwilling to waste the last precious days of good weather.

"Well, what do you think?" Len asked, standing behind and wrapping his arms around her.

"It's beautiful. I love it. Thank you."

"You're welcome." He kissed her neck. "I made reservations for a late dinner, so we don't have to put up with too many people. Wear one of your new dresses."

After she showered, she piled her hair on top of head, so she would look more sophisticated. Her wedding ring kept catching in the hairpins, so she took it off while she wrestled with the masses of curls. Maybe I should cut it, she thought.

"Do you think I should cut my hair", she asked Len, who was lounging on the bed blowing smoke rings at the ceiling.

"No. I like it the way it is. Don't ever cut it. It's more romantic long."

All right for you, you don't have to cope with it, she thought.

"Are you ready yet?" he asked. "I'm savage as a meataxe." At last she was.

The dining room was huge, the white-clothed tables appearing to stretch away forever. There were windows everywhere. They were seated so they could see the woods, the moon just starting to rise up over them, bathing them in a soft silvery light that magnified and distorted. A waiter moved around the room lighting candles.

Len ordered champagne. "Well, Mrs. Collins", he said as she took her first sip. "Are you a champagne girl, or would you rather have a chocolate malted?"

Edna had never tasted champagne before. The bubbles tickled her nose. It's like alcoholic gingerale she thought. But she liked it. "I could pretty much switch over to being a champagne girl for the rest of my life", she allowed.

Len grinned and ordered, shrimp cocktail to start and chateaubriand to follow. Edna didn't know what chateaubriand was.

"How do you know I'll like it?" she asked.

"Oh, you'll like it. You liked the champagne, didn't you?"

"You're awfully bossy."

"I'm your husband now. I'm allowed to be bossy."

"Oh really?"

"Oh really." He leaned forward over the table. "You have to do exactly what I want you to, you know. I'll show you what I mean later."

"Oh, you will, will you?" She felt a thrill of anticipation.

But they lingered over their dinner, chatting and laughing. Len was absolutely charming, pointing out other diners and inventing fantastic stories for them.

"He's a spy", he said of a florid man to their left. "That's why he sits in the corner, so he can't be taken by surprise. You watch, he'll pass something to the waiter any moment now. It's probably in code."

"They're having an affair", he said of a middle-aged couple by the wall. "They don't want to sit by a window because they're afraid someone might see them."

Edna looked at the mousy woman. "You'd think he could do better than that if he's going to have an affair", she pointed out.

"Well, maybe they're sitting by the wall because he doesn't want anyone to figure out that's the best he could do", Len laughed.

And all the time, he kept pouring champagne.

As soon as she stood up, she knew her legs were going to be unreliable.

"You got me tipsy", she accused.

"Yup." he said. "But not very. You'll be all right as soon as you start walking."

She leaned on him giggling. They wove into the lobby, Len whispering nonsense at her as she tried to regain some decorum. It was hopeless. She burst into laughter in front of the reception desk. To her surprise, the clerk smiled.

"He knows we're newlyweds. We can get away with murder."

"It's not murder I want to commit", Edna said, nibbling on his ear. All of her inhibitions seemed to have been turned off. All she wanted to do was to get this long-legged, wickedly handsome man upstairs to their room and tumble into bed with him. For once, “they” had been right. After the first time, it hadn’t hurt at all, and now the champagne had erased whatever apprehensions were left.

Afterwards, when she was almost asleep, nestled under his arm, he suddenly began stroking her cheek. "Eddie?" he said.

"Mmm."

"Eddie, are you happy?"

She rolled on her side and looked at him then, expecting to see the lopsided grin. It wasn't there. He was serious, there was no glint of humour in his eyes, no telltale twitching at the corner of his mouth.

She looked at the hazel eyes, the long brown face. "I think maybe I am, Len." She just wasn’t sure why it was important to him.

CHAPTER SIX

Vera swung her legs against the loading dock as she nibbled at her bologna sandwich. She hoped it would stay down. Yesterday she had packed egg salad, and there had been a panicky moment in the afternoon when the sulphurous aftertaste had almost gagged her, and she was sure she was going to have to leave the line and run to the dark, spider-infested washroom.

Mac had plain cheese, thick slabs of orange piled mountainously between slices of homemade bread. She tried not to watch as he devoured the first two sandwiches. There were another two that he would save for the afternoon break. It was his last day at the factory. At the beginning of the summer, had put his name in with the County Roads Department in the hopes that a job might open up there. County jobs didn't pay much, but it was full time and year round. He hadn't had any real hopes, but unexpectedly, one of the regular crew ran off with his brother's wife, and another was diagnosed with liver cancer, leaving gaps that needed to be filled before winter and the snow ploughing began. The foreman hired the first two reasonably qualified applicants who answered their phones. Fortunately, Mac had been home that day.

Vera knew she had to do something soon. She knew of plenty of girls who had children and no husband, but she had always looked down her nose at them. Their children were grubby and ill-clothed, carriers, she was sure, of the epidemics of scabies and lice that occasionally swept through the public school. The mothers themselves seemed to spend most of their time at the beer parlour, in some cases parking babies in their carriages outside the entrance while they whiled away the afternoon inside. She didn't know for sure where they got the money for beer, but she had her suspicions. Time was running out; they would be called back to work in a few minutes, and the afternoon break was no time for personal discussion. It was too short, and they all tended to stand around in a clump instead of breaking off into little groups like they did at lunch time.

She took a deep breath, then spoke in a rush."Mac, would you like to go to the church dance with me on Saturday night?"

His mouth was still full of cheese sandwich. He shoved it aside into his cheek so he could answer, making his moon face look even rounder.

"I'd like that," he managed to get out.

"Pick me up at my house at seven. Okay?"

He nodded, his eyes almost as round as his face, and watched her with wonder as she hopped off the loading dock and went back to work.

Mac arrived at her door with his hair slicked down and a corsage in his hand, in spite of the fact that it was only a church young people's dance. It was the corsage, already wilting in his sweaty hand, that gave her the courage to go ahead. She had been on the verge of phoning him all day and backing out, pleading some excuse or other, but the drooping orchid looked so sweet, and so pathetic that she warmed towards this innocent overgrown boy who stood so bashfully on her doorstep.

The music was already playing when they arrived at the church basement. The minister hovered over the portable phonograph, while parent chaperons watched to make sure couples didn't dance too closely together. They needn't have worried; as usual, most of the boys were lined up on one side of the hall, and the girls on the other, their heads framed by crayoned pictures from the Sunday School class.

The minister was glad to see Vera. She loved to dance and could be counted on to get things going. This was his first parish and he was anxious to make a success of these Saturday night events. He had gone out on a limb with the church board when he first suggested it, and he walked a fine line between making it enjoyable for the teenagers and acceptable for the chaperons. Vera always managed to impart a gaiety that proved to be infectious with the others, and soon after her arrival, the boys would often swallow their shyness and cross the floor to claim a partner.

But there was no gaiety in Vera tonight. She clung grimly to the gigantic boy she had brought with her, trying vainly to pilot him around the floor without getting her feet stepped on too often. Mac's face got redder and redder, and his tongue stuck out from the corner of his mouth as he concentrated on trying to move his body, and Vera's, with the music. They stopped for lemonade after the third dance. Vera killed some more time by retiring to the ladies' room, where she primped in the mirror and washed her hands a couple of times. Outside it was just starting to grow dark, twilight casting strange shadows against the cars in the parking lot. Three more dances, she thought, and that should do it.

Mac was doing his best to make conversation with the minister. This wasn't his church, and this was the first time he had attended any of the dances. He nodded politely as the minister explained the rationale of the church providing innocent amusement for its teenaged congregation, but he looked relieved when Vera retrieved him.

Around and around the floor they went, first a jitterbug, which they got through by the simple expedient of Mac holding her hand and swaying while she displayed the steps; then a simple one-two step, then a faster tempo. She waited until near the end of this third song before she turned her ankle over, grabbing at Mac to keep from crashing to the floor.

"Oh gosh, are you all right Vera?" His face was a mask of concern as he set her back on her feet.

"Ouch. I've really hurt my ankle." She stood with one foot on tiptoe, testing it to see if it would hold her weight, wincing when she tried to put her foot down.

"Oh gosh. Did I do that? I'm so clumsy. I'm sorry."

She smiled up at him. "No, it wasn't you. I just missed my step." She looked rueful. "But I don't think I can dance any more tonight."

She reassured the minister that it was a simple injury while Mac got her coat. They both helped her out to Mac's father's car.

"Do you want me to take you home?" he asked, when the minister had tucked her in the driver's side and returned to the dance.

"You know, now that I'm sitting down, my ankle doesn't hurt at all," she said. "It's a shame to waste the whole evening by going home. Let's just drive around for a while. Okay?" She smiled up at him.

Mac was sometimes slow on the uptake, but he was also a nineteen year old male, and he knew that Vera was suggesting that they go parking. He knew from locker room conversations at school that the other boys took their girls along one of the back roads that crisscrossed the ridge overlooking the town, and he was pretty sure he knew a place where he could pull the car off to the side of the road and they would be out of sight of any passing traffic. Here, he could put his arm around Vera and kiss her. He knew that the other boys often went further, depending on the girl. He didn't know if Vera would let him touch her breasts or not. Sometimes, he knew, the girl would let you unhook her bra, so you could really feel them, not just through her clothing, but he thought that probably wouldn't happen tonight. Not on the first date. He grew hot just thinking about what she might or might not let him do.

Vera turned the radio on while they drove. She hoped Mac wouldn't notice that her hands were shaking, but she needn't have worried; it was all he could do to keep the car on the road and his speed near the limit.

By using a farmer's access they were able to pull into a field, well-screened by a thick row of lilac bushes growing along the fenceline. Mac turned the ignition off, but kept the radio playing. Slowly he put his arm over the back of Vera's seat, more or less around her shoulders. She scooted across to him, nestling in his arms.

He had no finesse at all, and Vera wasn't sure he had ever even kissed a girl before. She broke away from his probing tongue and nibbled at his ear. He groaned and dared to brush his hand against her breast. She leaned in closer, and his hand found its target, massaging convulsively. She moved her hand to his thigh, and then to the already enormous bulge under his fly.

He was breathing heavily as his hand moved down across her stomach and between her legs, hardly daring to believe that he was being allowed this incursion. This was a whole lot more than an undone brassiere.

In spite of herself, Vera's body was responding, and she knew then that it was going to be all right, that she could go ahead with this. She let him explore until she was sure that he was about to explode, then hoisted her skirt and slid across his lap.

Mac meant to stop. He meant to ask her if she was sure she wanted to do this. He meant to ask about rubbers and whether or not they should wait until he had some, but Vera was straddling him before he had a chance to frame the words, and then the world exploded in a vast, white, blinding wave of ecstasy.

Hetty called the second Saturday after the wedding, to ask Len and Edna to dinner after church the next day. Edna was surprised at this conciliatory gesture on her mother's part. Was she prepared to accept her defeat, now that Edna was legally married and events had moved beyond her control? But no, she realized, Hetty was simply trying to set the ground rules on her own terms, while it was still early in the marriage, before Edna had a chance to consolidate her victory.

"I'll have to talk to Len first," she hedged.

"No", he said, when she told him about it.

"Why?" She didn't want to go anywhere near her mother, but she did want to hear his reasons for the refusal.

"I married you, not your family. I don't see why I should have to waste a whole Sunday with a bunch of people I don't like. Besides," he grinned at her. "It's more fun to lie around in bed on a Sunday, now isn't it?"

Edna relayed a politer version of this to her mother.

"Well", Hetty said, "I hope you're happy. He's cut you off from your family and your friends. You've made your bed, I guess you'll just have to lie in it."

Edna toyed with the idea of telling her that bed was an astoundingly delightful place these days and that she was perfectly happy to lie in it, especially on Sunday mornings, especially with Len, but decided not to rub it in. "I'll come over for a cup of tea real soon", she promised, although what on earth she would find to talk to her mother about, she didn't know.

She certainly couldn't talk to her about what went on when they lay in the bed she had made. Sometimes they would spend hours there, talking, cuddling, making love. Len told her stories sometimes; stories of shipwrecks, of long-forgotten crimes, of old political arguments, new political arguments, amusing events or even more amusing characters. She never knew when the things he said were true and when he was making them up. He never talked to her about his business. She still wasn't sure exactly what it was that Len did. He would disappear for hours at a time, but he never told her where he was going.

"Out," was all he would say when she asked. "I'll be back." As if there might be some doubt about it and she needed reassurance. He always seemed to have plenty of money, usually in cash.

At first she pottered around the little house, tidying and making an inventory of its contents. Len's kitchen was appallingly ill-equipped. One frying pan, two saucepans, a tea kettle and a handful of utensils were all she could find. The mismatched pieces of china were old and cracked in places.

That was all right. It fit her notion of his deprived bachelorhood. She took everything out of the cupboards and scrubbed them down with a solution of bleach. She scoured the linoleum and washed the kitchen curtains.

She hoped Len would notice when he came home, and compliment her on her housekeeping, but she was afraid that, like most men, he would fail to see the improvement and she would have to point it out. He noticed, but he didn't compliment.

"Look at your hands", he said. "God, you look like a cleaning woman."

It was true. The bleach had reddened and dried them out. They were chapped and sore looking.

"I didn't marry you because I needed a housekeeper, you know."

"Why did you marry me then?" She was puzzled by his reaction. Women were supposed to wash and scrub, weren't they? That was part of the bargain.

"Oh, no question," he said. "I married you so I could do rude things to your body."

"Well, you certainly do that all right."

"I haven't ever heard any objections," he pointed out.

"No. You've led me to the depths of depravity, that's why. I used to be a respectable girl."

"I like depraved girls better."

"I noticed." But she wondered what she was supposed to do with herself all day.

She continued cleaning the little house, mostly because she was bored, but after that she was careful to wear rubber gloves. She hardly ever cooked much. When he was there, they ate out. He would arrive home with basics like bread and milk or bacon and eggs tucked into a paper bag under his arm, so breakfast was always taken care of, but he didn't seem to expect her to set his dinner reverently in front of him every evening at six o'clock sharp, which was what she thought wives were supposed to do. There was no point in cooking dinner anyway; the chances of his actually being there at any given time were remote. They ate when they were hungry, drank when they were thirsty and made love whenever Len felt like it.

She spent hours on the phone, with Vera when she had time, sometimes with other girls from school, once she even phoned her mother. As she feared, she couldn't think of much to say. The other girls were eager to hear the details of her marriage. They were a little too eager, to Edna's mind, and she kept the conversation general. Vera was friendly enough, but there was a cool edge to their conversations that puzzled her.

Edna wondered if she was pregnant. She had always been led to believe that a single act of love could lead to conception. One indiscretion and her life would be ruined, or so she had been told. After the last couple of weeks, she thought, I certainly *should* be pregnant. It's a good thing the number of children you have isn't dependent on the number of times you have sex. I'd make the Dionnes look commonplace.

She discovered she wasn't a week and a half after the wedding when she woke up in a mess. Len had already gone, thank goodness. She looked all over the house, but couldn't find anything to use except for an old towel which she bunched up and pinned to her underwear, a stopgap measure that might hold her through the morning. She had no idea when Len would be back. She wondered how much a taxi to town would cost. Looking in her purse, she discovered that she had only forty-seven cents.

There was a jar full of change on the dresser. She scooped several handfuls, threw it in the bottom of her purse and called a cab. This is silly, she thought, I need to have some money of my own.

She went to Fletcher's Drug Store. Hannah Young was behind the counter. She had forgotten that Hannah was clerking for Fletcher's. She smiled and headed for the back, where sanitary supplies were discreetly stacked behind rows of vitamin supplements and tonics. Mrs. Henderson, the Rev. Mrs. Henderson, stood squarely in the aisle between Edna and the Kotex.

"Edna," she nodded coolly.

"Mrs. Henderson." Edna summoned up her best smile. Damned old bitch, she thought, don't you try and cold shoulder me. " I must apologize, Mrs. Henderson, " she said smoothly. "I'm so sorry I haven't been in church recently, but you see, now that I'm married, I must of course defer to my husband's wishes. I'm afraid you probably won't see me in your congregation any more."

She deliberated for a moment, leisurely picked up a box of pads so Mrs. Henderson would be sure to see it and left her standing open-mouthed in the aisle. We'll just lay that little rumour to rest, she thought.

She paid for the Kotex, dumping change on the counter.

"How are things going, Hannah?" she asked. Shy, tall Hannah had not been one of the girlfriends she talked to on the phone. They had been mildly friendly in school, and Edna wouldn't have minded talking to her, but she seemed to be always at work, and Mrs. Young apparently never relayed her messages.

Hannah rolled her eyes. "Oh, you know," she said.

Because Fletcher's had a soda fountain, there was a washroom available to customers. Edna desperately needed to use it, but she felt awkward about marching in, buying a box of pads, repairing to the bathroom and marching out again. She would get a pop at the soda fountain.

On impulse she turned back to Hannah. "Do you have a break soon?" she asked.

"Why, yes, I'm off in five minutes."

"Can I buy you a Coke or something?"

Hannah flushed and smiled. "Okay. I'll be there in a minute."

In the washroom, Edna was unsure what to do with the ruined towel. Finally she stuffed it into the paper bag reserved for napkin disposal and threw toilet paper on top of it.

Hannah was already seated in a booth when she came out. The blowsy blonde who had often served chocolate malteds to her and Len was at the counter.

"Who is that?" she whispered to Hannah, when the blonde had taken their order.

"Francine O'Brien. She's worked here for years. She's nice enough, I guess, but kind of....well....hard, if you know what I mean." Hannah giggled. "I've heard some pretty wild stuff about her."

"What kind of stuff?"

Hannah reddened. "Oh, you know, about drinking and men and stuff like that."

Edna wondered if Hannah had heard anything about her, if anybody was talking about how wild she was. She could have asked if it had been Vera sitting across from her, but she wasn't that close to Hannah.

"So are you just here for the summer?" she asked instead.

Hannah looked happy to have the subject changed. "No, I've been offered a fulltime job." She shrugged. "It's hard being on your feet all day, but I probably won't be able to find anything better. And they treat me pretty well."

She picked at the Formica tabletop. "You'll never guess who asked me to go to the movies with him!" she said in a gush. "Rick Fletcher!"

Rick was the heir-apparent to the drugstore. Reasonably good-looking. Not one of the popular boys at school but well-liked enough. He had always gone out with petite darkhaired girls, several times with Vera, but never with any one of them steadily. Edna was surprised that he would date the sandy-haired and looming Hannah. Surprise must have shown in her face.

"Oh, I know," Hannah said. "I'm not his type at all and he's probably just bored 'cause everybody's gone for the summer. But he's really nice and

I don't get asked that often." She looked at Edna with a flash of defiance. "Not like you."

"What do you mean, not like me? I never got asked that often."

"That's because they were all scared of you. God, they'd buzz around you, trying to get up enough nerve to ask you out, and half the time you didn't even notice they were there. It used to drive me crazy."

Edna thought for a moment, but what Hannah said didn't make any sense to her. She had dated a few guys, but couldn't remember boys "buzzing" around her. They certainly hadn't been scared of her, that she could remember. There was that Ice Princess crack that Charlie Cashen made at the class picnic. But scared? She sipped at her Coke, puzzled.

"It certainly wasn't any surprise to me to hear about you and Len Collins", Hannah went on. "He's probably the only guy around here who could handle you."

Handle? What was to handle? Edna had always known she was reasonably smart. She got good grades and she knew that put some boys off. She remembered, on a couple of occasions, trying not to sound too intelligent, but she had never considered herself scary. She had never even considered herself all that pretty. She became aware that Hannah had introduced the subject of Len because she was curious. Poor Hannah, isolated by her height and awkwardness. She decided that she really quite liked her. She told her then about her wedding and some of the details of her honeymoon. Hannah lapped it up, vicariously enjoying the romance.

Just as they finished their Cokes and Hannah was due to go back to work she asked, "What does Len do, anyway? None of us has ever been able to figure it out."

Neither could Edna.

Vera's wedding was just as plain and matter-of-fact as Edna's had been. She and Mac stood in front of the Justice of the Peace, Mac in an ill-fitting, off the rack suit, his round face red, his large hands clamped to his sides. Vera was pale, almost the same colour as her cream-coloured suit, and as she whispered her responses she sounded as though she were replying to a doctor who had just told her that she had a horrible cancer in an unmentionable part of her body.

Edna was holding a bouquet of small yellow roses, picked up from the florist's that morning, but they had no fragrance and all she could smell was furniture polish and old, stale sweat.

The ceremony was over in a matter of minutes. No music, no confetti, no celebration. Mac and Vera were going to Toronto for the weekend, that was all. Mac hadn't been at his new job long enough to request time off yet, and had to report to work on Monday morning. They would live with Vera's parents, so Vera could continue to help her mother.

The car was waiting for them as they came out of the county offices. Mac's brother had half-heartedly decorated it with a couple of old Baxter's tomato cans dangling from the rear. Vera was still pale.

Edna hugged her. "No matter what happens", she said, "we'll always be best friends. Always. You remember that, okay?"

Vera could only nod as she climbed into the car.

All the way to Toronto, she kept sneaking glances at Mac, his large hands wrapped tightly around the steering wheel of his father's car. Mac had not seemed surprised when she told him she was pregnant; it was the consequence he had expected from that night in the farmer's field. He was a little surprised that she had discovered it so soon, but it didn't matter, he was more than willing to do the right thing by her. He had a good job now, after all, and wasn't that a sign that he should be settling down? Besides, if he married Vera, they could do what they'd done in the car every night, something that Mac looked forward to with relish, now that he knew what it was like.

When they got to the city, they checked into the Royal York Hotel, the fanciest place they could think of. Vera had to tip the boy who stood waiting with his hands in his pockets long after he had shown them the bathroom, the closet and the light switches. Mac hadn't realized what he was waiting for.

They ate dinner at the hotel, since neither of them had been in the city before and didn't know where to go. Mac ordered roast beef; Vera tried coq au vin, but didn't like it. They considered getting a bottle of wine, but found the French names beyond them and settled for rye and coke. They were both appalled at the prices.

That night, she dawdled in the bathroom until she could hear the bed frame creak. She knew he was waiting for her. She looked in the mirror. Her eyes were huge, with shadows underneath. She daubed powder on her face, brushed her hair again, then timidly went into the bedroom.

He grinned at her and turned out the light as she crept beneath the covers. She shuddered as his huge hand found her breast. He kissed her, his breath still smelling of rye and the sticky-sweet aftertaste of Coke, then he switched his attention to underneath her night gown, pressing between her legs and rubbing. Vera felt nothing.

She could see his grin by the light of the moon which shone in through their window; the curtains had not closed all the way. She shut her eyes tightly as he entered her. She would get through this. Somehow.

Edna wanted to go Christmas shopping, so Len dropped her in the centre of town and promised to meet her for lunch afterwards. Once she would have delighted in the fact that she could buy anything, in any of the stores, that she wanted, but after an hour or so of looking, she realized there was very little she wanted. The goods in the local stores seemed shabby and ill-made. She supposed that sweaters from the department store might do for her mother and father, and Jack and Bill would certainly be happy with sports equipment from the hardware store, but she wanted to do better than that, to flaunt her new status as Mrs. Collins, who had plenty of money to spend on presents for her family, who had only to write a cheque and the world was hers. There wasn't a single thing she could see that would do for Len, either. I guess I'll have to get him to take me to Belleville or Kingston, she thought, but she wanted to surprise him, something she couldn't do if were hovering nearby while she shopped.

She had almost given up when she wandered into Elizabeth's, a new shop that had opened in early November. It was a gift shop. Most of the people on the island bought practical gifts, when they bought at all, things the recipient needed. A store dedicated to providing frivolous, and for the most part, expensive items for gift-giving was a new concept, and one that was the subject of a great deal of discussion along Main Street.

Edna found the store enchanting. She quickly settled on a set of canisters that looked like mushrooms, gaily painted and marked "Flour", "Sugar", "Coffee" and "Tea". Hetty kept her staples in old pickle and mayonnaise jars. Her father would be delighted, she was sure, with a walnut pipe rack, where he could stack his collection of old and smelly pipes instead of leaving them on tables and on the floor beside his chair. For Jack and Bill, she bought hockey sweaters, with "Toronto Maple Leafs" and the team emblem emblazoned on the front.

She debated buying Len some expensive men's cologne, but decided against it. She already liked the way he smelled, and didn't want to cover it up, no matter how rich and exotic the scents were. She liked the look of the little jack knife, with all of its attachments, that the saleslady, presumably Elizabeth, explained to her was a genuine Swiss Army knife, and she set it on the counter with her other purchases, but it wasn't enough. She needed something special for Len, even though it was really his money she was using to buy it. She needed him to know that she had spent some time and effort on the selection.

She had been concentrating on the stacked shelves and hadn't noticed the glassed in display under the counter until she put the knife down. There, in a handsome leather case, was a watch. A watch that showed the times in all the major cities of the world in a complicated arrangement of hands and dials, that was waterproof and shock resistant, and guaranteed for life. She pictured it on Len's wrist and knew it was perfect.

Feeling well-satisfied with her morning's work, she decided on one last purchase; an exquisite blue and white painted angel for the top of their first Christmas tree.

She was leaving the shop, her arms loaded with parcels, when she met

Vera on the sidewalk. She felt a little guilty when she saw her. She hadn't called her in at least a couple of weeks. Vera was carefully picking her way over a patch of ice on the sidewalk, her body clumsy with the added weight of her pregnancy. She looked round and dowdy, Edna thought, the collar of her winter coat frayed and the buttons straining over her belly. She also looked very, very tired. She smiled when she saw Edna.

"Hi. Whatcha got?"

"Oh... just some Christmas presents. You know, stuff for the folks. Where are you headed?"

"I have to go to the drug store. Dad's medicine." She shrugged. "I thought the fresh air would do me good, but I didn't realize it was so slippery."

On impulse Edna said, "Listen, I'm meeting Len for lunch, Why don't you come with us and he can give you a ride home afterwards."

"Oh, Edna, thank you, but I can't. Dad needs his medicine right away."

She felt guilty because she was so relieved. She wasn't sure what Len's reaction would be if she showed up at the restaurant with Vera in tow. "Listen, I'll call you tomorrow, okay? Maybe we can do something. Have you done your Christmas shopping yet?"

Vera looked evasive. "Yes, I got it all done last week."

Edna realized that she had said the wrong thing. She knew that money was tight at Vera's and now she knew just how tight it was. There would be very little, if anything, under her tree this Christmas.

Len was already on his second rye by the time she got to the restaurant. "So, how was shopping?" he asked as she sat down.

"Great. And no, you don't get to snoop through the packages."

"Oh goody," he crowed. "That means you bought me something! What is it? What is it?"

"Not 'til Christmas. But I will show you this." She pulled the angel out of its tissue wrappings. "It's for our first Christmas tree."

He smiled. "It's beautiful. Just like you. What else did you get?"

"God, you're just like a little kid. You'll have to wait until we get home. I'm not opening everything up in here, I'd never get things back in their packages. Oh, I saw Vera on the street."

"And how is the little mother?" He didn't sound very interested.

"She looked huge, and kind of depressed."

"Not surprising. I'd be depressed too at the thought of spending the rest of my life with Mac Dunlop. And there'll be a whole herd of squalling little Dunlops too, no doubt. Wouldn't it be awful if the baby looked like Mac?"

Suddenly Edna was glad that she was not, as yet, pregnant.

"Do you want to go look at cars?" Len said suddenly.

"Cars? What kind of cars?"

"I don't know. A lady's car."

"What lady are you buying a car for now?"

"A lady who might like to learn how to drive. If I got you a car, would you give it a try? It could be your Christmas present. One of them anyway," he amended.

Driving was something she had never considered before. Her mother had never learned how and her father took their old Chevy out of the garage only to drive sedately to the store and back, and on Sundays when they went to church. Every once in a long while the family would go on a picnic or to the beach, her father gripping the steering wheel and peering forward through the windshield, certain that disaster lurked around every bend and that only intense concentration would save them all from fiery destruction. Her mother would sit ramrod straight in the front seat while they wove down the road.

"I hope we can move into town within a couple of years," Len went on. "But in the meantime having a car would give you a little independence. I'm going to be pretty busy over the next while, and I'd feel better if I knew you could get yourself around."

Edna was pleased that he was concerned for her welfare and annoyed that he was going to be around even less than he already was.

"What are you going to be so busy at?" she asked.

"I'm thinking of running for Town Council."

If he'd said he was planning to be Pope, she couldn't have been more surprised. Len Collins on Town Council? Reckless, feckless Len?

"Don't you have to own property in town or something?" She vaguely remembered something from the section on municipal government in Grade 11 Civics class.

"I do."

"Where?"

"Several properties, actually. They're good investments. Or could be, if Council weren't such a bunch of stick-in-the-muds. They have no concept of progress."

"Do you think you could get elected?"

"Just leave that to me. All you have to do is stand by my side and be gracious. In the meantime, would you like a car?"

She would, but she had to learn to drive first.

They settled on a blue Chev, not unlike her father's. The salesman tried to steer them towards the black Olds that was parked enticingly at the front of the lot, but gave up when he realized that Len knew more about cars than he did.

"Too much car for a woman", Len said. "She needs something that's easy to handle. All she's going to use it for is to run to town."

She didn't think she would ever learn to drive. It was physically impossible, she was sure, to achieve the required balance between clutch and gas pedal while shifting gears and turning. Again and again, she stalled the car. Len became impatient.

"Just relax", he said. "You're too tense. You've got to get the feel of the car."

In the end, she banished him, and practiced by herself on the road in front of the house. Suddenly, one day, when she was distracted by bright sunlight gleaming off granular snow, she achieved a turn in one seamless motion and she was driving. Again and again and again she practiced, until she didn't have to think about what she was doing. Only then would she try her test, which she passed with flying colours, just before Christmas. It was the best present she could have received. As December passed into January and February, she grew more confident behind the wheel, until not even Len's presence in the seat beside her was enough to rattle her.

He was already campaigning, even though elections wouldn't be held until the following November. He got himself invited to join the Rotary Club, and attended faithfully, although privately he made fun of it.

"Did you know they sing at every meeting?" he said to Edna.

"Why?"

"Because it's just like a boys' club", he said. "I'm surprised they don't have a secret handshake."

She dutifully attended Ladies' Night with him. She knew few of the other "Rotariannes". They were mostly older women, her mother's age and she had little in common with them. Instead, she talked with the men, who were flattered by her interest, and who ran their eyes appreciatively up and down her figure. She developed a bantering tone with them that was alternately flirtatious and flippant. She soon realized that she could monopolize any man's attention simply by putting her hand on his arm, looking raptly into his eyes and hanging on his every word, no matter how banal.

They developed a routine; at any public gathering, they would split up and circulate the room, Len fetching drinks and holding chairs for the women, Edna delighting the men by standing very close and holding their eyes with her own while they talked. She made a point of smiling conspiratorially as she left them.

They joined the United Church, which was more stylish than the little Baptist church Edna's parents attended. She liked it. She liked the magnificent stained glass windows that rose three stories high in the sanctuary, she liked the outrageously large pipe organ and the chimes that called the town to worship on Sundays, she liked the United Church focus on the practical. Her mother was appalled. They went to services once a month or so.

There was a stir in the congregation the first time they walked in, people nudging their pewmates and sneaking glances over their shoulders. At the end of the service, when the Minister stood at the door shaking hands with each churchgoer, he had been effusive in his greeting.

Word quickly went round that she had "reformed" Len.

"All he needed was a nice girl", was one remark she overheard at the grocery store.

"My, but that girl is doing wonders with Len Collins", she heard at the Post Office. "She's settled him right down."

"Well, his mother was a minster's daughter", was the reply. "Nobody could ever figure out why she married that shiftless Harold."

Len was delighted with her, and Edna began to think he might actually get elected. They would lie in bed and compare notes.

"You're nothing but a flirt," he laughed. "I've seen the way you butter up all those old men."

"I learned how by watching you with the women", she shot back. "My God, they practically swoon at your feet. It's a good thing I'm not the jealous type."

"Oh those days are over. Haven't you heard? I've turned over a new leaf. All for the love of a good woman."

"I don't want to be a good woman." she said, snuggling close to him and stroking his chest. "I want to be a bad woman. I want to be a bad woman with you."

They would make love then in a tangle of sheets, Edna wild and passionate and needy. She was always mildly embarrassed when she thought of it later, but at the time would attack him hungrily, revelling in his smell and the feel of his long hard body against her.

And yet she could never bring herself to ask about those times when she awoke in the night to discover that he wasn't there.

CHAPTER SEVEN

Cara was astonished when her mother's lawyer called her a few days later to inform her that she had inherited yet another property.

"It was originally your grandfather's house," he explained to her. "Your father grew up there, I believe, but for the last eighteen years it has belonged to a Miss Francine O'Brien, who, unfortunately, passed on a few weeks ago. Her will leaves the property to you."

"To me? Why? I don't even know who she is."

"I'm not really entirely sure why myself," he said, "except that originally the property seems to have been held jointly with your father. When he died, of course, Ms. O'Brien automatically assumed full ownership. Perhaps she felt some sort of moral obligation to return it."

Cara remembered then that her father had not dealt with this lawyer, he had been retained by her mother in recent times. He wouldn't know all the ins and outs of her father's dealings. She doubted if anyone had ever known that. She knew that he had once owned a great deal of property, but thought it had all gone long ago, when everything else had come tumbling down.

"She has also specified that her personal property be left to you," the lawyer went on. "I should warn you that there isn't much, her furniture, a little money in a bank account. Ms. O'Brien was not a wealthy woman."

"But what about her family?" Cara wanted to know. "Won't they have something to say about all this?"

"I don't believe she has any family left. Certainly, the will is quite cut and dried and drawn up a number of years ago, several years before she became ill in fact. It's unlikely to be contested."

"Oh." She was nonplussed. "What should I do now?"

"Why don't you go have a look at it? " he suggested. "You can't do anything definitive until the will clears probate, but that shouldn't take long, and as far as I can tell, it's yours."

Curious, she dropped by his office that afternoon to pick up the key and to get directions. At one time the house must have been well out in the country, but straggling development along the highway had slowly encroached with gas stations, car dealerships and one storey bungalows. At first she missed the entrance to the driveway. Realizing she had gone too far she turned around and drove slowly back, finally locating the house behind a tangle of overgrown lilacs and poplars. It was long and low and the paint had long since peeled off , leaving the wood grey and weather beaten. It didn't look like anyone had used the front door for decades. A spirea bush planted beside the front step had now completely covered it as the insistent west wind twisted it against the house.

She opened the garage door. A couple of garbage cans and an old tire stood in the corner. She hadn't needed the key after all, as the side door was unlocked. She could never quite get over the fact that here people still left doors unlocked and keys in ignitions.

The entranceway from the garage led into a kitchen with wooden cupboards painted white and a small table under the window. The front half of the house was almost entirely living room with a large picture window framing the tangled growth of the front lawn. Closed doors guarded the hallway that led to the rest of the house. The first door gave in to a small pink bedroom, with a wrought iron bedstead, a dresser, a chair and not much else. The wallpaper had probably been very pretty when it was hung, but had now faded away to pink smudges. Over the dresser was a watercolour of iris and pink phlox around a pond. Cara examined the painting more closely; there was a quality to it that surprised her. She hadn't expected to find anything so fine in so modest a house. There was no signature on it, nothing to indicate the artist. She lifted it from the wall, revealing a delicate square of unfaded pink roses underneath. It had been here for some time then, long enough to protect the wallpaper from the bleaching effects of the sun.

She turned it over, seeking some clue, and there, in large scrawled letters were the words, "This pitcher painted by Naomi Collins, June 1934."

Her grandmother. She had been deaf, Cara knew, her father had told her that. And she had been fascinated by moving pictures, that was where she had met Cara's grandfather, or so the story went. This little watercolour certainly had a quality of movement to it, the flowerheads nodding over the pond as though a petal were about to fall into the clear waters, a sudden breeze about to blow, poplar leaves about to clatter in the wind. Cara couldn't remember her father saying anything about art in connection with his mother, but then in her father's day artists were usually odd fellows who drank too much, or spinsters with too much time on their hands. Naomi's unexpected abilities could certainly explain her father's sense of colour and her own artistic leanings. Had her grandmother been one of those rare creatures, a natural talent, or had the deprivation of one sense allowed another to be more fully developed? She supposed she would never know, there was no one left to ask, but she was delighted by the find and carefully set the painting by the door to take home with her.

Next to the little room was a bathroom, three piece, pink fixtures in a fifties style. The house ended with a large master bedroom across one end.

Double bed, two plain wooden dressers, a chair and a skirted dressing table. Perfume bottles, cold cream jars and bottles of nail polish were lined up in front of the mirrored table. Photographs were tucked into the frame of the mirror, nearly obscuring the surface and Cara was surprised to see several pictures of herself, school photos and snapshots. Who was this woman?

A small print of a black and white studio portrait showed a woman with light hair and over-plucked eyebrows. The rest of the pictures on the mirror were candid shots; someone, presumably Francine, dancing with a heavyset man in a pinstriped suit; Francine at the beach, in a bathing suit, posing like a pin-up girl; and down in the right-hand corner, Francine with Cara's father.

They were standing in front of a car that dated the picture to the late forties or early fifties. Her father was very young. He had his shirt sleeves rolled up, his felt hat pushed to the back of his head. He also had his arm around Francine and was laughing at the camera. She was not looking at the photographer, but at him, her attention focussed on his face, her hand lifted on its way to a caress.

Cara felt like a voyeur. It was such an intimate picture, a personal snapshot of the emotions of a woman she had never met, a glimpse into an aspect of her father's life that she had never considered.

The photograph showed a woman in love. Was he in love with her? It was impossible to tell from the photograph. Her father was mugging for the camera, his laughing face daring the lens to record anything but a young man with his arm around a pretty girl. Cara figured her father must have been in his early twenties. Francine looked to be well into her thirties. What was her father doing with this woman so much older than he? Where was her mother?

She knew that her parents had married in a grand romantic rush. Her father teased her mother about it at times, "I should have left you standing on the sidewalk with your suitcase", he would say to her, or, "There I was, a knight in shining armour, atop a graceful steed, appearing just in time to rescue the fair maiden."

"You weren't on a horse, you were sitting in a Buick", her mother would retort. "And you wouldn't even get out to put my suitcase in the car."

She knew that her mother's parents had disapproved of the marriage, but she had never been told why. She had never quite grasped the reasons her mother had been standing on a sidewalk with a suitcase, either.

"It was because she couldn't resist me", her father would say. "She ran away from home and begged me to marry her."

"No, I was running away to join the circus", her mother would say, "I just needed a ride, that's all."

Francine must have been a girlfriend from before her mother's time, she decided. But why had she been given joint ownership of her father's house? Had she remained special to him in some way? Was the tie so strong that it continued after her father's marriage? She would prefer to think that it was an act of kindness, of charity, a gesture to an old friend.

She tried to consider her father objectively. He always smelled good, she remembered that. She supposed he was handsome, but it was hard for her to judge, after all he was her father. She looked at the picture again. Oh yes, handsome was the word. Attractive. Everyone magnetically attracted to him. Energy. Action. Impulsiveness, perhaps. Charisma. He had been the sun in her universe when she was small. Was that the effect he had on grownup women as well?

Not on her mother. She could not remember argument or discord, ever. But there was always a certain wariness in her mother's approach, a holding back, a reserve. When she was five, Cara had been convinced that she would grow up and marry her father, so they could be together always. It was Rhonda, dear sweet dim Rhonda who explained to her that little girls couldn't marry their daddies, and that someday she would meet someone just as wonderful and fall in love. She had resented her mother a little then, for holding such a monopoly, for grabbing the prize before Cara was old enough to compete on level ground.

He must have devastated all the women, she decided. Especially Francine, who looked positively besotted in the picture. But for some reason, not her mother.

Len rolled over and lit two cigarettes. He handed one to Francine, who pulled the sheet up over her breasts before she took it.

"Hey, don't hide". He pulled it back down again.

"I'm cold."

"Well, come here, I'll warm you up again." He put his arm around her and pulled her closer, burying his face in her hair.

She pushed him away. "Enough. You're going to wear me out."

He laughed. "I doubt that. God knows, I've been trying as hard as I can and I haven't worn you out yet."

She pulled the sheet up again. She had always been a well built woman and worked hard to keep her figure, but she was slowly losing ground to middle age and gravity. Her breasts, although still shapely, were sagging slightly and her stomach had developed a roundness that no amount of diet or exercise could flatten. She pulled the sheet up again.

"Hey, I said don't." Len pulled it down again and buried his face in her ample bosom. "If you're all covered up I can't do this."

Francine had been Len's first lover, when he was sixteen. She met him at The Palace of the Moon, the dancehall at the dunes, when Len's father Harold had taken him along one night to help sell duty-free American whiskey from the back of their old pickup truck. The general consensus on the island was that Harold Collins was shiftless and lazy. The general consensus was quite correct; Harold held a commercial fishing license but only occasionally fished; more often he wandered across the lake to northern New York and wandered back again with whatever he could sell at a profit. Whiskey and American cigarettes were always popular, and he made enough to keep his family without too much effort on his part. He was not a greedy man and by keeping his smuggling activities low-key he ran little risk of running into serious trouble from authorities on either side of the lake.

Naomi Collins, Len's mother, had been a Pentecostal minister's daughter, one of twelve threadbare children who survived, but barely, on the tiny allowance provided by her father's congregation. She was a pretty, thin girl who was born with only partial hearing in one ear, and none in the other, an affliction that no amount of praying seemed able to cure. Overwhelmed with children, poverty and God, her parents gradually accepted Naomi's disability as a cross they had been given to bear. This acceptance also allowed them to ignore it.

She attended only a few days of grade school before teachers advised that they were unable to teach her much of anything and that she should be enrolled in a school for the deaf. For a Pentecostal minister, it was out of the question, from both a financial and a philosophical point of view. From then on, Naomi was a prisoner of the parsonage, taught to care for the endless parade of babies her parents seemed unable to stop producing. She became indispensable to church suppers and revivals, content to set tables and wash dishes, since she was unable to grasp the meaning of the wild gesticulations her father led his congregation through. She quickly picked up the mechanics of any task she was shown, but complex concepts of theology remained forever beyond her ken.

Whenever her parents thought about her future, which was not often, they consoled themselves with the fact that Naomi's life could be devoted to the church and the comfort of her parents in their old age, since they felt she was unlikely to be the bride of anyone but Christ. God had given her this affliction, they reasoned, and God would look after her, in the same way that angels frequently safeguarded fools.

But Naomi was no fool. Although she had never been taught to read, she could certainly see, and it was this fact that framed her salvation. She was not often sent on errands; she had difficulty making change and was dependent on the honesty and good will of storekeepers to give her fair value. Occasionally, though, her mother would send her to Merrill's General Store for sugar or salt. The Merrills were members of the Pentecostal congregation and could be counted upon to return the correct amount of money to the Pastor's daughter.

The route to Merrill's took Naomi past the Regent Theatre, with its garish posters and festive air. She would always linger there for as long as she could, trying to imagine what the posters were about and why the women looked so different from everyone she knew. The women in her father's church were dowdy, their plain faces made plainer by their repudiation of anything resembling style and their refusal to alter in any way the faces God had given them. The poster women had ruby red lips and smoky blackened eyes. They seemed dressed, always, in filmy garments that exposed the shoulders and sometimes, the tops of their breasts.

Naomi tried, once, to go inside the theatre to see more, but was stopped at the door by the usher, who tried to tell her that she needed five cents to go further. She couldn't fathom what he was saying to her until, in desperation, he grabbed the sugar money out of her hand and held up a nickel. She understood then, that this mysterious coinage was her passport to another world, but that she was without a country to issue it; no nickels ever came her way that weren't strictly accounted for.

The Pentecostal congregation was not affluent, but it was devoted. Naomi's father received free housing and a small salary, but his household's needs were mostly met from the collection box that passed down the aisles every Sunday. Most often pennies were placed in it, but every week there would be a sprinkling of nickels and dimes, dull from the sweat of hands that clutched them in the effort to make them last until Sunday. Naomi's father took the box home and left it in his study. Naomi's mother fed the family from it.

The study was off limits to the children and they were admonished if they even went near the door, but Naomi had no difficulty finding an opportunity to slip in and remove the coveted nickel. Unaware that both theft and theatre were anathema to the Pentecostal Church, she merely walked out the door one afternoon and walked in through another, finding a world she had never dreamt existed.

She was enthralled by the flickering images on the screen. The first movie she saw was "Son of the Sheik". She was delighted to see camels. She had seen the strange looking beasts in the pictures at Sunday School, but she had no idea that they moved in such a deliberate and lumbering fashion. The man in the movie was unlike anyone she had ever met. Smoldering eyes pierced through her, he had broad shoulders and he happily rushed to the rescue of any voluptuous female who was silly enough to let herself be abducted by fierce looking men with brandishing swords. She couldn't understand exactly what the menace was, or why these women would wring their hands instead of trying to escape, but it didn't matter. She was hooked.

From then on she took a nickel and went to the movies at least once a week. She made no attempt to prevaricate, or even realized that there was a need to. In her mind she was fulfilling a need, in the same way that the money from the box provided coal to keep them warm and food to fill their bellies. Her mother was a little alarmed at her disappearances when she eventually noticed them. She assumed that, at sixteen, Naomi had reached the dangerous age, when hormones do battle with dogma, and young girls must be prayed for. She dutifully prayed for her daughter, but reasoned that there was little else she could do, since she was unable to communicate any of her fears to Naomi, and besides, no young man was likely to take an interest in such a wild, damaged being. Best to leave her alone for now. There was little trouble she could get into in broad daylight.

Harold Collins noticed her one day when he was supplying three bottles of whiskey to the cast of a travelling show that had been booked into the theatre. Originally built for vaudeville, the owner of the Regent had quickly realized the potential of moving pictures and had made renovations that would accommodate them, but had hedged his bets by leaving the enormous stage intact. It was still a regular and lucrative stop for stage shows, which preempted movies and always sold out.

Naomi had been unable to understand why she couldn't get in. By then, the ushers had noted her as a regular customer, and did their best to explain to her that she could see stories with real people that evening if she returned at eight o'clock with a quarter. She had never seen a quarter before and had no idea how to get one.

There was something in her manner that attracted Harold. There were no tears, no signs of disappointment or resignation, just a determination to deal with a difficult situation. From the expressions that flitted across her face, he could see her piecing out the train of events that she would need to initiate in order to gain admittance to her magic kingdom. He liked that, since he seldom took no for an answer himself. He asked one of the ushers about her.

"It's the Pentecostal Minister's deaf mute kid", the usher replied. "She comes to the movies all the time. I don't know how she follows the story, but she seems to like it and she don't ever cause any trouble. She's really kind of sweet when you get right down to it. I'd like to let her in tonight, but it would mean my job if the boss found out."

"Pentecostal, huh? Does her old man know she's here?"

The usher grinned. "I doubt it. He'd have a conniption I expect, but Jeez, he's got a million kids and I expect this one don't have much of a life. What harm can it do if she sees a movie now and again?" He shrugged. "I doubt she'll come up with the quarter for tonight, though."

Harold collected his whiskey money from a patronizing and hungover actor at the stage door, then sauntered into the lobby. Naomi was still there, staring at the show poster. He took a quarter out of his pocket and walked over to her, holding it up.

She had never been given money or much of anything else before and was unsure why this man was approaching her. Finally, Harold had to put the quarter in her hand and point to the poster to get her to understand that he was treating her to the admission price. He was unprepared for the way her face lit up when she grasped what he was offering.

"It was as if I was Jesus Christ hisself", he related to Len one time. "I never seen anything like it."

He led her to the booth where she purchased a ticket for the evening's show. He bought a second for himself, and by pointing first to himself and then to her, made her understand that he would meet her that evening.

After she had washed the mountain of supper dishes that night, Naomi simply walked out the door. Occupied with getting the smaller children to bed, her mother didn't even notice her leave.

Harold was waiting for her in the lobby and together they were led down the aisle by an usher with a flashlight. Naomi was startled when the orchestra began tuning their instruments. She could feel the vibration through the floor and when the music began, she connected with the rhythm, swaying and rocking in time. The show was a comedy, and she had no difficulty following the slapstick antics of the actors, at times laughing out loud, although she was only dimly aware of doing so.

Harold saw none of the entertainment he had paid for. Watching Naomi's face was all the show he needed. During the second act, he reached over and took her hand. Over the next few months, Harold Collins bought two tickets for every movie that came to the Regent Theatre. He didn't actually see a single one of them.

Unsure how to move things along with a girl who couldn't understand what he was saying, Harold felt their romance might have stalled there, gradually sputtering to a halt from sheer inertia, had Naomi's mother not finally become alarmed at her silent daughter's absences. She recruited one of the younger children to follow his sister and when it was reported that Naomi was not only going to forbidden movies, but meeting a man there, the reaction was swift, vicious and predictable. She was locked in the room she shared with five sisters. After two days of this, she had had enough. On the third afternoon when the older girls were in school and the younger ones napping, when her father was in his study and her mother was in the kitchen, she packed up her meagre belongings and jumped out the window, spraining her ankle on the landing. When she limped into the theatre lobby with her pitiful bundle, Harold made up his mind. He made arrangements for a marriage license and sent a note to the Pentecostal Minister to tell him what had happened to his daughter. The entire Pentecostal congregation prayed for her redemption and her parents never spoke to her again.

Naomi's deafness was no detriment as far as Harold was concerned. As he put it, "I never could stand a woman who yapped all the time." Gradually, they worked out a complicated series of signs that allowed them to communicate with each other as they needed to, but most often they simply moved together in the unspoken unison of nearly perfect compatibility. By everyone else's standards, Harold was shiftless, lazy and a crook; by Naomi's, he was the living incarnation of the smouldering heroes on the movie screen. He had rescued her, not from brigands with brandishing swords, but from a lifetime of church suppers and dirty laundry.

Harold drank, but he was never a mean drunk; he was always tender with his vulnerable bride. He never held a job, but always came home with a few dollars in his pocket and after all those years in the poverty-stricken parsonage, Naomi found it more than adequate for their needs. There was more than enough money for a movie at least once a week, too and Harold often came home with little gifts for her. These were an odd assortment, a set of silver hairbrushes, a jigsaw puzzle, a box of watercolours.

"Picked you up a little something," he would say, "Didn't cost much, but I thought you might get a kick out of it." Naomi had never received gifts this before, and the fact that he would turn up with them for no reason at all elevated him in her eyes to a demi-God. She worshipped him. Harold had certainly never been worshipped before, and found it a novel and amazingly satisfying experience.

Their happiness intensified when it became clear that Naomi was going to produce a child. She was familiar enough with her mother's innumerable pregnancies to understand the signs and welcomed the chance to look after a baby of her own. Her only fear was that she would somehow pass on her deafness, and she worried about this for some time until Harold noticed her distraction, and deduced the cause.

"It don't matter none," he made her understand. "We get along all right, and if the little one is deaf, then I'll just have to do the talkin' for all of us."

When the baby came, he named it Leonard, after his father. "It means lion", he said, and showed Naomi pictures of magnificently-maned creatures in an old National Geographic he had rescued from the dump. She agreed that it was an apt name for the tawny child they had produced.

Her happiness was crowned one day when Harold dropped a plate on the kitchen floor. The sound of the shattering china startled the child, and he erupted in a storm of sobs and wails. He could hear.

She luxuriated in her good fortune. There were no more babies, but Len was a beautiful child and she was content with only one. When he was only a few weeks old she packed him up and took him along to the Regent Theatre with her, and as he grew older, he became as fascinated as she. More than anywhere else, this was where Len's education began. Naomi's world was one of silence and her child learned to speak, not so much from his taciturn father as from Friday night features. The men in these movies never said "I seen" or "yous" and they wielded their knives and forks with an elegant and surgical precision. They held doors open, polished their shoes and always made sure their haircuts and clothing were impeccable. Other men treated them with respect. Len copied them in every way he could, often reenacting the entire story later in the kitchen as his parents watched with amusement.

Their world was a perfect one until Len was twelve, when a summer cold quickly developed into pneumonia and Naomi was carried away within a week. Both father and son were devastated.

As a single father, Harold adopted the traditional method of parenting and simply let his son tag along with him whenever he wanted to, truant officers be damned. By the age of fourteen, Len was an experienced sailor and a savvy smuggler, who could calculate the risks against the probable profit margins and come up with a winning formula nearly every time.

They bootlegged liquor only occasionally at places like The Palace of the Moon. Dance halls were a little too public and a little too closely watched by local police. Harold liked to sell his wares directly to hotel owners, who would reserve it for their special customers. He had been stung on the last trip out, though, dealing with an American he had never done business with before, a man who had come recommended, but who at the last minute stuck him with a load of inferior whiskey. Not up to the standards of his usual buyers, he was forced to get rid of it a bottle at a time out of the back of the truck.

The Palace of the Moon was their last stop and they were lucky; they had only two bottles left when the local constable collared them. Harold cursed himself for being careless, but wasn't worried. Two bottles meant he could readily convince a judge that they had been purchased for personal consumption; it wasn't his fault that the duty stickers had fallen off. At the most, he was probably looking at a fine for drinking in a public place. Len was another matter. He was underage and Harold didn't want to add "contributing to the delinquency of a minor" to the charge. Some judges took a dim view of fathers who supplied booze to their sons.

Francine had just been approaching the truck to buy one of the last two bottles when the policeman leapt out of the bushes. He should have waited until money changed hands, but he was young and inexperienced, excited by the prospect of catching a real and notorious criminal. In mid-stride, Francine changed course from Harold to Len, smoothly taking him by the arm. In answer to the policeman's queries, she maintained that Len was her date, and had only been waiting for her to return from a call of nature behind a dune. The policeman was dubious.

"Come on, he can't be much more than sixteen or seventeen."

"Yes, that's true." Francine held Len closer.

"And you're....well...you're..."

"Yes? I'm what?" She fixed the constable with an icy stare.

"... a little older," he finished lamely.

"Yes, a little," she agreed.

Len played along. "I've always liked older women", he said. "They're ...... comfier." He threw his arm around her and squeezed.

In the end, the policeman took only Harold in.

"I'll get somebody to bail you out in a couple of hours", Len promised.

He walked Francine back to the dancehall. "Thanks. That was quick thinking."

"Hell, I didn't want to get nabbed either", she said. "What are you doing now?"

Len had no plans, other than to hang around until the police had time to book his father. When Francine suggested a dance, he shrugged.

"I don't know how."

"I'll show you. "

He picked up the waltz step quickly, and Francine relaxed into his arms. This boy was tall and had an easy grace. He smelled good, too, better than the beery, middle-aged men she usually danced with.

When the band swung into a jive beat, he suggested they walk on the beach instead. "One dance a night is all I can learn," he protested. "Besides, it's too hot in here." They'd walked in the moonlight down the beach, then sat on a dune as the first red streaks of the sun lightened the horizon. "Boyfriend, huh?" Len laughed. "I can't believe he bought that."

Francine was tired and a little nettled by his tone. "And why not?" she asked.

"Well, I don't know. You are older than me."

"So what?"

"So... I don't know. So... what would you do if I kissed you right now? Just like a boyfriend would?"

"Why don't you try it and find out?"

He kissed her tentatively at first, then more aggressively. She had a few qualms and protested a little when he began to undo the buttons of her blouse but quickly forgot them when his hand reached her breast.

Afterwards, she turned to him. "How old did you say you were?" she asked.

He grinned. "Sixteen."

Harold had been at the police station for five hours when Len finally arrived with Joe Mason to bail him out. He was furious.

To Francine's surprise, Len turned up at her apartment the next night.

"Do you mind?" he asked. "I really enjoyed last evening." He had a bottle of bourbon with him. She allowed him to mix her a drink while she thought about whether or not she minded. She had been feeling a little guilty about the previous night, he was so young, just a boy. On the other hand, she reasoned, what better way to introduce a young man to the mysteries of romance than with someone who knew what she was doing?

In the end, she let him stay the night.

They saw each other regularly after that. She taught Len how to dance. She indicated that a lady appreciated a man who would bring her flowers and flatter her. She showed him what pleased her in bed, and in all things he proved to be an apt pupil. He had plans she knew, he told them to her. He wanted more out of life than to shuffle through it like his father had. He did not want to be Harold Collins standing at a hotel service entrance making deliveries of smuggled liquor; he wanted to be one of the men inside, who wore nicely-cut suits and ate at tables with snow-white linen cloths while they sipped their illegal American whiskey. He watched these men carefully, to see how they carried themselves. But mostly he patterned himself after the men he had seen on the movie screen.

It was because of Francine that Len hadn't been along on Harold's last trip across the lake. When she wanted to go dancing one night, Len had opted out of a planned run into Oswego. Harold was a little upset; he had come to rely on his son when the weather was rough. Len was young and strong and a better sailor than he was. Apparently the boy had an eye for the women, and that made things inconvenient sometimes, but then again, Harold had been young once too. He shrugged and checked the weather forecast. Fair, light winds. Let him go dancing, he could manage this one himself.

Halfway out, he realized he was wrong. The wind had been rising for some time, growing steadily stronger, piling the waves up under the fishing boat. Harold was a prudent sailor and Main Duck Island was close. He decided to put in at the island's little harbour to wait out the storm. By the time he got there, the wind had switched to the northeast and he knew he would find no shelter. His anchor would never hold on the muddy bottom.

If he could make Timber Island and shelter in its lee, he would be fine, he figured, but there were nearly seventeen miles of open lake to be sailed across first. The wind by now was vicious and the waves were at least twelve feet high, washing over the boat, pummelling it and depositing gallons of water with each wash. He knew he needed to tie a lifeline to himself, but was afraid to let go of the wheel as the little craft yawed and scrambled through the heavy seas.

Should have made Len come after all, was Harold Collins' last thought as he was washed overboard into the cold dark water.

Against all odds, the boat survived. She was sighted from the shore by two fishermen out of Point Traverse, who watched uneasily for a while until it became evident that the ship was adrift in the foamy swell. They brought it in to the little harbour and called the police, who called Len.

Harold had disappeared in two hundred metres of water. At that depth the cold water of Lake Ontario seldom gives up its bodies, but the authorities ruled that he could not be declared dead and the estate settled until it could be proved definitively that he had passed on. No one was sure quite what to do with Len, who was now nearly eighteen and well able to fend for himself. His mother's family refused to get involved. There was nobody left in Harold's family. In the end, Francine agreed to act as trustee and official guardian. The two fishermen, out of deference for a local man, declined to claim salvage and Len continued to make the midnight runs across Lake Ontario, convincing Harold's customers that they could continue to do business with him on the same footing that they had dealt with his father. He upped the stakes though, carrying larger cargoes than Harold had ever dared to, often transferring the goods in mid-lake to another boat, or hiding them on one of the out islands to retrieve later.

He bought a car, a big purring Buick. He drove it far too fast. He drank too much, but as far as Francine could tell, it never affected his judgement. He still visited her bed on a regular basis, but he never hid the fact that he was now seeing other women as well, young, pretty women, usually only for a date or two, but a constant stream of them.

She had been expecting it and was surprised that it upset her. She had known all along that someday Len would be no more than a warm memory and she tried to feel grateful that she would have even that. But it was hard when she saw him with some little snip of a thing on his arm, someone she knew was no more than a passing challenge, who would soon be replaced by some other giggling girl. She tried her hardest not to be jealous, or at least not to show it. After all, Len was never serious about any of them. Not until the Charles girl.

This was something different right away. She wasn't sure what Len was up to, but it was odd that he never took Edna to the dancehalls like he did the other girls. Instead, he sat sedately with her in a booth at the drug store, sipping chocolate malteds. He had grown bored with every other girl after a few dates, but week after week went by and he still continued to wait for Edna outside the optometrist's office. She was sure he hadn't yet lured her into bed and that was unusual too; Len wasn't often denied, and when he was, he simply moved on to the next girl.

When he abruptly married her, Francine was sure it was finally over. She toyed with the idea of marrying Joe Mason, who had asked her on several occasions, after all she was getting on, maybe it was time to settle down a little, to look for a little security in her life. But Joe was so colourless in comparison, so stolid and unexciting. With a pang she realized that, despite her best intentions, she had fallen in love with Len.

Why Francine O'Brien, you old fool, she chided herself, what made you think you could ever hang on to a boy like that? You were nothing but a convenience, and it only stood to reason that he'd find somebody sooner or later. He's gone, so get used to it.

But he wasn't. Every once in a while he'd turn up on her doorstep with a grin and a bottle.

"Why are you here?" she asked one time. "Edna's a pretty girl. What do you need an old broad like me for?"

"Because I like old broads like you," he had replied.

"Then why did you marry a young one?"

"Because I need Edna, too. But for different reasons. Don't worry about it, I won't leave you high and dry. I owe you."

She would have liked far more than gratitude, but she was willing to take what she could get.

Vera met Mac at the door every evening when he came home from work, determined to uphold her part of the bargain and be the perfect wife.

She was already perfect, as far as Mac was concerned. Vera's mother was occupied most of the time with her speechless husband and paid little attention to Vera's running of the house. By now too large and uncomfortable to bother with much heavy cleaning, she concentrated her efforts in the kitchen, serving up mammoth portions of meat, potatoes and two vegetables exactly one half hour after Mac arrived home from work every night.

This was as it should be, according to Mac, who had been treated in the same fashion by his mother. If asked, he would be unable to explain the series of events that had led him to this life of perfect contentment. He recalled asking Vera for a date, but after that, the details were hazy and before he knew it he was standing in front of a minister with Vera by his side. Not that he ever attempted to reconstruct the scenario, or even thought about it much. He had a pretty good job with the roads department. He liked working outside and he liked the men he worked with. He was waited on hand and foot at home and at night he took his pleasure in Vera's soft little body. She had been a little reluctant lately, of course, what with the baby and all, but that would pass, he was sure. In the meantime, he good-naturedly laughed along with his coworkers' ribald remarks about his virility.

"Hey, Mac, old boy, you must have knocked her up on the first go."

"Way to go, Mac. Get a couple of kids on them right away and they settle right down."

"What a man, eh? What a man! Made the most of his honeymoon all right!"

Every night he would settle down in his easy chair, with his beer, his newspaper and a sigh of contentment.

Mac seen to, Vera would lower herself awkwardly onto the chesterfield. She had indigestion and her ankles were swollen. She watched her husband as he read, one large hand wrapped around his beer glass.

Sometimes she had difficulty believing that so large and red a creature had any connection with her. She knew she should be grateful to Mac. He uncomplainingly handed his paycheque over to her every week, content to take only enough out of it for beer and papers. She didn't know what she and her mother would have done without him. She certainly couldn't work, a pregnant woman would never be hired anyway, and even after she had the baby, who would look after it? Not her mother, who was at the limits of her endurance already. Her father had continued to suffer small strokes and seizures, each one leaving him more helpless than the last.

Her mother had seemed unsurprised when she announced her impending marriage to Mac Dunlop. Vera didn't know if her mother had known why, but if she did, she never said a word about it.

"Are you living here or with the Dunlops?" she had asked, and there was relief in her eyes when Vera, who hadn't really thought about it at all, said she thought they'd come here, so that she could continue to help with her father. Mac had agreed. He could see that his mother-in-law couldn't cope on her own. He assumed that he was now the breadwinner, the man of the house, responsible for them all. His paycheque didn't go far, eroded constantly by medicines and the ever-spiralling doctor's bill, but what he had was theirs.

On the night Vera woke to a cramping pain, she ignored it as long as she could. She had been experiencing intermittent pains for the last month. The doctor had assured her that it was normal and nothing really to worry about, just one more uncomfortable manifestation of an uncomfortable state.

Mac was snoring again. She closed her eyes and wondered if she would be able to go back to sleep. Sleeping had been a problem for a while now. She obviously couldn't lie on her stomach, but if she lay on her back, she felt like she was suffocating. If she tried lying on her left side, the baby kicked too much, but if she lay on the right she received the full fanfare of the noises coming from Mac's deviated septum. She had adopted a half-sitting position, propped up on pillows. It was only marginally more comfortable, but at least she could doze a little.

Another cramp. She shifted slightly so she could look out the window. The moon was rising in a tiny sliver high in the cold February sky, casting almost no light. There were a few stars scattered here and there, but the street lighting made them difficult to see. Her back was killing her. She started to count. She couldn't see the clock, but she knew she could count pretty accurately in her head. All those games in the woods that required her to wait until she went looking for Edna.

Five minutes and another cramp. I'll wait for a couple more, Vera decided. There's no point getting everyone upset for nothing. It would be nice if she could hold off for just another couple of weeks.

Two more, five minutes apart. Okay, here we go, let's get this over with, she thought. She leaned over and shook Mac.

He continued snoring.

"Mac." She shook him a little harder.

"Wha...wha?" Mac was always befuddled and confused when he awoke. Physical labour in the outdoors combined with rich, heavy food and beer guaranteed that he slept like the dead.

"The baby's coming." He looked at her, but his eyes weren't focussing.

"I said the baby's coming!"

"Wha...? No, Vera, it's not time yet."

"The baby doesn't care whether it's time or not, Mac. It's coming and it's coming now."

What she was saying sunk in and he leapt out of bed. "Okay, what do we need to do?"

"Get my suitcase out of the closet please, and I'll start packing my things."

She should have had all her things ready, all the books told you to be packed ahead of time, but Vera had been afraid to do it so early, in case her mother or Mac found the suitcase and questioned her. She threw in underwear, a couple of nightgowns, slippers and a dressing gown. Toothbrush, toothpaste, hairbrush. What else? She shrugged. She could always send Mac to get what she forgot.

She needed to go to the bathroom, but just as she got there she felt a gush of liquid. When she looked it was colourless and copious. The pain in her back intensified. She was sweating.

She nearly fell going down the front steps, they were icy and covered with a thin layer of snow. Just as she stepped from the top, she was hit with a pain and her heavy bulk had affected her sense of balance. She grabbed the rail and sank to the top step.

"Are you all right?" Mac asked, rushing to her.

"No, I'm not", Vera said. "I'm not all right at all." And she began to cry.

She cried all the way to the hospital. She cried with each pain, she cried when they shaved her, she cried when the doctor examined her and she cried when they wheeled her into the delivery room. She had never felt such pain. There is no way this baby is ever going to come, she thought. She could feel her pelvic bones shifting, widening, inexorably pried apart by the enormous thing inside her.

And then, suddenly, it was over. The pain stopped and she lay in a pool of tears and blood as the doctor fussed over what had come out of her.

"It's a boy and he looks just fine", the doctor said. "We'll weigh him in a minute, but he looks a good size for an early baby." He winked at her. "Must take after Mac."

And then he put a bundle in her arms. It didn't look like anything she had ever seen. She had expected something pink and white and round. This baby was covered with a viscous yellow goo and its head was mashed into a point.

She started crying again.

Mac visited after work every evening. His stock had risen even further at the Roads Department.

"What a man", they all exclaimed. "Catches her first go and produces a son right off the bat."

He bought cigars and passed them around, and his coworkers had taken him out to the beer parlour and stood rounds. He had never been so happy in his life.

He held the baby occasionally when they brought it in for its evening feed. The hospital had it on a strict schedule and he was careful to arrive after eight, after the feeding was finished and he wouldn't be in the way.

They discussed names. Vera would like to have picked an unusual name, something from one of the books she had read, like Trevor or Jason.

Mac was scornful. "Those are sissy names", he said. "The other kids will make fun of him."

Mac's first name was Maclean, but that was because his mother had followed the local tradition of recycling surnames into first names, and he had not suffered among other boys who had names like Harrison and Robertson and Taylor. Inevitably these were shortened or transformed into nicknames that stuck.

Vera couldn't see calling a small baby "Matlin", although she supposed it would soon be shortened to "Mat".

"My mother's maiden name was Stevens", she said doubtfully. She turned it over in her mind. Steven. Steven Dunlop. Little Stevie Dunlop. Not bad. At least it wasn't another Bill or Bob or John.

"Steven. That's his name, "Steven Maclean Dunlop".

Mac grinned and turned with Little Stevie towards the window. The streetlight bathed the baby in light for a moment and Vera realized that his body was long and narrow and finely shaped, and that no one who took a good look would ever be able to say that he took after Mac.

CHAPTER EIGHT

"Upset Victories in Progressive Sweep".

In a surprising victory, John Moore, 56, led the polls in the town's municipal elections on Monday. Moore garnered nearly 500 votes, outpolling Incumbent Ray Langton by 50 votes. Moore's count was a clear victory for the progressive element in town.

In his victory address, Moore promised to lead the town to prosperity.

"Progress is the key to the future", he said. "Industrial expansion and increased development means more jobs and more wealth for everyone. It's up to Council to attract new business to this area, and I'll do my best to lead the way."

Another surprise on Monday was the election of 25 year old Len Collins, one of the youngest men ever to serve on Town Council. Collins has made no secret of his alignment with the Progressives and promised Moore his full support. For more election results, see page 3.

The flaking scrap of yellow newspaper had, for some reason, been tucked inside a soup tureen in the china cabinet. Cara had been about to throw it away when her father's name in the column of text caught her eye.

The article predicted booming times ahead, now that Town Council consisted of young, forward-looking representatives like Len Collins. She had to laugh at the breathless prose of the time; "progress" (read "uncontrolled development") was just around the corner for the town, it seemed to imply. All it needed to do was elect the right officials (read "middle-class white men") and opportunity would soon come knocking. Along with pollution and globalization, she thought, but these things were non-issues in 1954, when the world was still putting the war behind it and any forward motion looked good.

Her father was described as a "businessman". The article included a blurred and faded photograph, an official campaign head and shoulders shot. Unlike most photographs of its kind, the subject was smiling. She hadn't realized before how much Mickey looked like his grandfather. She'd always thought he looked like Randy.

She'd called Mickey the night before. He'd sounded tired and grumpy and wanted to know when she was coming home.

"How much longer do I have to stay with Auntie Cass?" he asked. "I don't like it here."

"I don't know for sure sweetie. I've still got a lot of stuff to sort out."

She was less than halfway through the house. She hadn't yet done anything with the other property at the edge of town, except to take away the watercolour and hang it in her bedroom. Silly, she'd just have to move it again later, but she liked looking at it.

"Look, as soon as school's over, why don't I get Cass to put you on the train. I really have no idea how much longer this is going to take."

"On the train? All by myself?"

"Sure, why not? You're all grown up now. Cass will be there at the start and I'll be there at the end and the conductor will look after you in between. Okay?"

He thought for a moment. "Okay. Love you."

"Love you. Night, night sweetie."

It would be good to have Mickey with her again, she thought as she hung up the phone. She could show him the picture of his grandfather.

Edna found the campaign exhausting, although Len seemed to thrive on it. He had had signs printed, she didn't know how many but it seemed there were thousands, and hired kids to put them up on walls and telephone poles wherever they could. He worked the town systematically, knocking on doors and shaking hands. Edna went with him when he judged it helpful, usually in the better neighbourhoods where the presence of a dutiful and smiling and mostly silent wife was judged an asset. At these places he presented the new improved Len Collins. The Len Collins who had chosen a wife from one of the better families in town and who had settled down to become a respectable and respected citizen. Who was one of the young, upcoming breed who had a vision of prosperity and the energy to make it happen. They would drink cup after cup of tea in these neighbourhoods, perching the fragile porcelain on their knees, while Len nodded in chorus with the opinions of the owners, interjecting only occasionally when it seemed they needed verbal agreement.

"I tell you, that young Collins boy has a head on his shoulders," Edna overheard at Fletcher's. "He's an up and comer, all right."

The other men drinking coffee at the counter nodded their heads in sage agreement.

Len laughed when she breathlessly reported the conversation.

"They still won't vote for me, you know. They'll go ahead and vote for their buddies the way they always have. But thanks, if they're talking that way, it's a good sign."

Edna stayed home when Len canvassed the poorer areas. His roots were his greatest asset here, along with his charm. The people in these neighbourhoods could relate to a young fellow who was busy pulling himself up by his bootstraps. They remembered that his father was a "character" and that his mother was a "sweetheart". Oh, everybody knew that Len had led a rackety old kind of life for a while, but that was just a young man getting the wild oats out of his system, wasn't it, and wouldn't it be nice for once to have a fella on Council who understood that a man's dignity depended on his ability to put bread on the table, and that what this place needed was jobs? These men listened carefully while he talked, interjecting only occasionally with comments of their own.

But wherever he went, he zeroed in on the women. Old, young, rich, poor, as long as they were over twenty-one, they had a vote, and Len was determined to go after each and every one of them. He canvassed mostly during the day, when the husbands (and his opponents) were at work. He surprised women washing the breakfast dishes; he surprised women doing the laundry; he surprised women in their housedresses with their hair still in pins. It didn't matter what he surprised them at, when they opened the door, he would look them up and down and break into a slow, lopsided grin, a grin that implied intimacy, a promise, a might-have-been. He would chat with them for a few minutes and leave a campaign pamphlet that had that same lopsided grin printed right on the front. The women would save the pamphlet because of the picture, sneaking peeks at it from time to time and smiling to themselves. When their men came home from work, they would say that Len Collins had been around to the door and left a pamphlet and shouldn't we have a look at what he was saying? Some of the men would snort and throw the pamphlet away. Some of them would read it. Whatever they did, it didn't matter. The women were voting for Collins.

On the day of the election, it was nearly midnight before they got the results. They waited at home. It was considered in bad taste for the candidates to hang around the clerk's office while he counted the votes, and most of those running wouldn't learn the final outcome until the following day. Len had sent Joe Mason to wait with the newspaper reporters on the steps of the Town Offices.

Len spent the evening pacing. Edna knew he would like to have gone driving, funnelling his impatience into a wild ride of cut corners and gravelly skids, but he was unwilling to be too far from the phone. Instead he drank too many whiskeys, smoked too many cigarettes and walked round and round and back again. Into the kitchen, down the hall to the bedroom, back to the living room again. She tried to read, but couldn't concentrate on the story. Whenever she finally started to lose herself in the book, Len would interrupt with some remark about the campaign. It was the first time she had seen him less than confident. In a way, it was kind of endearing, but she wondered at his nervousness. She knew he wanted to win, but if he didn't, it wouldn't make much difference in the grander scheme of things, would it? She didn't know.

When the telephone rang at quarter to twelve, she knew he needn't have worried. He broke into a grin as he heard Joe's news. The grin got wider as he told her about it.

"It worked, Eddie, can you believe it? It's good times ahead for us!" She smiled sleepily and kissed him and announced she was going to bed.

"I'm going to town just to run over the results with Joe," he said.

It was the first time he had ever offered her an excuse.

Mac snorted when he read the paper. "I can't believe it."

"What dear?" Vera was feeding the baby. She had just given him a bath and hoped that the pablum she had laced his bottle with would be enough to ensure her a reasonable stretch of uninterrupted sleep.

"That Len Collins got elected! What the dickens is this world coming to when a hellion like Len Collins can get himself on Council?"

Vera, immersed in the sweet smell of clean baby was only half listening. "What's wrong with Len being on Council?" she asked.

Mac sputtered. "He's a crook! He makes all his money bootlegging. Everybody knows that." He shook his head in dismay. "Somebody better keep a close eye on things, or he's apt to run off with all the taxes."

"Oh, Mac! Len wouldn't steal."

"How do you know? He smuggles, that's just as bad."

Vera rocked the baby, whose eyes were slowly closing. "You don't know that for sure. That's just talk."

But Mac had heard it down at the yard, and if the guys at the yard said it, it must be true.

"Why are you defending him, anyway?" he asked.

"Well, Edna is my friend."

"Yeah, poor Edna. One of these days she's going to regret getting tangled up with that crook." Another thought struck him then. "Oh, God, I hope they don't put him on the Public Works Committee."

"Why? Vera's attention had switched back to the baby.

"Because then he'd be my boss, that's why!"

But Len didn't want to be on the Public Works Committee, the committee that looked after the town's roads and snowploughs. He'd already arranged to serve with John Moore on the Planning Committee.

February was sullen, gray and cold, a month of high winds and sudden snow showers. Edna was bored. Len was often gone during the evenings, called to this committee meeting or that, and when there were no town meetings, to meet with gray-haired men in business suits. Sometimes he needed her presence at a dinner or reception, and she would pile her hair up on top of her head, dress up in something wonderful he had bought her and walk into the room on his arm, turning heads and conversation their way. It was just like the games of dress-up she had played so often with Vera. Who are we today? Who can we pretend to be? But Len seemed proud of her and for some reason her appearance oiled the wheels of whatever he was up to.

In the meantime, she had little to do. She tidied the house for an hour or so each morning, that was all it took, but she found it difficult to fill in the rest of the day. She longed for spring and the garden.

One day on impulse she drove to the hardware store and bought paint. She didn't know what colour Len's kitchen had been originally. Whatever it was had faded to a uniform beige, punctuated by splotches of grease. She bought a pale, sunshiny yellow for the walls, and a deep goldenrod for the cupboards. Halfway home, she realized she had no idea whether or not there were any paintbrushes in the jumble of boxes in the garage. She turned around and drove back to the hardware store, and to the library for a book of painting tips.

By this time it was late afternoon, and she was dying for a cup of tea. She hadn't seen much of Vera or the baby lately. She turned down Vera's street, and hoped her friend wouldn't mind an unexpected visit.

The baby was screaming. He had just fallen for the seventeenth time that day and Vera was at her wit's end with him. He hadn't napped at all again that afternoon, and now, as dinnertime drew near, he was exhausted and overwrought, and so was his mother.

Edna scooped the child out of Vera's arms and jounced him as they walked down the hall, patting his back and swaying with him as Vera's mother put the kettle on to boil. Gradually he subsided into hiccoughs. He was fascinated by Edna's earrings, grabbing at them and pulling whenever she let her guard down for a moment.

Vera subsided into a chair. Mrs. Matlin excused herself.

"I'll let you girls talk," she said, smiling at Edna. "You don't get much chance, do you?" She disappeared into the back bedroom.

"What's new?" Vera asked. Edna nearly always had something to tell, an amusing story, a piece of gossip, tidings of classmates who had married or given birth.

"I decided to paint the kitchen," Edna said, shifting the baby away from her earrings.

"Why? You don't spend any time in it anyway." Vera was pregnant again and grumpy, although she had no intention of telling Edna the reason for her sour mood. She had assumed that after Little Stevie was born, Mac's attentions would wane, but as soon as the doctor had given the okay he was at her nearly every night again. She had come to hate the little front bedroom with the cabbage rose wallpaper that she had played in so happily as a little girl.

They had put the baby in the room across the hall. Vera could get to him quickly if he cried in the night, so he wouldn't disturb her mother, who most nights didn't go to bed at all, but dozed on the chesterfield downstairs. Her mother who was just as exhausted as she was each night. They performed virtually the same tasks; the changing of diapers, the feeding of the helpless. Whenever Vera had pictured motherhood, she had thought of a pink and contented baby lying serenely in her arms, swaddled in a soft flannelette blanket, cooing and blowing bubbles. She hadn't thought of diapers, she hadn't thought of two a.m. feedings, she hadn't thought of screaming fits of colic that lasted for hours. She hadn't realized the meaning of the term "bone-weary" before, but now she understood. It was a weariness so deep and so profound that it penetrated every cell of her body.

She didn't know how she was going to cope with another baby. Stevie was only thirteen months old, a loud, noisy, active baby who had crawled at seven months and walked at nine. He had to be watched every moment. He pulled cloths off tables, mugs off counters and glasses off faces. He crawled into cupboards, under beds, and once, when Vera had been trying to make jam, out the front door and across the street.

Mac was delighted with him. "He's real boy, Vera, a real boy!" And he would throw him high in the air or bounce him on his foot until Stevie was sick with excitement. Then Mac would hand him back to Vera who would spend at least an hour calming him down before she could get him to go to sleep. She loved Little Stevie dearly, of course, but one Little Stevie was enough.

No point in taking it all out on Edna though, and Vera tried to pull herself together and show some interest. "What colour are you going to paint it ?" she asked.

"Yellow. Pale yellow for the walls. Deep yellow for the cupboards."

Edna's kitchen faced east and Vera tried to visualize the sun pouring through the window in the morning, its amber light reflecting and intensifying yellow walls.

"Don't you think it'll be kind of bright?"

Edna agreed. "Yes. That's why I want it."

"What does Len think?"

"To hell with Len. He's not there often enough to notice anyway."

It was the first time Edna had ever voiced any sort of criticism. Vera wondered, as she had often wondered, what it would be like to live with such an energetic husband. She expected Len was at Edna just as often, no, even more often than Mac was at her. Of course, Edna didn't have nearly as much to do as she did. She wasn't so exhausted at the end of each day. Maybe she liked having Len at her all the time. Odd, that there were no signs of a baby yet.

"Well, I'll have to see it when you're finished," she said, pouring herself another cup of tea. "I just can't quite imagine it right now."

Edna smiled. "Maybe I'll have enough paint left over for your cupboard doors." She had suddenly realized how gray and dingy Vera's kitchen was.

"Thanks, but don't bother. I wouldn't have time to do it anyway."

Little Stevie had been contentedly gumming an arrowroot biscuit while they talked, smearing the sticky paste across his face and his clothes. He seemed so quiet that Edna had let her guard down, and now the baby saw his chance. He grabbed at her earring and clenched it in his chubby fist.

"Stevie, no." Edna tried to catch his hand, but before she could he flung the earring across the table, yelling loudly in triumph.

"Stevie, no!" Vera scooped the child up and shook him roughly, then burst into tears.

Alarmed, Stevie joined her with sympathetic wails.

"Vera! It's all right. It's only an earring." It had ricocheted off the wall and rolled under the table. Edna stooped and retrieved it. "It's all right. See?" She held it up so Vera could see that no damage had been done. "He's only a baby after all."

"I know," Vera wiped her eyes with a tea towel. "He's only a baby and he'll be a baby for a long time, and now I'm going to have another one, and then I'll have two babies, and I don't know what I'm going to do." She hadn't meant to say anything, but once started, it all came out in a gush.

"You're having another baby? Already?"

She started crying again. "Yes. Oh, Edna I don't know what I'm going to do. I can barely cope with it all now. We don't have any money and there's too much work for mother and me and Mac won't leave me alone..."She tried to stem the flood of tears, mashing the tea towel into a sodden wad. "I'm sorry. You came here for a cup of tea, not to have me weep and wail all over you."

"No," Edna said, getting up and putting her arms around her, "I'm here to be your friend."

She racked her brains after that to try and figure out how to help. She knew she had to be careful, for Vera had her share of stubborn pride. She thought about it on the drive home. When she got there, she realized she'd forgotten to buy a paint roller.

One afternoon about a week later she went to Vera's and knocked on the door.

"Hi, I'm going to the park. Do you and Stevie want to go with me?"

Vera shook her head. "I can't. I'm in the middle of a wash."

"Oh." Edna allowed herself to look downcast. "Gee, I was really looking forward to some company. Gee. Maybe I could just take Stevie...."

After that, she took Stevie a couple of afternoons every week. Sometimes they went to the park, where they would feed the ducks with chunks of bread and watch while they squabbled and fought over the scraps. Sometimes they went to the school playground, where Edna pushed Stevie in the swing that had been set up for the smaller children, or guided him carefully down the slide. In the beginning, she did it because it was a help to Vera, but she came to enjoy her afternoons with the little boy. He was very bright and very lively and she understood why he tired Vera out so much. She always made sure that he had a chance to run and jump and tumble, so that when she returned him he was tired enough to sleep soundly at night.

Len found her at the park one afternoon. The sun was shining brightly, odd for March, and there was a whiff of spring in the air. Stevie was bundled into his snowsuit with a red and white scarf wound round and round his neck, his mittens dangling on strings from his sleeves. The wind was still cold enough to turn his cheeks bright red. He looks for all the world like a little gnome, Edna thought as she pushed his stroller down the street. Stevie knew where they were going and shouted his pleasure at passersby, who found his good humour contagious and smiled back at the little boy.

When they reached the park, they headed straight for the slide, his favourite. He would liked to have gone down the big slide, but Edna limited him to the kindergarten version, carefully guiding him up the ladder and down the slippery incline.

She didn't notice the Buick as it pulled into the curb. It wasn't until Len was right behind her that she noticed anything but Stevie, hooting with laughter.

"What the hell are you doing?"

She spun around, alarmed, then realized who it was.

"I'm playing on the slide."

"Who's the kid?"

"Stevie Dunlop. Vera's little boy." She hadn't told Len about her afternoon outings with Stevie. She wasn't sure why. She guessed it was because he probably wouldn't be interested.

"How come you got stuck with Vera's brat?"

"He's not a brat and I didn't get stuck with him. I started taking him out to give Vera a break, now I find I really enjoy it."

Len looked irritated. "What a waste of time."

"Not really. I enjoy it, he enjoys it. Vera enjoys it. What's your problem?"

There was an expression on his face she couldn't read, but then that was often the case these days. "I don't have a problem," he said. "I just don't understand why you would be bothered with somebody else's snotty-nosed kid, that's all."

Edna suddenly realized that snotty nose or not, Little Stevie was nowhere to be seen.

"Oh, damn", she said. "Now look what you've done." Frantic, she ran around the corner of the school just in time to see Stevie let go of the handles at the top of the big slide and go whizzing, laughing the whole time, down to the end. His laughter turned to wails as his feet hit the sand at the bottom and he went tumbling, head over heels, across the grass. One small rubber boot flew off into the air.

"Oh, God." Edna ran to him and bundled him in her arms. She looked him over quickly. There didn't seem to be any open wounds or broken bones, and she sat on the end of the slide with him, rocking and soothing him until his wails dissipated into intermittent sobs.

Len retrieved the boot and put it back on the little boy's foot.

"Thank you. Now go away." She glared at him until he shrugged and stalked off.

That night he turned to her in bed. "Do you want a baby?" he asked.

"Of course I want a baby. Isn't that what's supposed to happen when you get married? Sooner or later, you have a family?"

"I guess," he said. "Maybe we should have one."

"Maybe? We haven't exactly been doing anything to prevent it, have we?"

He chuckled then. "No, we haven't. I wonder why you're not pregnant yet?" He said it as if it hadn't occurred to him before. It probably hadn't, she thought. "Well, let's get started. We've got a lot of work to do here." He ran his hand along her thigh.

"Oh, I get it. That's the excuse now is it?"

"Well, yes. I can see I've been remiss. It's obviously my duty as a husband to impregnate you and then keep you barefoot and in the kitchen for the rest of your life."

"Brute." She flung herself on top of him and pinned his arms to his sides. "I'll show you who's boss around here."

"Yes, ma'am. I'll do anything you say." But he raised his arms, easily lifting her off him, and rolling her over on her back.

"Okay, okay, I surrender", she laughed.

"You're darn right you surrender. We've got ourselves a baby to make."

But in spite of their best efforts, the baby refused to be made.

CHAPTER NINE

The very silence was keeping Cara awake at night. After years of living in a city where traffic rumbled constantly and there was always the scream of far-off sirens, the quiet of the small town night was eerily unnerving and she would lay awake in the small hours of the morning listening to the refrigerator running, the wind blowing and the scratchings of small, nocturnal animals.

Her mind would work overtime then, cataloguing what she had not yet done, what she hadn't sorted, or disposed of, or arranged to have something done with. She knew there were at least two Christmas catalogue designs waiting for her and she fretted about not having started them yet. She worried about Mickey.

Although he was seven now, and of course, completely grown up as they both well knew, he still liked to snuggle up close after his bath and have her read a bedtime story. He smelled achingly sweet then, an odour of shampoo and flannelette pyjama and little boy, and she would fuss with the still damp hair at the nape of his neck while she recounted the adventures of Peter Pan or Winnie the Pooh. She told him the old stories too, the stories her father had told her when she was little, but he was more interested in these when they were on the island, where the immediacy of geography made them somehow more real.

She needed to take her mother's stories back, she realized at four a.m. one morning, those library books that had collected under her bed as she lay dying. The next morning she gathered them up and walked downtown. "Upstreet" was what everyone here called it. She remembered the first time she had used the term in the city. Her friends had hooted in derision.

"Where's upstreet? Just west of Hicksville?" one laughed.

She had been careful after that to say "downtown", anxious to appear city-born and bred. Now as she walked along, she understood why, in this place, upstreet was more appropriate. The town had, indeed, grown up from the harbour, climbing the hillside on its way to the high central plateau of the island.

Upstreet wasn't much of a walk. The Collins house was only a couple of blocks away from the main drag and Cara was used to walking in good weather. She had never maintained a car in the city and it wasn't worth taking the subway or a bus for only a few blocks unless it was snowing or raining. Here, driving was more natural than walking. Cara's mother had occasionally walked somewhere, her father, never. Usually they would get the cars out even if they were just going a short distance, circling and circling the block until they found a parking space in front of wherever they wanted to go into, preferably a space with time still left on the metre.

As she walked along, Cara noticed that the houses along her street were all still present as remembered, but that their functions had changed. The neighbourhood now boasted several Bed and Breakfasts, a few offices and a couple of craft shops tucked into corners of ground floors. The Victorians had been gaily painted in blues, tans, yellows and plums. Quaint and elegant signs hung from iron posts in front of many. Too large by far for the modern family, and no doubt too expensive to maintain, their owners had found new uses that would have appalled the original inhabitants. At least they were still intact, she reflected and their characters lovingly restored, no matter the motivation.

She rounded the corner to Main Street. Once a crowded and nondescript collection of shoe stores, offices and pool halls, in recent years the street had been widened, trees planted and benches installed. She noted a book store, several art galleries and gift shops and a couple of nice looking restaurants. For the tourist trade, she supposed, but unlike many tourist towns, you could still find hardware stores and a dry cleaner.

Further up the street the squat library faced off against the towering post office, both vying for domination of the town's centre. When she was a teenager, the library had been a fusty and uninviting place, where she had gone only for material for some hastily-completed assignment. The librarian had been forbidding and disapproving of teenagers, shushing and herding them into the reference room, where they quickly scribbled down bits of information and left as soon as possible.

The reading room was a hubbub today. Pensioners sat at the tables with the latest papers, their shopping piled around their feet. Two teenage girls were investigating the Internet at a computer terminal, giggling at the cyberspace selection of information sites. A middle-aged man scrolled the microfilm machine through pages of ancient documents. There were five or six people waiting at the desk to take books out, chatting and gossiping. The librarian greeted each of them by name and made small talk about the weather, their illnesses and children.

"Hello, dear. How are you doing?" Cara turned to find Vera Dunlop's round face smiling up at her.

"Vera. Hello. I'm fine. How are you?"

Vera's arms were piled high with novels and shopping bags, balanced against the cane in her left hand.

"I always take too many books," she said. "I used to read so much, I'd go through five or six books a week, but now my eyesight isn't so good, you know, and it takes me a lot longer, but I still haven't got out of the habit. The librarian here is so sweet, though, she lets me keep them as long as I need to."

"What are doing with a cane?" Cara asked. She hadn't ever seen her use one before, in spite of the fact that Vera's balance had been precarious for some time.

"Oh, I fell and twisted my ankle yesterday. I was setting out a dish of milk for this little stray cat that keeps coming around my door. The poor little thing is so skinny, I haven't the heart to chase it away. I've been looking for a home for it, but I'm afraid I may be stuck. The cane was my father's and I found it in the back of the hall closet. You never knew my father did you? No, of course not, he died when you were just a girl."

"Could I give you a hand?"

"Why, thank you dear, but I'm all right. Mac is supposed to meet me here in a few minutes. He has the car. Why don't you come back with us and I'll make us a cup of tea?"

Cara was loathe to waste the rest of the day drinking tea. It was nearly eleven already and she hadn't accomplished anything, but she needed a graceful way to put Vera off. "Oh, I'm sorry, I can't today." she said with what she hoped was regret in her voice. "I have to..... I have to go see Uncle Jack at the store. I'll take a raincheck though."

"Why don't you come over for supper tomorrow night?" Vera said. "Steve and Marcie are down and I know he'd love to see you. Unless you were planning on heading back to the city right away. I know how busy you are, dear."

Cara hesitated. How many years had it been since she'd run across Steve Dunlop? Their visits home had never seemed to coincide. How odd it would be, she thought, to sit at a dinner table with Steve and Marcie, the wife she had never met, and make small talk. She had been in love with Steve, once. It would be kind of nice to see him again, she decided, to find out how his life had turned out. And she could use some conversation, small or not. She had been spending far too much time with old memories.

"What time do you want me?" she asked.

Vera beamed. "Six o'clock. We'll see you then." She patted Cara's arm and handed her parcels and books to Mac, who had finally come to retrieve her.

Cara placed the books she was carrying on the returns counter and took out her wallet, expecting to pay the overdue fine, but the librarian waved her away.

"No, no" she said, "Mitigating circumstances. We can't take your money for those." Cara smiled and thanked her.

She decided that since she'd told Vera she was going to the store, she might just as well do it. It was probably about time to touch base with Jack anyway. As she wandered along the street, she kept meeting people she knew, or who knew her. Her mother's friends, Mrs. Fletcher, Mrs. Jackson, the man who cut her mother's lawn, the real estate agent, a couple of people she had gone to high school with. People she didn't know smiled and nodded as they walked by. It took her half an hour to walk the two blocks to Charles and Sons Fine Furniture.

She stood for a moment looking at the building before she went in. The storefront was distinctly shabby. The trim needed painting and the windows wanted washing. Inside was just as unappealing, the showroom furniture arranged in regimented rows and strict order; living room suites in front, then tables and chairs, lamps and beds at the back. A young girl with a pony tail intercepted her as she walked down the centre aisle.

"Ken I help ya?" she asked, snapping her gum.

"That's all right. I'm Cara Collins. Is Jack Charles in?"

"He's in the office right now. If you just go to the back and up the stairs..."

"That's okay. I know the way."

The girl shrugged and went back to leaning against a sofa and staring out the window.

Jack was hunched over a ledger, but waved her in, smiling.

"Cara! How are you? How nice to see you!"

"Hi, Uncle Jack, how's it going?"

"Well, it's going. You know. Please, sit down, sit down." He swept the office cat from the chair across from him, and made a half-hearted attempt to brush the hair off the seat. "Now, what can I do for you?" he asked when she had settled.

"I just thought I'd drop in and see you. You know, find out how things are going and get a feel for where things go from here." Oh my, this is awkward, she thought. Jack had been running Charles Furniture ever since her father died, what was that, over twenty years now? Technically, Cara was his boss now, the owner of the company, the person to whom he must answer, but she had no idea even what questions to ask.

"Well, I'm glad you dropped in, dear. We need to have a chat about the store, but I didn't want to intrude, you know. I didn't know if you were ready for it yet."

She nodded, grateful that Jack had slid gracefully into the topic. "For starters, I guess, how is the store doing?"

"It makes a profit every year, not a huge one, mind you, but a profit. A lot of people still come here out of loyalty or habit or something. I guess they like to buy local or else they don't like driving to Belleville. But there are less and less of them every year. We're being squeezed by the big chains, like every other small business in the world. But maybe you'll have the energy to fight it."

"I would really like to just leave things the way they are," she protested. "I know you've been running the business for a long time and I don't really see any reason to change that. I wouldn't know where to start anyway."

He looked uncomfortable and played with the piles of paper on the desk.

"Well, Cara, " he said slowly. "I appreciate that and I'm sure the people who work here appreciate it too. They've been kind of worried about their jobs. But there are a few things you probably don't know. I haven't been well..."

Her face must have shown her dismay, because he chuckled and patted her arm. "Nothing disastrous, or at least I don't think so, but apparently the old ticker isn't as good as it should be. Now I've managed to put some by, and your Aunt Margaret's uncle passed on last year and left her some money and to be blunt, I'd like out, so I can slow down and take it easy for whatever time I have left. We'd like to spend the winters in Florida. That's the thing that gets you when you start getting old, you know, the darn winters. It would make life a whole lot easier for Margaret too."

"Oh." Cara didn't know what to say. She had assumed that the store would go on pretty much as it always had. "What do you think I should do?"

"Well, that's up to you of course," Jack said. "You could sell out, but I'm telling you right now, I don't think it would fetch much, other than the value of the land. It used to be you could count on a certain amount for good will, but that doesn't seem to hold anymore. There's the stock of course, but when you get right down to it, it's not worth that much. The building needs a lot of work. I expect it would be cheaper to just tear it down and start over, but that would require a fairly large infusion of capital. The other option of course is to just close it down. I don't know if you were counting on any income from it or not."

"I hadn't really thought about it", Cara said. "I've been making my own living for an awfully long time now. It never occurred to me that I had, what did the Victorians call it... "expectations"." Somehow the notion of closing the store appalled her. Charles and Sons Fine Furniture had survived, albeit precariously, for four generations now. It had been there as long as Cara could remember. But what was the alternative? Uncle Jack clearly wanted out. She could hardly run the store herself. She had no head for numbers and besides, she liked being an artist and made an okay living at it. She didn't want to go into business.

"Do I have to make a decision right away, Uncle Jack?"

"No, no of course not. I just wanted you to be aware of the situation, and have some time to think about it, that's all." He shifted in his chair. " In fact, it would be better if we could keep things going at least over this winter. In terms of the staff, I mean. They'd stand a better chance of picking up other work in the spring, if you decided to close down. And the building looks better with some greenery around it if you decide to sell."

Oh God, Cara thought. The staff. I have a staff. What I decide will dictate what happens with their lives. Cara the employer, the boss, the giver of wages and salaries. How on earth did that ever happen?

"I promise you I'll give it some serious thought over the next little while", she said, rising. "I'll let you know as soon as I've figured things out."

"That'd be grand, Cara. And now, can I take you to lunch?"

"Are you sure you have time?"

"For my favourite niece? Of course I do. Besides, I don't often get to walk into a restaurant with a pretty girl on my arm, now do I?"

In a different time and place, Cara might have been offended by being called a "pretty girl". At thirty-nine she was certainly no girl and "pretty" was an adjective she had always found patronizing, but somehow Jack's gentle smile turned the diminutive into a mark of affection and she took the remark in the spirit in which it was offered.

They lunched at Grenadine's, a new place on Main Street that Cara had noticed as she walked by earlier. She expected that Jack would have preferred the greasy spoon down the street, where they served hot beef sandwiches and cheeseburgers, but he was obviously taking her city sensibilities into account. She ordered a glass of white wine and a salad; Jack grunted appreciatively when his smoked meat sandwich proved to be piled four inches high.

"I haven't ever eaten here, before", he confessed. "But I'd heard it was good. They certainly give you a fair serving."

They groped for conversation for the first few minutes. Cara had never had much to do with her uncles. As a child her world had been filled by her father. As an adolescent, she had been absorbed by her own activities, and later on, she had been immersed in her own life.

"Tell me what my mother was like when she was a girl," she said, more to make conversation than because she was curious.

"Oh, she was always a looker, that's for sure", Jack said after a moment's thought. "And high-spirited. Why, I remember she used to drive Mum crazy. She would never just do what she was told, she always had to have a reason why. And the reason had to make sense." He chuckled. "Dad always said that Edna was just like his sister. Aunt Ellen had a peculiar way of looking at the world, as if she was standing on the outside of it, looking in, and not afraid to comment about what she saw, either. I don't think anyone was real surprised when Edna ran off with your father. Oh, they were a real matched set, all right."

Cara was puzzled. She didn't remember her mother as high-spirited at all. It was her father who had been meteoric and unpredictable.

"Why did the store go to my mother?" she asked. "Wouldn't it have made more sense to leave it to the boys?"

Jack looked uncomfortable. "Well, now, I don't know. It was some arrangement between Len and your grandfather. I never did get the details straight. I suppose it only made sense after your grandfather took sick. I was only eighteen you know, and Billy was sixteen. And after your father took over, the store made more money than it ever had before. He took me on right after I finished school and I can't say I've ever had any complaints about the arrangement. After all, it stayed in the family and I've had a good living from it all these years. I doubt Bill would have hung around anyway."

The younger of Cara's uncles had left school at seventeen and eventually found work at the General Motors plant in Oshawa. He had married a girl there and fathered four children, drab cousins that Cara seldom saw. They hadn't even come to Edna's funeral.

"What was it like, growing up here, when you were a boy?" She was suddenly curious about her uncles' lives.

"Not much different than when you were a kid I expect", he said. "Everybody always knew what you were up to, but that was okay, I guess, because it kept you out of trouble. As a boy, my goodness, it was paradise. Always lots to do, mischief to get into. I remember we'd play pickup hockey in the winter and pickup baseball in the summer. And you could always walk down the hill and go swimming in the bay. It was a great place for kids."

Cara compared Mickey's life, with its organized games and schedule of activities and wondered if his childhood was as carefree as Jack's sounded. Her own had seemed complicated and difficult, but she supposed that Jack was right, it had been a great place for kids.

"As a teenager, it was a little different", he went on. "There just wasn't much for us to do, other than church socials and hanging around the pool hall, unless of course, you had a reckless bent and then you went out dancing at some of the wilder places like The Palace of the Moon.

"What was the Palace of the Moon?" she asked. That had been the name on the postcard she'd found in her mother's closet. The place where she was supposed to meet someone called Sacha.

He looked bemused. "That was the old dance hall out at the Outlet, sorry it's all called Sandbanks now, isn't it? It was a rackety place I guess. I never went out there. I never drank that much, and The Palace of the Moon had a real reputation. It was for an older crowd, really, not us teenagers. I guess people thought teenagers didn't need much to do in those days, and most of us couldn't wait to get out of here and go to the city to find our fortunes. I don't think many who left did all that well, though, and most of them scuttle back here just as soon as they retire."

"But you stayed?"

"Yes, I stayed". He looked at her earnestly. "I'll always thank your father for that, Cara. I was already in love with your Aunt Margaret by then, and all I wanted to do was find a steady job so we could get married. Your father made that possible for us, and I'll be grateful to him for the rest of my days."

Cara thought about her own relationships, flash-in-the-pans, nothing that ever lasted for more than a few months. Briefly, she envied this kindly-faced uncle who had taken her to lunch.

Edna had taken the call at seven in the morning, before she'd even had time for a cup of tea. Len was long gone, off on the business of the day.

"Your father's been taken bad", her mother's voice said over the phone. "We're at the hospital now. You'd better come."

"Bad? Bad how?" The words didn't make any sense. She wasn't awake enough yet.

"It's his heart. He woke up in the night and couldn't get his breath, but waited until this morning before he told me. They've admitted him."

Shaking, Edna dressed quickly and drove as fast as she dared. There were no spaces left in the visitor's parking, so she had to find a place for the car out on the street. She rushed in through the Emergency door and was directed to a room on the second floor. She hated hospitals; the pervasive smell of uncontrolled feces and urine, the pungent tang of disinfectant, the aroma of powerful and dangerous medicines. She felt nauseous as she walked down the corridor with its shiny floor and bilious green walls, past rooms holding not only the very ill, but the old and the dying, their lives sputtering away in coughs and discharges and pain.

Her father was in a private room, lying inertly in the hospital bed, an oxygen mask over his face, tubes running in and out of his arms. His sweat-soaked hair was pasted to his pallid forehead. He seemed smaller somehow, shrunken, dwarfed by the buzzing machinery and the starched linen. Jack and Bill huddled in a corner, looking confused and awkward. Edna's mother sat stiffly in a chair beside her husband.

Edna tiptoed to the foot of the bed and looked down at her father.

"They say they've got him stabilized, but it was a bad one, Edna," Hetty said. "All the stress of the last little while you know."

Edna was numb and the implied causality of her mother's remark escaped her.

Her father opened his eyes and smiled at her.

"He's awake", her mother said. "Go closer. I think there's something he wants to say."

Edna moved closer to the edge of the bed and looked down at her father's face, faintly foolish, unfocused and vague as it had been all his life. She stroked his hair. "What is it father?" she whispered.

He struggled to remove the oxygen mask cupped over his mouth. She held it away for him. "Sorry to be so much trouble," he whispered.

Alarmed at his struggle for breath, she let the mask slip back into place. How typical, she thought. He had drifted through his life, always taking the path of least resistance, wanting only a tranquil existence, his unwillingness to be a bother nearly costing him his life.

"You're no trouble, Daddy, no trouble at all," she said. "Don't you worry about anything. Don't worry about mother or the boys or the store, we'll look after it all, okay? You just get better." Tears filled her eyes and her voice.

With that he seemed reassured and closed his eyes again.

"Will you, now?"

Startled, Edna turned to her mother.

"Your father isn't going to be able to work for a long time, you know. The store won't support us and a manager too and Jack and Bill are too young to be much help. Besides they have to finish school. I don't know who you think is going to look after everything unless you're prepared to roll up your fancy sleeves and go to work."

Edna glanced at her father; mercifully he seemed to be asleep. She muscled her mother out of the room and down the corridor to the waiting area.

"Well, what did you expect me to say to him?" she hissed when she got her alone. "'Thanks to your heart attack the family business is down the drain and we're all going to starve?' Don't be ridiculous, mother. Have a little charity."

"Charity may be what we'll have to take," Hetty replied. "Small as it was, we can't manage without your father's income. I'll have to take in boarders, I guess, but I have no idea how we're ever going to pay the hospital or the doctor."

Suddenly, Edna felt sorry for her mother, and found her agitated vulnerability almost touching. Hetty had hitched her wagon to the Charles fortunes at an early age and at the time must have assumed that she would be set for life. It hadn't turned out to be such a wonderful fortune after all, had it? Is that why she was always so disapproving and bitter? Edna wondered. She didn't want me to make the same mistakes she had? She was on the point of grappling with this sudden insight when Len burst through the door.

"I just heard the news," he said. "Why didn't you call me?"

"Because I didn't know where you were."

He hugged her. "Are you all right, Eddie?" he asked, patting her back.

Under other circumstances, she would have been amused at the look on her mother's face; it was not Edna's role to be comforted in this. How dare Len be so solicitous? She was, after all, a mere daughter, and an estranged one at that. It was Hetty was who was supposed to be the star of this show, but obviously someone had neglected to give her son-in-law the script.

"He's resting comfortably now, and the doctors say he's going to be all right. I really think the best thing we can do is leave him alone for a while and let him get some sleep," Edna said to Len.

"How bad was it?"

"Bad enough." Her mother finally found her voice. "He's going to have to take it easy for some time."

"Who's running the store?"

Trust Len to get right to the nitty-gritty, Edna thought. The store would have been the last of her considerations, yet it was taking up more conversation than her father's heart attack.

"Nobody," Hetty said. A tear slid down her face.

"Don't worry. I'll drop in and make sure the staff isn't stealing you blind." Awkwardly her patted her on the shoulder. "I'll make sure things stay on track until we can sort something out, okay? We'll talk later, but don't worry about it now."

Hetty finally let the tears come then. Wordlessly, she nodded and groped for a handkerchief.

Edna's father was in hospital for two weeks. He might just as well have stayed forever. After he came home, Hetty kept him in bed for the first ten days. After that, he got up in the morning, but only to pad down the stairs to the front parlour, where he sat for hours beside the radio. He showed no response to his wife's constant fussings and cossetings and eventually these stopped, the household slowly assuming an orbit that excluded him. Ever uninvolved in the world, Bert Charles had finally achieved what he had been striving for all his life; he became virtually invisible, an obstacle to be dusted or swept around, and nobody paid any attention to him at all.

Len took over management of the store, "until someone can be found to run it", as he said to Hetty. "I have no interest in being a shopkeeper. I'll keep an eye on things, but I need to find a good manager."

In the meantime, he forcibly hauled the company into the twentieth century.

First, he removed the old wooden signage from over the front door and installed bright neon lights that beckoned to passersby and lured them inside with promises of chrome and flash.

He replaced the old wooden counters with metal and steel shelving and covered the creaking wooden floor with linoleum. The stolid walnut dining room suites he replaced with flashy chromium dinette sets, set out on display complete with place settings and floral centrepieces.

He expanded the store's stock, adding row after row of shiny new electric appliances to the inventory. Stoves and refrigerators had always been good sellers, but now Len brought in electric toasters, osterizers and juice extractors as well.

All this might have passed by unnoticed except for the one addition guaranteed to astonish everyone - a television. Len set it up right in the front showroom window, so that every passerby would be drawn by its mesmerizing images.

The older staff protested. "Why would anyone want to buy one if all they have to do is stand on the sidewalk and watch", they asked.

"They can watch all they want. They can't hear it, though can they?" he pointed out. "They have to come into the store to do that."

His strategy worked. The curious might come inside once and leave without buying anything. The very curious had to have an excuse after that. Sales of small appliances, lampshades and throw cushions, all items with a big mark-up, soared. Word went round that Charles Furniture was now very stylish, and those in the market for a new chesterfield or refrigerator, who wanted something modern like they saw in all the magazines, checked at the local store first. They nearly always found just what they were looking for. If they didn't, Len was happy to order it for them.

His stock soared. He was touted as a fine example of the new progressive spirit of the community. A young man who, despite humble beginnings, through his own hard work and sheer determination had become a pillar of the community. It amused Edna enormously. Would they all be so complimentary if they knew that he sometimes made love to his wife in the back of the car or on the kitchen floor? Did they know that he kept a mickey of rye in the glove compartment of his car, "in case of snakebite" as he facetiously explained to her? Did they know, and Edna only occasionally admitted this to herself, that he was frequently gone all night with no explanation and was very probably out tom-catting somewhere, although at least he was smart enough to be discreet about it. She expected many of them knew this perfectly well, but his success made him immune to any overt criticism.

He never discussed his absences with Edna, and she too was unwilling to bring it up. It was a fact of her marriage, that was all. Sometimes Len was there at night and sometimes not. It was certainly a very different arrangement than her parents had had, but then everything about her relationship with Len was quite unlike her parents'. She could never dominate the household the way her mother had; even if she had been inclined to do so, Len's impulsiveness would have made it impossible. Besides, in most respects, she was perfectly happy with their arrangements, and even if she didn't like to admit to herself that Len strayed, she could take comfort in the fact that he never strayed far.

Len put Charles and Sons on a paying basis right away, but he waited until it became clear that Edna's father was not coming back to work to put his ultimate plan into motion. Store clerks and neighbours alike were surprised one morning when two bulldozers rumbled down the roadway by the Charles building and tore into the brush behind the loading dock, ruthlessly uprooting the small shrubs and tall grasses to expose the thin soil and rock that lay underneath. Back and forth they thundered, chewing everything in their paths.

Vera, who could see the destruction from her kitchen window, phoned Edna.

"What is Len doing behind the store, Edna? He's got bulldozers in there ripping things apart."

Edna had been enjoying a lazy morning in bed with a pot of tea and a magazine, and was mildly irked by Vera's call, not so much by the interruption, but by the fact that she had no idea what the answer to Vera's question was.

"I don't know. But I'll find out. I'll call you back."

She dressed quickly and drove to the store. The staff sent her out back, where Len was standing on the loading dock, watching the work.

"What's going on?" She had to shout it at him to be heard over the noisy machinery.

"I'm developing this piece of property."

"Developing it into what?"

"A subdivision." He waved an arm. "Next year, this time, the whole hillside will be houses."

"But what about the woods?" She knew that the woods were worthless, nothing but scrub, probably not even good for firewood, but it was a special place for her and she was a little disturbed that it was being discarded so cavalierly and torn apart so efficiently.

"Come on inside, and I'll show you the plans."

She followed him up the stairs to the office, where he spread out a large set of blueprints. It took her a few minutes to orient herself and to understand the meaning of the many lines drawn so precisely on the paper. When she did comprehend it, her breath was taken away by the scope of the project. She could see that several avenues of houses were slated to march up the hill, in prescribed lots of a quarter acre, each house boasting a tiny front yard and a larger back, each with a garage and a breezeway.

"So many? There must be forty houses here Len. Who's going to buy them all?"

He rolled the blueprint back up and pulled out the elevations.

"These houses are going to be real affordable", he said. "I expect all those people who are living in pokey little houses all over town are going to jump at them. All they need is a downpayment, and they have a brand new house with all the modern conveniences and I expect they should be able carry them for not much more than the rent they're paying now."

Forty houses times however much it took to build a house, Edna didn't know how much, but she knew it was a lot.

"Len, what happens if you build all these houses and nobody buys them? You can't afford to lose that much money." But she realized, even as she was saying it, that she had no idea whether he could or not. He never discussed his business with her, just handed her a chequebook and told her to buy whatever she wanted.

He chuckled. "Don't worry about it, Eddie. I'm not bankrolling the entire project. I got some partners to come in with me and it's all set up as an incorporated company."

She was struck by another thought. "Is the woods yours? Is that the property you told me about owning? When you decided to run for Council?"

"Among others. But it was the one with the most potential. All I needed was access to it. Well, that and a bylaw amendment."

Access down the roadway beside Charles and Sons Fine Furniture. Lucky for Len that he happened to marry into the Charles Family, wasn't it? And that his bid for election had been successful. She felt a disturbing nibble of suspicion, but thrust it away from her. It was a ridiculous thought, still, it wouldn't have been possible without her, would it? She told herself she was just being silly and sentimental about the woods. It had been worthless, after all, worthless to everyone but the children who played there and Len, who saw what could be done with it. He was going to make a great deal of money from this, she could see. If it worked.

The project was a major topic of conversation around town.

"About time somebody did something with those fields," they said at Fletcher's.

"Those houses are going to sell like hotcakes," they said at the post office.

"Just hope Len Collins don't lose his shirt," they said, privately, around the supper tables.

On any given day, three or four men would stand around the site, watching first as the large trees were removed and the building sites levelled, then providing unsolicited advice as gaping holes were dug for foundations. Len refused to chase these sidewalk experts away.

"If they weren't out at the site, they'd be sitting in the beer parlour," he pointed out. "It's a community service to keep them sober."

The local newspaper lauded Len's efforts, congratulating him on his progressive outlook and pointing out that the new subdivision would provide much-needed affordable housing as well as broadening the tax base and contributing to the future prosperity of the town.

"One of the major stumbling blocks to attracting new industry has been the lack of facilities for the employees of that industry", one editorial read. *"Businesses looking to re- locate in this community can now rest assured that their workers will be adequately*

and affordably housed. Counsellor Collins is to be congratulated on leading our fair town to a new era of economic growth."

Edna wasn't so sure. She continued to be vaguely disquieted, not only by the subdivision itself, but by the way in which Len had quietly, almost secretly, directed the events that had made it happen. She was sure he had a master plan, and had manipulated the pieces one by one to fit his blueprint. She had little time to think about it, though, because finally, after she had begun to give up hope, she realized she was pregnant.

CHAPTER TEN

Edna had been suspicious, but she had had her suspicions before and been wrong. Month after month, she had hoped, only to discover once again that she had failed. Sometimes she would be late, she had never been terribly regular, and then she would be almost sick with excitement, not daring to mention anything to Len, in case she was wrong, then grateful that she hadn't when once again her period started. After too many false alarms, she refused even to read the signs, and stopped keeping track of when she was due.

This time was different. She wasn't sure how late she was, but by backtracking, realized that it was at least three weeks. After sicking up her breakfast three mornings in a row, she knew it was time to see Dr. Simpson. He confirmed her diagnosis and advised her to limit breakfast to water and a handful of soda crackers. His advice was next to useless. No matter what she ate or didn't eat, she continued to throw up, not only in the morning, but in the afternoon as well. When she reported this fact, the doctor assured her that the nausea would soon go away, but again he was wrong. It dragged on for weeks.

She expected Len to be disgusted by her infirmity, but surprisingly, he was considerate and gentle with her, excited by the prospect of a family.

"Now that we've got started, let's have lots and lots", he said. "There was only me at home, you know, it would have been nice to have a brother or two."

She wasn't sure that she liked being pregnant or that she was going to survive having this baby. She wasn't sure she liked the sound of "lots and lots".

Initially, Vera was a little put out at Edna's news. She had had a far easier birth with Susan than with Stevie, in fact, everything with Susan was different than it had been with Stevie. Susan was a round-faced pudding of a baby, who bore an uncanny resemblance to Mac's father. Placid, where Stevie had been frenetic, Vera found her an easy child, who conformed to the strictures of a timetable with little complaint. She had always felt a certain smugness about her family, it allowed her to feel a patronizing sympathy toward the childless Edna. She was certain that Edna was envious of her children and devastated because it seemed she could have none of her own. Late at night, when she was too tired to fall asleep easily, she would indulge herself with vague fantasies in which Len would somehow, someday realize the worth of a real woman, one who could fulfil her biological mandate, one who could produce babies, seemingly, at the drop of a hat. In these fantasies, she pictured herself as a madonna-like figure, tenderly gazing at a swaddled, faceless and silent child while Len knelt worshipping at her feet. He would say he was sorry then, and beg her, and her children, to come away with him. She would spurn him, send him crestfallen and crushed back to his barren wife. These midnight fantasies would have been more satisfying had they not been punctuated by Mac's snores.

When she heard that Edna was, at long last, pregnant she did her best to sound happy for her friend, and to her credit, downplayed the perils of childbirth.

"Oh, you know, it hurts", she said. "But the end result is worth it, and you soon forget all the discomfort when you see the baby." Edna was sure the large black circles under her eyes would never go away, and wasn't sure any end result was worth feeling so nauseous all the time.

Still, as her stomach swelled, she allowed herself to imagine her child. A boy, surely, for would Len have anything else? Somehow, her mind's eye wanted to skip the baby stage; she pictured her son at around three, the same age as Vera's little Stevie, with the same hazel eyes and long limbs.

Len began to talk to her belly, regaling the lump with all the adventures they would have together.

"We'll go hunting and fishing, " he said to it, " and I'll teach you how to drive a car."

Edna shuddered at the thought of Len teaching anyone to drive and said so.

"I taught you, didn't I?" he protested.

"No, I taught myself. You were too impatient, so I kicked you out of the car."

"Oh. Well, our son will learn a lot faster than you did, so I won't get so impatient." And he went on to describe to her stomach the many sailing trips they would take across the lake and the proper procedure for pitching a tent.

When Francine O'Brien heard the news, she was once again certain that she had finally lost Len.

If she had been certain when he married Edna, she was even more sure of it when he was elected to Town Council. She was astounded when he turned up late on the night of the election.

"You shouldn't be here", she protested.

"Why not?"

"Well.... you're supposed to be respectable now, aren't you?"

"No", he corrected. "I'm supposed to look respectable. What I do privately is my own business. Besides, who's going to say anything, and who would they say it to?"

"But what if all those women who voted for you find out that you're cheating on your wife," she pointed out.

He laughed then. "Oh, they might squawk in public, but deep down they'd be having fantasies about how much fun it would be to cheat with me themselves."

She had to admit that he was probably right. He seemed to have the world by the tail, and apparently his young wife either didn't know what was going on, or didn't care.

She'd heard the news about Edna at the drug store. There was a group of men, retired storekeepers, pensioners, farmers who had moved into town, who met every morning for coffee at Fletcher's soda fountain and it was here that much of the town's real business was conducted. Rumours were discussed, speculations made and gossip exchanged between eight-thirty and ten o'clock every morning. She was squatting behind the counter, taking clean cups from the shelf when Jim McDonald and Morris Albright came in.

"Looks like Len Collins is going to have to tone things down a little now", Jim was saying as they ambled up to the counter. His wife had been in the waiting room the last time Edna had seen Dr. Simpson.

"Yup, the little woman is going to want to have him home after that baby comes," said Morris, who had heard the news from the mailman.

"What, Edna Charles finally took?" Marshall Benson hadn't heard yet.

"Yep", Morris settled his ample bulk comfortably on a stool. "You know, I always figured Len must have bastards scattered all over the countryside, but it took him long enough to knock his wife up. Funny, ain't it?"

"Don't matter", said Marshall, slurping his coffee. "This one's legit, that's all that counts."

Francine stood up then, and they changed the subject. It was common knowledge that she had run with Len at one time, and most were pretty sure the race was still on.

By that evening, she had convinced herself that her relationship with Len was truly at an end, and steeled herself for a long stretch of loneliness. She regretted that she had few mementos; a couple of snapshots, a corsage he had once brought her that she had pressed between the pages of an encyclopedia, a stuffed elephant he had won for her at the fair.

Maybe I should have married Joe Mason after all, she thought, but the idea depressed her and she was on her fifth rye and coke by the time Len arrived at midnight. She had so convinced herself that she would never see him again that she was almost taken aback when she opened the door and saw him standing there. She wasted no time in making him feel welcome.

Paradoxically, Hetty Charles was ecstatic when she heard the news. For the first time in her life, she was almost happy. She had far more money than when Bert had run the business. Len had taken Jack in hand as soon as he graduated, schooling him in the art of management and accounting between stints on the delivery truck. Jack wanted to get married, Hetty knew, to that Carson girl, who was probably no better than she should be, but soon he would be off her hands, and in the meantime he paid her board from his earnings. Bill was already talking about leaving next year. Bert was still a worry, when she got around to worrying about him, but he required little from her, and his illness made her the object of concerned inquiries at the Ladies' Aid meetings. She had enough money to hire help with the heavy housework, freeing her to spend more time at the church where she took a great deal of satisfaction in organizing not only rummage sales and Sunday School pageants, but the minister himself.

Every night, she got down on her knees and thanked the Lord for sending Len into her life, although she still had a bone to pick with Him about the way He had arranged it. Now, a child would solidify the union between Len and the Charles family, make it much harder for her flibbertigibbet daughter to upset the apple cart.

She was convinced that the child would be a girl, a fresh start for Hetty, who had somehow failed with Edna. She had wished her daughter to be compliant, quiet and supportive, putting the needs of her family ahead of her own. Instead, Edna had somehow grown into a willful, defiant and wayward woman, who, in her mother's estimation, was undeserving of a wonderful husband like Len Collins. Her fate should have been the one Hetty predicted: ruin and disgrace. That her marriage had turned out to be brilliant and advantageous for the whole family could never have been due to effort or discernment on Edna's part, she felt, but rather some sort of divine intervention in answer to years of prayer.

This time it would be different, she decided. This child would be the daughter she had always wished for. She was determined to make it so. In the meantime she knit sweater after tiny sweater, in soft pink wool.

The late September sky was grey, so leaden that it cast little light into Edna's pretty yellow kitchen. She was brewing an afternoon cup of tea when she felt a stabbing pain in her back. She had felt so unwell for the past few months that she was able to convince herself that it was nothing, a holdover from a restless night, a result of having lain in an awkward position. It abated, just as she thought it would, but as she was reaching for the sugar, the second wave erupted. This pain brought her nearly to her knees. Reluctant to call the doctor about something she was sure was transient, she instead called Vera for advice. It never occurred to her to call her mother.

Vera was alarmed. She had been uncomfortable with her pregnancies, but she had never experienced the unremitting nausea that Edna described, and she was unsure whether or not this new symptom was ominous. She called a cab after Edna admitted that she was lying on the kitchen floor and would need help getting up.

When she arrived, one look at Edna's face was enough to send her to the telephone again. Dr. Simpson arrived within minutes and Vera knew then that something was terribly wrong. Instructed to find Len, she tried first at the store. He wasn't in. She asked Jack to have a look around the construction site, but he was nowhere to be found.

The doctor gave Edna a sedative and ordered complete bedrest. "There's a problem with the way the baby is lying", he explained to Vera, for lack of anyone else to explain it to. "Mrs. Collins needs to stay in bed, probably until she delivers. Have you found that husband of hers yet?"

She hadn't and was still with Edna when Len finally came home at midnight, whistling jauntily as he ambled into the kitchen.

"What are you doing here?" he said when he saw her.

Vera was a little nettled by his tone, but she explained as best she could what had happened and the doctor's advice.

Len paled. "Is she going to be all right?" he asked, and briefly she envied her friend the obvious concern her husband showed. She offered to stay if he wanted. He didn't want, and hustled her into her coat and out the door as soon as a taxi arrived.

He might've thanked me at least, she thought. He could have offered me a ride home, but then she recalled that Edna could not be left alone. She wondered what Mac's reaction would have been if it had been her lying in the bed down the hall, her life in peril. Would he have turned white like Len did? Would he have been so obviously distraught? Would he have rushed down the hall to her room?

She tried to picture it, but Mac never rushed anywhere and she had never seen him distraught about anything. As to turning white, he spent so much time outside that he was permanently reddened by the sun, so no one would be able to tell anyway. He would have left it all to my mother, she realized. He would have thrown his huge yet helpless fists up in the air and left the women's business to the women, hopeful that his dinner wouldn't be forgotten in the confusion. She felt disgruntled and annoyed as she scrabbled in the bottom of her purse for enough change to pay the cab fare.

Len was sitting in a chair by the bed when Edna surfaced from a strange and confusing twilit dream.

"Oh my God, what time is it?" she asked. "I meant to stay awake until you got home. I'm sorry." But when she tried to get up, he pushed her gently back, explaining to her what he understood from Vera's garbled version of the doctor's instructions.

She burst into tears. "I'm going to lose this baby, aren't I?" she sobbed. "After all this time, and now I'm going to lose it."

Len sat down beside her on the bed and took her in his arms. "No you won't, Eddie, no you won't, I promise. I'll do everything to make sure that doesn't happen. I want this baby too, and you know I always get what I want, don't I?"

She smiled a little then, because it was the truest thing she knew.

Len called Edna's mother as a matter of courtesy, but discouraged her from visiting. Hetty was affronted. She was quite prepared to move in with Edna to look after her. One couldn't expect Len to do it, he was a man, and besides, wasn't he needed at the store, to keep it running smoothly and the money coming in? She became quite insistent, until Len flatly told her no and forbade her from coming around, or even telephoning.

"I'll call you once a day to let you know how things are going", he said. "And I'll certainly let you know as soon as anything happens, but I don't want you setting foot in this house."

She hesitated. For a moment she considered giving him a piece of her mind, but in his new role as provider for all of them he had acquired an authority that even Hetty dare not challenge.

He solved the problem neatly by hiring Bernice Davis. Bernice's husband had been a heavy drinker who had finally given it up when he wrapped his car around a tree trunk late one night, cracking a bottle of whiskey, the frame of the car and his own skull. Bernice had been left with a tiny house on the edge of town and eleven year old Rhonda, a good-natured, clumsy child who was not quite old enough, or mature enough to leave on her own. Bernice was ecstatic when Len Collins called and asked her to look after his ailing wife. Edna was a local girl, who would understand that she was not a servant, to be bossed and bullied, but, as local parlance had it, "help". There was no stigma attached to being "help". At the age of fourteen she had moved in with a neighbouring farm family to "help" and she had been "helping" ever since, accepted as a part of each family she worked for. When Len raised no objections to having Rhonda there after school, she knew she had found a new family.

She and Edna liked each other right away. Bernice's duties were never fully delineated, but she understood that Edna must never, never be left alone, and that she needed rest and tranquillity. Bernice occupied herself in keeping the little house clean while Edna was sleeping. She rejoiced in scrubbing the kitchen floor every other day and vacuuming the closets once a week. The house was so small, it took her little time to get it done, and she could spend most afternoons on the telephone, checking in with her numerous sisters.

Her only difficulty lay in terminology. "Mrs. Collins" seemed too formal for so young and helpless a girl, but some mark of respect was due her employer's wife and eventually she took to calling her "Mrs. Len", an appellation that amused nearly everyone, especially Len.

"Mrs. Len is a real lady," Bernice would report at the grocery store. "Lady" was the highest approbation she could think of. Always please and thank you, grateful for any little thing you did for her. Why Mrs. Len didn't even get upset when Rhonda, anxious to be of help to her mother, smashed two good china teacups on the kitchen floor when she tripped over her own shoelace and fell.

Bernice had been very annoyed with Rhonda. She had gathered up the pieces of china in an old newspaper and went to Edna.

"Mrs. Len, I'm so sorry. Rhonda is such a clumsy girl. I won't ever let her carry any of the dishes again." She showed her the broken pieces.

"What happened?"

"I don't know, Mrs. Len. She was carrying them teacups into the kitchen for me and she just tripped and fell."

"Oh my goodness, is she all right? She didn't cut herself or anything did she?" Edna asked, and won Bernice's heart forever.

It was as well that Edna took the attitude she did. Rhonda was never let near the china again, but everything else took a beating. No matter how careful Rhonda was, and she tried so hard to be careful, she managed to crack, break, scratch, burn, rip or shrink everything she touched. She became a byword for anything that malfunctioned.

When Len's car wouldn't start one morning, he shrugged. "Rhonda must have been in the garage," he said.

When a large crack was found in the kitchen window one day, he and Edna speculated that Rhonda must have looked through it.

When an early winter gale unexpectedly piled snow in five foot drifts, paralyzing traffic and stranding them all in the house for two days, they shrugged. "Rhonda must have listened to the weather forecast," they said.

But Edna was careful never to say such things in front of Rhonda and that, in Bernice Davis' book, was the mark a real lady.

Len curtailed his activities significantly, only occasionally asking the housekeeper to stay all night in the little guest bedroom.

"I'm sorry, Mrs. Davis, but I really must go out of town this evening," he would say at these times, "Business, you know. Don't wait up, I'll be late. By all means, Rhonda can stay too."

Bernice was a heavy sleeper and never knew what time he returned. She never thought to ask what sort of business was conducted so late at night. He was always there when she got up in the morning, whistling cheerfully as he made bacon and eggs. She would shoo him out of the kitchen and finish cooking his breakfast for him while he shared a cup of tea with Edna. He spent hours sitting with her, trying to relieve the unremitting boredom that complete bedrest imposed.

Edna was a reader and had always thought that paradise would be having time to read as much as she wanted; now she found that she could read only so long each day before her eyes tired and her mind wandered. Len tried bringing a television set from the store and setting it up in the bedroom so she could easily see it, but daytime programming, what there was of it, bored her. She leafed through magazines sporadically, but the women's magazines everyone brought her were full of recipes she would never try and silly advice on how to be a perfect wife. She tried writing, something she had always thought she would like to do, but couldn't keep her attention focused long enough to produce a coherent story.

She lived for when Len came home. He would burst in the door, shouting a hello at Bernice and then hurry down the hall to see how she was doing. The room seemed to explode in an uproar as soon as he entered. Bernice would bring Len a drink (no alcohol for Edna, other than a brandy at bedtime, prescribed by the doctor) and he would tell her of the day's activities, spinning the most mundane event into an entertaining and frequently scurrilous story.

"You know that truck driver I told you about?" he would say. "The one who delivers the small appliances from the wholesaler? I think he has the hots for Mabel." Mabel was the tall, cadaverous sales clerk in charge of lamps and upholstery materials. Edna would giggle then, trying to picture a beefy, red-faced trucker in an amorous embrace with the bony and bespectacled clerk.

"He came to deliver the packing slip this afternoon just as she was coming out of the bathroom. They nearly collided in the hall and he grinned at her and winked. I thought she was going to have a heart attack. Love at first sight, I tell you, I can recognize it every time."

He would tell her about work at the subdivision too.

"I can't believe it, I walked into one of the houses, and the guys were all sitting around playing poker. I don't know where the hell the foreman was. You should have seen the look on their faces when I walked in."

"What did you do?"

"Well, they were sure they were all going to be fired on the spot, you know, but I thought what the hell and sat down and joined the game. I cleaned them out. Took them for every last cent they had, then I told them if I ever caught them playing cards on my time again, I'd boot their butts down the hill into the bay. They won't be doing that again in a hurry, I'll tell you."

"But what would you have done if you'd lost?" Edna wanted to know.

He grinned. "I couldn't lose."

"Why not?"

"Because I cheat." She had hooted with laughter, bringing Bernice at a trot to see what the commotion was.

Len had offered to sleep in the other room, so Edna could rest at night, but she had refused. It was a comfort, after such a long day of nothing, to have his long, lean body next to her. In spite of her still-constant nausea and intermittent physical discomfort, she longed to take him in her arms and make love to him. At times, the longing was unbearable, and she wondered at herself, at this wanton creature who so craved physical sensation. Sometimes the feeling was so overwhelming that she almost considered risking it.

She wondered if Len felt the same way. She suspected he did, but she knew that men were different and that they had ways of seeking release. She wondered if that was what Len did, but she doubted it. She decided not to think about what he was doing instead.

When the pains started, Len was, after all, away. Unavoidable business required a trip to Toronto, he said, but he would hurry back as soon as he could.

"Just don't do anything 'til I get back".

"I don't have a lot of choice in the matter", Edna pointed out.

"Well, just try okay?"

It was the middle of the night and she woke in a panic, drenched in sweat and uterine fluid. Thank God Bernice is here, she thought. The housekeeper handled the crisis as efficiently as she did everything else. A cab was called, Edna bundled into it with her suitcase, and Bernice accompanied her to the hospital, signing her in, galvanizing the nurses into action.

When Dr. Simpson came, he took one look at her and ordered her to the delivery room.

The pain was unbearable. Edna had not grasped how such a large object could slide out through such a small opening, but now she understood. It forced its way, not caring what it ripped and tore in the process.

"Wait, wait, don't push", the nurse ordered. She might just as well have been talking to herself, for Edna couldn't have stopped pushing if her life depended on it. She didn't realize that it did.

She came to from a strange grey foggy place, where faces floated in a small frame directly in front of her eyes. Oh, there's Len, she thought in surprise. I thought he was away. He looked concerned, but smiled anyway.

"Hi", he said, stoking her hair.

She meant to say hi back, but all that came from her mouth was a moan. Her insides hurt, hurt horribly. Haven't I had the baby yet? she thought. Oh God. A nurse bustled in and poked a needle in her hip, and she sank back into fog.

She woke again, swearing at the pain. Len was still there, and he started to laugh. "Watch out, or you'll shock all these nurses. They probably think you don't know those words."

Her stomach still hurt, but not as badly as before.

"Did I have the baby?" she asked.

"Yes, darlin', a beautiful seven pound girl."

"A girl? Oh, I'm sorry, Len."

"No, no, don't be, she's beautiful. An absolute doll." He hesitated. "She gave you kind of a rough time, though."

The doctor came in then." Mrs. Collins, you're with us again!" he said. "Nearly lost you there."

Lost me? Edna thought. How could you lose me? Don't hospitals keep track of their patients? Isn't that why they put those bracelets on your wrist?

Dr. Simpson went on, something about the afterbirth being in the wrong place, and they were lucky they got the baby out, how there was excessive bleeding and how they had had to operate quickly, imperatively, there was no time to explain, no time to get a consent. Edna finally understood that there would be no more babies, too much damage had been done.

Strangely, it didn't bother her much.

Len lived at the hospital, leaving only when he was ordered to do so, which wasn't often. His charm worked magic with the staff and it seemed he couldn't get enough of the little scrap of humanity he had fathered, a fact that amused the nurses no end. Whenever they brought the baby out of the nursery, they handed her to Len, not to Edna. She was being bottle-fed, because the doctors said that was best, given Edna's condition, and besides, that was the modern scientific way. She was a red-faced little thing, with a thick head of dark hair. Len swore she looked just like his mother. Edna thought she didn't look like anything on earth until one evening when Len lounged in the armchair at the foot of her bed, the baby cradled against his chest. They had both fallen asleep. They have the same shaped face, and the same hands, she realized. And then she understood that this baby was not hers, it was Len's, and that was the way it would always be.

They had a great debate over names, a responsibility they had not given much thought to.

"I'd like Naomi to be in there somewhere," Len said, "after my mother."

"It would be nice as a middle name, but it's too old-fashioned for a first name," she objected.

"Let's call her Edna after you, then."

"Not a chance. I've always hated it. Besides, can you see calling a little tiny baby "Edna"?"

"Your mother did."

"Well, we all know about my mother, don't we?"

"What about your middle name? Elizabeth?"

Edna wrinkled her nose. "Elizabeth always ends up being "Liz". Like "lizard".

One by one names were trotted out, only to be discarded for one reason or another. Len liked the older names, like Deborah and Suzannah; Edna wanted something more modern. "Linda" was a popular name, just then but Len vetoed it.

"Every other baby these days is called "Linda", he said. "I don't want our daughter to be just like everybody else."

"No, hardly any of the boy babies are called Linda," she pointed out. "But I don't want to give her too weird a name. It'll make her odd."

"Well, okay. Let's just call her Charlie or Ralph and be done with it. Those are nice common names."

"Charlie Collins, yeah that's a great name for a little girl." She paused as a thought struck her. "What's the female version of Charles?"

"Caroline. " She could see him turning it over in his mind, savouring it. "Caroline Collins. It has a nice ring to it, doesn't it? Caroline Naomi Collins. It includes you in it, too, sort of. I like it."

And so, long after the nurses had expected all the papers to be filled in and returned, they named the baby "Caroline". It quickly turned into "Cara".

After they were allowed to take the baby home, Len would rush down the hall in the same old way, not to Edna, but to Cara. Over time she lost the thick thatch of black hair she had been born with, and the new growth came in brown and wavy.

At least something's mine, Edna thought. For everything else was pure Collins. The hazel eyes, the brown skin that always seemed slightly tanned, the long legs, but most of all the charm.

Cara was the most charming of babies. She soon had Rhonda and Bernice dancing to her tune, and all she had to do was let her lower lip quiver, and someone was there to pick her up. Len wouldn't let her cry, no matter what, and if a slight cold made her irritable he would walk the floor for hours or take her for a drive in the car to calm her down.

"I don't want you driving around with the baby at night", Edna objected. "I know how you drive."

"It's just around town", Len said. "And I'm careful when I have her with me."

Edna gave up. She was just as happy to let him go ahead, in fact. She wondered why she didn't feel the wonderful maternal rush of feelings she had been promised in all the books. She would pick Cara up and feed her and look after her, but when she thought about her, it was only as a mildly amusing responsibility. Sort of like a slightly irritating but adorable puppy. Better to leave it all to Len.

CHAPTER ELEVEN

Cara couldn't remember any home but the big brick house her mother had died in, although she had been told that they had moved there when she was eighteen months old.

The house stood on a corner, set back from the street, almost obscured by large maple trees that had been planted in the front yard more than a century before. In a neighbourhood of Victorian frivolity, its Georgian proportions seemed austere compared to the gingerbread and turrets that spilled off the other houses.

"It's huge!" Edna said, when Len took her to look at it. "What do we need this big a house for?"

"We don't need it, we want it", he said. "We can't entertain where we are now and this is perfect."

"Entertain who?" she wanted to know, but he didn't answer.

"Are you sure you wouldn't rather have that ranch-style we looked at?" she asked. "It's brand new and it has that nice big living room."

"And it's cheaply built and will go out of style in about fifteen years", he said. "I want a house that's more substantial than that. Besides, this place is a bargain."

"Then why did we bother looking at the other one?"

"Because you'd give me hell if I bought a house without consulting you," he said ingenuously.

The house Len wanted had an elegant front hall, with stained glass sidelights dimmed by greasy dirt. To the right of the hall was a large double parlour with a marble fireplace that had been blocked off with plywood. To the left was a small room that Edna supposed was a study, behind it the dining room, with peeling wallpaper and a nasty looking stain on the floor. The kitchen was located at the back, in a one and a half storey addition. A formica table stood in the centre of this, littered with papers. Two cupboards against the wall held cracked china and grimy glassware. The cubbyhole under the sink was curtained off with a stained calico print.

"I don't know what Bernice will say about this", Edna said doubtfully. Len had kept her on after the baby was born, at first to help Edna through the initial stages of infancy, and then because he never quite got around to letting her go.

"Don't worry, by the time I'm through, Bernice will have a dream kitchen", he said. She could see that he had made up his mind.

A stairway with an intricately carved newel post led upstairs from the front hall. There were two large bedrooms at the front of the house, two smaller ones at the rear, used, they could see, mostly for storage. A small bathroom had been carved out of the upstairs hallway with a flimsy partition. The half storey at the back had never been finished, although a tiny staircase led from it down to the kitchen.

Temporary repairs and hasty renovations had kept the house going for the previous thirty years. It had belonged to two sisters, neither of whom had married. Edna remembered them well. Addie and Amelia Lambert were as alike as two peas in a pod, their wispy hair scraped back into topknots, their watery eyes magnified by thick, wire-rimmed lenses. Their father had been the owner of a button factory, she recalled, and the house had once been elegant, but the two girls, for that was how they referred to themselves, had been left with only just enough to live on, if they were careful. It never occurred to them to move from their childhood home to somewhere smaller, warmer and cheaper, and over the years the house had slowly degenerated, the only maintenance provided by kindly neighbours who knew their circumstances.

Nowhere was this more apparent than in the garden. The back fence had long since fallen apart and schoolchildren had worn a path through the lawn as they cut across the corner on their way to school. A scrubby and dying hedge separated the house from the driveway and what had once been a large coach house. There was litter everywhere; chocolate bar wrappers were half covered with last years leaves; broken pop and beer bottles had fetched up under what was left of the fence; a couple of old inner tubes flapped against the stone bird bath.

The door handle came away, padlock and all, when Len opened the coach house, a two storey brick building that had housed the gardener/ chauffeur/handyman in better times.

"Hey", Len said, "what do you think about doing this over for Bernice and Rhonda? The house she's living in now is going to fall apart one of these days, and this way she'd be handy whenever we needed her. I could keep her on full-time if I made housing part of her salary."

Edna was astounded. A full time housekeeper was unheard of. Almost anyone with a little money hired a cleaning lady or someone to help with the heavier jobs. Nobody had live-in help.

"Do we want Bernice and Rhonda around all the time?" she asked.

"Well, we probably want Bernice. Unfortunately Rhonda is part of the package, but I don't see why it wouldn't work. They'd have their privacy and we'd have ours."

"Can we afford it?" she wanted to know.

He shrugged. "We're going to have to get a crew in here to renovate anyway. It won't cost much more to get them to work on the coach house while they're at it." He thought for a moment." Yeah, I can swing it."

"Do you think she'll go for it?"

"Are you kidding?" he laughed. "She'll shout hallelujah. If she sells her place, she'll probably only get what the land is worth, but that's still more than she has now and she'll live cheaper here anyway."

As Len predicted, Bernice Davis was ecstatic when he told her his plans. She had been living in fear that she would be let go, now that Cara was older and the first hectic months had gone by. Edna could easily handle the baby herself and the Collins house wasn't big enough to require much keeping. Oh, she expected she would still be called in now and again for spring cleaning, or to babysit if Mr. and Mrs. Len wanted to go away, but that wasn't enough to keep body and soul together, not with Rhonda to look after. She had been making discreet enquiries around town, asking who needed some extra help, in preparation for the day the Collins realized they no longer needed her.

Now there was this new, big house to look after, and a little thing like Mrs. Len couldn't possibly do it all by herself. She knew they'd been looking at houses, and hoped against hope that there would be more work for her to do, but she hadn't expected such a windfall. A renovated garage would be perfect for herself and Rhonda, she assured Len. She'd be delighted to stay on. No, she didn't mind working whenever they wanted her, and she'd be happy to accept her accommodation in lieu of part of her wages. She looked forward to keeping a house that was all brand new done over and best of all, she could continue to look after that darling little girl. She could scarcely believe her good fortune.

Len oversaw almost all of the renovations to the property himself. A new oil furnace was installed to replace the old coal-burner, the roof was reclad, the trim repainted. Floors were stripped of layers of old varnish to reveal their lovely golden grain. The kitchen was completely rebuilt with new cupboards and a breakfast nook by the window. Upstairs one of the smaller back bedrooms was converted to a modern bathroom and a hallway punched through to make an extra bedroom in the half-storey over the kitchen. The upstairs front hall was once again a front hall, and a couple of comfortable armchairs were placed to bask in the sun that poured in through the massive front window. Len even had the gardens professionally landscaped, although Edna would liked to have had a chance to dig around a little and discover what had been there.

They moved in the spring. She hadn't been able to picture any of their old furniture in the new house. With the exception of the fourposter bed, Len hadn't either, for everything else was new. He got a surprising amount of it from Charles and Sons Fine Furniture.

"A lot of this stuff was packed away at the back of the storeroom", he said. "I doubt I can sell it, it's too old fashioned and out of style. But these solid old pieces suit the house, don't they?"

"But what are we going to do with all our old furniture?," Edna asked. "Some of it was nice."

"That was for that house, this is for this house," he said. "We'll leave it behind and I can rent the old place furnished."

She shrugged and hoped he had enough money for it all.

They attended auctions until he found the dining room suite he wanted. It was cherrywood, from the estate of an old woman who had been married to a Member of Parliament. The table was huge, and would sit twelve comfortably. It came with several side pieces; a large glass-fronted buffet, a sideboard and a wheeled coffee cart.

"I'll be afraid to set a dish down in case I scratch the tabletop," Edna protested. Len just laughed at her and bought it anyway. He had the seats reupholstered in a rich, dark green satin, to coordinate with the brocaded paper he hung on the walls.

She had to admit that Len's taste was wonderful, albeit not in the current fashion. She had initially protested the formality of his choices. She had liked the spareness of the old house, and was leery of too much fussiness. The last thing she wanted was a bigger version of her mother's house, with its bric-a-brac and warring patterns. Besides, when she leafed through the latest magazines, the full-colour pictures all showed pale teak with a Scandanavian design. But when all the wallpaper had been hung, the painting completed and the furniture installed, she could see that the house had a finished look to it. Rather than treat each room separately, he had considered the house as a whole, so that one room seemed to float effortlessly into another, one colour picking up seamlessly from the last and flowing into the next.

"We need some good artwork, and dishes and things, but I'll have to pick that up as we go along," he said. Little of what he had bought had actually cost him that much. The rage for chrome and formica and plastic made the heavy pieces found at auction sales little more than white elephants and they seldom fetched what they were worth.

Edna invited Vera to tea two weeks after they moved in.

"My God, it's enormous", she said, "How will you ever keep it clean?"

"Bernice is staying on to help", Edna said. She didn't mention that the housekeeper was fulltime, and living on the premises. It seemed too much like bragging.

Vera was impressed. She would have dearly loved some "help", but she had only Mac's paycheque from the County to keep her house with. It barely covered food, coal and hydro, never mind the doctor's bill from her pregnancies and her father's illness. Even though Mr. Matlin had finally, mercifully, passed on just after Christmas these bills were enormous and would probably never be paid off. She followed Edna glumly from room to airy room and only cheered up a little when they sat in the new breakfast nook and drank a pot of tea, which Edna served with tiny, buttery shortbread cookies. It felt good to sit down for a few minutes and not have to worry about Stevie and Susan, who were upstairs playing with Cara under Rhonda's supervision.

With a cup of tea in her, she felt better and decided she had been ungracious and unfair. "The house is wonderful, Edna," she said.

"It's all Len. I didn't really have that much to do with it. I don't know how he ended up with such wonderful taste, but he certainly has an eye."

Vera agreed, although her preference too, would have been for something more modern. She was still living with her mother's old furniture, upholstered rockers festooned with antimacassars, fussy Victorian tables that were difficult to dust. She couldn't afford anything new and anyway there was no point, not with two children who were forever leaving sticky fingerprints on everything and an aging mother who was starting to have small accidents on the kitchen chairs.

She sipped her tea, nice Earl Grey, and half listened while Edna chattered on about the house. Her friend certainly seemed to be living a fairy tale existence. Edna had it all - beautiful house, beautiful child, beautiful husband. I wonder if she knows who he's moved into the old house on the edge of town? she thought idly.

Francine O'Brien was approaching forty when Cara was born, and thought she was long past yearning for children. She had accepted that Len was a part-time, sometimes sort of thing, apt to disappear at any moment and was always surprised and grateful when he didn't. She had nothing at all against his pretty wife. She understood why he had married her. After all, who would want an old floozy like herself for anything but a good time?

Francine, born plain Frances, had come from a family of eight girls, their father wearing himself out in a fruitless attempt to coax a crop out of the poor rocky soil of his grandfather's farm, their mother worn down by her constant effort to can and preserve enough from the kitchen garden to see them through the winter. Although the O'Brien children attended the local one room school, they went to church at St. Gregory's, their father hitching the old plough horse to a hay wagon and driving them the ten miles to town every Sunday. Their Catholicism was never an issue with the children at school, or their parents either for that matter, other than a mild curiosity about something that seemed to them so foreign and mysterious. All of the other children were United Church, as was most of the island itself, and the O'Brien children did occasionally find themselves excluded in conversation, not part of the constant round of church suppers and Sunday School picnics that their schoolmates referred to so casually. Their poverty was no social handicap; most of the other families were in the same sort of circumstances, scraping away at the land or trying their hands at fishing in order to make ends meet.

What did set the O'Brien's apart was early puberty, accompanied by swift transformations from skinny, pigtailed girls into ripe, full-bosomed women, seemingly overnight.

Boys their own age seldom bothered them. They were too much in awe of such blatant womanhood, preferring instead to pester the little girls who still looked like little girls. It was the older boys and men who reacted in a peculiar manner.

Frances' older sister Mary had driven their schoolteacher to distraction. Only nineteen, Arthur Peterson had attended Teacher's College for the requisite year and hoped to earn enough from teaching to go to university, where he hoped to become a doctor. Marshall's Corners was his first school and he found the work both boring and exhausting. There was a paucity of teaching materials, the farmhouse where he boarded was cold and cheerless, and the children, although rather sweet, were none too bright, destined by and large to take over their fathers' farms or become labourers.

He had never taken any notice, much, of girls, mostly because he hadn't had time for it. When eleven year old Mary O'Brien suddenly developed a thirty-eight inch bustline, Arthur tried not to notice, but it was difficult when she asked for help with her arithmetic and bent over his desk, unaware that her large breasts were flapping in his face. He looked the other way in the schoolyard when the girls found an old skipping rope and Mary took her turn, her chest bouncing up and down in abandon. She developed hips, too; shapely round ones that wiggled when she walked.

He began to be haunted by Mary O'Brien. He dreamt about her lush figure at night and woke in the morning confused and embarrassed. It wasn't that he had an unnatural interest in little girls, it was just that Mary was no little girl, she was a woman in blossom.

Mary was blissfully unaware of the effect she was having on her teacher. She was puzzled but grateful when Mr. Peterson moved her seat closer to the stove. Those seats were normally reserved for the little ones. How could she know that this gave him a better view of her legs? Frances, who was by far the smartest of the O'Brien children, knew exactly why he had put her there, and when she too bloomed a few months later , was determined to take full advantage of it.

Frances, with her blonde hair, was also prettier than Mary and discovered that she could make Mr. Peterson blush just by brushing against him. She began asking for extra help after school, which he refused, then complained when she failed tests. After that, she always received a passing mark, no matter how poorly she had done.

She hated games, and was promptly excused from them when she said she wasn't feeling well, "girl problems, you know", and Arthur, in a rush of embarrassment, finally understood what she was talking about.

She was the first to remove her stockings and shoes in the spring, stretching her long bare legs out in front of the teacher's desk, where he would nearly trip over them on his way to the blackboard. She would ask, then, to be excused, and would spend a good fifteen minutes, not in the outhouse, but outside lounging in the sun.

When the next youngest sister, Grace, developed in the same explosive way the following year, it was too much for Arthur Peterson. He hastily requested a transfer and was replaced by a stern-faced spinster of forty-five.

But Frances had learned a little about power, and how to use it. She was determined not to end up like her mother, worn out from babies and kitchen work by the time she was thirty-five. When she turned sixteen, she changed her name to Francine and marched into Fletcher's Drugstore to ask for a job at the soda fountain.

"I can probably help attract some customers", she said to Gord Fletcher, leaning forward to give him a good view down the front of her V-necked dress.

Gord Fletcher agreed that she probably could and hired her on the spot. Armed for the first time with money of her own, she promptly left home and rented an apartment. Her parents scarcely noticed she was gone.

From then on, Francine did exactly as she pleased. What pleased her most was drinking, dancing and fast cars. That, and men who appreciated her figure and made their appreciation known in concrete ways. Francine was not for sale, she went only with men she genuinely liked, but she did expect her escorts to pay for dinner and keep her amused with small gifts. In return, she never enquired too closely into their personal lives and was always discreet.

After she took up with Len, her other gentlemen friends gradually faded away, not through any active discouragement on her part, but just because she seemed less interested in them, and would cancel dates at the drop of a hat if Len were available. She knew from the start that he was a dead end for her. He had ambitions, he was going places, she wasn't the sort of person he needed as a wife, so much older and a Catholic, because, yes, in certain circles that was still a disadvantage.

She did have a few little piques of jealousy, especially in the early days - he always seemed to have a million young girls after him - but by and large he was peculiarly faithful to her, in his own way. She managed to convince herself without too much difficulty that his marriage to Edna was purely strategic and that he really cared nothing for his young wife.

Cara was another matter. He was besotted with the child, taking her with him whenever he could. He even brought her to visit Francine one afternoon. She had been prepared to hate the child, this small rival, but when she saw the little girl who looked so much like Len, she had melted. She had once vowed that she would never be caught in the net that trapped most women, but now she began to regret the years she had thrown away and fantasized about a child, a little girl who looked just like Cara, but who would be hers. Hers and Len's.

When he and Edna moved into their new house, and he offered her the old one on the edge of town, she quickly accepted. It would tie her more firmly not only to Len, but to the little girl.

In time, she felt that the baby was almost hers, and was eager for any news of her. Len was happy to oblige, since it was one of his favourite topics. He reported her first tooth, her first word, the fact that she walked at ten months, her first day at kindergarten, and later, small triumphs at ballet recitals and school concerts.

Later when Cara and her father were at such odds, Francine would take the girl's side. "What are you so upset about", she would ask him when Cara was caught skipping classes. "She's no different than you were, still are, who do think she takes after?"

"That's different", he would grumble.

"Why is it different? Because she's a girl? You men are all the same, you love wild women as long as they aren't your wives or daughters. Leave her alone."

"Leave her alone", Edna would echo at home. Len tried, but it was hard when you knew how evil the world was.

Bernice Davis loved to bake and had a gift for pastry. Mrs. Len's new electric stove was a wonder, with its lovely even temperature at the turn of a knob. Not like the old iron cookstove she had cooked on at home, where you had to watch the pies like a hawk to make sure they didn't burn on the bottom.

"This whole house is a wonder", she would say to Rhonda. "Everything so clean and new to start with, why it's a breeze to keep it clean."

She and Rhonda had moved into the apartment in the coach house, where things were also new and clean. The ground floor consisted of a fair sized living room and a small kitchen, which Bernice barely used.

"Why should I cook double?" she would ask. "It's just as easy to make enough for four all at once," and four for Bernice was eight by anyone else's standards.

The second floor contained two small bedrooms and a bathroom, one bedroom and one bathroom more than Bernice had ever had before. At the back of the building was a large shed, unfinished, but useful for storage.

"You and I landed lucky", she said to Rhonda. "No drafty old house no more and easy work, and Mrs. Len don't interfere. You mind you behave yourself, and for heaven's sake, try to stop breaking things."

Rhonda would nod solemnly, but no matter how hard she tried, things came to pieces, as if her hands contained some sort of cosmic solvent that unglued the universe. Bernice would sigh, and throw herself into her cooking, producing pie after flaky pie, cake after mile-high cake, day after day, that they could never hope to eat up.

One day, Edna bundled Cara up, packed up three-quarters of an apple pie, two cream puffs and some chocolate chip cookies and walked to Vera's, pushing the baby carriage through the mounds of leaves that had fallen on the sidewalks and clogged the gutters.

"Bernice has done it again," she said when Vera answered the door . "That woman bakes enough for an army. Please take this or I'm just going to have to throw it out."

Vera was dubious. "Surely you can eat it up tomorrow." she said.

"No, we can't, that's the problem. She'll bake another three or four pies by then. I'm going to end up weighing three hundred pounds if I try and eat everything she makes."

Vera unpacked the food and put it away. Mac would eat almost anything she served up in the way of a main course, but he did enjoy his dessert and Bernice certainly had a way with a pie. Her own pastry was grey and hard, and having a dessert already on hand meant that she could take the time to sit and have a cup of tea with Edna.

Four year old Susan was fascinated by the baby. The little girl brewed an imaginary pot of tea and poured it out, holding a tiny plastic teacup to Cara's lips while the baby cooed and tried to grab it. Stevie roared from room to room, alternately ignoring the girls and pestering them.

"You bad," Susan said. "Go 'way. Mummy make Stevie go 'way."

Vera tried to shush him out of the room, but he danced around her and ripped the teacup from Susan's fat fist.

"You're not doing it right", he shouted. Stevie never just spoke, he shouted. "Here's how you do it."

Susan wailed and snatched at the cup. It went flying out of Stevie's fist and hit Cara squarely on the nose. Vera jumped up, spilling her tea. Edna grabbed up the screaming baby. Susan screeched. Vera whacked Stevie across the bottom and he too started to shriek, the noise building into a deafening roar.

Finally, Vera sent Stevie to his room and gave Susan a chocolate chip cookie, which she ate sitting under the kitchen table, chewing between big, gulping sobs.

A red mark the shape of a small tea cup handle had formed on Cara's nose.

"Oh dear," Edna said. She had no idea if the injury was serious. "Should I do anything with this?"

Vera looked. "She's going to have a mark there for a few days, but I wouldn't worry about it. It'll go away."

Edna wondered how Vera could be so casual, but reflected that poor Susan had probably been taking knocks as big or bigger for most of her short life, and so far she seemed to have survived.

Vera cleaned up the spilled tea and poured more, and they tried to make conversation between interruptions from Susan, who wanted another cookie, Stevie, who demanded to know when he could come downstairs, and Cara, who needed to be changed. Finally, they gave up and Edna went home.

Len was incensed when he saw the mark on Cara's nose.

"Why weren't you watching her?" he demanded.

"I was sitting right there", Edna said. 'It all happened so fast."

"What were you doing over there anyway? If you drag her all over town, you know, she's going to get hurt or catch some horrible disease or something."

"You drag her all over town."

"That's different. I never take her to play with other children."

She was exasperated. "Len, I am not going to sit in this house all day with nothing to do. Besides Vera's my oldest friend."

"I don't know why you even bother with her", he grumbled. "You know lots of women who are a hell of a lot more interesting than Vera Dunlop."

"But I don't like them nearly as well", she pointed out. And she didn't. They were acquaintances, not friends. People they played golf with, or who they met at the cocktail parties they attended. Edna always felt she was in competition with these women; who had the most successful husband, who had the most expensive clothes, whose house was the nicest? There weren't any of them she could sit down with and have a cosy cup of tea like she could with Vera. And all the drinking and flirting got on her nerves.

She flirted too, it was part of her duties as a wife to make Len's friends feel comfortable. But there was never anything to it. She wasn't sure it was quite so innocent when it came to Len and the other women, but she preferred not to know any of the details.

"I just don't understand what the attraction is," he said. "She's such a pudding."

That was true, she had let herself go, Edna thought, but so what? It wasn't as though they ever saw the Dunlops on a formal basis. Mac would have been like a fish out of water at a dinner or a party, but she and Vera seldom needed evening dress to drink tea in the kitchen. "Pudding or not, she's been my friend for a long time, you know," she replied.

"I just can't figure out what you find to talk to her about," he said. "The price of coal? Recipes for hamburger casserole?"

"You've got a lot of nerve, you know, it's not like you were born with a silver spoon in your mouth. Don't be such a snob."

"What do you mean by that?"

She was a little alarmed at the look on his face. "We all come from pretty run of the mill circumstances," she said quickly. "Unless you've renounced some foreign title you haven't told me about."

He softened then. "Didn't I ever tell you I was once Lord Collins of Cressy? I gave it all up for you, you know."

"I know. And you've never regretted it either, have you?"

It was all right between them then, but his attitude continued to puzzle her. Well, I don't care what he says, Edna thought, I'll visit Vera whenever I damn well please. Besides, it was good for Cara to be around other children.

And Bernice, who was no fool, always made sure there was too much of something on hand so Mrs. Len could take it with her.

CHAPTER TWELVE

Cara kept getting sidetracked by old memories. School yearbooks proved to be a major distraction. She would leaf through them, laughing at the hairstyles and fashions and wonder what had become of her classmates. Some of them had married each other, she knew, and many of them still lived on the island, but as to any of the other details, she had long since lost track. She found hundreds of photographs, some of them carefully pasted in albums, but most of them squirreled away in drawers and closets. She spent hours sitting cross-legged on the floor looking at them while the cardboard box beside her remained empty.

The early snapshots she found distinctly embarrassing and she fully intended to burn them before they fell into the wrong hands. Stark naked in front of the marble fireplace in the living room, Bernice bathing her in the kitchen sink, (her parents must have been away, she decided, her father would never have allowed that if he'd been there), at the beach, at the shore, on a boat. There were many pictures of herself with Susan and Steve Dunlop, at different ages. In most of them, Steve was a blur. He never stood still long enough for the camera to catch him. Susan always hovered, never far away from Cara, not looking at the camera. She set these group shots aside to take to Vera.

In most of the family pictures her father held her, laughing. Her mother had nearly always been the photographer. She had had an old box camera, a Brownie, and Cara remembered having to squint into the sun while her mother peered in through the little window on top to make sure they were centred in the frame. She could recall in detail many of the occasions which had been recorded. There were a number showing the south shore, where they often went for picnics or to go fishing. Her favourite was one taken when she must have been around four, still small enough to be hoisted up and carried on her father's shoulders.

"Sit still, honey". She had drummed her feet against his chest while they waited for the shot, her hands clutched in his hair.

"Turn around just a little will you?" Her mother was fiddling with something on the camera.

"Why?"

"I want to get those rocks in the picture."

Her father turned left. Cara hooted in derision.

"Silly Daddy, not that way!"

"Which way then?" He looked up at her and his face was all upside down, his eyes becoming a mouth and his nose tilted the wrong way like a pig's.

"The other way."

"Right or left?"

"Hmmmm..."That way," she pointed. Cara knew her numbers and letters, but was still confused over left and right. She liked to do everything with her left hand, whereas, for some reason the rest of the world seemed to prefer the right.

"Okay, I got it", Edna said. "You can put her down now."

Len tilted her forward suddenly, catching her by the back of the head just before she hit the ground. It was an old game and she shrieked with laughter.

"Want to go looking for sunken treasure?" he had asked.

"Yes." Hand in hand they walked along the shore, picking their way carefully through the loose, rounded stones. Cara looked back to wave at her mother, but Edna had settled herself on a blanket to read, and wasn't watching. Her mother was always reading, it seemed, and she could hardly wait until she knew how, so she could find out what held her mother's interest so.

"Careful, Cara Mia." They were at the slippery part now, the part where the loose shingle changed abruptly to flat limestone slab, slick with seaweed. Above them rose the cliffs, eroded constantly by water and wave, exposing the layers of rock in which tenacious wildflowers and scraggly bushes had somehow clung long enough to put down roots and grow.

"Oh, look, there's a boat."

Cara squinted as hard as she could, but couldn't see anything. Len squatted beside her and she followed his outstretched arm, past the pointed finger, until she located the tiny black dot on the horizon.

"Have you got it?"

She nodded. "Okay, here, take the binoculars and tell me what it is."

She looked through the glasses and adjusted them expertly. It took her a moment to locate the boat again, but when she did it magically resolved itself into a black hull with red markings, with two men aboard.

"It's a fishing boat", she said. "Can we go fishing with them, Daddy?"

"Nope. Not until you can swim, at least a little bit." The answer was always the same, she thought. You can't do this until you can do that. You must learn to do one thing before you can do another. There were so many conditions for everything.

"As soon as you can swim", her father went on, "we can go fishing on a boat and I'll take you sailing, all the way out to Main Duck Island."

Main Duck, which lay halfway across Lake Ontario, loomed large in her imagination. Her father had regaled her with tales of the storms and shipwrecks which seemed to frequent this part of the lake. She knew that Main Duck was a haven for anyone caught out on the water in a sudden storm, but only if the wind wasn't blowing from the east. Then the unlucky sailor would probably make a run for the lee of Timber Island, close to her own, larger island, or put in at the tiny fishing harbour on the southeast point. She knew that, long ago, some French sailors had been wrecked on Main Duck and perished one by one at Graveyard Point. She also knew that one must never, never mistake the treacherous False Ducks for Main Duck Island, for there was no anchorage there, only thousands and thousands of birds.

"Can I be a sailor when I grow up, Daddy?" she wanted to know.

"Of course", he said. "I'll be the captain and you can be the crew and together we'll sail the seven seas."

Along the shore they climbed, over the jumbled rock, picking out the speckled bits of pink granite that were occasionally thrown up on shore. As they went along they threw driftwood into piles to pick up on the way back for their campfire. Cara found a bird's feather, black and sleek, not a seagull's and stroked it against the grain, ruffling it, then smoothing it back again. They walked until they reached the point where they would have to go into the water to get past a jutting cliff, and there they turned back.

She could see that her mother was still reading, but she looked up and waved at them as they walked along the beach. Cara ran on ahead, slipping and sliding on the stones, the feather held aloft, her other hand clutching a piece of driftwood. Suddenly, the stones under her feet shifted sideways and she went down hard. Edna leapt from the blanket and she and Len reached her at the same moment.

Cara seldom cried. She had never really been allowed to cry very much when she was a baby, and had never acquired the habit of using tears to get attention. It was generally unnecessary anyway; all of her needs were usually anticipated.

She had scraped her knee, not badly, but it stung. Edna went back to the blanket and got a towel, which Len took from her and dipped into the lake to clean off the scrape.

"You okay, sweetheart?" her father asked.

"Yup." She snivelled, just a little bit, so that he would know she was being brave.

He noticed. "God, you're a tough little monkey aren't you? We'll just get this cleaned up and then we'll start the fire so we can cook some hotdogs, okay?"

She nodded. "And some marshmallows?"

"And some marshmallows. But you'll have to go find us some wienie sticks."

She rummaged through the scrubby trees until she found the branches she was looking for. Wienie sticks had to be taken from a living tree, still green, so they wouldn't catch fire. She found three that were forked at the end and took them back to her father. "Doubles! I found three doubles, so we can cook two at a time," she said, waving the sticks in the air.

" Good girl. Now what do you say about a swim?"

They waded into the lake. The first part was tricky because the rocks were covered in seaweed and slippery, so Len hoisted her to his shoulders and carried her until he was waist deep in the water.

"Throw me, Daddy!" She drummed a tattoo on his chest with her feet.

"Okay, ready?" She stood on his hands, balancing herself with one hand on his head.

"One, two three....jump!" She was thrown backwards, flying in an arc until, after a flight that seemed to last forever, she tumbled into the water. Down, down she went, propelled by the force of the throw, until her feet touched the stony bottom. It was a green world down here, murky and dark and full of shadow, the light dim and unrevealing. She pushed her feet as hard as she could against the bottom and shot back up to the surface again, to be caught by her father just as she ran out of air.

"Again, Daddy, again!" Three, four, five times he threw her, until she was out of breath and waterlogged. Her mother watched from the shore. She would come in later, when the roughhousing was done and hold Cara by the middle while she practiced real swimming.

"The fire's ready. Come and get some dogs."

They huddled around the coals, dripping and watched the hot dogs sizzle and split in the fire.

"As soon as I can swim Daddy and I are going to sail the seven seas", Cara announced to her mother. "He's the captain and I'm the crew. Would you like to come with us?"

"Oh, I don't think so", her mother said. "I think it would be more fun to wait at home in case you sent me a message in a bottle."

"In a bottle?". She was intrigued. "How do I do that?"

"Back in the old days, that's how people sent messages," Edna explained. "Especially sailors. They would write a note, put it in an empty bottle, put the cork in and throw it overboard. When it floated ashore, whoever found it would mail it to the person it was addressed to."

"Is that true, Daddy?" Cara never accepted anything her mother said without verifying it with her father.

"Yep, that's true, and I'll tell you a story about a message in a bottle."

"Yes! A story." She hunkered back on her heels in anticipation. No picnic was complete without a story.

"Way back in 1901, there were three ships over at Charlotte. There was the Acacia, the Annie Minnes, and the Schooner Picton."

"Charlotte Harbour across the lake, right?" Cara always liked to have the details of a story firmly in her grasp.

"That is quite right. Right across the lake from us. Now, there had been a bad storm the night before, but the weather that morning was pretty good, and Jack Sidley , who was captain of The Picton was anxious to get going. You see, he had his twelve year old son Vesey, with him."

"Vesey, like Cape Vesey?"

"Yes, he was named after Cape Vesey, up the shore aways. They were short-handed, you see, because one of the regular crew stayed home."

"Why?" Cara wanted to know.

"Um... because he was sick. So Captain Sidley wanted to get his son home, because he was missing out on a lot of school. Now the Picton was a lot faster than the other boats, but still the Acacia was only about ten minutes behind her, and the Annie Minnes about half an hour behind that. The boats were halfway across the lake, out near Main Duck Island......

She knew it. Main Duck Island had to be involved somehow.

"... when the crew aboard the other two ships noticed the Picton's topsails coming off, and then her lower sails settling down.

"The sails came off? How?"

"That's boat talk for taking them down."

"Oh." Cara could tell from her father's tone that something strange was going to happen now and she rocked back and forth on her heels, waiting for it.

"And then", Len went on, "while they watched, the Schooner Picton disappeared. It was just like a big hole in the lake had opened up and swallowed her."

"And then what happened", Cara gasped.

"And then the Captain of the Acacia called out to lower the sails and they'd go and see what happened, and the Captain of the Annie Minnes did the same. But when they got to where the Picton should have been, they couldn't find anything. No wreckage, no nothing. She'd just completely vanished into thin air."

"Oh no!" Cara could hardly breathe, her face scrunched up with worry.

"They searched far and wide," her father went on, " but they couldn't find a trace of the Picton. But the strangest thing about this story is still to come. About three weeks later, a little fisherman's boy over at Sackett's Harbour saw a bottle bobbing out in the water."

"What was his name?"

"Tommy. Tommy didn't think anything about the bottle at first, but it was still there the next day, and the next and the next. Finally, his father said, 'Why don't you row out and get it and we'll see what it is?' So Tommy did, and what he found was a glass bottle with a note in it. The note was written in pencil, and it said 'Have lashed Vesey to me with heaving line so we will be found together' and it was signed 'Captain J. Sidley, The Schooner Picton. "

"But how did he have time?" Cara couldn't write anything but her own name. She couldn't have written a whole long note at the best of times, never mind when the boat was going down beneath her feet.

"That's the mystery," her father said. "That's what makes the story so strange."

Cara shuddered then, and tried to imagine what it was like to be in a sinking ship. What would it be like to drown? Would it be the same as when her father threw her off his shoulders, sinking down to the green, murky bottom, only you never came back up again? Would you know you were drowning, or would you be convinced that eventually your feet would find bottom and you could shoot back up to the surface again where strong arms would be waiting to catch you?

She had puzzled over the story of The Picton for years, and had even gone to the library when she was twelve to see if there was any record of the schooner. By that time, Len was no longer her oracle, and she questioned everything everybody said. To her surprise, it was a well-documented story and The Picton's disappearance had occurred more or less exactly the way her father had told her.

She sifted through the pictures again. There were so few of her mother, so little record. She had always been on the edge of things, at least as far as Cara was concerned. Her preference was to spend all of her time with her father anyway, but when he insisted that she stay home, she always had Bernice and Rhonda to pester in the kitchen. They helped her make towering sculptures of papier mache, shaping the sodden newspaper into fantastic images of castles and volcanoes. Sometimes they let her make cookies, too. When Bernice and Rhonda were busy, she would watch endless reruns of Howdy Doody and The Friendly Giant, doodling on a piece of paper while she kept one eye on the flickering screen. Soon the doodles took shape, and she was drawing Howdy and Rusty, making up her own stories to go with the pictures.

Her mother realized how much Cara was by herself, but was at a loss. As a little girl, Edna had always had Vera in constant tow and she wasn't sure how to cope with her daughter's utter self-possession. She enrolled her in ballet class and arranged for piano lessons, hoping that a schedule of activities might connect her with some kindred spirit. Cara found ballet a torment. She still confused left and right, and in spite of the physical grace she had inherited from Len, she often found herself at the receiving end of the dance teacher's exasperation.

"Cara, no! Turn left, dear. Can't you see what the other little girls are doing?" The other children would giggle, then, and make fun of her. She stuck it out for one season, making it all the way through to the recital so she could wear a pink tutu, then refused to go back.

Piano lessons were a little more successful. At least it was a solitary pursuit and she was not obliged to fall into any conformity other than that dictated by the music itself. She liked marches. She could crash and bang as much as she wanted, something the piano teacher discouraged when it came to minuets and waltzes. She became quite competent at reading music, but it quickly became evident that for her, music would be a social grace and not a vocation. Hetty Charles expected no Mozart, content that Cara could magically translate the confusing black notes into old and familiar hymns. Hetty would sit in Edna's living room with the little girl while she pounded through "The Happy Farmer", then turn to a page in the Hymn Book.

"Play this, Cara", she would say. "I always liked this one." And Cara would struggle through "Soldiers of Christ" or "Bringing in the Sheaves".

Edna tried not to be uneasy about the amount of time Hetty spent with her grandchild. She knew Len wouldn't approve, but she knew that her mother was lonely. Her brother Bill had moved out six months or so after their father's heart attack.

"I can't stand it anymore", he said to Edna. "It's like living with a ghost with Dad sitting in the parlour all day. And all mother does is fuss."

"Do you want me to speak to Len?" she had asked. "I'm sure there's room for you at the store."

"Nah. Thanks, but I think I'll just get out of this place and see where I fetch up."

As time went on, Bert occupied less and less of Hetty's attention. He demanded nothing and expected nothing and slowly faded away until one day he just wasn't there any more. Hetty discovered him in his chair by the radio, quite dead and was afterwards tormented by the fact that he could well have been dead for hours before she had realized he was gone.

After the funeral she began dropping broad hints."My, my" she said, "It must cost you an awful lot to have that Bernice Davis doing all your housework. I know you can't manage it all yourself, Edna, it's such a big house, but my goodness, the expense."

And another time, "That coach house turned out to be such a cosy little place. And all brand new services. Maybe I'll look around for a place like that now that I don't need so much room."

Edna knew what she was angling for and ignored the comments, but she did let her spend more time with her granddaughter. They would walk in the park or read Bible stories in Hetty's uncomfortable kitchen, Cara nibbling politely at the rock hard ginger cookies her grandmother invariably produced.

"Maybe she'd like a pet", Len speculated one night after dinner. "We should get her a puppy."

Edna shuddered at the thought of a puppy peeing on carpets and chewing on the antique furniture. "What about a kitten?" she said. "They're a lot easier than puppies."

"The only thing wrong with kittens is that they grow up to be cats", he said as Rhonda cleared away the dinner plates. "Besides, we already have a cat and when was the last time it was company for anybody but itself?"

Secretly that was something Edna quite liked about cats, but Len wanted a golden retriever or a black lab, something that was big enough to be a watchdog, he said, but could perhaps double as a hunting dog.

"I thought it was supposed to be Cara's dog", she pointed out. "It can't very well be company for her and go hunting with you too."

"Well, I don't know, something like that anyway. I'll keep my eyes open for something nice."

Rhonda beat him to it. Rhonda was as clumsy and well-meaning as ever, a large sixteen year old who had somehow fallen into the role of housekeeper's assistant without any of them quite noticing how. Len paid her a small amount to act as bartender or waiter when they had large parties, although he grumbled that she spilled more than she served. The rest of the time she quite cheerfully helped Bernice. She was constantly reminded by her mother that they had "landed lucky" and she agreed; she adored the entire Collins family, Cara most of all.

"Why, I'd cut off my right hand for any one of 'em", she said to her mother one day.

Bernice was all too afraid that one day Rhonda might do just that, inadvertently, and forbade her the use of the carving knife.

The puppy arrived with her one Sunday evening, after she had spent the afternoon visiting some cousins who lived in the country. It was a tiny scrap of whimpering fur with the oddest coat Edna had ever seen on a dog. Thin, sparse and hair-like, its fur barely covered its body, except at the ears, where it grew in a glorious profusion of ginger coloured tufts that stood straight up. Its tail had been docked, but the outrageous ears had been left uncropped.

"It's the runt of the litter", Rhonda explained. "Uncle Quentin's Doberman got out and got mixed up with something, we're not sure what. She had a litter of ten and Uncle Norm says he'll put this one down if he can't find a home for him."

The puppy squealed, then staggered across the linoleum and peed in the corner.

"What does 'put down' mean Mummy?" Cara asked.

"It means put it to sleep."

"Like I go to sleep at night?"

"No, asleep forever."

Cara frowned. The puppy whined. "You can't kill it." she said decisively.

"You can't. Rhonda brought him for me!"

"I know, sweetheart, but I don't think it's what your father had in mind when he talked about getting a dog. I think he wanted a purebred, you know, one that has papers."

But the puppy had found Cara and was sitting in her lap, licking her face.

"I want this dog. You can't kill it." She was adamant.

Edna sighed. She knew Len wouldn't like it, but Cara was holding the puppy in a protective embrace, ready to do battle to save its life, even if it meant defying her father. Len doesn't stand a chance, she thought as she looked at the determined set of her daughter's chin. "All right," she said, " but I'm afraid our names will be mud."

Cara misunderstood the remark. She thought the puppy had come already named.

"That's a disgusting dog", Len snorted when he saw it. "What on earth did that Doberman get tangled up with - a chihuahua? It's got no fur."

"No, Daddy, he's beautiful", Cara corrected, "and he's a him not an it. Mummy says his name is Mud."

Cara loved Mud and soon, Mud loved Cara and that was that, much as Len grumbled.

As the runt of the litter, Mud had existed in a state of semi-starvation, constantly nudged aside by his more robust littermates. He was far too small for a three month old puppy, and Edna hoped he would stay that way, but regular feedings, along with extra tidbits Bernice, Rhonda and Cara slipped him on the sly soon had their effect. In the first month he put on fifteen pounds. His legs grew long and he began to knock Cara over when he jumped up to lick her ears. By the time he was six months old, he stood three feet high. His fur remained hair-like and thin, and they had to be careful to dry him off when he went out in the rain, because his coat seemed to have no natural waterproofing. He would shake with cold and pant with heat. He developed enormous, ginger-coloured eyebrows to match the tufts at his ears, the markings contrasting strangely with the dark brown on the rest of his body.

He had a maniacal devotion to chewing pens and pencils, spewing splinters and ink throughout the house whenever he could. His favourites were red ballpoints. Len tried to confine him to the kitchen at night in order to minimize the damage, but he would howl and moan until one of them got up and put him in Cara's room, where he settled ecstatically on the foot of her bed until the early hours of the morning, when he would somehow open her door and tiptoe downstairs on a quest for writing utensils.

"How does he get out?" Len would ask. But nobody could answer.

As the dog grew older, his Doberman parentage became more obvious, but he remained an odd-looking and odder-acting dog. He would often stand and peer through his tufty eyebrows from slightly crazed golden eyes, the only clue to his state of mind the wagging stump of tail. He was afraid of everything; of thunder, of the washing machine; of umbrellas; and of cats. When Bernice turned on the vacuum cleaner, Mud had to be banished to the back porch. He was so afraid of the noise he would howl.

The only thing he was not afraid of was the mailman. Cara felt it was really the mailman's own fault. Mud had been in the front yard with her one afternoon when the man came along the street, whistling while he stuffed letters and circulars through mail slots and between doors. Mud stood stock still, carefully watching the approach of this unfamiliar and threatening creature. He peered intently, trying to gauge the degree of danger.

The mailman stopped at the front gate. Like all mailmen, he had a healthy respect for dogs, and this one was big. It had crazy eyes. It was peering at him strangely. He briefly considered handing the Collins' mail to the little girl in the front yard, but decided she was too small to be trusted with it. If she got playing and left it under a bush or something there would be hell to pay. After all, Mr. Collins was an important man. He had important mail. The mailman also knew from experience that many dogs were nothing but bluff, and that if you stood your ground, they would capitulate. Slowly, he put his hand on the gate.

Mud growled. His parentage may have been mixed, but his growl was pure Doberman, low and menacing and originating from somewhere deep within his belly. The mailman felt the hairs on the back of his neck rising. Mud growled again, peering fixedly at the blue menace at his gate.

Had the mailman continued through the gate, said hello to the dog and to Cara and continued up the front steps, Mud would have disappeared around the corner of the house, to hide under the hedge until he was gone. But the man couldn't quite bring himself to open the latch and walk in. This dog was too big, with too many teeth and an obviously uncertain temperament, and every time he moved, there was that heart-stopping growl. Finally, he threw the mail in Cara's general direction, asked her to take it into the house, and with as much dignity as possible, continued down the street.

Mud barked wildly at his back, delighted that there was finally something he had managed to chase away.

After that, no one in uniform was safe.

The man who came to read the hydro metre was unnerved when a low snarl issued from behind the garbage can in the Collins back porch; when the furnace man came to service the furnace, Mud somehow slipped past the basement door and stood, halfway down the stairs, holding the man hostage, barking every time he moved.

But Mud saved his special vengeance for the hapless mailman. He would hide under the bushes by the gate, waiting, for he knew that sooner or later, the hated uniform would make its appearance. Mud had a nice sense of timing, and would wait until the mailman's hand was reaching for the gatelatch before issuing his best and most menacing growl. No matter how often this happened, the mailman would still jump, setting Mud off into a paroxysm of barking.

The mailman complained.

His supervisor called Len and explained the problem.

"Oh for crying out loud, you've got to be kidding", Len said. "That dog is afraid of its own shadow. Just tell the man to yell at it and it'll go and hide somewhere."

The supervisor told the mailman to stop being hysterical.

He tried varying his route, so he would arrive at the Collins' at a different time each day.

But Mud always knew when he was near. Somewhere in the dim recesses of his brain, he could sense when the enemy approached and would whine and scratch at the door until someone let him out. He would take up his station in the bushes, poised and watchful, waiting until the most disconcerting moment possible to begin his menacing rumble.

The mailman appealed again to his supervisor. Reluctantly, the supervisor called Len again.

"Your dog is a menace", he said. "My man is going to have a heart attack or something if you don't do something about your dog."

Len decreed that the dog wasn't to be let out during the hours when the mailman might be coming down their street, but Mud always found a way. None of them knew how.

"He's the size of an elephant, how does he get out all the time?" Len asked, exasperated. No one could say.

Finally, he installed a mailbox at the gate, so the man wouldn't have to come into the yard. The supervisor at the post office was dubious.

"We can't leave mail right out by the street", he said. "What if someone took it?"

"As it stands right now, I'm not getting my mail anyway", Len pointed out. "Your man is always leaving it with the neighbours or not delivering it at all. At least this way, I stand an even chance of catching up with my correspondence."

And so Mud's great delight in life, next to red ballpoint pens, continued. The mailman was relieved that he wasn't expected to go into the yard anymore, and although he never got used to hearing the bushes growl, at least he could do his job.

And Mud acquired a second name; according to Len he was "that damned dog".

CHAPTER THIRTEEN

Edna generally spent a good deal of the morning lying in bed with a pot of tea and a book. Len rose at first light and was gone by seven-thirty or eight, touselling her hair and kissing her goodbye before he left, but he seldom insisted that she achieve any great degree of consciousness for this. Bernice was happy to get Cara ready for school, and since the high school and public school were within a block of each other, Rhonda was happy to walk her there. Bernice would watch them down the street, and when she was satisfied that they had reached the corner without mishap she would pour Mrs. Len's tea and take it to her. Edna would happily browse through a magazine or catalogue for an hour or so before she took a leisurely bath. Then she would carefully dress for the day, apply a dash of makeup, consult with Bernice regarding dinner menus and housekeeping details, and go for a walk.

Sometimes she would go to Vera's, but not more than a couple of times a week. She didn't want to bother her too much. Vera still had her hands full with her family, although her load had been lifted somewhat when her mother, like her father, had suffered a stroke. Unlike her father, Vera's mother had, mercifully, succumbed to the initial assault.

"I sometimes worry if it runs in the family, you know," she confided to Edna one day. "If it does, I hope I go like she did. I couldn't stand wasting away like Dad. Months in bed with somebody having to do every little thing for me."

Edna assured her that as far as she knew, strokes weren't hereditary, and anyway it would be years before she had to worry about it.

On many days, they would sit contentedly in the kitchen sipping tea while they giggled over the latest fashions and gossiped about old schoolmates. Sometimes it was almost like it had been back when they were girls playing in the woods, so in tune that they would finish each other's sentences. At other times, the conversation veered dangerously towards subjects that neither wanted to fully discuss.

Mac still worked for the County, filling potholes in the summer and ploughing snow in the winter. Wages were better, much better, than they had been when he started, and there were only the four of them now so Vera could indulge in the occasional luxury for herself, but on many weeks Mac's paycheque was stretched and pulled in unexpected and unforeseen ways. A prescription, a muffler or even an unseasonable cold snap was enough to poke a hole in her carefully calculated budget.

Edna tried to avoid any mention of money during their conversations. She didn't want to look like she was rubbing it in.

Vera was also cool whenever Len was mentioned, so Edna didn't talk much about him, either. It certainly limited their choice of topics, since Len and the money he was apparently making were the talk of the island. Len's prediction had been correct; many of the families who lived in tumbledown rental properties had scraped together downpayments and somehow managed to qualify for mortgages. All of the cookie-cutter houses had sold. It was better than they had before, Edna supposed, with new wiring and plumbing that worked and roofs that kept the rain out, but she found the development depressing. All the houses looked alike, and heavy spring rains had washed down the hillside creating ugly gullies and small landslides. Here and there proud homeowners had planted trees in the still tentative-looking lawns, but they would be saplings for many years to come. She was sure the houses were unbearably hot in the summertime.

When Vera was busy, or her own inclination was for solitude, Edna's walks took her to the outskirts of town, where the sidewalks ended and she could stroll down a farmer's laneway into the woods. These were real woods, not like the woods behind her father's store. Here, only the occasional ray of sunshine penetrated through the overhanging maples and birch, casting a pall of shadow that shimmered and shifted as she passed.

She seldom told anyone where she went. She had, at one time, and had been surprised, then amused by Bernice's reaction.

"You don't want to go walking in them woods, Mrs. Len. You never know what's in there waiting to prey on defenceless women."

She had a far better idea now what was meant by "preying" than when she had received this same warning from her mother. She doubted that anything was waiting to prey on her, but to allay Bernice's fears, she started taking Mud with her. She was fairly certain that if anyone needed protection, it was Mud, but the mere sight of a Doberman was probably enough to make even the most fearless attacker think twice.

She enjoyed her walks; she could let both her feet and her mind wander down whatever path they chose. Sudden images and cunning metaphors would occur to her, and she sometimes wondered if she should try writing again, but when she tried to set these thoughts down on paper, nothing coherent ever emerged. She did try her hand at poetry, but her efforts seemed sophomoric and trite; only one of her poems came close to being acceptable from a literary standpoint, she felt, and this she printed out carefully and stuck away in the drawer of her dressing table. The rest she ripped into tiny pieces and threw in the garbage. She was afraid Len would laugh at her if he found them.

She really had very little to do, other than to play helpmeet, the gracious appendage who smoothed the way at dinners and parties. She was not unintelligent; she could easily have understood the mechanics of Len's enterprises had he ever chosen to share the information with her, but he kept her excluded from this part of his life.

She had asked, once.

"Oh, it's not important," he had said. "And actually it's sort of hard to describe, because it changes all the time. Don't worry about it. I'll always make sure we have enough money. " And he had distracted her by burying his face in her hair and nibbling on her ear.

But there had been a tone to his answer that had alarmed her. She hoped that whatever he was doing was legal, but in the end she had to trust to the fact that he always seemed to know what he was doing and that it always turned out all right. This realization saddened her; when they were first married, she had felt like a partner in a new and wonderful adventure. Now she was merely witness to Len's triumphs, social grease for his financial stratagems.

It was Hannah Fletcher who first invited Edna to join a bridge club.

"It's so much fun", she gushed. Hannah nearly always gushed. It was a habit she had developed after her unexpected marriage to Rick Fletcher. "We take turns playing at each other's houses, and we have a lunch afterwards. We need somebody to fill in on Thursday, Marion Abberhart's away."

"But I don't know how to play," Edna pointed out. Cards had been banned in her mother's Baptist household and she had never had the opportunity to pick it up anywhere else.

"Oh, I'll teach you, it's easy. Besides, nobody takes it very seriously."

Len hooted when she told him of Hannah's offer. "Good God, why on earth would you want to spend your afternoons with all those gossiping biddies," he said. "Haven't you got anything better to do?"

The problem was she didn't.

Hannah had been as good as her word, showing up at Edna's house the next afternoon to explain the mysteries of bidding and making a contract. They sat at the table in the kitchen, Cara hovering nearby. It was less mysterious than Edna had feared and she quickly mastered the concept of trumps and how to keep a running count of how many had been played in the course of a hand. She found she liked the game, the way one could turn a poor deal into an advantage by clever bidding, and the patterns each hand sorted itself into. Cara picked it up nearly as quickly as she did, and they practiced together, playing double dummy on the kitchen table nearly every afternoon after school. She also borrowed a copy of "Goren On Bridge" from the library.

By Thursday, she was ready. She acquitted herself well, her scores by the end of the afternoon sitting respectably in the middle tallies of the two tables in play.

She found the afternoon more entertaining than she expected. The other women, concentrating on their cards, were less apt to gossip and silence was seen as a dedication to the game rather than a social shortcoming. In less than a month, she was invited to become a regular member of the club, Marion Abberhart's absence made permanent by her divorce and subsequent move to the city.

From then on, she played bridge whenever she was invited, spending afternoon after afternoon slapping cards down on the table.

She was on her way home from a marathon bridge game when she first noticed him in front of the old candy store. A tiny building on Catherine Street, whose front door was dwarfed by two enormous plate glass windows, it had been abandoned since the Harris family had closed the business after the war.

She had never seen the man before. He was supervising the installation of a small sign over the door. It read "St. Petersburg Gallery" in a flowing and vaguely foreign-looking script.

St. Petersburg? St. Petersburg, Florida? she thought. But no, the strange lettering indicated something far more exotic. St. Petersburg in Russia. Called something else now, she knew, but the old name had stuck with her from the handful of Russian novels she had once attempted to read. Why would someone call a gallery in Eastern Ontario "St. Petersburg"? she wondered. Most people wouldn't even know where St. Petersburg was. Or Russia either, for that matter. What sort of gallery could it be?

She drove around the block so she could get a better look. The man was foreign looking too; very fair hair, long, or at least longer than most men wore it. Small, almost delicate looking. She couldn't get close enough to see much more.

She didn't dare risk another circuit around the block, he might notice and besides, she had to go home and get ready for the evening ahead. It was the annual Business Association dinner-dance and she and Len tried to attend when they could. Although little of Len's business was done locally any more, there was still Charles Furniture, and the event would have been judged incomplete without their presence.

She was late and so was Len, as usual, and she forgot about the gallery in the rush to bathe, dress and coif for the evening. Len had been held up with a last minute long distance phone call, Rhonda blubberingly confessed that she had scorched the lace on one of Edna's nightgowns in an attempt to help her mother with the ironing, Cara was feverish and sick-looking from an incipient cold and Mud had chewed Len's toothbrush. They were always late. "Making an entrance" Len called it, but Edna's mother would have called it lack of organization.

They swept in to the dance and heads turned. Edna had piled her hair in an elaborate swirl on top of her head, and she wore a creamy white, skintight sheath that stretched from one wrist, swooped daringly across her bosom and ended, leaving the other arm bare. She had found the dress in Montreal the previous month, on one of the occasions when she had gone away for the weekend with Len. She had hesitated, just for a moment, when she looked at the price tag, but she knew it was unlike anything she could find closer to home, and was sure to cause a sensation. Most of the other women dressed in some version of basic black with pearls, "always safe, always appropriate" according to the women's magazines they all read.

Len immediately left her side. It was their party routine. He circulated around the room, greeting everyone by name, flirting with the women, joking. Edna moved in the opposite direction, smiling, nodding, gracious. They covered a lot of ground that way, and no one left a party feeling that they had been ignored by the Collins.

And then she saw him. He was standing with Helen Rensell, his back turned to her. She glided over to the group around him. Helen turned.

"Oh, Edna, there's someone here you simply must meet. He's an artist, dear, and clever old Isabel found him in Vancouver when she and Fred were on vacation. She persuaded him to come back with her and open a gallery right here in town!"

"Really?" Edna murmured. "How exciting."

He turned, bowed and kissed her hand. What an outrageous thing to do, she thought. But then, he is an artist. Allowances must be made.

He straightened and smiled at her and Edna fell into the largest, brownest pool of eyes she had ever seen.

Marion tittered. "Sacha Karensky, this is Edna Collins. Edna's husband is a prominent businessman here in town."

"How do you do." He had just a hint of an accent, a slight formality to his speech, that indicated that his English was a second language, learned well and probably at an early age, but learned with the inflection of another tongue.

"Charmed, I'm sure", Edna replied, echoing his formality.

"May I get you a drink?" He skillfully cut her away from the group and led her towards the bar.

"A martini, please. Heavy on the vermouth."

The crowd at the bar parted as he approached, the women looking admiringly, the men confused, but ceding ground nonetheless. Edna glanced around the room. Everyone was watching.

He turned from the bar with her martini and a glass of wine for himself. Wine? She was amused. Wine was something that eased you through dinner, but hardly qualified as a drink. Certainly not something one drank by preference. Not if you were a man.

Sacha tasted the drink and wrinkled his nose.

"Oh dear", he said, "I must speak to the bartender about his cellar. This is not good, not good at all."

"Helen tells me you're friends with Isabel." It was a stupid thing to say; he had been standing right there when Helen had said it, but Edna suddenly couldn't think of anything else.

"Ah, yes, the divine Isabel "discovered" me, although I knew perfectly well where I was. The discovery, however, was new to her."

"What kind of artist are you?"

"I paint in oils", he replied. "Portraits, alas."

"Why alas?"

"Ah, because I have discovered that Canadians do not buy portraits, unless it is of someone they know. They prefer landscapes. I am not sure why, when all they have to do is look out the window to see the most marvellous landscapes on earth. But, no, it is not enough to have an everchanging panorama in front of their noses, they must hang it in their drawing rooms as well. However, I shall make a small but adequate living painting heads of companies and their pigtailed children by day and beautiful women by night."

"So, your best work is done at night?"

"Always." He looked at her with amusement and she realized her unintentional double entendre. She blushed.

Isabel Jackson swooped down on them.

"Edna, you are very naughty, monopolizing Sacha this way. Do come with me, Sacha, there is someone you simply must meet."

He gave Edna a slight shrug and allowed himself to be towed off by the unstoppable Isabel.

She circulated the party then, in remote control, always watching him out of the corner of her eye. He made no attempt to come back to her, and when they sat down at dinner, she was disappointed when he was seated several tables away. She made desultory conversation with the man to her right. He was the guest speaker for the evening and she had somehow missed his name and the topic of his speech. The man was puzzled. He had been told he would be sitting beside the dashing Mrs. Collins, and would have a wonderful time. She was certainly pretty enough, but appeared to have all the personality of a turnip. Finally, he gave up and made small talk with Hannah Fletcher on his left.

She had to wait until the speeches were finished and the awards given out before she had a chance to speak to Sacha again. The band was warming up, and most of the women had retired to the ladies' room to primp in preparation for the dancing. He was standing at the window, looking out into the darkness. None of the men seemed particularly interested in him. She joined him, watching, not the darkness, but his reflection in the glass.

"Most artists are terribly concerned with light", he said, without turning to her. She supposed he could see her reflection as well as she could see his. "They don't realize that dark is far more interesting. One must look for the meaning in shadows."

She didn't know how to reply to that. It was a statement so completely outside her conversational experience that she almost turned around and went back to her table.

He turned to her then and smiled, a slow sad smile with a little shrug. "You must excuse me. I sometimes get so wrapped up in my work that I forget who I am speaking with. I must try and remember that I am in a colonial society where the subtle distinctions of light and dark are unimportant. I must learn to speak knowledgably about automobiles and the stock market and, how do you say it, the intricacies of politics."

She bridled at "colonial". "We aren't all barbarians, you know. There are some of us who are interested in art and music and literature," but even as she said it, she realized it wasn't really true. They had paintings in their home, of course. Len's taste ran to stark abstracts, while she herself preferred the landscapes Sacha had referred to so disparagingly. She couldn't remember the last time she had attended a concert or read anything other than bestsellers.

He became apologetic though. "Pardon me, please. I don't know what comes over me. Artists! Here I am with a beautiful woman all to myself and I waste the time talking about my work." He took her hand. "Forgive me?"

"Of course." He looked, Edna thought, almost exactly like Mud caught in the act of chewing a red pen. Contrite, certainly, but apt to do it again at the first opportunity, and a hint of mischief somewhere in the set of the mouth. "There's a price for forgiveness, though," she said.

"Yes?"

"You must dance with me."

He smiled. "If that is the price of forgiveness, I must remember to sin more often."

They sat out the first two numbers. It always took two or three tunes to get people past their post-dinner stupor, and the band waited until several couples were up doing the twist before they dropped into a slow, dreamy waltz. Sacha took her hand and led her to the floor. He held her much closer than was customary for a social dance, and she had no option but to dance cheek to cheek with him. He was more solidly built than he looked, and she could feel the muscles in his shoulder and chest rippling slightly as he piloted her around the room. He smelled faintly spicy, a combination of soap and something akin to cloves. She liked the feel of his cheek against hers. It was smooth and soft, no sign of the stubble that Len pared off his face twice a day. His hair was very blonde and very straight and cut very beautifully. She sighed and relaxed into the music.

A tap on the shoulder. It was Fred Jackson, Isabel's husband, cutting in smoothly, whirling her away and leaving Sacha standing in the middle of the dance floor with a quizzical look on his face. He shrugged slightly, and took up the waltz again with Hannah.

Fred loved to dance, but Isabel didn't and wasn't very good at it. He especially loved to dance with Edna, and she always gave him five or six turns throughout an evening, but tonight she could have strangled him.

"Didn't think you'd mind me cutting in," he said. "That arty fella was holding you kind of close."

"I think it's just because Europeans dance differently than we do," she said.

"Do you think so?" Fred had been drinking heavily, probably before he even arrived at the dinner. "He looks like a bit of a pansy, to me. 'Course, if he was a pansy, he wouldn't be holding you so close, now would he?" He giggled. "It's hard to tell with these foreign types, you know."

Mercifully, the music ended before she had to reply and Fred staggered off towards the bar. Sacha was being towed around the dance floor by Helen Rensell, who was grimly determined to lead.

Edna couldn't get near him again all night, the other women tittering and swooping around him, but just as Len was helping her into her coat, he came into the foyer.

"Thank you for a delightful evening," he said. "It was a pleasure to meet you." And again he took her hand, bowed slightly and kissed it. She could sense Len's amusement and she hoped they would make it through the door and out of earshot before he laughed openly or said something embarrassing.

"I do hope you'll come to my Grand Opening," Sacha said. "I'll be sure and send you an invitation." He looked at Len. "Both of you." And with a faint nod, he was gone.

The night was cold and there was a heavy layer of frost on the windshield. Len had to wait for the car to warm up before the defroster would clear it away.

"So what kind of art does this guy do?" he asked while they waited.

"Portraits, apparently."

He snorted. "Portraits. And this guy expects to make his rent this winter?"

"I have no idea," she said coolly. "I only had a short conversation with him. We didn't get to the subject of his finances."

"If I were Fred Jackson, I'd be watching my bank account like a hawk. Isabel is such a silly woman, she's apt to bankroll this guy just so she can pretend she's some sort of patron of the arts."

"Some people take great pride in being patrons of the arts, you know," she replied stiffly.

"Oh my God," Len said with a sideways glance. "You fell for this guy! A little hand-kissing and bowing, and you're a bowlful of jelly! I'll have to remember that the next time I want to get you in the mood."

"Oh shut up!" she said. "And if you ever try and kiss my hand, I'll swat you alongside the head!"

He laughed all the way home.

She waited a week before she drove past the old candy store again. She remembered it well, it was where she and Vera used to go on Saturdays, to spend the dimes each of them were given once a week. She supposed it had had staples like bread and milk, but they hadn't noticed such mundane items, intent as they were on assessing and calculating the maximum number of sugary sweets they could buy with ten cents. Strawberry hearts were only three for a penny, licorice sticks a cent apiece. A nickel would buy a small chocolate bar, but that would use up far too much of their money. They agonized and chose, put back and agonized more before finally, tiny hands laden, they would spread their choices on the old wooden counter, waiting anxiously while the obese old man who owned the store recounted and validated their purchases. Afterwards they would go to the woods and sit on a log by the creek while they ate their candy, blackball juice rolling down their chins, fingers sticky with sugar. Eating was never as good as choosing, Edna thought. It was a dime's worth of candy but a dollar's worth of fun.

She drove along , looking for a parking space under one of the old maples that still, in places, overhung the street.

He saw her right away.

"Edna", he smiled from the front step, "How nice to see you again. Have you come to see my new gallery?"

"It's nice to see you again too, Mr. Karensky".

He laughed. "Don't you think Mr. Karensky is a bit formal for someone who is about to become my most important patron?"

Edna was nettled a little by his presumption. "Who says I'll be a patron at all?"

"Oh, but you will. Do come in and see what I've done with this absolutely fabulous space." He put his arm around her shoulder and ushered her through the door before she could protest about appointments, schedules, busyness.

The change was astounding. The old store had had creaking wooden floors, peeling plaster. There had always been a fustiness about the place that spoke of broken water pipes and mildew. It had seemed small, shelves piled high.

Sacha had stripped the floors and varnished them to a high gloss. The walls were painted a deep avocado green, a backdrop for the artwork that was hung, not in profusion, but delicately and precisely placed to take advantage of the astounding light that poured in from small skylights in the roof. The room had been opened to the rafters at the front, left as an open loft at the back, with a graceful cast iron staircase leading up. Edna had never seen anything like it.

"Fortunately, the building faces south", Sacha was saying. "It was perfect for having a display in the main part of the store, while I could reserve the back part, with its beautiful northern light, for my studio. Would you like to see?"

"Just a moment, I want to look at the pictures", Edna said. "If you expect me to be a patron, shouldn't I at least look at the pictures first?" She mentally kicked herself as soon as she said it. Now she had more or less obliged him.

Nevertheless, she slowly circled the gallery. Her only experience with art had been through Len, and she had always left the choice of paintings to him. He had definite ideas about what he liked, would discuss form and the use of light with any of the few people they came in contact with who expressed an interest. He seemed to have a catholic taste, choosing only that which appealed to his dramatic eye.

Sacha's works were, to Edna, bizarre. Many of them were portraits, as he had said, but portraits unlike anything she had ever seen. The subjects were painted from odd angles and in strange lights. In some of them the proportions seemed to be out of kilter and skewed.

He was right behind her. "You see, as I said, I paint portraits, but not portraits in the traditional sense. I try to capture the essence of the personality and reflect that in the work. Otherwise, I would not be an artist, you see, but merely a drawer."

Edna was confused for a moment. She thought he had said "drawer" like "chest of drawers" and it took her a moment to catch his meaning. He seemed disappointed that she did not comment on his comment. She moved on. There were some landscapes, but not with the usual Canadian subjects of autumn forests or spring wildflowers. These scenes were blasted and black, with twisted, gnarled branches and greenish outcroppings of granite.

"My pictures are not pretty", Sacha went on, "not like in Canada where life is so wonderful that art has nothing to do but reflect the beauty of nature. I paint what is inside, and I can only mirror my experience."

Edna had had enough practice with flirtation to understand that she was supposed to ask, at this juncture, about his experience, what he could possibly have undergone that would culminate in these horrific landscapes.

She knew that he would then sigh, and change the subject, leaving her to wonder about the tragic secrets in his mysterious past. She decided not to play.

"They have a certain awesome beauty of their own", she said. "I really don't find them threatening at all."

She was amused by his look of disappointment.

"Do come upstairs and see my studio." He recovered quickly. "It really is quite wonderful.

They climbed the stairs after a slight jockeying. Edna stood back and let Sacha go first.

There were more and larger skylights, all facing north. The upstairs space was completely open except for a small closet-like corner, the bathroom, she guessed. The loft was obviously both studio and living quarters. A daybed, covered with a paisley throw was in the centre of the room, surrounded by books, half-burnt candles and wine bottles. There was no other furniture in the room except for a wooden stool that stood in front of an easel. Whatever picture Sacha was working on at the moment was covered with an old quilt.

"I do not allow anyone to see my work until it is finished, until I am satisfied", he explained. "I keep my works-in-progress covered until I can unveil them in their finished states."

A counter flanked a large laundry-sized sink against one wall. It was crowded with brushes, paint and cans of turpentine along with tins of soup and boxes of crackers.

"You live here?" she asked.

"Oh yes, when one is an artist, one never stops being an artist, so one gives in and lets the art take over one's life. Most people do not realize the enormous burden that creativity imposes."

That was just a bit too much.

"Well, thank you very much for the tour, Mr. Karensky", she said briskly. "Now, I really must be off." She thrust her hand forward for a businesslike handshake. As at the dance, he held her hand tenderly and kissed it goodbye.

"I see that artist has finally got his gallery open", Len said that night, one of the few nights that week they were dining alone.

"Yes, I happened to be going by and dropped in to see it."

" His stuff any good?"

"I don't know. It certainly was different."

"Hmmph", he said as he carved his steak. "I can't imagine how he expects to make a living in this town. People around here buy artwork to match their sofas. He doesn't happen to use a lot of beige, does he?"

"No, actually, it's all kind of black and stark."

"Hmm, maybe I'll drop by and have a look. I could always get your portrait painted for Christmas. I wonder if he does nudes?"

"What's nude?" Cara asked.

"Bare naked. In her birthday suit. With her bum showing." Len laughed at the outraged look on his daughter's face.

"Uh-uh." Cara shook her head. "We can't have a picture of mummy with her bum showing. Everybody would laugh."

"Oh I don't know, Cara Mia, I can't imagine anybody laughing at the sight of your mother's bum. Not if they were in their right minds."

"Len!"

"Well, I wouldn't laugh, that's for sure," he leered.

"Me either, Mummy. I wouldn't laugh at you," Cara said earnestly.

"Well neither of you will be put to the test, will you, because I have no intention of posing in the nude. Or posing at all."

"I don't know," Len said. "It might be kind of nice to have your portrait done. If this fellow isn't any good, I can always ask around. Someone must do them, you see them in banks all the time." He paused for a moment. "Oh no, sorry, that's post offices. And they're wanted posters, not portraits. My mistake."

"In that case," Edna said. "It would be have to be your portrait, not mine."

She waited until Sacha held his grand opening before going back. When she arrived, the gallery was full of people, mostly women, mostly those who had met Sacha at the dance. Isabel Jackson was in full flower as grand patron, taking a proprietary air with Sacha, introducing him, clinging to his arm.

Edna made it a perfunctory duty call, greeting her friends politely, taking a business card from the wicker basket at the door, sipping a half glass of wine. And then she left before Sacha could kiss her hand again.

"I dropped by that studio today", Len said a few evenings later. The conversation was flagging. George Almont, who seemed to transact a great deal of business with Len, had arrived for dinner with a girl half his age and with an eighth of his personality. George and Len had discussed a pending deal over cocktails while Edna tried to entertain the young friend. She seemed never to have been anywhere, done anything, or found any area of life that held the remotest interest for her. Edna gave her a detailed account of how they had just redecorated the living room. Len noticed her difficulties, and tried to pick up the conversational ball at dinner, but the girl was so dull, or shy perhaps, that even his attentions failed to make her sparkle.

"Yes, we have an artist in town now," Edna commented, jumping on Len's remark. " A Russian. He paints portraits."

George looked puzzled. "How in hell, excuse my French please, can an artist make a living in this burg? Of course, I suppose artists live on next to nothing anyway."

"I don't think a good artist could make a living here, and this one is definitely going to be on the relief rolls in short order," Len said.

"Why?" Edna was interested in his opinion of the work. Several paintings he picked up for a few dollars had later skyrocketed in value after the artist had been hailed by the critics.

"They're crap. Pure unadulterated crap," he said.

"If you ask me, that's what most of it is these days", George said. "I don't have anything against this modern art, mind you, it's just that I can't seem to connect with a lot of the stuff."

Edna wasn't sure exactly what sort of art George would connect with, considering his taste in women. Dogs smoking cigars and playing poker perhaps. She spent the rest of the evening trying to figure out why she was vaguely annoyed with Len.

She was back at the studio in two days, and Sacha looked like he had been expecting her.

"Exquisite timing", he said as he ushered her in the door. "I still have wine left from the grand opening. Come upstairs."

"No, I just want to look around, thanks", she said. She felt that having been given the obligatory tour of the studio, she would be wise not to go up there again. At least not right away. She made a show of studying paintings. She still found them faintly disturbing. She compared them with the artwork Len had hung at home. Very different, but she couldn't qualify it in any way. I guess I just don't know enough to make a judgement, she thought, but surely they can't be "crap" as he so elegantly put it.

This time they had price tags on them. She was no stranger to the concept of paying good money for beautiful things, but these prices made her gasp. How on earth is he ever going to sell any of these around here? she wondered, then realized that she sounded just like Len.

He brought her a glass of wine.

"Not very good, I'm afraid", he said. "The local liquor store has an astounding selection of rye whiskey, but not much in the way of decent wines."

Edna agreed. Len bought all their dinner wine in Montreal. She grimaced as she took the first sip.

Sacha took the glass from her hand. "Ah, I knew it. Not suitable for a lady of your taste at all." He set the glass on the table by the door. "I know, come upstairs and I will make you an espresso, that's the thing to do." He bounded up the iron staircase.

Oh well, Edna thought as she followed. Oh well.

Sacha was fiddling with a complicated looking machine that teetered on a small table by the counter.

"I love espresso", he said. "The liquid you call coffee in this country is nothing but an insipid coloured water. You'll love this. And just wait until I unpack my samovar, so I can make you a tisane."

She had no idea what a tisane was, or a samovar either for that matter. She stood awkwardly at the head of the stairs. There was nowhere to sit except on the studio bed.

"Please, please, sit down", he gestured towards the bed. "Make yourself at home."

She perched on the edge while he fiddled with the machine, chatting away, explaining the mechanics of what he was doing, which coffee was best to use, the history of the beverage. Finally, after what seemed an eternity and an enormous amount of fuss, he brought her a small cup of thick, black liquid. She took a small sip, but found the coffee bitter and unpleasant. She expected that Sacha would come and sit beside her and she stiffened, prepared to assume her starchiest and most prudish demeanour. Instead, he paced the room, holding his coffee and talking.

"I'm experimenting with perspective right now", he said. "Most portraits are done in a very traditional manner, either a full frontal view or sometimes, in the old days, in profile. I'm trying different angles, different lights, in an attempt to capture the true essence of the person I am painting. It's a technique that has been used in studies, but you hardly ever see it in the finished product."

Edna nodded, puzzled and off balance. Why was he talking to her about art? And why was she disappointed by this?

Suddenly he stopped in mid-stride, his coffee cup sliding dangerously to the edge of the saucer.

"My God", he said, looking at her, " my God!"

"What?"

"This light. You in this light. Unbelievable. I must paint you."

"Oh, I don't know." She moved to get up.

"No, no, stay right where you are! You look like a madonna. I knew it, as soon as I saw you. You have a quality that I want to capture on canvas forever."

"I'm a middle-aged woman with a husband and child", Edna protested, "You're being ridiculous."

"Please, I am not interested in your husband or your child or your age. Only in what I see. Please, please think about it. It could be my master work. Like DaVinci's Mona Lisa or Botticelli's Venus."

"I think I should go now." She set the unfinished cup of espresso on the floor.

He followed her down the stairs and opened the door for her. Just as she was leaving he clasped her hand and kissed it in that same way he did with all the women, or did he hold on to it a moment longer than before? Her imagination was really running wild, she decided.

She kept away for nearly a week while she tried to sort out what she was feeling. Why did this odd man confuse her so? She was certainly no stranger to flirtation, and she was sure that Sacha was flirting with her. Many of Len's business associates and more than a few of the men they met socially flirted with her at the drop of a hat. She was expert at responding in such a way as to leave the impression that she was interested and attracted, of course, but, alas, unavailable. This was different, somehow. She wasn't sure Sacha knew the rules of the game.

She found herself driving out of her way past his studio, just on the off chance that she might catch a glimpse of him. What would she do then? she wondered. Would she stop and talk to him, beep the horn and wave, or sweep regally by, pretending that she hadn't seen him?

Whenever his name came up in conversation, her heart would race. His name came up often; Sacha and his studio were the talk of the town. Several of Edna's friends said they were considering having their portraits done.

"We may never have another chance to have a real artist paint us," gushed Helen Rensell. "Who knows, someday the portraits could be worth a fortune."

This is silly, she thought in her saner moments. He's just another man, a little more exotic than I usually run across, but he puts his pants on one leg at a time, just like anybody else. She immediately regretted the metaphor. Putting his pants on, one leg at a time or not, evoked an image of Sacha with his pants off, a prospect she wasn't yet ready to think about.

Vera and Edna met Friday for lunch. Edna picked at her salad, but Vera tucked into her meal with gusto.

She should really try and cut back a little, Edna thought. She had gained at least thirty pounds since she got married. She reminded Edna of the dumplings her mother served up with her chicken stew, pasty and grey.

Vera was full of her children; Little Stevie was, of course, the most amazing child anyone had ever produced, the best looking, the smartest, the most precocious. Susie was "difficult", but then she was delicate and one had to make allowances for that. Susie remained a short and pudding-like little girl and Edna privately thought she was about as delicate as a front end loader.

"And how is Cara doing?" Vera always asked, and Edna always knew it was just to be polite.

"Fine." It was the only answer she ever gave. Cara was in perfect health and seemed to be developing quite normally. If she experienced any childhood traumas or triumphs, she certainly didn't ever share them with her mother.

"Have you been to the art gallery?" Edna asked.

"No, but I hear the artist is quite handsome. What are his paintings like?" Vera dipped a chip in the gravy that covered her hot beef sandwich.

"I find them very disturbing."

"Oh really, in what way?"

"I don't know, it's hard to describe." She debated whether or not to tell Vera that he had offered to paint her portrait. She finally decided to float the topic out gently.

"I'm thinking of hiring him to do a portrait of me", she said. "It would make such a lovely Christmas gift for Len."

Vera's chip was arrested halfway to her mouth. "You can't be serious."

"Why?"

"Everyone knows what artists are like."

"Why, what are they like?"

"I can't imagine Len allowing you to do anything of the sort."

"I'm not talking about taking my clothes off or anything you know. Just a nice sedate studio portrait of my head and shoulders."

"Oh, I know," Vera said. "That would be it at first, but how long would it take before he had you undressed and lounging on a sofa? And you know what would happen after that. I'm amazed at you, Edna, how could you even consider doing something like that ?"

"It was only an idea". She was amused, and a little taken aback by Vera's reaction.

So was Vera and she thought about it that night as she tried to fall asleep. She wondered if it was just jealousy. She knew that she was jealous of Edna, who seemed to have everything, who never had to worry about the hydro bill or the price of hamburger, who lived in a fairy tale with her big house and her cocktail parties and her bridge club. She tried hard not to be, and most of the time, in the daylight at least, she was able to convince herself that she had a good life; Mac certainly wasn't a romantic, dashing figure by any stretch of the imagination, but he was a hard worker and a good provider and thought a lot of his family, spending most of his spare time teaching Stevie how to play hockey and baseball and allowing Susan to tag along with her dolls. He asked for little in return except for a beer and a good meal and, now and again but not too often, access to Vera's round body. There was more money now, and that made things easier. Mac always made sure there was more in her housekeeping envelope than she needed to run the house, so she could indulge herself in small ways. Although she made a great show of deferring to him, she knew that most of the time he wanted her to make the big decisions, to tell him what to do, just like his mother had done. This was only as it should be. Most women would be more than satisfied with Mac Dunlop, and most of the time, Vera was.

But this smugness could be unsettled in a moment. She loved it when Edna arrived at her door and she could take a little time to sit in the kitchen and drink tea with her. Often they chattered and giggled just like they had when they were children, the conversation flowing freely and tangentially from topic to topic. At these times they fell into a strange verbal shorthand, one word or phrase enough to evoke a mutual experience or a shared memory, even a look could send them off into gales of laughter, and these afternoons left Vera feeling warm and cherished.

At other times, some chance remark would remind her of the very different ways their lives had turned out, and then she found it hard not to be bitter and resentful. She knew that Edna was very careful not to flaunt her good fortune, but Vera didn't want a careful friendship, and on those days when some train of thought led to dangerous ground, she could be depressed for hours afterwards. Worst of all was mention of Len. Whereas Mac had grown heavier and more bear-like as he grew older, Len seemed to have stayed the same tall, slim boy he had always been, laughing, hands thrust in pockets, hat shoved to the back of his head. On the few occasions Vera permitted herself to look in the full-length mirror on the back of the closet door, she was appalled at the way the dimpled fat had crept around her hips and stomach, bunching into a roll that no girdle seemed able to contain. She had once been pleasantly round, a neat little package that she was pretty sure had been quite attractive. There were her ankles of course, they had always been a little on the thick side, but she had disguised this in her choice of shoes, enduring higher heels than the other girls wore, confident that they made her look taller.

She wore nothing but flats, now. There was no point in disguising the breadth of her ankles. Mac surely wouldn't notice and who else would be liable to look at her legs? During the daylight, as she washed the dishes or swept the kitchen floor, she could persuade herself that it wasn't Edna's possession of Len she envied, but the loss of her own youth. In the abyss of a sleepless night it was different. Then, the sour gall of what-might-have-been tormented her. It should have been her in the big house, with servants and fancy furniture, with beautiful clothes and manicured hands, and most of all, best of all, with Len.

She knew from the gossip at the Post Office that Len strayed. She tried not to imagine that someday he might stray in her direction, but in spite of herself, she sometimes fantasized a grand, romantic affair. Yes, Edna was her best friend and always would be, but there was no fighting this magnetic attraction, was there? They must be careful, discreet, protect her from the truth. They must meet secretly, in another town, in another place, never at home. Vera tried to place them in a sumptuous hotel room, with a huge, canopied and rumpled bed, but her only experience with hotels was her honeymoon at the Royal York, where the neon light outside had flashed in time to Mac's snores. She certainly couldn't imagine Len here, in her own bedroom. The cabbage rose wallpaper was peeling away around the window and the sheets were worn thin.

Again and again, her imagination returned to the dunes, with the moon shining down and the band playing Stardust in the background. They would melt into each other's arms, just like they had that night, and Len would slowly undress her, her body miraculously lengthened and tightened and smoothed. Her breasts would be full and round and strain towards his hands, her slim, shapely legs would part willingly for his rampant manhood and their love would be wildly and passionately consummated to the rhythm of the crashing waves.

In the dark of the night, this seemed right and good and possible. In the early morning light, it was embarrassing that she had even thought it, and she would be grumpy with Mac and short with the children.

And now there was this artist fellow that Edna was all excited about. She wasn't at all sure that there was really anything to it. After all, if you were married to someone like Len, why would even look at anyone else? Still, there was something in Edna's voice that was alarming and, Vera realized with a pang, that she recognized all too well.

It was after Christmas when Edna finally agreed to have her portrait done. She saw Sacha occasionally at parties, and had dropped by the gallery a couple of times, where he charmingly offered her a glass of wine or a cup of coffee while she studied his paintings. She would stay away for a couple of weeks at a time, convincing herself that it was only the novelty of his presence that intrigued her. He had such an air of world-weary sophistication. Such a contrast to the hard- headed, straight-to-the point pragmatism of all the other men she knew. Len was dashing, of course, everyone agreed on that, but it was in a brash and direct way that confronted each situation head on, with no patience for obstacles or interference. Len could sweep you off your feet; Sacha, she was sure, would make you go weak-kneed so that you collapsed of your own accord. His manners were so elegant, his gestures so refined. And there was that deep, underlying sadness that made her want to take him in her arms and hold him until the sadness went away.

When absence failed to get him off her mind, she would return, drawn like a moth to a flame. This is silly, she thought. You're behaving like a fourteen year old with a hopeless crush. But she couldn't stay away for long. She finally went ahead and asked about a portrait. With any luck, the long hours of his company would serve to inoculate her and the novelty would wear off. He seemed annoyingly unsurprised by her request and suggested they start the following week.

When she arrived, he said little, just sat her on the studio couch to start the preliminary sketches. She was awkward and self-conscious, aware of the need to retain a pose, but unable to relax into a position that was easy and natural. As the work progressed, she gradually became more comfortable, and by the time he was ready to start painting, she was ready to start sitting in earnest. She let her mind roam outside the room while he worked, and most days she enjoyed the freedom it gave her to float through her thoughts.

She had chosen to wear an emerald green silk blouse. It was a colour that suited her, but by the end of January, when the weather turned bitterly cold, she wished she had chosen something warmer, something like a woolly skating sweater for instance. Sacha had installed a small electric heater, but the loft was barn-like and chilly. She had let her hair down and at least that kept the back of her neck warm.

He refused to let her see any of the work, covering it with an old quilt after every session. She sighed. This was harder work than she had thought.

"Have you had enough for today?"

"Yes, I should be going soon." Bernice thought she was playing bridge and Edna hadn't disabused her, although why it would matter, she wasn't sure. Len was unlikely to question where she went in the afternoon, and even if he did, what harm could it do to have her portrait painted? He had suggested it himself, hadn't he? She persuaded herself that the reason she told no one was because it was to be a surprise. For Len.

"No. It's early." Sacha checked his watch. "I know, for once I have some decent wine. It will warm you up."

He went to the counter and poured two glasses, then came and sat beside her, carefully balancing the wine bottle on a stack of books beside the couch.

"You are the most astounding subject, you know. It will take all of my skill as an artist just to capture the way the light reflects from your face. Your beautiful face." Tentatively he lifted his hand and stroked her cheek, then moved to her hair.

She turned her head into his hand, caressing it in return, then turning, hesitating, she met his eyes.

He sighed. "Perhaps you should go, after all," he said. "Please forgive me, I forgot for one brief ecstatic moment that you are forbidden. I will try not to let it happen again." He rose, picked up the wine bottle and walked over to the sink where he stood with his back turned to her.

She was both annoyed and relieved. She was never sure what Sacha's motivations were; there was an aura about him, a disguised sensuality that both attracted and repelled her. Certain that he had designs on her, she had expected him to make a move long before this. Now, just as it seemed he was about to press his attack, he had abruptly broken it off.

Edna was very adept at sexual innuendo, and very good at controlling it. What she didn't know was how to unleash it. She shrugged herself into her coat and was at the head of the stairs before he spoke again.

"You will come back on Thursday?"

"Yes, of course. I'll be here at one."

Len was away that night, the second time that week. She lay awake until nearly two, replaying the scene with Sacha over and over in her head.

What did she want? She didn't know. She wasn't the sort of woman who had affairs, at least she didn't think she was. She tried to imagine what it would be like to have Sacha make love to her, but her only experience was of Len. What if Sacha found her awkward and gauche? He was so continental, so sophisticated. What if he laughed at some practice of hers, something she didn't even know was backwater and hopelessly provincial?

The fact that Len obviously found her adequate was no comfort. He presumably had had all sorts of experience, but it was all with local girls like herself. Or as far as she knew, anyway. Besides, she was a wife. Men had different standards for their wives, she knew that from the many novels and magazines she had read. Mistresses were a different story. Mistresses were alluring and worldly and passionate. They were more understanding, accepting a man's foibles without criticism, offering them a haven where tenderness and understanding sheltered them from the vicissitudes of their complex lives. "Be your own husband's mistress" the magazines urged. "Offer him what he needs at home and he'll never wander."

She was pretty sure Len wandered, in spite of the fact that she never went around the house with curlers in her hair and made sure that she kept her legs shaved. She wondered if Len loved her. He never said so, except in that offhand, joking way he had. She supposed they had a pretty good marriage. They still made love frequently. He certainly provided her with everything she needed and more. She never nagged. He seldom confided in her, but then his business affairs seemed so complex and convoluted she doubted if she would have made an adequate confidant anyway.

Why was she even thinking about Sacha when she had Len?

You're nothing but a ridiculous middle-aged woman,she lectured herself. Here you are with a beautiful home and a handsome husband and a lovely child and everything your heart desires, and you're having adulterous thoughts about a man you hardly know. She resolved then to stop going to Sacha's studio, portrait be damned. I'll pay him the full price, so he's not out of pocket, she thought, but I'll explain to him that things are getting out of hand and I can't continue. On Thursday. At one.

But her resolve weakened in the light of day, when her fantasies of the night before seemed silly and unwarranted. Perhaps she had misinterpreted his actions, not made enough allowance for his foreignness. She was unwilling to discover that she had been mistaken and was afraid of making a fool of herself. When she reached the studio, she shrugged off her coat and assumed her usual modelling position on the daybed.

Sacha made no comment about their last session. He corrected her pose and removed the quilt over the painting, fussing with brushes and mixing colours. Edna wasn't sure where to look. She was uncomfortable gazing at him; in her midnight fantasies she had visualized him naked, and now this image returned to her unbidden.

He worked for nearly twenty minutes, then laid his brushes down.

"What's wrong?" he asked.

"Nothing's wrong."

"But you are so stiff today. I can't get the paint to flow when you sit like that."

"I'm sorry."

"Do I need to make an apology for myself? For the other day?"

"No, of course not."

"Good." He sat beside her and took her hand. "Because I have no intention of apologizing for what I said. It is true. You are very beautiful, and under other circumstances, I would have made love to you long ago."

There, it was out in the open, finally. Edna laughed at herself. She had been so afraid of putting a foot wrong, of making an assumption, and now she felt vindicated. He wanted her, after all.

He stroked her hand. "I know it is wrong, but I can't help myself. There are nights when I lay awake, after you have been here, thinking about you. It tortures me."

Edna was impressed. As far as she was aware, she had never tortured anyone before.

"I can't sleep, I can't eat, all I can do is think about you. Worship you from afar." He stopped stroking her hand and began stroking her hair.

He had a nice touch. Firm, yet gentle, and as his hand moved, she caught the elusive clovish smell she had noticed before. His eyes were such a deep, dark brown. You could drown in eyes like that.

She closed her eyes and moved her face closer to him. Their lips met then, Sacha's head turned to one side. He kissed her tenderly, almost reverently.

"We should not be doing this," he said again.

She kissed him again, this time harder.

"No, no we cannot." He stood up and looked at her. "But you are so beautiful."

She smiled up at him, waiting, knowing that all she had to do now was wait. He stood over her for a moment, then bent down as she slid backwards to lie on the daybed. She shivered as he slowly undressed her, kissing each part of her as it was exposed. She told herself it was the cold.

"Ahhh", it was less than a groan but more than a sigh. "Exquisite."

She closed her eyes and when she opened them again Sacha, too was naked above her. He caressed her body slowly. She had been shaking with anticipation, but now his soft touch calmed her. His hands reached her breasts and she realized that her nipples were hard and erect and she thrust them towards his mouth. He obliged, first licking, then sucking and biting. She moaned and tried to pull him down on top of her, but he resisted, abandoning her breasts and kissing instead between her legs. Edna had never been so aroused, her arousal growing as his mouth latched onto her. Oh delicious, oh unbelievable, when was the last time it felt like this? And then she exploded in sensation and one small part of her could hear her own cries as the pleasure rolled over her in a vast tidal wave.

"Ahhh", the whispery moan again, as he stroked her, extending her pleasure for as long as he could. Edna felt detached, far, far away in a tranquil and unreachable place.

And then he was inside her, filling her.

As he climaxed, she realized that she had forgotten to notice how he'd managed to get his shoes and socks off so fast.

CHAPTER FOURTEEN

Bernice Davis smelled trouble.

She was good at smelling trouble. It had been the one thing that had enabled her to survive her drunken husband, who would often arrive home late at night prepared to cause a great deal of it. In the early years of her marriage Bernice had occasionally been caught unprepared for this, and had allowed herself to be found fast asleep in bed. Chester would crash into the bedroom and enraged by her slumbering form, grab her by the hair and pull her to her feet, demanding that she make him coffee, or bacon and eggs or perform some other unreasonable service.

There was a pattern to Chester's drunkenness that coincided with his weekly paycheque, earned tending the grounds at the town cemetery. This paycheque was both a prize and a torment to him.

"I work my ass off all day and they pay me peanuts," he would storm at Bernice. "Peanuts! This isn't enough for a man to live on!"

It was, only just, if the man didn't drink it all away.

"I have half a mind to go down there tomorrow and quit," he would rage. "I'll tell them to take their bloody job and stick it!" But he never did. He would be sidetracked by the siren call of the beer parlour, where most of his paycheque would be poured into a shotglass. Those nights were the worst, when he finally got home. Those, and the next couple of nights. After that, Chester would be broke again, and try to wheedle his way back into Bernice's good graces so he could borrow some money from her. She would give him a few dollars from the money she made cleaning other women's houses, just enough to hold him until the next payday when he erupted all over again.

After Rhonda was born, late in her life, she decided enough was enough, and on the nights when she expected Chester to arrive home in an uproar, she arranged for Rhonda and herself to spend the night with one of her sisters. Since she had many sisters, Chester was never sure where to find her, and would run out of steam after checking with one or two of them. After the storm was over, she and the little girl would return home as if nothing had happened.

"Why do you stay with him?" her sister Martha asked. "You're paying your own way anyway."

Bernice wasn't sure why, except that she had promised for better and for worse, and sometimes, when he hadn't been drinking too much, he could be kind of nice. Besides, the ramshackle house they lived in was in Chester's name. The money she earned was enough to keep them in food, but Bernice knew it wouldn't stretch to cover rent.

She had been saddened when Chester died, but relieved as well. The town had provided a small insurance policy, and this was enough to bury him. The house was now hers, such as it was, and her housekeeping money was enough to keep them as well as it ever had. She would have been all right no matter what, she figured. She and Rhonda could have managed. But when Len Collins asked her to look after his ailing wife, and subsequently his household, it meant the difference between merely managing and finally being on her feet. She could even put money by for a rainy day. Bernice was alert to any nuance or undercurrent that might threaten this new-found security.

The trouble she smelled at the Collins house was different from Chester's trouble, but she recognized it for what it was right away. She was deeply worried about Mrs. Len.

Bernice knew Mr. Len's reputation; gossip at the grocery store kept her up to date with what he was up to most of the time, or at least the rumour mill version of what he was up to. She knew he philandered. Chester never had, and she wasn't sure what her reaction would have been if he had, but it was hard for her to be too critical when it came to her employer. He was good to her and Rhonda, and good to his wife and little girl too. Besides, he was so handsome, she suspected that women just threw themselves at his feet. What man wouldn't take advantage of that once in a while?

She wasn't sure whether or not Mrs. Len was aware of the gossip. She thought that probably she wasn't and Bernice certainly wasn't going to tell her. She adored Mrs. Len too, and knew, instinctively, that interference on her part could easily upset the delicate balance that existed between man and wife. That, and the fact that it was really none of Bernice Davis' business anyway, now was it? she would chide herself as she pounded out the dough for a batch of rolls.

But Mrs. Len was upsetting things in a way that Bernice had never dreamed could happen. If she wasn't mistaken, and experience with her numerous sisters meant that she was seldom mistaken in these things, Edna was in love.

She paced. She wandered from room to room. She became snappish when Bernice asked her little questions about housekeeping routine. She blew up at Rhonda, who pulled the living room curtain completely off its track in an attempt to close it one night, then immediately burst into tears and apologized. In love or pregnant were the only two explanations Bernice could come up with, and pregnant, from what she understood of the circumstances surrounding Cara's birth, was an impossibility.

She wondered that Mr. Len didn't notice, but then he paid little attention to anyone's moods, other than his own. If he had, Bernice surmised, he would have put it down to "women's troubles" and ignored it, like men always ignored anything they didn't want to be bothered with.

Edna was indeed in love. She had never felt this way before, certainly not about Len. Oh, she supposed she loved him in a way, but it was a comfortable old- pair- of -slippers kind of love, not the crushing, suffocating feeling she had when she thought of Sacha.

When she knew she would be seeing him, she would become almost sick with excitement. Unsettled, even the night before, she would be unable to focus on anything. She would surface in the middle of a conversation with Len or Cara or Mrs. Davis not having the vaguest notion of what they had been talking about. She would try to read, but would be unable to recount the plot. She would drink innumerable cups of tea and smoke innumerable cigarettes. When she couldn't see him because of some commitment or other, she drove slowly around the town, hoping for a glimpse of him. Success brought both euphoria and despair; euphoria at having seen him, despair that she would have to wait to see him again.

She began to take him little gifts. Wine, at first, because he so obviously enjoyed it and so obviously couldn't afford the pricier vintages. He would compliment her on her selection, although she usually grabbed the first bottle she came across in the rack Len had installed in the basement. He would uncork it as soon as she arrived, allowing it to breathe and warm to room temperature while he slowly undressed her, caressing and lightly kissing each part of her, from her earlobes to her toes. When he judged the wine was ready to drink, he would carefully pour out two glasses, dipping his fingers in it and tracing intricate patterns on her skin, then gently he would run his mouth along the pattern, imbibing the wine from the soft cushion of her flesh. He would hold the glass to her lips while she sipped the musky liquid and when she swallowed, seek out the last traces of it with his tongue. She would be eager for him, but he moved with slow deliberation, spinning out each moment until she hovered on the edge of frenzy; then he would take her, roughly and abruptly, sending her tumbling into a tumultuous ecstasy.

He used the dreamlike stupor of sexual aftermath to work on her portrait. She had no difficulty then holding the pose for long periods. She would be content merely to sit and listen to the sounds of his loft; the wind blowing a branch against the window, the ticking of the clock, the shifting of the old building as it contracted in the cold. She was sure she could hear the sound of his brushes striking the canvas.

He had not been prepared for the harshness of Ontario winters, so she bought him a coat, a lovely wool and cashmere camel hair, and a soft woollen scarf to tuck in at the neck. On the day she gave him the coat, she packed a wicker basket with pate and brie and crackers to go with them, along with a bottle of wine, and they drove to the dunes looking for a sheltered place out of the wind for their winter picnic. The dunes were bleak and deserted in December, a light layer of snow lying in the shaded valleys between them. The lake was dark and angry-looking, its swells beating against the fragile shore, determined to erase every sign of summer frolic. They walked along the beach, leaning into the wind, until in the distance, they could see a weather-beaten shack nestled against a dune.

"What's that?" Sacha wanted to know.

"The Palace of the Moon. It's an old dance hall."

"But what a wonderful name! Palace of the Moon. Palace of soft light and deceptive shadow, where nothing is ever quite as it seems." He was delighted, stopping in the sand to consider this small, unexpected gift on an afternoon of gift-giving. "It's too bad the reality doesn't live up to the name, but perhaps this is a deception as well?"

"I don't know," Edna said. "I've never been inside. "

"Then we must go." He grabbed her hand and they began running down the beach towards the old building.

The Palace of the Moon had never achieved elegance, even at the height of its popularity, but now years of neglect and abuse had made it derelict. Winters of punishing wind and wild storms had blown away the wooden stilts that once supported the walkway, but drifting sand had piled against the side of the building, and they were able to climb to the door. This had once had a padlock, but moisture from the nearby lake quickly rusted it through and the door stood half open, sand blown into a small pile in front of it. They were not the first intruders; evidence of vandalism, both animal and human, was everywhere. Raccoons had revelled here, mice had nested, skunks had waddled, lovers had coupled. The heavy cardboard signs at the deserted snack bar had been ripped and scattered across the counter. " ot dogs 2..." they now read and "..joy an ice-cold Co...". Empty whiskey and beer bottles were piled in a corner, along with old blankets and discarded articles of clothing. A fine layer of sand covered the hardwood dance floor, its golden blanket marred by scores of tiny footprints.

It was dark in the old building. A lone shaft of wan sunlight spilled through the half-open door, and if Edna closed her eyes she could imagine music, couples swaying in time, holding each other close as the moon cycled its way across the warm summer sky. While she stood there dreaming, Sacha slipped behind her. He unwound the soft scarf she had given him and tied it across her eyes, knotting it firmly but gently behind her head. Then he took her hand and led her to the platform that still stood at one end of the hall. She was amused and slightly alarmed. She could hear the picnic basket opening, and the sound of the cloth being snapped open and spread. He pulled her down then onto to the hard wood of the platform, opening her coat and slipping his hands inside.

He teased her, stroking first her breasts, then her thighs. She didn't know where the next touch would be, if it would be gentle or abrupt, if he would kiss her softly or pull her clothing roughly aside as he grasped her, bit her, entered her. The thin table cloth he had spread on the floor was little cushion against the unyielding wood of the platform and she gasped as her back was rammed into it. She was aware of being cold, her nipples wrinkled and hard in protest at the frosty air. The scarf was scratchy and the knot at the back of her head had caught up stray strands of hair which pulled and hurt. She had never been so excited.

She had arrived home sticky and sore and bruised, and when she inspected herself in the mirror while her bath was running, she realized that Sacha had left bite marks on her neck and breasts. I can't keep doing this, she thought as she lowered her aching back into the warm water, I'm going to get caught. And then she sank into a drowsy review of the afternoon, fixing the delicious details of their lovemaking in her memory, eliminating the squalor of their surroundings and the stench of the hall.

She rocketed from panic to passion with alarming regularity. At times, she would resolve to end the affair, knowing that it could end only in heartbreak or disaster. She would arrive at the studio, determined to tell him it was over, but as soon as she saw him all of her resolve melted away. He seemed to know when these times were, and it was then that he appeared to be most passionate and most vulnerable.

At other times, in spite of herself, she would wonder what it would be like to live with him. What would it feel like to wake up every day and see his face on the pillow next to her? What was he like in the morning? Grouchy until his first cup of coffee? Cheerful? She hoped not, since she wasn't. What would it be like to have breakfast with him? That's assuming of course, that she would actually get up and have breakfast with him, God knows, she never did with Len. What would it be like to live in the loft over the studio? Or rather, she corrected herself, a loft over some studio somewhere, since if it ever happened, they undoubtedly would move on. Not if. Not ever. But still.....

What would she find to occupy herself with while he painted? If they lived in a loft over a studio, she assumed she would have to vacate while he was working. Would she need a job? Probably, since Sacha never had money. It had been so long since she worked, she could hardly remember what it was like. She did remember that she hadn't liked it much.

No, this was nonsense, it was never going to happen, there were too many practical details to get in the way. Why on earth would she give up her comfortable home and comfortable life for the rackety existence of an artist's wife? Girlfriend. Lover.

But her mind kept slipping into a daydream of what it could be like. She knew it was silly, but she found herself playing schoolgirls' games, like she and Vera used to play in the hut back in the woods when they were on the brink of adolescence and discovering the intricate rules of courtship. He loves me, he loves me not. Love, hate, friendship, marriage. How many letters in our names agree?

Bernice came to her with a question about linen. "Cara's sheets are getting quite worn", she said. "I really think they need to be replaced."

"Um huh", Edna had replied.

"Is that um huh, yes, or um huh, no?"

"Sorry, what?"

Cara, who had been lying on the living room floor colouring a picture of The Friendly Giant, started to laugh.

"Mummy's gone away again," she said.

"What do you mean, gone away?" Edna was puzzled and defensive.

"Sometimes you're just not here", Cara said. "You're somewhere else. Just like when you're reading, only you don't have a book."

Len finally noticed her abstraction and was a little concerned. Edna had always been dreamy and somewhat absent-minded, but now it seemed to be getting out of hand. "Are you feeling all right?" he asked. "Maybe you should go get a check up."

"I just had a check up."

"Well, what's wrong with you? You're not taking after your father, are you? I'm not going to find you stone cold dead in front of the radio with nobody noticing for days am I?"

"No, I just sort of tune out sometimes. What's wrong with that? Don't you ever just sit and think?"

"No," Len replied, and it was the truth.

She smiled at his honesty. “I'm okay,” she said. “It's just the winter blahs.”

He shrugged and left it at that.

"Edna we have to talk about mother." The telephone had jangled Edna awake. She looked over at the clock on the bedside table. Eight a.m. She sighed.

"Hi, Jack, what's up?"

"The neighbours found her walking around on the sidewalk in her nightgown again. They called me at six-thirty this morning. I've just come from getting her back into the house."

Hetty Charles had taken to wandering, not only in body, but in her mind as well. She had gone back to the days when she had been Hetty Becker, pretty Hetty Becker, who could wind that Charles boy right around her little finger. Hetty, who wasn't above pinching her cheeks a little to make them pinker or putting mineral oil on her eyelashes to make them darker. Who would sit on the back stoop for hours, looking at the moon and dreaming about her life away from the hardscrabble little farm her father half-heartedly worked.

She thought Jack was his father and flirted with him shamelessly. She no longer recognized Edna at all, except as a potential rival, and treated her with an icy disdain. Unable to sleep, she would fumble her way to her front door in the dark, forgetting that the flick of a switch would illuminate her way. Her determination to reach the front porch would falter once she was there and forgot why she had come out. Turned around and confused, she would be unable to find her way back. The rest of the night she would march purposefully up and down the sidewalk, fiercely intent on she knew not what. Eventually, one of her neighbours would notice and call Jack or Edna.

This was one of many things in her life that Edna had been ignoring in her obsession with Sacha. She knew that Jack, along with everybody else was waiting for her to do something. As the oldest, she guessed it was her responsibility to take some kind of definitive action. She had no idea what that would be. They couldn't put her mother in the County Home; for a woman of Hetty's generation it was unthinkable. The County Home was where you ended up when you were indigent or your family didn't care. There was a nice new nursing home that had been built on the edge of town a couple of years ago, but Edna wasn't sure anybody understood the distinction between the two.

"I'm sorry you had to deal with it today, Jack," she said. "I'll try and think of something."

Grumpily she wandered downstairs to the kitchen, to put the kettle on for more tea and to think about her mother. If it hadn't been so sad, Hetty's regression to an earlier time might have amused Edna. She had known her only as the stern-faced matriarch who took her comfort in the arms of the church. Who was this simpering and flirtatious girl who had lain buried for so long? What had happened to the bright-eyed and hopeful young thing who had dared raise her sights to the lofty goal of marriage with a Charles? What internal urges prompted her to relive her young adulthood on the front porch every night?

She took her tea and sat at the kitchen table, moving aside a towering papier mache castle that Rhonda had been helping Cara to build. One corner of it was chewed to a pulpy mass. Undoubtedly Mud had got to it in the night, but Edna knew that neither Rhonda nor Cara would have the heart to chastise him. There was no point anyway; unless you caught Mud in the act, yelling did no good. He would hunker down on the floor and whimper piteously, but make no connection between their harsh tones and any action of his. Mud and my mother are operating on just about the same level, she thought glumly, with Rhonda only a rung or two above that.

She knew her mother's neighbours were talking. They wondered why none of Hetty's children were taking her with them to live; it was what they would have done, in fact, had done, with their difficult relatives. Edna knew that she was coming in for the bulk of the criticism. After all, she had a huge house with almost nobody in it, and live-in help besides.

She shuddered at the idea of sharing house-space with her mother again. Besides, Len would never stand for it. She supposed that under other circumstances, Jack and Margaret might be persuaded to move in with Hetty, but Margaret was not well herself. She was a diabetic and a brittle one at that. No matter how carefully she watched her diet, no matter how painstakingly she measured the dose of insulin into the syringe, no matter how faithfully she injected herself each day, her blood sugars would fluctuate wildly and she would have to be rushed to the hospital. It wasn't fair to ask Margaret.

She would have to talk to Len, that's all there was to it, but she was certain what his reaction would be. Oh, she thought, why can't they all just leave me alone?

She was seeing Sacha that afternoon and she shoved the problem of her mother out of her mind again. Sacha was very strict about fixing the arrangements for their meetings. She had once, on the spur of the moment, stopped at the gallery on a Tuesday morning. She had been going by anyway on her way from the liquor store, where she had discovered a lone bottle of the French burgundy he liked so well. It was a present for him ; she would deliver it early.

To her surprise, the gallery door was locked. She rang the bell for what seemed forever, and finally he appeared, tousled and flushed.

"Hi, I was going by and I thought I'd bring you this," she said. She thrust the bottle at him.

He looked at it as if he didn't recognize what it was and at her the same way. Stammering, she backed away and left.

Later he had apologized. "I was working," he said. "I was in the middle of creation and in another world. You brought me back to this one so abruptly with your ringing at the door, I hardly knew where I was." He smiled ruefully. "If I let you, you would fill my every day and night, but I can't let you. I would never get my work done, do you see? Perhaps it would be better if you came only at the appointed times."

And so, Mondays, Wednesdays and Thursdays were Edna's "times". At one o'clock sharp in the afternoon, home by five, no exceptions.

She was still floating on the sensation of that afternoon's session when Len came home. He was fighting a cold and grumpy. Had she been more herself, and not wrapped up in the soft, warm cocoon of an interlude with Sacha, she might have picked a better moment, with poorer results.

They were dining alone that night, so Cara was with them, the three of them at the ridiculously large dining room table. She waited until Rhonda had served the soup before she began.

"Mother had another episode last night."

Len groaned. "Why don't you and Jack just put her away somewhere?"

"We can't do that. Besides she wouldn't stay anywhere we put her."

"They have guards at those places, you know."

"Are you going to put grandma in jail?" Cara asked, her eyes wide.

"Now look what you've done," Edna said to Len.

"No darlin'," Len said to Cara. "We're just trying to figure out how to look after her. She's kind of sick, but not sick enough to go to the hospital."

"Like when I had chickenpox?" Cara asked.

"Well, sort of."

"Chickenpox is icky," she said. "But it was nice when Rhonda looked after me." Rhonda had volunteered to sleep on a cot in Cara's room for a week, so she could be on hand in case the little girl needed something in the night.

Len looked at Edna.

"You can't be serious," she said.

"No, I guess you're right."

They stopped talking as Rhonda came in to clear away the soup plates and to serve the main course, a hamburger casserole that Bernice referred to grandly as "beef stroganoff". Anxious to appear efficient, Rhonda moved far too fast, whisking the soup plates away with one hand and serving the dinner plates with the other. Disaster struck, as usual, when she got to Len. The empty soup plate struck his wine glass on the way up, knocking it over and spilling the dark red liquid on the white tablecloth. Rhonda made a valiant grab for the glass as it teetered, forgetting about the plate in her other hand. The messy casserole slid gracefully off the plate and landed squarely in Len's lap.

He roared and stood up, dumping the mess on the carpet. Rhonda burst into tears and fled to the kitchen, where Edna hoped she would remember to get a wet cloth. In the meantime, she stuck a linen napkin under the spreading wine stain and attempted to scoop the stroganoff back onto the plate.

"For God's sake, I'm surrounded by the insane and the incompetent," Len shouted. Cara giggled. He glared at her, and stamped off up the stairs to change his trousers.

Bernice bustled in from the kitchen, clucking, and efficiently cleared away the mess. Len stamped back down the stairs and disappeared into the den, slamming the door behind him. It slammed open again immediately.

"That goddam dog has been in here again," he shouted. "There's red ink all over everything. Cara!"

Cara slid off her chair and ran towards the kitchen, just as Len appeared in the dining room doorway. He was about to go after her when Bernice emerged with a fresh serving of stroganoff. She set it down away from the wine stain and got fresh sliverware and another glass, making a new and pristine table setting.

"Come and sit down, Mr. Len," she said. "there's no harm done here. Eat your dinner and I'll go and clean up the den."

"Jesus,"Len muttered, but he sat and downed the wine.

"Sorry." Edna said.

"Is it too much to ask for a peaceful evening at home?" he said.

"Don't be silly, you'd be bored to tears. You'd better call your daughter back, her dinner's getting cold."

"What's she done, thrown herself bodily over the damn dog so I can't get at him?"

"Probably."

"She can wait a minute." He sighed and refilled his wine glass. "Okay, problem number one, your mother. We've got to do something or she's going to get run over or die of exposure or something, and then, God forbid, the neighbours will talk. Problem number two, Rhonda, who is getting clumsier all the time. Problem number three, the stupid dog, who's getting stupider all the time. My solution is this: we ship problem number two and three over to problem number one's house and everybody's happy."

"Len."

"Okay, okay," he said. "But what about the idea of sending Rhonda over to your mother's at night? Surely she could manage to keep the front door locked so she can't get out."

Edna considered for a moment. It was true that most of Hetty's wanderings took place in the dark hours after midnight. During the day, long years of household routine held her in a familiar pattern of cooking and cleaning, tidying the house and sweeping the floors. Only at night, unfettered by tasks, did her mind slide away.

"We could give it a try," she said doubtfully. "I don't know what Bernice will think."

"I'll sweeten the pot, pay Rhonda a little for doing it, and we'll see how it goes. We'll just have to hope the pair of them don't burn the place down between them."

Bernice was dubious, but agreed to try it for a while. To everyone's surprise, Rhonda proved a surprisingly ideal caretaker. Every night she would pack up the dinner her mother made and carry it over to Hetty's, where she would serve it up on trays in front of the television. The two of them would watch Lawrence Welk or Don Messer in a companionable silence. After the dinner dishes were washed, Rhonda would do her homework or watch more TV with Hetty until it was time to go to bed. Bernice had tied a couple of tin plates to Hetty's bedroom door, and on the nights when she wandered, Rhonda was alerted by the banging of the tins and simply followed Hetty down stairs and out the front door. She would let her stand on the sidewalk for a few minutes, then gently turn her around and lead her back up the stairs to bed. Her duties over for the night, she would promptly go back to sleep.

In the midst of her confusion, Hetty had somehow got hold of the notion that Rhonda was her sister Arlene, and so she was not surprised to see her out on the step, or to be led gently back to bed by her.

"Don't tell, Arlene," Hetty would say. "Don't tell Papa I was outside."

"I won't," Rhonda promised. "Now come back to bed."

Hetty's mistake was understandable; her sister Arlene had been nearly as clumsy as Rhonda, and she made no comment and showed no surprise when things were knocked over or broken. Without her mother's constant admonishments, however, Rhonda gradually relaxed and things stopped jumping out of her hands and crashing to the floor. She no longer had to fret about looking like an overgrown Shetland pony next to the elegant Mrs. Len, she no longer tensed in anticipation of Mr. Len's abrupt comings and goings, she no longer had to worry about dropping or burning things or about her mother yelling at her. At Hetty's house, Rhonda was in charge, and she showed an intuitive understanding and casual acceptance of the older woman's infirmities that astounded everyone but Rhonda herself. It didn't bother her at all that Hetty called her Arlene or that long hours would pass without a word spoken between them. She didn't mind a bit that Hetty put the snow shovel in the broom cupboard and the broom on the front porch. She was unembarrassed by Hetty standing on the front walk in her nightgown and undisturbed by the constant interruption of sleep. Rhonda had found her calling.

Bernice was more surprised than anyone, and more grateful than ever before at the way the Collins' seemed so magically to find solutions for all her problems. She continued to worry about Edna, but realized that there was little she could do, and besides, if things got out of hand, she was sure things could somehow be put right again in the same magical way. She would put her faith in Mr. Len. And if anyone asked where Mrs. Len disappeared to on so many winter afternoons, the answer would be "playing bridge".

Vera worried, too, although she had no idea what she was supposed to do about it. She missed their kitchen conferences, the sipping of tea, the sharing of gossip. Edna had even cancelled out several of their scheduled lunches, occasions Vera adored. She asked Mac if he had heard anything about the Collins. He often heard things down at the yard.

Mac pondered for a moment. "They say Len is building a big shopping mall just outside of Kingston, he and another bunch of big shots. One of these days he's going to take on too much and we'll see what happens to all his fancy friends. He'll be left holding the bag, all right. I hope for Edna's sake it doesn't happen, but if it does, it's long overdue."

This wasn't the sort of information Vera wanted, but it surprised her nonetheless. If that was what the crew down at Public Works was saying, then it must be the general consensus around town, too. She hadn't realized Len was flying so far or so fast. She wondered if she should say something. But what? "Edna, my dear, I'm sorry, but don't you know that your husband is in over his head and everybody in town knows you're having an affair?" Not that they did, not really, but there was enough speculation to cause concern.

She wondered what Len's reaction would be if he found out. Would he accost Sacha, demand to know what he thought he was doing, would there be an argument, an altercation, would it end in tragedy, with Sacha hemorrhaging and dying of bullet wounds while Len was led away in handcuffs by grim-faced policemen? Of course not, that was ridiculous, but she did spend a few moments wondering what it would be like to be fought over in such a dramatic fashion. Would he vent his anger at Edna, his passion so fierce that he couldn't bear to see her with another, would she be found with Len's fingerprints about her neck, telltale symbols of his intolerable, unbearable jealousy? "He killed for love!" the headlines would scream, and everyone would wonder what had prompted a woman like Edna, a woman who had it all, a woman who had a husband as handsome and dashing and rich as Len, to throw it away so carelessly and with such disdain. No, she decided, that wasn't Len's style either.

She entertained, for a second or two anyway, a delicious vision of Len, a hurt and bewildered Len, sobbing while she cradled him in her arms.

"Oh, Vera," he would say. "You're the only one who ever understands me." And she would pat his back and croon while she rocked his grief away, then lead him upstairs (damn, that peeling wallpaper again) and make love to him tenderly, restoring his faith in the honesty of women.

She regretted now the barriers she and Edna had set between them, the subjects that were never discussed. She wished that Edna had confided in her more, that she had let her talk about Len. If she had talked about Len, then maybe she would have talked about this other thing too. Vera was overwhelmed with curiosity about it. Where did they meet? How often? What was it like? Was he tender, worshipping her with his caresses? Or did he take her roughly, arrogantly, demanding what he knew she wanted to give? She was dying for the details, but unable to ask.

Francine heard rumours too, and asked Len if everything was all right, something she seldom did.

"Oh, everybody seems to think I've lost my mind with this shopping mall thing," he laughed. "They think I'm financing the whole thing myself, you know. I've put together a group of investors who are putting their money in, I just happen to own the land it's being built on, that's all." He grinned. "That and a lot of the stock."

That wasn't what she was asking him, but she let it lie. "What happens if it doesn't work out?"

"It'll work, don't worry."

But she did worry. Len had always been supremely self-confident, and she had to admit that things always did seem to work out for him. He always got what he wanted, no matter what stood in the way, but he was so busy with all of his shopping centres and subdivisions and real estate deals, she wondered if he was paying any attention at all to his wife. Francine had an almost psychic connection to the local grapevine; she could seldom specify where she had picked up a rumour or piece of news, but her connection was remarkably accurate. She had easily caught the ripple of speculation about the foreigner who had opened an art gallery. Edna was involved somehow, as were two or three other women around town. It could just be a little flap because he was such an odd character, but she doubted it. In her experience, where there was smoke, there was fire, at least ninety-five percent of the time.

She wasn't sure how Len would react if the ripple developed into a groundswell. She had discovered a long time ago that jealousy was not part of his nature. He hadn't batted an eyelash when she went out with other men; in the early days of their relationship, he laughed it off when she objected to the constant stream of pretty girls on his arm. But she wasn't his wife.

Wives were subject to different rules; it was one of the reasons she had never married, although she probably would have jumped into it fast enough if Len had ever asked her. Maybe. Not that there ever seemed to be many constraints on Edna, mind you, but what would happen if she became less discreet, if the full flower of her love affair became a topic of conversation, not in the backrooms and bars, but in front parlours and on the steps of the post office? How would Len react to the embarrassment of a wife who was known to dally? What would he do if she did something silly like run off with this artist fellow? She couldn't see Len in the role of cuckold.

Or would he ignore the whole thing, like he always did when something happened that didn't suit his purposes? Laugh it off, make a joke, shrug his shoulders? In all fairness, he had never been faithful to Edna, so how could he expect fidelity from her in return? But the rules of love were never fair, were they?

The only thing Francine knew for sure was that she wasn't going to be the one to tell Len Collins that his wife was fooling around.

Edna knew something was wrong as soon as walked in the door. The studio had lost it's peaceful sheltering feeling. Sacha was fiddling with the kettle, making tea, and barely turned around when she entered. He seemed agitated, and kept dropping things, the tea strainer, the spoon.

"What's wrong?" she asked, but he refused to answer. Instead, he sat her down on the day bed and picked up his brushes, then put them down again and went to lean on the railing of the loft, his hands clenched around the wood.

She got up and went to stand beside him.

"What's wrong?" she asked again.

"Maybe you should just go," he said, without looking at her. "I'm not in the mood today."

"If there's something wrong, maybe I can help." She rubbed his back, a soothing gesture, like one would use with a small child.

He sighed. "No, I don't think so."

"Try me."

He broke away from her and started to pace around the room. "No, I can't," he muttered.

"Can't what?" She wanted to scream at him to let it out, tell her what the problem was. Was it her? Had she done something wrong? Was it over?

He ran his hands through his hair. "It is just such a stupid thing, or at least it will seem that way to someone in your position."

It wasn't her then. She wanted to weep with relief.

"You see," he went on, "I sold a painting, or at least I thought I had sold a painting through an acquaintance in Toronto. His friend owns a gallery and he hangs many of my works, which he sells on, how do you call it? Consignment. This friend called me last month to tell me the good news, that someone would buy. And then today, this same friend calls me to tell me that the painting has been returned. The buyer has decided not to take it."

"Why?"

"He didn't say. It could be for a thousand different reasons. The wife didn't like it, or it wasn't the right colour to match with the walls, who knows?"

"Well, someone else will buy it, surely. Can't your friend just put it back in the gallery?"

"But you don't understand. When I thought the painting was sold, and that the money would be coming, I celebrated. I treated myself. I went out to dinner and bought new clothing and indulged in flowers and wine. Food for the soul. And now I don't have food for the body, you see."

She finally understood. Sacha had blown all the money before he had it in hand.

"I am so embarrassed. I cannot believe I was so stupid. But it is so hard, being an artist, and being in poverty all of the time when I love beautiful things so much."

"This is very simple," Edna said. "I'll make you a straight business proposition. I'll pay you the rest of the money for my portrait now, in advance."

"Oh, no, I cannot do that," he said. "That is not right. That is not how it is done."

"Nevertheless, that is how we're going to do it." She reached for her bag to get her chequebook. "I'm in a position to help you out a little, and that's the very least you must allow me to do." She would write him a cheque on her personal account, and Len would never know. Technically, she supposed, it was his money, since she had saved it out of the excess from the housekeeping account and her clothing allowance, which was always more than she ever spent, but it was in an account in her name and she would do what she wanted with it.

She wrote the date decisively, then hesitated.

"Is Sacha your full first name?" she finally had to ask. Stupid, she'd never thought about it before.

"Alexandre, with an "re" not an "er". Oh God, this is so embarrassing. I don't know how I'll ever repay you."

She signed her name with a flourish, and handed him the cheque. "I can think of a way," she said.

He folded the cheque carefully and put it in his pocket, and then he led her to the daybed.

The Annual Valentine's Dance was that night. She was sitting at her dressing table, trying to get the studs of her pearl earrings through her ears when Len came in. She had had her ears pierced when he started buying her expensive jewellery. She was afraid she might lose clip-ons. The holes had a tendency to grow over and she often had to punch through a thin layer of skin, especially if she hadn't been wearing earrings for a while.

Len had just showered and came into the room in nothing but a towel wrapped around his middle. He stood behind her, looking at her in the mirror.

"What are you looking at?"

"You." He put his arms around her. "Mmmm, you smell yummy."

"Don't, your going to mess up my hair and knock my earrings out. I'll lose them."

"I'll buy you a new pair." He nuzzled her neck.

"I'll never get ready if you keep doing that."

He slid his hands down the front of her dressing gown.

"Or that."

"Can we be late?" he asked.

"We're probably going to be anyway."

"Good."

Edna stiffened. So far, she had managed to keep Len and Sacha separate, apart, pigeon-holed into discrete compartments in her life, one here, the other across town, separated by distance and time. This was too soon, too much overlap. She pulled away.

"What's the matter?"

Get hold of yourself, she thought, you can do this. Don't let him know. She looked up at him and smiled.

He pulled her over to the bed and unwrapped her dressing gown, then pulled her down onto the spread.

Fortunately, all of the usual physical responses were there. Len was too good a lover and knew her too well not to arouse her, and her body became an ally in her deception. Her mind remained detached. Two men in one day, she thought. One right after the other. Well, well, well. It was bound to happen, I guess. What does this make me? A wanton? A harlot? Heavens, maybe even a trollop? She giggled, which Len mistook for encouragement.

They were very late for the dance. It had taken Edna nearly an hour to repair the damage to her makeup and hair and get dressed in her party clothes.

Isabel Jackson was there with Sacha in tow. Edna was hailed by Fred, who was delighted to see his favourite dance partner. He whirled her out onto the dance floor, where she could see both Len and Sacha as she turned. She began to giggle again. Two men, and now they were both in the same room with her. She felt unbelievably sexy.

"What's so funny?"

She looked down into Fred's plain, good-natured face and smiled at him.

"Nothing, Fred. I'm just having one hell of a good time, that's all."

He grinned back and whirled her round and round the room, faster and faster, the lights blurring as they spun, until the orchestra ended the song with a flourish and segued into a tango. Most of the other dancers left the floor, but Fred smiled up at her. "Ready for this?"

"Always."

They were one of the only couples on the floor who could tango, the other dancers contenting themselves with a choppy waltz step in time to the music. They hammed it up, sweeping dramatically in a diagonal across the floor. Edna wished she had a rose to clench in her teeth, like they always did in the movies. It was a complicated dance and required her to focus all of her attention on following Fred as he introduced impromptu steps and flourishes. When the music crescendoed, they finished in a triumphant sweep that ended with Edna bent backwards over Fred's arm.

It was then that she noticed Len and Sacha. They were standing together by the bar, deep in conversation. They looked so odd, from her upside down perspective, one tall and brown, one blonde and slender. My two men, she thought. My two men talking. Together. And then panic. What could they be talking about?

Fred wanted to hold the pose, to soak up the scattered applause that greeted their melodramatic performance, but she got one foot under her to regain her balance and pushed herself up.

"Thanks, Fred." She smiled at him and turned, walking towards the bar. She hoped she looked nonchalant, but she realized her hands were shaking. What if Sacha said something that gave them away?

They were talking about Russia, or at least Len was.

"Karl says there'll be war, sooner or later. The collectives are failing and the U.S.S.R. can't produce enough food to feed itself. It's as simple as that."

"Um huh."

Who was Karl, she wondered. Sacha looked bored.

"Hi guys," she said. "Who's going to get me a drink?"

"I will," Sacha said. "What would you like?"

"A glass of wine, please."

Len looked surprised. She never drank wine, except with dinner. Or with Sacha, she thought. Be careful.

"What were you talking about?" she asked. "Who's Karl?"

"He's an old guy in Montreal I've done some business with. Got out of Russia just before the war and got out of Europe just after. We've had dinner a couple of times and he filled me in on what was going on over there. Your artist fellow sure doesn't seem to know much about his own country."

"I don't think he ever actually lived there," she replied vaguely. "I think he said at one point that he grew up in Paris."

"His mother should have given him some geography lessons, then. He doesn't even seem to know that Odessa is on the Black Sea."

Sacha returned with her wine. He smiled as he handed it to her. "Madame", he said with a little bow. "Excuse me please, I must go and amuse my hostess." He bowed again towards Len and went off in search of Isabel.

Len's eyes narrowed as he watched him walk away. "If that's a Russian," he said, "I'm a yellowbellied sapsucker."

CHAPTER FIFTEEN

Vera woke up one morning in a determined frame of mind. She packed Mac's lunch for him and sent him off to work with three massive bologna sandwiches and a piece of apple pie left over from supper the night before. She checked that Stevie and Susan had scrubbed behind their ears and that they had their homework with them and watched out the front window as they walked down the block and out of sight. She piled the breakfast dishes in the sink and ran hot water over them.

Then she climbed the stairs to the tiny bathroom tucked under the eaves at the back of the house and started the water running in the bathtub. She still had a packet of bath salts left over from Christmas and this she tore open carefully, emptying the fragrant crystals into the water, watching as they foamed and swirled under the tap. She tried not to look in the mirror as she lowered herself into the tub. Sometimes when she was taking a bath she would forget and catch a glimpse of herself. The doughy whiteness of her torso always startled her.

She lay back in the hot water and tried not to think of laundry and dusting. It could all wait for today. She kept adding more hot water until the bathroom was thick with steam, and the mirror obscured. When she felt she had soaked long enough to let the fragrance of the bath salts seep into her skin, she took a washcloth and pushed back her overgrown cuticles. Her hands were rough, the nails ragged, but she would buff them smooth and shining and bathe them in hand lotion.

She was quite pink and cosily warm as she padded into her bedroom in a towel. This was the hardest part. She hadn't had a new dress in a long time. There were a depressing number of cheap cotton housedresses hanging in the closet. She pushed them aside, bunching them up against Mac's shirts. There. In the back. A little old-fashioned maybe, but quite lovely and it should fit if she wore a girdle. It was the last nice dress her mother had bought, before her father's stroke, when there had been money for things like nice dresses. It was a lovely rosy red and cut so that it hung from the shoulders, designed to hide bulging waistlines and sagging bosoms. Her mother had been a little smaller than she was, and the sleeves weren't quite long enough, but when Vera looked at herself in the mirror on the back of the closet door, she was well-satisfied with what she saw. She had her mother's colouring and the red suited her.

Shoes. Her feet hadn't changed in size, surely, there must be a pair of heels back in the closet somewhere. She had once spent quite a lot of money on nice shoes, always with heels, so that she would look taller. There were two pairs there, one brown, one a shiny black patent leather. The brown ones were out of the question with the red dress. The black shoes were just a little too dressy, she thought, but there was no alternative. She winced as she jammed her feet into them and teetered a little as she walked down the stairs.

She rummaged in the pockets of all their coats and between the dimes and quarters she found there and some from the old coffee can where she kept the housekeeping money, she scraped together five dollars. She would have her hair done.

She had no coat except the one she always wore, a grey check that she decided didn't look too bad with her black shoes. She added a silver brooch to the lapel. It wasn't real silver, but it was quite nice if you didn't look too closely.

She picked her way down the sidewalk. She knew that salt stains would show on her shoes later, but it hadn't snowed in the last few days and there were whole sections that were bare to the pavement. By the time she reached the beauty parlour, her feet were in agony.

She sank into the chair and luxuriated in having someone else wash her hair, massaging the shampoo deep into her scalp, warm rinse water sluicing over her neck. She loved the smell of Agnes Bartlett's little shop; the fragrant aroma of potions and creams blending with the sticky-sweet of hairspray and the odour of hot metal from the dryers. She could have fallen asleep while Agnes rolled the curlers in, except that Isabel Jackson was having a perm in the other chair. Isabel was full of gossip. Hannah Tyler had just had her kitchen remodelled, my, it must keep Rick going to keep up with her, musn't it? Morris Albright was in the hospital, everybody had thought it was cancer, but it turned out to be a double hernia, wasn't that a relief? Town Council was finally doing something about the sidewalk in front of the Post Office, it was about time.

Agnes, her mouth full of hairpins, grunted noncommittally in response to each item.

Vera, who for once in her life felt no need to join the conversation, had almost nodded off when Isabel started on Len.

"That Len Collins is sure making a splash," she said. "Why that shopping centre he's building must cost millions. Where on earth would Len Collins get money like that? I hope for Edna's sake he knows what he's doing."

So the men down at the yard had it right, Vera thought. Len was flying high and fast.

"If I were Edna, I'd bring that man up short and sharp," Isabel went on. "I don't know how she puts up with it, the way he carries on. I know I wouldn't take that from Fred."

Vera stiffened in her chair, then jumped when Agnes mistakenly jabbed her with a hair pin.

"Nosirree, husbands should be kept on a real short leash if you ask me." Isabel laughed. "That way they know who's boss."

Vera tried to picture Len on any sort of leash and snorted. No, the image better fitted Fred Jackson, who was short and bandy-legged and completely cowed by the unflappable Isabel. She thought she might point this out, but Isabel had gone on before anybody had a chance to reply.

"I said to Sacha the other day, Sacha my dear, I says, it's a good thing you're not mine. I'd have to keep you locked up to keep the women away from you. You've seen him haven't you, Agnes? The Russian artist? My goodness, it's a good thing I'm a married woman. Poor Fred, you should have seen the look on his face when I said that." She tittered then, and blushed a little.

Vera wanted to hear more of what Isabel was saying, but Agnes had finished rolling her hair, and put her under the dryer where the whir of blowing air drowned out any conversation. By the time she was done, Isabel had gone on to other topics.

She almost changed her mind then, but she had invested too much in the morning. Better to see it through.

When she reached the old candy store, she hesitated on the sidewalk. Was there anyone there? There was no way to tell from the look of the place, but then she noticed the small piece of cardboard in the window of the front door. "Open" it said, in tiny elegant lettering. Squaring her shoulders, she went in.

She hadn't known what to expect. Thick, gilt frames perhaps, sectioned off with heavy red rope suspended between solid, stainless steel posts. A doorman in a uniform with brass buttons. But that was silly, she realized. This wasn't an art museum, just a small gallery in a small town.

He was talking with a woman. She didn't know who it was, but she had had her hair streaked and was wearing a fur coat. Vera pretended to examine the paintings, although she was appalled at the ugliness of them. The prices made her gasp. Her feet hurt again. She undid her coat, letting it lie open so that the colour of her dress showed. She watched Sacha, for it must be Sacha, out of the corner of her eye.

He was flirting with the woman in the fur coat, even Vera could tell that. Occasionally, in the course of their conversation he would touch her on the arm or the shoulder, casually, yet letting his hand lie for just a fraction of a second longer than seemed natural. He held the woman's eyes while he talked, a faint smile lifting the corners of his mouth. Vera could see that the woman loved it, leaning in closer to him while she talked, laughing a little too loudly.

She moved along the wall, leaning forward to peer at the paintings. There was an iron staircase in the corner of the room that led up to the second floor. That must be where he lives, she thought. That must be where Edna goes to be painted, for there was no evidence of brushes or easels on the ground floor. That must be where she meets him, where they...... if they.....

She had to admit it would be terribly romantic, meeting a clandestine artist lover in a garret. She hadn't ever been entirely sure what a garret was, but had always imagined it as high and airy and very much like this. Did he flip the little cardboard sign over when they were together, she wondered. Would the front door be locked with the announcement "Closed" tucked in the corner to keep everyone away? Was that the signal that the artist was occupied, not with art, but with Edna? Or Isabel. Or the woman with the streaked hair and the fur coat.

Finally the woman was leaving. Sacha walked her towards the door, stopping her just before she left to take her hand and kiss it goodbye.

Oh, brother, Vera thought, but she was impressed nonetheless.

He turned to her then. "May I help you?" he asked.

"I'm, um, I'm just looking," Vera said, peering up at him. She leaned in to him and smiled, expecting that he would smile in return, and let his hand touch her shoulder or her arm, letting it lie there just a little longer than seemed natural, that he would hold her eyes with his while they talked and that she would laugh just a little too loudly. But his eyes swept over her, taking in her shabby coat and her black patent shoes and her cheap purse. They saw the work-reddened hands that, in spite of her best intentions, she had forgotten to slather with cream, the dress that was just a little too tight, the tawdry pin she had fastened to her lapel. She knew she smelled, not of flowery bath salts, but of cheap hairspray.

And he dismissed her. "Let me know if you see anything you like," he said and he turned his back and went to stand by the front window.

Vera fled. The cardboard sign on the front door fluttered to the floor as she slammed the door behind her. She went down the steps as fast as she could without tripping on her heels and then ran until she was at the corner and out of sight. She stepped squarely in a muddy pile of slush as she crossed the sidestreet. Somewhere between the second and third blocks she realized that she had dropped a glove, but her feet hurt too badly for her to go back to look for it. It started to snow.

She was crying by the time she reached her front step. Inside the front hall she kicked off the black patent shoes and threw her coat over the bannister. She removed her stockings and wiggled out of her girdle and threw them on top of the coat. She went into the kitchen and made herself tea while the tears rolled down her face.

What had she been thinking? She didn't know. She had known only that she wanted to see him, to place him in a context so that she could understand what was happening to Edna, or so she reassured herself. It wasn't as if she would ever be interested in someone like that, God knows, she had just wanted her suspicions confirmed. How could she have known that he would look at her as if she were insignificant, as if she wasn't important enough for even the smallest of courtesies, as if she wasn't fit to breathe the air in his gallery? But she should have known. It was the same way Len looked at her.

She wept for real then, giving in to shuddering sobs, humiliated, mortified, and then, for some reason, sorry for Edna. Did she know she wasn't the only one? Vera was sure of that. Poor Edna, destined never to be the only one. Just like I'm destined to be the one nobody wants, she thought, and cried a little harder. She went through a whole box of kleenex before she finally got up and did the breakfast dishes.

She had the beds made and her girdle and shoes put away by the time Stevie and Susan came home from school. She had supper started and her coat hung up by the time Mac came home from work. She was fussing with getting the potatoes started when he came in. He stopped in the doorway instead of heading straight for the fridge to get a beer, as he usually did. Startled, she looked up at him.

He had a smile on his face. "Is this some sorta special day?" he asked.

Of course. She hadn't changed out of the red dress yet, she realized, and she had had her hair done.

She managed a smile in return. "No, nothing special."

He shrugged. "I just wondered. You look beautiful." And he continued on his way to the fridge.

She thought she had cried all the tears she could that afternoon, but she found she had one or two left, and she brushed them away as she covered the potatoes with boiling water. For once in his life, Mac Dunlop had thought of the perfect thing to say.

Francine was curious too, but not curious enough to go to much trouble over it. She'd seen the artist a few times around town. Occasionally he would come into the drug store and rummage through the after-shave lotions until he found an elusive bottle of men's cologne. There wasn't much of a selection for him. The men on the island didn't go in much for cologne.

Hannah Tyler, if she was in the store, would swoop over as soon as she saw him, taking him protectively by the arm and pulling him close to her to speak of toiletries in hushed tones. Francine wasn't the only one who noticed.

"Is that that artsy-fartsy Russian fella?" Jim Macdonald asked one time when not only Hannah, but Marion Rensall had cornered Sacha by the razor blades.

"Yup," said Marshall Benson as he slurped his coffee. "I'm gonna get me a paint brush, I am. Of course," and here his eyes twinkled, "then I'd have to find a paint pot to dip it into wouldn't I?"

He'd caught Cory Taylor by surprise. Cory snorted the mouthful of coffee he had just taken out through his nose and all over the counter, and Francine had to go find a wet cloth to mop it up with.

Jim leaned back on his stool, so he could get a better look. "Now what colour paint do you suppose that fella uses most?" he asked with an air of innocence.

"Pink, I expect," said Marshall and they had all hooted.

But Francine knew better. In spite of his long hair and his elegant clothes, in spite of his exaggerated mannerisms and his precise speech, Sacha Karensky was all man. She could practically smell the musk rising off him. Just like Len, she thought, but this one's probably not nearly so amusing.

She'd seen him again at the Tyler's party. Rick Tyler sometimes asked her to tend bar when they had large gatherings, and she really didn't mind as long as Len and Edna weren't there. They weren't at parties often these days; Len was frequently out of town and Edna seemed to have dropped out of sight.

She'd been working behind the makeshift bar Rick had set up in the hallway that led from the front door past the living and dining rooms to the kitchen. Hannah had set up a buffet on the dining room table and most of the guests were clustered around it, picking at trays of cheese and pickles and crackers. She'd been busy mixing drinks up until then, but now took advantage of the lull to stretch her legs. She'd wandered into the kitchen but had stopped abruptly when she realized that Sacha and Isabel Jackson were there, huddled in close conversation. They hadn't seen her. She slipped back to her place behind the bar, but if she leaned back against the wall, she could just see them.

Isabel took something from her purse and laid it on the kitchen table. A chequebook. She signed her name with a flourish, then tucked the cheque into Sacha's front pocket. He took her face in his hands and kissed her forehead.

It was only then that Francine realized that someone else was watching, too. Fred Jackson was standing in the dining room doorway, his face a mask of disbelief and disgust. Francine ducked away out of sight.

I wonder how many of them he's taking money from? she thought. I wonder if I should say something to Len? She began to giggle to herself. No, we'll just let Len find out all by himself, she decided. It'll serve him right to be on the other end of a con for once.

She giggled away intermittently for the rest of the party.

Edna knew he was gone as soon as she drove up. The gallery had a shuttered, closed-in look, that same look of abandonment that summer cottages have in the wintertime, the nobody's home look. She ran to the front door and rang the bell, knowing even as she did it that there would be no answer. She scraped the frost away from one of the front windows and peered inside, her hands cupped around her eyes to block the glare from the bright winter sun. All of the ugly and disturbing pictures that had hung on the white walls of the gallery were gone.

She tried the front door, but it was locked, so she ran around to the back, where there was a little door and entranceway with a broom and garbage pail. This door was locked too, but the broom had been left outside, probably so that Sacha could knock the snow from his boots before he went back into the gallery. She looked around. The house next door was quite close, but there were no windows overlooking her and she was hidden from the street by a garden shed. She picked up the broom and smashed in the glass window of the door with the wooden handle, hoping that the sound of breaking glass wouldn't attract any attention. It didn't. She reached inside and unlocked the door.

The walls, which had looked so fresh and cool and clean with paintings on them, now looked stained, hooks hanging askew and brighter patches outlining where the pictures had once been. She ran up the iron staircase to the studio. The daybed was still there, but when she looked in the closet, the camel hair coat and the rest of his clothes were gone. The little curtained-off bathroom held no sign of his presence; no razor or toothbrush or lotion. Dirty dishes were piled in the sink, but gone too were the cans of turpentine and the pile of brushes that had littered the counter. The wooden easel had been taken away, but the old quilt that had covered her portrait was thrown in the corner. She lifted it and looked.

There was a pile of canvasses stacked underneath, and she pulled them out and spread them across the floor. The only way she could tell which one was hers was by the splash of emerald green at the bottom, the green of the silk blouse she had shivered in all winter. The rest of the painting was as twisted and grotesque as the landscapes downstairs had been, but only a fraction as complete. Her head was marked by a slash of brown paint across the canvass, what she assumed were her eyes were far too close together and dwarfed by a clumsily drawn nose. Everything was wrong; the colour, the light, and especially the perspective, which foreshortened everything and pulled it up, away from the viewer, so that it seemed as though you were looking at it from somewhere on the floor. The others were the same, with only the differing details of colour.

She sank to the floor on her knees and pulled the quilt over her head, inhaling the lingering scents of oil paint and turpentine.

No. It was the only thought she was capable of. No, no, no, no, no, no, the drumming of this single syllable in the darkness of the quilt and her mind. She didn't know how long she knelt there, rocking with the rhythm of denial, but her next conscious thought was that she couldn't breathe. It took her a moment to realize that this was probably because of the quilt over her head. What does it matter? she thought, but she pulled the quilt away and lay with her head on it for a while. She wanted to cry, but no tears would come.

When she finally moved, she was stiff and dizzy. She stood swaying for a moment, blinking in the sunlight, which had marched across the gallery floor and now reached the edge of the loft. Slowly, she bent down and picked up her distorted canvas image, and without a backward glance, went down the wrought iron stairs and out the front door, leaving it ajar. Somehow she found her car keys and somehow she drove home. Slipping in the front door, she mounted the stairs and went straight to the darkest corner of the attic, where she propped the canvas against the wall and threw an old slip cover over it.

Len was full of news at dinner that night.

"I was talking to Fred Jackson this morning," he said as he carved his pork chop. "He says that so-called Russian artist has disappeared in a hurry. Took off in the middle of the night with a thousand bucks of Fred's money. Left umpteen contractors on the hook too. Apparently he never got around to paying for all those renovations he made to the old Harris place."

"Is that so." Edna had been pretending to eat dinner, shoving food around her plate, but now she gave up even that pretence and sat very still. "Does anyone know where he's gone?"

"No and it's a good thing too. Fred is livid. Apparently that silly Isabel had him painting her picture and gave him the money up front. Now there's no artist, no money and no picture. If Fred gets his hands on him, he'll kill him." He chuckled. "God knows how many others he had on the hook. I expect we'll hear as time goes on and husbands start checking their bank accounts. God some women are silly."

Edna thought she was going to faint.

"Hey, are you okay?" Len asked. "You look kind of pale."

"I'm really not feeling very well," she said.

"Me, neither," said Cara. "I don't think I can possibly eat carrots."

"Eat." Len said. "They help you see in the dark."

Edna excused herself and went to bed. I am bereft, she thought as she huddled under the covers. Bereft was one of those wonderful words from English novels that seemed so quaint on first acquaintance, but proved to be entirely appropriate when you needed them. If bereft meant a shuddering constriction of the heart, a great, boneshaking emptiness, then she was truly bereft.

Her mind went round and round in an attempt to make some kind of sense of Sacha's abrupt departure. There had been no note, no sign left for her, no signal that she had meant anything to him at all. Am I truly stupid, or just naive? she wondered. Did he love me at all? Was I just another foolish, bored housewife, someone to toy with, someone with whom to idle away the boredom of winter afternoons in a small town? Someone to foot the bill? She swung from mood to mood, first hurt, then embarrassed, then angry, then hurt again, but over every mood lay a thick and suffocating layer of longing.

She tried to recall and catalogue every moment of her time with Sacha. She recreated scenes of their lovemaking on the daybed, filling herself with such empty yearning and despair that she was sure that at any moment she would stop breathing from the pain. She pictured scenes of reconciliation, where his sudden absence would be explained away, revealed as a silly misunderstanding, an overreaction, a jealous and hysterical misinterpretation. He would get in touch with her, she was sure, let her know where he was, provide an explanation for his sudden disappearance. He couldn't just leave her without a word.

She told Bernice she had the flu, but that bought her only a limited respite. After three days of lying in bed, she knew the time was coming when she would have to get up and at least make a pretence of getting on with life. She toyed briefly with the idea of spending the rest of her days in a decline, like a romantic heroine in a European novel. What was the term? Melancholia. Diagnosis for a lifetime of invalidism, of lying on a sofa or bed in a flowing gown, while bearded doctors huddled in consultation outside the door, recommending the taking of baths in Germany or fresh air cures in Switzerland. It appealed to her, this notion of genteel decay, but she knew it would never fly. Len would simply call in Dr. Simpson who would prescribe antibiotics or tonics or God forbid, antidepressants, pat her on the head, tell her she was a good girl and expect her to be up and about in two or three days. No, she was going to have to deal with this, find some way to cope.

Besides, by the third day she was exhausted by her own sorrow. She discovered then that she could take the sorrow and isolate it, put it in a box and lock it away in a corner of her heart, to be taken out only when she had time to dissect and examine it, away from distractions and digressions. It took practice, this knack of walling off, and used up an enormous amount of energy, but at least it allowed her to get out of bed.

Len did his best to cheer her up.

"Tell you what", he said. " I have to go to Montreal next week. Why don't you come with me?"

But Edna couldn't. She might miss the ring of the phone. Sacha might call and she wouldn't be here and Bernice might forget to give her the message. Or a letter might arrive, and Rhonda, who had been known to do such things, might think it was just another piece of junk mail and throw it away. Or Mud would chew it up before she had a chance to read it. Or it would somehow get mixed up with Len's business mail and be taken to his office at the store, where Mabel would open it and blushingly show it to her boss. It was one thing to move slowly back into the rhythm of the household and resume some semblance of domestic routine; it was quite another to go traipsing off to another province where the effort of making conversation with strangers, and most of all with Len, would require reserves that she quite simply didn't have yet.

"No", she said to Len. "I still don't feel well enough."

He shrugged. "Suit yourself."

Instead she busied herself with a thousand household tasks. She told Bernice she was going to clean the attic and in the process of sweeping and scrubbing and reorganizing, buried her grotesque portrait behind a stack of boxes and a crate of old toys. She polished already gleaming silver and dismantled the glass chandelier in the dining room, bathing each sculpted crystal in a solution of water and vinegar. She sorted Cara's clothing, setting aside outgrown items for the church rummage sale. She swept the basement. Nothing was tidy enough, nothing clean enough. Bernice might have been offended by all this frantic cleaning, seeing it as a reflection on her performance as a housekeeper, except that she understood that Edna was dealing with some inner despair that required mindless, numbing, bustling activity to quell.

When Edna could find no more busy work, she walked, further and longer than she had ever walked before. These were the times when she allowed herself to unlock the sorrow box and peek inside. She stayed away from her own neighbourhood and never walked upstreet, where she would run into too many people with whom she might have to speak. She thought that these people should be able to see that she was heartbroken, just by looking at her, but they didn't seem to and if she ventured down the main street, they were constantly intruding with banal comments about the weather. Even a simple "Good morning" was too distracting. Framing a reply could open a hole in her mind where a tiny memory of Sacha might slip away, unnoticed, forever.

Len realized she was behaving a bit oddly, when he had time to think about it at all, but he was always busy and away a lot. Cara knew only that her mother had retreated even further into somewhere else, a place she had always been excluded from anyway. Bernice watched Edna carefully, but had an intuition that the trouble that had knocked on their door had somehow passed them by.

Vera knew what had happened. Someday Edna might tell her about it, just as someday Vera might tell her about Len, but that would occur at some distant point in the future, when she was sure it wouldn't matter anymore.

In the meantime, each of them decided they would just leave well enough alone.

CHAPTER SIXTEEN

One morning the sun rose and Edna realized it was spring. Winter nearly always parted abruptly from the island, decamping suddenly in the middle of the night, leaving behind only slushy grey mementos in shady corners that soon melted away in the balmy air. Crocuses bloomed exuberantly with raucous encouragement from choruses of returning birds. There was a different quality to the wind, a hint of warmth and the subtle scent of awakening buds. Winter would still make a half-hearted attempt to reclaim the island, briefly, as if it regretted its hasty departure, but it would be scorned and finally skulk away like an unwelcome lover.

She had intended to go for a walk, but as she stood on the back step in a patch of warm sunlight, she found herself idly wondering if she should do something with the garden. The grounds had been landscaped, of course, Len would see to that and the front flowerbeds had been planted with junipers and spruces, clustered around the foundation to frame and protect the house. Bill Braxton, who cut their lawn, would plant geraniums and marigolds and petunias in clumps in front of the shrubs, and keep the weeds out of the beds, but that was as far as he would go.

The back yard was largely ignored, except to keep it tidy and mown. Weedy maples lined up across the back fence, shading the scraggly forsythia and the cast-iron birdbath, which no bird ever used. There's not enough cover here for them, Edna thought, that's why they don't use it. Somewhere inside her mind, she felt the nibble of a fledgling interest. She had once enjoyed working in an old garden. She seemed to remember that it had kept her hands busy while her mind was free to wander.

She took a trowel from the shed behind the coach house and started digging in a back corner, where her efforts wouldn't be too noticeable and where there was nothing but an overgrown snowball bush. She chopped it back to manageable proportions with a pair of clippers and excavated the soil around it, finding comfort in the feel of the sandy loam as she sifted it with her fingers, meticulously removing tiny weeds and grass roots. She knew it was still too early and too wet for gardening, but was reluctant to let go of the tiny piece of enthusiasm she had latched onto.

Peat moss would help this, she thought and she drove to the florists' hauling several bags into the back garden by herself and digging the spongy stuff deep into the soil.

What to plant? She didn't know. She knew what she didn't want. She didn't want the mawkish marigolds and petunias and pansies Bill Braxton grudgingly planted at the front of the house. Or geraniums. She went to the library and was directed to the garden section, leafing through book after book that described how to grow vegetables, perennials, herbs, fruit trees and even Japanese meditation gardens. Most of these books recommended complicated sprays and chemical treatments as the only way to deal with pests, but she found this as repellent as the bugs apparently did.

And then, on the very bottom library shelf, she found an old tattered copy of a book called "Companion Planting", which explained that if you planted garlic with rose bushes, it would keep the aphids away; if you put basil with your tomato plants, it would help them grow; and if you set a row of the despised marigolds around a vegetable garden, insects would positively flee the area.

I know how they feel, she thought, but she liked the idea of counterbalancing one plant with another. Floral talismen to keep evil away. If only life worked like that.

She decided that the truncated snowball was the perfect centrepiece for an experiment in daylilies. The orange ones were readily available; they were an old pioneer favourite and had long since escaped the bounds of farmhouse dooryards and spread through abandoned fields and ditches along back roads, where the County workmen did not, as was usual along the main highways, ruthlessly cut and spray. There were pockets of yellow ones as well, though these were less common.

The lilies hadn't bloomed yet of course, but she could find them easily enough by the distinctive spiky leaves that lay in brown and withered mounds. She thought they should probably be moved in the fall, but she didn't want to wait, so she drove country roads until she found an enormous clump along the driveway of an old farm. When she knocked at the door, an elderly woman in a flowered housedress answered.

"My lilies? My goodness, child, you're welcome to all you can take. I can't keep the darn things under any kind of control. As soon as you dig them up, they produce ten more bulbs. Are you sure you want them?"

Edna was sure, and had brought a shovel, but was ill-prepared for the hard, stony ground, so different from her own loamy soil.

"Clayton will be up from the barn soon. Why don't you let him dig them up for you? You'll ruin your back," the woman called.

But Edna liked the way the lilies clung tenaciously to the rocky soil, admired their ability to grow under such adverse conditions, and in the end, after an hour's muddy labour, triumphantly extracted several large knots of the bulbs.

"Mind, now, you keep on top of them things. They'll take your garden over. Are you sure you won't stay for tea?"

In the end, she did, after carefully wrapping the lilies in damp newspaper. The woman wanted to give her tea in the parlour, a room that was reserved for company and was covered in antimacassars, but Edna preferred to stay in the cosy kitchen and sip her tea at the enormous pine table. The woman cleared away seed catalogues and pieces of farm equipment and wiped down the oilcloth while the tea steeped.

"How long have you lived here? Edna asked her.

"Oh, ever since Clayton and I was married. I was seventeen. Clayton's lived here all his life, you know. This was his father's farm and his father before that and way on back further than anybody can remember." The woman brought out a plate of shortbread cookies on a cracked blue and white plate.

"Did you ever want to live anywhere else?" What Edna really meant was "Did you ever want to live with anyone else?", but she could hardly ask that.

"Well, yes", the woman chewed her shortbread thoughtfully. "At one time I thought it would be so nice to have one of them new bungalows they built behind the Charles block, you know, with lots of water and no worry about the hydro and all, and no farm muck tracked in, but I don't know what Clayton would have done with hisself in town. The only thing he's ever worked at is farming, and I guess he don't know much else. In the end, we stayed here and I expect I'll die here and that will be the end of the farm unless one of the kids wants to take over."

"How many children do you have?" She was curious about this woman, whose life seemed so straight-forward and uncomplicated.

"Four. Two boys, two girls. Nice and even."

"Do they still live around here?"

"Just the one. Bob got a good job in Kingston at the penitentiary, and Dale went into the army. Roseanne married one of the Harding boys and they moved out west. The only one that stayed around is Dot. Her husband helps Clayton out with haying and such and he may want to take over altogether if he can't find a steady job. All the kids would liked to have stayed here, but there's no work, you know, and farming don't pay no more." She put down her teacup and smiled at Edna. "But you don't want to hear my troubles. Tell me about your garden."

Edna explained what she wanted to do. The woman nodded.

"Certainly if you're just starting it out, them orange lilies will fill some holes in real fast, but mind you keep on top of them, or they'll take over. And come back if you want some more."

Edna finished her tea and hurried home to put the lilies in. When she got there, Len was pacing in the garden.

"Who dug all this up?" he demanded when he saw her. "Kids? What a mess!"

"I dug it up."

"You? Why?"

"Because I'm going to plant a garden."

He looked puzzled. "Look, if you want to do something with that back corner, that's fine, but let me put Bill on for a few extra hours and he can do the heavy work. There's no need for you to be scrabbling around in the dirt."

"But I want to."

He was even more puzzled. "But you'll ruin your hands if you keep digging. Especially without gloves." He grabbed her hand. Sure enough, dirt had wedged itself under her fingernails and her knuckles were stained a grimy brown.

She pulled her hand away. "Look, I really want to do this, okay. I want to take just one little corner of this huge yard and make it mine. God knows I don't do anything else."

"I don't care", he said finally. "You can do whatever you want, but at least wear gloves so you don't look like some farmer's wife when we go out."

She thought of the farm woman in her untidy kitchen, her workworn hands and the lines of peaceful resignation on her face. She had long since accepted her lot in life and had achieved a serene balance with it, or so it seemed. She wouldn't mind looking like that, not at all, but Edna supposed she could give in to Len on this one point.

"All right. I'll wear gloves so I won't embarass you when we go out."

Then he noticed the bundle of newspapers she was carrying.

"What's in there?"

"Orange day lilies."

"Oh, for crying out loud, not those damn things. My mother planted those in the garden and they took the whole place over. She spent more time digging them out than she did anything else," He threw his hands up in mock despair. "My wife, the farmer. For God's sake, wear a hat so you don't get sunstroke. Unless it's too late."

She separated the bulbs into four clumps and planted them against the hydrangea backdrop. Vera's aunt had yellow lilies in her backyard and Edna added those as well. She would include some more exotic asiatic ones too. To fill in between the lilies she dug in primrose and snowdrops. They should have been planted in the fall, but she hoped that it was still early enough that they would provide some sort of colour in her little corner.

Len was impatient with the piles of books and magazines lying around and puzzled that Edna had found such an odd occupation, but she knew that he was a little relieved that she was more like her old self. She didn't really care what he thought. The feel of the cool earth as it slipped between her fingers soothed her. The rhythm of digging and sifting lulled her into calmness. She expanded her original garden and made plans for the fall. She would scatter daffodils across the lawn, she decided, in a natural random pattern that would explode in yellow in the spring. Iris and bluebells could go over by the coachhouse, where it was sunnier. She planted forsythia and mock orange bushes in a crescent around the birdbath and was rewarded one hot July morning when a goldfinch swooped down to drink, its bright yellow plumage flashing against the grey cement.

Her lilies bloomed for her that summer, but little else did. Still, the bright orange of their flamboyant heads cheered her, and she began to see the pattern her garden would take, how it should be sculpted so that it all seemed wild, as if nature had thrown a palette against the earth, smudging it with colour. The next spring the back yard was yellow with daffodils. They slowly faded, only to be replaced by the exuberant purple of old-fashioned iris, segueing into anemone and coneflower and coreopsis.

Sacha did not preoccupy her now. She thought of him at odd moments, when some reminder would ambush her thoughts, and briefly she would experience the old heavy sadness, but this happened less and less often.

Then, after more than a year had gone by, the postcard arrived. It showed a tourist's view of Niagara Falls. On the back was a brief, scribbled note.

"You are still the best model I ever had. Meet me at Palace of the Moon at nine on Thursday. I'll wait for an hour.. Sacha"

Cara had finally learned how to swim.

"Can we go out on the lake, Daddy?" she pestered. "I can swim now."

"Soon, Cara Mia, soon."

"When?"

It was a dinnertime refrain that was growing tedious for everyone but Cara.

"You said, Daddy, you said."

"I did, indeed," Len would reply. "We'll go soon."

In the meantime, Cara practiced swimming whenever she could, so she could be ready. She wasn't sure what she was supposed to be ready for, but if swimming was a required part of it, she would master the art.

"Are you sure she's big enough to take out there?" Edna asked privately.

"Of course she is. I was out there with Dad at that age. Don't worry, I won't let anything happen to her."

As it turned out, the timing couldn't have been better.

"I don't have anywhere I have to be until the weekend," Len said to her on Tuesday evening. The weather forecast looks pretty good. I thought Cara and I could go to Main Ducks on Thursday. We'll stay overnight, she'd like that, and we'll come back Friday. That okay?"

It was more than okay, in spite of the reservations Edna had about Cara out on the lake. It cleared her of the need for excuses and manipulations. Her Thursday night would be free. There was no question of her going with them; this was Cara's trip, an adventure with her swashbuckling father.

Cara was beside herself with excitement. Edna helped her pack her clothes, not in a heavy suitcase that might shoot dangerously across the cabin in a heavy sea, but in a soft duffel bag, with a rope at the top so it could be tied down. Bernice organized a mountain of food; a chicken to be eaten cold, hotdogs and marshmallows for roasting on shore, cookies and a chocolate cake.

Len was scornful. "We don't need all this stuff," he said. "We can just catch fish."

"But what if you don't?" Edna pointed out. "What are you going to do then?"

"I don't even like fish, Daddy."

"Aw, but you've never had it done the right way, rolled in cornmeal and fried in lard," Len said. Cara still looked dubious.

"Okay, okay. We'll let Bernice pack us off with enough food to feed the Canadian navy. What the heck, we need the ballast."

Cara had been on short excursions with her father often enough to know the departure drill; cast off the lines, scramble aboard, pull in the heavy rubber bumpers that hung between the hull and the dock. This done, she stood on the bow and watched as the town and her mother receded, growing smaller and smaller until finally they disappeared. After they were out in the bay, her father let her steer the boat. She knew the rules about buoys; which one was which depended on whether you were coming or going.

The first part of their voyage was routine. She had been "down bay" many times and occasionally as far as the cove at the eastern tip of the island, where they would tie up for the night, lazily swimming and eating until it was time to fall asleep to the gentle slap, slap, slap of the waves against the hull.

This time they went right past the cove and kept going, on around the point and out into the gap, where her island ended and the next one hadn't begun yet. She realized the difference right away. The swell increased and the wind blew stronger, coming straight in from the broad expanse of Lake Ontario.

They kept fairly close to shore, so Len could point out the landmarks that told them where they were. Cape Vesey, or The Rock, as it was known locally, pugnaciously jutted out into the water. They skirted around Waupoos Island and Smith's Bay. Len told her the story of poor Sarah Pierce, who, one day in 1866 had taken her family out in a rowboat and lost them in the twinkling, deceptive waters. There were six Pierce children in the boat that afternoon, as well as three neighbours, and when the boat overturned, Sarah was able to reach only Michael Harrington, holding him to herself and the drifting boat until finally they washed ashore. Five sons and a daughter claimed by the lake. Only one little girl left at home.

Cara wondered what it was like for that little girl, growing up with a grief-stricken mother. Did she hear tales of her lost brothers and sister? Was she constantly reminded that she had been spared, where the others were taken? Or was there a vast and arid conspiracy of silence surrounding them, lest the gods were reminded that they had missed one, and be tempted to make their vengeance complete? Cara wondered if she too had had a brood of siblings who had somehow been snatched away and now no one would mention their names or comment on their existence.

Her father laughed when she asked this. "No, Cara Mia, you've always been the only one. When you arrived, we realized that we had a little girl who was so perfect, we didn't need any more kids. They would have paled in comparison."

She was comforted by this, but still she wondered what it would be like to live in a bustling and crowded household, with many sisters and brothers, all of whom had their own concerns and endeavours. After she thought about it for a while, she decided she wouldn't like it much. Too noisy.

They headed for McMahon Bluff, then Little Bluff and Halfmoon Point, where they often went swimming or picnicking. From there they headed southeast, around the lake side of Timber Island where there had once been bald eagles, and past Gull Shoal, barely above water, but with thousands and thousands of birds squawking and quacking at their noisy approach.

After that it was open water and Cara could convince herself that they were really out on the seven seas, she and her father, pirates looking for a hapless Spanish galleon to board and capture. The swell was a constant thump now, and she had to be careful walking across the cockpit, adjusting her stride to take advantage of the times when the boat was climbing a wave so she could reach a handhold to steady herself before it slid down again to slap against the bottom of a trough.

"False Duck coming up on starboard," Len called.

She looked, and could just make out a lighthouse off in the distance. It was a few minutes before she could see the island itself, low-lying, covered with scrub and twisted, stunted trees. The land seemed to be undulating and shimmering in the sunlight, and it wasn't until they were close that she realized that every tree and rock was covered with birds, roosting, nesting, preening, squabbling birds. Vast flocks would rise as one, circle the island and with a great flapping of wings, settle again, displacing other flocks, which in turn would rise, circle and return.

False Ducks passed by and they were into the most dangerous part of their journey. She knew from the stories she had been told that the eastern end of Ontario's lakebed rose abruptly. Still deep at Rochester, its bottom tilted up to meet the conjunction where the lake drained into the St. Lawrence River. Storms and high winds had the entire length of the lake to gather force before the agitated water smashed into the tilted lakebed and churned the water into a maelstrom that could capsize a ship, or drive it onto evil rocks where it would be battered to pieces. These rocks, and the lakebed itself, held their own treachery. They were full of iron, enough to deceive a compass, and could falsely lure sailors to destruction.

The lake was mannerly today. Len had been worried that Cara might be seasick, the swell took some getting used to, but she sat beside him at the wheel of the boat drinking in the sunlight on the water and the vast blue that surrounded them.

"Look," he said pointing. "You can just see the lighthouse."

She oriented her sight along his outstretched arm, until she spotted the white cap, which slowly resolved itself into a red and white striped tower, and beside it a house, with large windows that looked out unblinkingly at their approach.

The boat slid past the limestone cliffs on the north shore. Len throttled the engine back. "Look over the starboard side. I want to show you something."

She hung over the rail, searching the water until she spotted timbers lying on the bottom.

"What is it?" she asked.

"A shipwreck. The Schooner John Randall. She went down in '21 in a storm."

Cara gasped. Stories were one thing, seeing an actual boat submerged in water, never to rise again, was another. So close to shore. They had almost made it.

The tiny harbour lay at the northeast end of Main Ducks, the smaller Yorkshire Island guarding its entrance. The mouth was only twenty or so feet wide. Cara had expected a larger bay, more like the one that lay at the foot of her town, with room for many boats and ships. She could see bottom as they manoeuvred through the buoys and coasted into the dock. Surprisingly, there were no other boats there.

It took her a moment to adjust to the lack of movement and absence of swell when she stepped off the boat. She ran up the grassy bank to look at the huddled fishermen's cottages while Len secured their lines. It's like a little village, she thought. It must have been fun to live out here in the summer. But then she thought of the winter, with its gales and snowfalls and shuddered. Whoever was here in bad weather would have hunkered down in the cottages and closed the doors tightly against the blow, trying not to think about being stranded on this tiny dot in the middle of the lake.

Something slithered at her feet; a snake. She wasn't afraid of them, like the silly girls at school, but its sudden movement startled her. She must remember to walk carefully; the island was full of water snakes, known to be bad-tempered on land. She ran down the dock again and danced along it while Len adjusted bumpers and ropes.

"What do you want to do first?" he asked when he had finished.

"Explore!"

They walked along the edge of the harbour until they found the road that led around it and across the fields to the lighthouse.

"The road cuts through the middle," Len said. "But let's walk along the south shore."

They cut through brush until they reached the stony beach. Cara knew that Galloo Island lay somewhere off in the distance; the islands were like stepping stones across the lake, Main Duck, Galloo, Stony and then to Henderson Harbour in New York, but as she stood on the south shore, she could see nothing but water and sky, stretching away until they met at the horizon. They could have been in the middle of an ocean.

They picked their way along the shore, clambering over rocks, and sliding on loose stones. This coast would offer no peace for a storm-tossed ship, she could see. Boulders, large and small, lay half-submerged all along the shore, forming pools and lagoons that provided a shallow haven for frenzied, mating carp and certain destruction for any vessel approaching from the south. The wind and the waves joined in a constant assault on the shoreline and trees which had grown to maturity in the safety of solid ground now teetered dangerously at the shore's edge, the earth around their roots inexorably washed away. Several times they had to wade out into the water to get past those that had finally succumbed and fallen over into the lake.

As they worked their way along the shore, the land began to rise in shelves of layered limestone. They climbed up these from the shore and suddenly, as they rounded the point, there was the lighthouse. Cara was amazed at how tall it was when she stood at the bottom of it, craning her neck upwards to see the top. Len opened a small duffel he had been carrying and set out a bag of potato chips, a pop and a bottle of beer.

"Oh dear," he said worriedly. "I'm not sure who's supposed to get what."

"I'll take the beer," Cara cried.

"Okay, that means I get the pop. Oh wait a minute, no, that can't be right. How about I take the beer and you get the pop?"

Cara pretended to consider this for a moment. "Oh, okay," she said reluctantly.

They sat at the base of the lighthouse for their impromptu picnic, looking back wordlessly at the water they had just crossed. Len lit a cigarette and leaned back against the stones, the wind blowing the smoke in a swirl around his face.

Cara was so happy she thought she should die at this moment, then hastily retracted her thought, in case she jinxed herself. She closed her eyes and held her face up to the wind. I wish we could stay here forever, she thought, just me and Daddy. I'd even eat fish.

"Do you want a swig of beer?" Len asked her.

She took the bottle and gulped a mouthful, wrinkling her nose at the bitterness.

"Okay, now I get a swig of your pop. Fair's fair."

She handed the bottle to him and he drank.

He made a face."Ugh. I think I better stick with beer and you better stick with pop."

"Deal. Race you to the house."

She scrambled up the bank and ran along the path, Len in hot pursuit. The lighthouse keeper was there, cleaning fish on the back step. He waved at Len.

"Haven't seen you for a while," the man said. "Where you been?"

"Sailing the seven seas with my first mate here," Len replied. "Worked her way up from cabin boy." Cara swelled with pride and smiled happily at the man.

"Now that's what I need, a good crew," the man said. "Any chance I can hire her away from you?"

"Nope. Can't let good crew go."

The man smiled back at her. "Guess you'll have to ship with your Dad, then. But if you ever change your mind, you let me know, eh?"

Cara nodded and hung on her father's arm. He chuckled, and pulled her to him, ruffling her hair.

"Come on down to the harbour later will you? I've got a bottle of whiskey with your name on it."

The man saluted and nodded his assent. Cara wondered if her father knew everybody in the whole world.

The sun was beginning to set as they followed the road back to the harbour. This was a very different landscape, sere and brown. From this perspective, Cara could see how flat the island was, and how the wind had pushed all the trees in the same direction. As they neared the harbour, they could see that another boat had tied up at the dock, a sleek sailboat, its fibreglass hull and steel masts twinkling in the last rays of the sun.

"It's the Natty J", Len said. His eyes narrowed.

"How do you know?"

"I recognize her. I can tell by the shape."

To Cara it looked like any other sailboat. "Do you know the people?" she asked.

"Yeah, it's Art Marsden. I've run into him here and there." He didn't sound very enthusiastic.

A large man hailed them from the dock.

"Hey, Len. I thought it was your boat." He walked up to meet them. "And who's this pretty little lady?"

"This is my daughter, Cara. Cara this is Mr. Marsden from Oswego." Her father's voice was toneless and flat.

The man looked surprised. "Your daughter? Hard to imagine you as a family man, Len."

Cara was outraged. Of course her father was a family man. He was her father, wasn't he? But maybe this red-faced man didn't understand about families. "I'm his second in command," she said proudly.

"Ah, a pirate in training. Following in your dad's footsteps, huh? Did you know your old man is a pirate, Cara?"

She slipped her hand into her father's. She didn't like this man. He had a big belly that hung out over the top of his belt and a funny way of talking, the vowels in his speech stretched out and nasal. From the way he stood, she didn't think her father liked him much either.

"Can I go for a swim, Daddy?" She hoped he would come with her, so she could jump backwards from his hands, and so they wouldn't have to talk to Mr. Marsden.

"Sure, but stay close to shore, okay?" She climbed aboard the boat to get her bathing suit, but Len made no move to come with her.

She paddled in the shallows, while Mr. Marsden poured her father a drink. The two men sat in the roomy cockpit of the sailboat, and she could catch snatches of their conversation here and there.

"You on a run, Len...."

"No, just out for a ride with my daughter....."

"Thought she was a lot younger than your usual girls....pretty little thing...."

And later:

"No, I'm not interested, I've got bigger fish to fry...."

She was puzzled. They hadn't caught any fish, and her father had promised her she wouldn't have to eat any. She wasn't even sure they were talking about real fish; there was a menace to their conversation that she didn't understand, and she could sense that her father was tense and disturbed by the unexpected appearance of this drawling American. She held her nose and put her head under, but the water was murky and she couldn't see much.

She was pleased when Mr. Marsden declined to join their wiener roast on shore, instead opting to walk the road up to the lighthouse. She scoured the beach for driftwood and found two perfect roasting sticks. She threaded the wieners on to the ends while her father stacked the dead wood carefully within the confines of the ring of rocks he had built, tucking dead grass and bark underneath and around them. The fire caught easily. As usual, Cara couldn't wait for it to burn down to coals, but thrust her hot dog straight into the flames, leaving it charred on the outside and cold on the inside. It was perfect.

By the time they had roasted their marshmallows, darkness was falling and Cara was yawning. Her father drew buckets of water from the harbour and poured it over the fire while she padded down the dock and clambered aboard the boat. She rolled her sleeping bag out on the V-berth at the bow and debated about whether or not she should put on the flannelette pyjamas her mother had packed for her.

"Should I wear jammies, Daddy?" she asked when he came aboard.

"Pirates don't need jammies," he scoffed, so she kicked off her shoes and climbed into the sleeping bag in her clothes while he lit a kerosene lamp and placed it by the galley sink.

She lay drowsily in her bunk, the gentle rocking of the boat a lullaby while she replayed the day, but the sun and the water and the excitement had exhausted her and soon she was asleep. Later that night she awakened again and knew that her father had gone to sit on the sailboat with Mr. Marsden and that their conversation had resumed.

"Think about it anyway..." There was an urgency to the American's loud voice.

"I'm pretty sure I'm not interested, Art ."

"Jesus, Len, it's easy pickings."

"I said no." Her father's voice rose and she wondered if they were going to have an argument. She couldn't imagine anybody arguing with her father, because, as far as she was aware, nobody ever had. Alarmed, she scrambled out of her sleeping bag and up the companionway ladder. If there was going to be a fight, she would battle it out by her father's side.

They were both startled when she jumped down to the dock.

"What's the matter, Daddy?" she asked.

Len stood up and stretched. "Nothin' Cara Mia, nothin' at all. We were just talking. I thought you were long gone."

"I woke up again."

"Well, I think it's time I turned in too. Thanks Art," he said turning to Mr. Marsden.

"Think about what I said."

"I'll think, but don't be surprised if that's all I do."

The American shrugged.

When she woke the next morning, the sailboat had gone, leaving them to dawdle happily in the morning sun before they cast off for home.

Edna slid down the dune, her feet looking for purchase in the loose sand. She wished she had worn sandals; already her shoes were full of grit, which settled unpleasantly between her toes. Luckily the moon was full, otherwise she could never have found her way without a flashlight. She should have brought one, but it was the sort of thing that never occurred to her. It was the sort of thing Len would have thought of.

The pungent smell of dead fish and seaweed was much stronger here on the beach. Small silver bodies lay rotting along the water's edge, shad, driven by some unfathomable instinct to swim to their deaths in the shallow bay. Alewives was the correct term for them, Edna knew. She had heard that once from one of Len's dinner guests. With the opening of the St. Lawrence Seaway, alewives, marine fish by nature, had made their way through the locks and into the Great Lakes. Used to the cold depths of the ocean, every year thousands of them floundered as they unwittingly swam into the warm waters of Ontario bays.

She had decided to park her car halfway along the beach and walk the rest of the way. The dunes were full of visitors at this time of year and she thought it unlikely that she would run into anyone she knew, but locals did sometimes walk here in the evening, when it was hot in town and cool by the shore.

Off to her left she could see a weatherbeaten building half smothered with sand. The Palace of the Moon. It looked more desolate than ever in the twilight. Part of the roof had caved in over the winter, the rotting timbers finally giving way to the weight of wind-blown sand and snow.

She had almost convinced herself not to come. What good could it do after all these months? What could he possibly say to her that would make a difference? If she had any sense at all, she would leave him waiting with no explanation, no word, just as he had left her. But in weaker moments, she fantasized that he was coming back for her, to beg her to go away with him. What would her reaction be then? Would she fall into his arms and run off into the night, leaving her husband and child to discover her absence upon their return? Or would she scorn him in payment for his perfidy? Perhaps he only wanted to settle down again close by so that they could resume their sly and clandestine afternoon meetings. She had no idea what he wanted.

At the last moment, just as she had known deep down that she would, she had walked to her car and driven towards the beach. There was no predicting what would happen. She knew only that she had to see him again.

She wandered down to the shore, and stood looking at the lake until it was a few minutes to nine. She was about to head back towards The Palace of the Moon when he spoke.

"Edna?" She turned and there he was. She hadn't heard his approach over the rustle of the poplars and the roar of the water. He hesitated in the shadows, unsure of his welcome.

"Sacha? Oh Sacha!" She ran to him and threw her arms around him, wallowing in the familiar feel and smell of his body. He was different, thinner, and when the rising moonlight caught his face, she could see that his face looked haggard.

"Oh, Edna, please, I missed you so much." She had forgotten that he spoke with that slightly stilted, slightly foreign inflection.

"Are you all right? Where have you been? You left so suddenly."

He held her close. "I know, I'm sorry. The situation here was so difficult, I thought it best to leave quickly. I felt terrible, doing that to you."

Now that she was in his arms again, nothing else mattered, she thought.

"But now you're back." She looked up into his face. "You are back, aren't you? Tell me you'll stay." She could tell by the uncomfortable expression on his face that there was something more, something he hadn't told her yet. "What is it?"

"This is terrible, believe me, I know how terrible this is, to hurt you so badly and then come running back to ask for help."

"I'll help you. You know I will. Just tell me what's wrong."

He let her go and half-turned from her, running his hand through his hair. "I got into trouble," he said finally. "I owe money. They are going to hurt me if I don't pay by next week. "

"Why?" She was sickened by the thought that anyone might hurt him, inflict pain on his beautiful, beloved body.

"It's the same wherever I go. Philistines. They are all philistines. They do not understand the artist or the artist's ways."

"Sacha, what happened?"

A shuddering sigh. "There was this beautiful woman. A madonna. My interest in her was purely artistic you understand", he said quickly, "but the way the light caught her face, the shadow of her hair." He shrugged helplessly. "Her husband did not understand. He thought that because she was without clothes, you see, that it meant we were lovers. But I swear, Edna, there was never anyone but you. The others were only models. For the art, you know."

For the art? She thought of the crude slashes of colour on canvas, the half-finished daubs that had been piled in the corner of his loft, the ugly, twisted, repellant landscapes. She wondered if he had depicted this new madonna with a fore-shortened perspective and eyes that were too close together.

"Go on," she said, suddenly wary.

He was agitated now, pacing along the beach, occasionally running his hands through his hair again in despair. The effect was somewhat ruined, she thought, by the fact that he had to keep stepping over piles of dead fish.

"The husband burst into the room one night and started yelling," he recounted. "Then he took a hammer and smashed all of my paintings. Ruined, with large holes in them. It was awful."

He stopped pacing and embraced her again. "I don't understand why this keeps happening to me. Why can't these bourgeoisie understand that I am an artist? What would I want with this woman?"

He would want the same thing he had wanted from me, she realized. Money. And afternoons of passion on an old studio daybed.

"So you see", he continued, "I have no way to pay back the money I had borrowed to open my studio. And now the men I borrowed it from are after me. Oh, Edna, I hate to ask this of you, but I don't know where else to turn. Can you help me, please."

Edna watched as the moon slid under a cloud. The shadow made Sacha's face look narrow and sly. She wasn't reacting the way he expected, she realized, there was some element in his script that she was failing to grasp. When she didn't answer him, he went on.

“If I could just take care of this one problem, I would be all right, you see. And then I could come for you. We could make a life together. You would be my model, I could spend the rest of my life painting only you, and no one else.”

This was what she had once dreamed about, but now that the moment was here it all seemed wrong, as out of perspective as one of his paintings. She thought of the months she had waited, the days she had wasted, the hours spent huddled in a hurting mass under the blankets. The humiliation of knowing that he could walk away from her without a word. And then she thought of his arms around her, his lips against hers, their bodies together, frenzied and needy.

"How much do you need?"

"He doesn't need money,” said a voice through the darkness. “He needs a kick in the pants."

Edna gasped and spun towards the voice. For some reason Vera was standing there on the beach.

"Come on, Edna."

"What ....what are you doing here?" Vera's sudden presence was so incongruous, so unexpected that Edna had difficulty making any sense of it.

"C'mon let's go. Then I'll tell you a few things you need to know. A few things you should have been smart enough to figure out for yourself."

"What are you talking about?"

"Oh, Edna." Vera looked like a small and angry bantam rooster, red in the face, her feet braced solidly in the sand. "You weren't the only one, you know that. Did you honestly think that whole business with Isabel Jackson was just a matter of money? Do you think Fred would be that upset over a thousand dollars? You should go ask your fancy friends how many of them he had. And you knew it, Edna, you knew it all the time."

Edna did know, and she realized that Vera was right. She had known it from the start.

"And lo and behold he turns up again", she went on, "ready to dip right back into the honey pot. And surprise, surprise, he's looking for money. Len's money. For God's sake Edna, you and I are both too old to fall for this kind of sweet talk again."

And then Edna understood. She understood everything.

Sacha moved slightly towards Vera. "Now, lady, I don't who you are, but can't you just calm down a little? We can talk about this. It is not the way you make it seem."

"Oh, isn't it? Fine, Mr. "I'm Just a Misunderstood Artist", tell me how it is then. Tell me how you'll romance anything that walks by, as long as she has a healthy bank account." She glared at him as she spoke, her arms on her hips, daring him to go on. He stopped, uncertain what to do.

Edna looked out on the lake again. This wasn't turning out in any of the ways she'd rehearsed, though she herself wasn't sure what ending, exactly, she had been hoping for. She certainly hadn't expected Vera to turn up, but then she hadn't expected Sacha's story to be so transparent either. She tried to think it through coherently, to discover what it was she really wanted, but she kept being distracted by an odd light to the south. It changed every few minutes, first faintly red, then green. Was it a ship far out in the middle of the lake? A reflection of moonlight on the water? She watched as it changed to red again, and then she knew what it was. She had heard that this happened when the atmospheric conditions were just right, but had not really believed it was possible. What she was seeing was Rochester, all the way across the lake, and the changing red and green were the reflections of traffic lights at some intersection that stood in the perfect, precise place to reflect off the sky. She thought, for a moment, that she would point out this interesting phenomenon to Vera and Sacha, and then realized that they were far too caught up in the drama of the moment to be interested in meteorological oddities.

She turned to look at Vera, small and determined, her hands still planted on her hips, then at Sacha, for once unsure and waiting warily. From the corner of her eye she could see that the strange lights had turned from red to green again.

Slowly and deliberately she bent and picked up a dead shad. Once it would have sickened her, but working in the garden had dispelled any squeamishness she might have had. Death was a part of life and things must rot away in order to nourish new growth, musn't they?

Sacha shifted uneasily, not sure what she intended to do.

She looked at him for a moment, lifted her arm and threw. It struck him in the chest. His mouth dropped open and he looked, she thought, like a fish himself, his eyes wide and unblinking. She stooped and picked up another shad.

He held his arms in front of him, warding her off. "Edna, don't, I can explain. Just give me a chance will you?" She noticed that his accent had disappeared in the stress of the moment. She threw again. It caught him in the face this time.

And then Vera was throwing too. She ran to Edna's side and gleefully joined in a stoop, pick, throw rhythm that left Sacha with little choice but to run. Laughing, they chased him, grabbing fish and throwing on the run, their aim wild. He soon outdistanced them and disappeared over the dunes. They followed, but lost their footing in the loose, gritty bank.

Abruptly, Edna sat down.

Vera stood, uncertain.

"Come and sit beside me, Vera, I think we have a lot to talk about."

"I smell like fish."

"So do I. We better wash before we go home."

Vera sat down while Edna tried to decide where to start. How to go back and retrieve it all? Start at the beginning and work it through to the end, that was the way.

"Stevie is Len's, right?" she asked after a while.

Vera nodded.

"When did it happen? No, never mind, none of my business."

"Oh, but it is." She told Edna then, about the Palace of the Moon, and the treachery of the shimmering sand dunes, about "Stardust" playing in the background. About how she had been so charmed by Len, and wanted so badly to be grown up. About Francine. "It was before he even met you."

"I know," Edna said, "but why didn't you ever tell me?"

Vera shrugged. "What was there to say? You'd already burnt your bridges. He wouldn't have married me anyway, would he?"

Edna thought that was probably true, but it distressed her to hear the bleakness in her friend's tone.

"Does Mac know?" she asked finally.

"No. And I won't ever tell him. There's no point in making us both miserable."

"Oh Vera. Miserable? Are you really miserable?"

Vera sighed. "I was for the longest time. I don't think I am any more." She paused, for once struggling with what she wanted to say. "Do you remember my wedding?"

"Well of course I do. I was Matron of Honour."

"Do you remember what the weather was like that day?"

Edna was puzzled. "No, I can't say I do."

"I do. It wasn't too hot. It wasn't too cold. It wasn't exactly sunny, but it wasn't raining either. It was all right. And I thought for the longest time that that pretty much summed up my life with Mac."

"Oh Vera." It all sounded so sad.

"But it's all right now," Vera insisted. "In a lot of ways it's really all right.

Mac is a nice man. He's good to me. He's good to the kids. He loves me, I think, in his own way and every once in a while he can surprise me." She laughed ruefully. "It's not the way I thought my life would turn out. I don't exactly get grand, passionate love in the moonlight, but then I had that once, didn't I, and look what happened."

"Does Len know about Stevie?"

"I don't know. Maybe. I never told him. There didn't seem to be any point." She thought about it for a moment. "No, I'll be honest, since that's what we're being tonight. As long as I didn't confront him, I didn't have to admit to myself that I was just another silly girl in a long line of silly girls who fell for him. I never meant anything to him, and I never will."

"You know," Edna said, wiggling her toes in the sand. "I've never really been sure why he married me. I don't even know if he loves me. If he does, he has a funny way of showing it, doesn't he?"

"Do you love him?"

"I don't know. I just really don't know. Oh God, Vera I was so sure about Sacha. He was so handsome, and so ..... I don't know, exotic. He made me feel.... like I was special. Treasured. Can you understand how exciting that was?"

"Oh yeah, excitement," Vera said with a wave of the hand. "You don't have to tell me. How do you think we got into all this trouble in the first place?"

Edna looked at her closely. "Did Len ever.... you know, after we were married, did he ever......?

Vera shook her head. "Never. And you know something? That was probably the thing that hurt the most."

She could understand that. It was what Sacha had done to her when he left. She had felt discarded, jettisoned, thrown away like a piece of unwanted scrap, but at least she had the satisfaction of being the one to end it finally, to send him scornfully on his way. Poor Vera. "Are all men such bastards?" she wondered aloud.

"No, only the ones you pick out."

Edna was about to protest when she realized it was a joke.

"After all," Vera went on, "at least I had sense enough to pick a good one the second time around."

"Oh come on. That was a complete accident and you know it!"

"Yeah, actually it was," she admitted. "I'd have fallen for grand passion in the moonlight all over again if anybody had given me half a chance."

"All right," Edna said, "I've got most of it straight, but tell me one thing. How did you know where I was going tonight?"

Vera laughed. "I was outside your house when the mailman stopped me and asked if I'd take your mail in for him. That damned dog of Cara's was snarling under a bush, and you know how frightened he is of it. You know, you could at least have told your boyfriend to send a sealed letter instead of sticking it all on the back of a postcard for the whole world to see. What if Len had seen it?"

Edna thought back. The mail had been lying on the front hall table when she got back from seeing Len and Cara off on the boat. Bernice had said that Vera had been around, but in the excitement of seeing the postcard, she had paid little attention. She shuddered. What, indeed, if Len had seen it? "So now I know how," she said, "but I still don't know why."

It took Vera a while to answer. Edna's toes had made little patterns in the sand, and now she took a twig and brushed them over while she waited.

"I'm not sure," she said slowly. "Partly because I didn't want to see you throw your life away on somebody that wasn't worth it, I guess. And partly because... well... as long as you have Len, I guess I don't mind so much that I don't." She chuckled. "And mostly because I went to the gallery one day and Sacha really ticked me off when he didn't pay any attention to me."

Edna laughed and shook her head. "Hell hath no fury? You know, Vera, we're both smart women. How in hell did we end up being so stupid about men?"

"I don't know. All those great plans we had, and look where we are now."

"Of course, you were young when it happened to you," Edna pointed out. "I should be old enough to know better."

Vera looked at her slyly then. "So... was he worth it?"

"What do you mean?"

"You know what I mean."

"You snoopy old thing, you! What makes you think I'm going to tell you that?"

"Oh, come on," Vera giggled. "I'm your best friend. No more secrets, okay?"

"No more secrets," Edna agreed, and then she grinned. "He was incredible. Absolutely, unbelievably incredible."

They hooted with laughter then, the sounds of their mirth floating out over the moonlit bay.

CHAPTER SEVENTEEN

Cara arrived at Vera's with a bottle of red wine promptly at six o'clock. She couldn't remember for sure whether or not Vera and Mac drank, but she would bet that Steve did, from what she could remember of him anyway.

Mac's big face split into a grin when he saw her. Mac Dunlop had always been a shadowy figure to her, hanging around on the periphery of things, but only as an adjunct to Vera. She could never remember discussing anything more than the weather with him, yet he always seemed happy to see her.

Steve was sitting in the living room with a small, dark woman and a little girl of about eight or so, drinking beer and watching the baseball game. He rose to greet her. He hadn't changed much as far as Cara could see, a little heavier perhaps, a few worry lines around the eyes.

"Cara! How good to see you. I'm so sorry about your mother."

"Well, you know, under the circumstances, it was a blessing that she didn't last any longer."

She hated herself for saying anything so trite, and yet it seemed true. Death in a small town left survivors peeling back the clouds to look for the silver lining; "That's the way he would like to have gone", they would say of the man who had unexpectedly dropped dead of a heart attack. "You wouldn't have wanted her to linger any longer", they would say of the woman who had been rendered a vegetable by stroke. Sometimes it took a lot of work to find this positive slant, but in her mother's case, death really had been a blessing. There had been no hope of recovery.

The dark-haired woman was smiling shyly.

"This is Marcie", Steve said, "and this little munchkin over here is Amanda."

The child looked up briefly and smiled, then stuck her thumb in her mouth and refocused her attention on the screen.

"Mandy", her mother chided softly.

Guiltily, the little girl removed the thumb and smiled again.

"So, do want a beer?" Steve asked, as Cara settled on the chintz-covered chesterfield. "Mother's not sure she approves, but I just can't watch a baseball game without a beer in my hand. Just doesn't seem right somehow."

"I'll get it", said Mac, who had been lurking in the hallway. "And I'll see how mother's doing with supper."

"So, Steve," Cara said. "I only know the bits and pieces I've heard from Vera. How's life treating you?"

"Not great," he smiled ruefully. "Thought I had the world by the tail there for a while, but all this corporate restructuring has been difficult." He swigged his beer. "To tell you the truth, I'm out of work right now. I was on the fast track to become a Vice President, then we were bought out, no, let me amend that, we were taken over, by an American company who brought in their own management."

It was a story Cara had heard all too often. Whiz kids with business degrees who were suddenly let go in an orgy of downsizing and realignment. She knew exactly what sort of pickle Steve and Marcie were in. Big mortgage on a house in the suburbs, car loans, everything bought with a nickel down and a nickel when you catch me and now the payments were killing them.

"What do you do, Marcie?" she asked.

"I do some bookkeeping for a car dealership", she said. "So far, my job's okay, but its only part-time."

"How old is Amanda?"

Marcie smiled. "She's eight. It's a nice age."

"My Mickey is seven. You're right. They're still sweet at this point, but I expect all that will change when they hit puberty."

"I don't want to think about it", Steve said. "Man, when I remember all the stunts I pulled when I was teenager."

Cara was surprised when he said that. She remembered him as serious, a jock who got good marks and kept his nose clean. Good-looking, Lord yes, but never one of the wild bunch, not like she'd been.

"You wouldn't believe Cara as a teenager", he said to Marcie. "If there was trouble, she was always in the middle of it. And the way the boys used to flock around her. Yours truly not excepted." He saluted her with his beer bottle and took another swig.

Marcie smiled, a little uncomfortably.

"You should have seen Steve back then," Cara said quickly. "Long hair, wide belts, big boots."

"My hair was never that long," he protested.

"No, but it was long enough. A sort of compromise length, if I remember correctly. Not long enough to be called a hippy, but enough there to be fashionable."

He laughed. "Well, I hadn't discovered the joys of three piece suits yet."

"We'll have to get your mother's photograph albums out," Marcie said. "I bet there are pictures Cara hasn't seen."

"Not more photographs," Cara groaned. "It seems like all I've done in the last couple of weeks is sort out old photographs."

"Have you got much left to do over at the house?" Steve asked.

She sighed. "I'm getting there, but it's difficult. The real estate agent advised leaving most of the furniture. Apparently it "shows better" whatever that means. I've got a lot of the junk cleared out, but I still have to deal with mother's personal stuff." She hesitated. "That's a little more difficult than I thought it was going to be. And then there's this whole other house on the outskirts of town I've apparently inherited."

"Really?" Steve said. "Where?"

"Out on the west end. Apparently it belonged to some friend of my father's. Funny thing is, now she's died and left everything to me. And I don't even know who she was."

"Bizarre. Maybe mother will know something about it."

"Something about what?" Vera stood in the doorway, beaming at them all.

"Vera!" Cara jumped up and, on impulse, hugged the round little woman. Mac, carrying a trayful of beer glasses, grinned in the background.

"Get away with you," Vera protested. "You're all so big! You knock the wind right out of me."

"Hey Mum, Cara was just saying she's inherited another property on the outskirts of town, but she's not sure why. Do you know anything about it?"

"Oh?" Vera suddenly stopped beaming. "Where exactly is it dear?"

"Out in that strip where the Jiffy Mart is."

"Oh, yes." She considered for a moment before she spoke again. "I believe that was your father's home at one time. It's where he grew up, but I thought he'd sold it long ago. Either that or lost it when everything else went."

"It belonged to a woman by the name of Francis O'Brien. I have no idea who she is or why she would have left it to me."

It was Mac who replied. "Francis? Oh, Francine! Francine O'Brien. Oh yeah, she worked at Fletcher's Drug Store for a long time. I think she sort of looked after things for Len when his father died. I don't think she had much family, or not around here anyway, so I guess you'd call her sort of a family friend, maybe."

It was by far the longest speech Cara had ever heard from Mac. She was disappointed that there was so little information in it. She was desperately curious about Francis, alias Francine. "I don't recall ever even meeting her," she said.

"Well, well," he said. "These things happen, don't they? What are planning to do with all your property?"

She threw up her hands. "I have no idea. No idea at all. Up until now, everything I've owned could be moved in a medium-sized van." They laughed. "Fortunately Uncle Jack made sure mother's estate was all in order, so it's not tied up."

"Is he going to stay on and run the store for you, dear?" Vera wanted to know.

"Yes, for now, although he'd like to retire." Cara was suddenly struck by an idea, but tucked it away to think about later. "Hey Vera, do you know anything about The Palace of the Moon?"

"The Palace of the Moon? Where did you ever hear about that old place?"

"It was mentioned on a postcard I found with mother's things, and then Uncle Jack was talking about it, but he didn't tell me much. I gather it was a pretty wild place."

"The Palace of the Moon?" Marcie said. "What a name! What was it?"

Vera laughed. "It was a dance hall out at the beach. It was only there for a few years, but Cara's right, it was a wild place when it was going."

"Wild? How wild?" Steve was intrigued.

"Oh you know." Vera blushed a little. "A lot of drinking and stuff. But the music was great."

Mac looked surprised. "I didn't know you ever went out there," he said.

"It was before I married you, dear," Vera said patting his hand. "And I only went once. It was a little too much for me."

"Palace of the Moon," Marcie repeated the name, savouring the sound of it. "It sounds all sort of dreamy, doesn't it?"

"Well," Vera said. "The name was the only dreamy thing about it. It was a ramshackle place, all built up on stilts over the sand. I remember it had a really nice dance floor though."

"What happened to it?" Cara wanted to know.

"Well, now, let me see." Vera wrinkled her forehead as she thought. "Was there a fire? No, that's not right. Isn't that funny, I don't really remember. It closed down in the early fifties, I know that." She laughed. "Isn't that awful? I don't know. Maybe I just never heard."

"I know what it is mother," Steve said. "You're just trying to hide your disreputable past from your children."

Cara had to laugh at the notion of plump little Vera with a shady past. Everyone else laughed too. Vera looked uncomfortable and blushed even more.

"Now what about these photographs I keep hearing about," Cara said, "I don't suppose you've got a picture of a wild woman in there, have you?"

Vera was beaming again as she brought the albums out. She settled herself beside Cara on the chesterfield, so she could explain as they went along. Steve and Marcie looked at each other and grinned.

They went through the first few pages quickly. There were a few photographs of Vera, some as a child, some as a teenager. Cara was struck by how pretty Vera had been when she was younger. Petite and slim, with a saucy smile and an elfin look. Suddenly she could well imagine Vera in the arms of some tall, dark stranger, dancing away the night in a seedy dancehall, kissing him under the light of the moon. There was only one snapshot of Vera and Mac at their wedding. Cara thought she looked surprisingly grim for a bride. A younger, slimmer Mac beamed beside her, his arm protectively around his new wife. Idly, Cara wondered what Vera had ever seen in him. Even then he looked awkward and bear-like.

The rest of the album contained pictures of Steve and Susan in various stages of development. The camera only emphasized how different they were, Steve forever caught in the middle of some impulsive action, Susan sedate and stolid-looking. In these shots Vera had begun to assume the appearance Cara was more familiar with. It must have been kids that did it to her, she thought. Funny, how some women fall apart when they start having kids. Like me. With my fifteen extra pounds.

"Now, this is where you come in," Vera said pointing to a picture. "You see, here you are in your carriage, now you must have only been about three months old there."

She had been turned backwards and was lying on her stomach, peering out at the camera, her body raised on stiffened arms. Susan stood behind the carriage and to one side, her hand clenched around the handle.

"We used to be afraid that you'd crawl right out sometime when we weren't watching. You were always so strong for such a little thing. Susan liked to push you along, even though she could barely make the carriage move by herself. Of course, we didn't dare let Stevie anywhere near you. It seemed like every time your mother came to visit, you ended up scratched or bruised or banged somehow."

Cara made a face at him. "You brute."

He stuck his tongue out at her.

Vera didn't notice. "Your father would just have a fit if your mother took you home and you had as much as a scratch on you," she went on. "He was always afraid you were going to get hurt if he wasn't there to look after you, but your mother and I knew how tough you were."

Tough. For some reason she was always being described as tough. "You're a tough little monkey," her father had said when she refused to cry over some little hurt. He would say it proudly, and Cara quickly learned that he thought tough was a good thing to be. "God, you're tough" her boyfriends had said when she refused to simper and kowtow to them. And Randy, who complained that she was too tough, she had no feelings, she didn't understand what it was like for him. Even Mickey, who bragged that he had a tough mom, who could look after mysterious things like plumbing and household carpentry all by herself. She wondered why she so seldom felt as tough as she looked.

There were only a few photographs of Edna in Vera's album, and when she did appear, she was usually off to the side, not part of the grouping. On the few occasions when she was actually looking into the camera, it was warily, as if she had secrets that needed to be protected from the camera's probing eye.

Mac interrupted. "I think there's something burning, mother."

"Oh my goodness, I left the gravy on!" Vera hoisted herself up and bustled down the hallway to the kitchen.

"Can I help you?" Marcie called after her.

The reply was muffled and unintelligible.

"I'm pretty sure that was a "no" Mac said. "You girls sit still."

When Vera finally emerged from the kitchen again, it was to announce that supper was ready. Mac took his rightful place at the head of the table, Cara noted, with Vera at the foot and the rest of them in between. She was surprised when Amanda asked if she could sit beside her.

"It's all right as long as Cara doesn't mind," Marcie said.

Cara didn't. Amanda seemed like a nice little girl, with her mother's looks and quiet manner.

"What grade are you in, Amanda?" she asked.

"I'm in Grade Three and my teacher's name is Miss Randall and my best friend is Miranda McCain."

Steve and Marcie lived in a sprawling suburban development, probably full of look-alike houses with the garages in front, Cara guessed and sport utility vehicles and little girls called Miranda and Melissa and Jessica, all of them dressed in OshKosh and Gap and carrying the same lunchpail. Mickey seldom mentioned his classmates. Like her, he seemed content with his own company.

"I have a little boy who's seven," she said. "Sometime you two should meet."

"I know, Mummy told me. But I don't like boys."

Mac cut the roast pork into huge steaming slabs and passed the plates to Vera, who scooped up mounds of mashed potatoes and turnip. Gravy, and the ubiquitous jellied salad were sent around the table, farmer style. Her city friends would have scoffed at the supper, with its prosaic ingredients and plain jane preparation, but tonight Cara felt comforted by the familiar food. There was a companionable silence as they all dug into the piles on their plates.

"So what have you been doing to pass the time now that you're retired, Mac?" she asked when she had scraped her plate clean.

"Making a mess in the garage," Vera answered for him. "At least it keeps him out of my hair."

"Dad's restoring old cars," Steve explained, and Cara wondered if Mac ever got a chance to speak for himself, or if it was just taken for granted that someone else would answer for him. He didn't ever seem to mind. "He got hold of an old Model A and started tinkering with it. Now he goes off on car rallies when the weather's nice and they don't have to worry about those new-fangled things like windshield wipers and headlights."

"It passes the time," was all Mac said.

"I keep telling you you should get into some of the later model classic cars," Steve said. "They'll be worth big money some day."

"Could be right," he replied.

"Can I ask you something?" It was a whisper, barely audible, at her left elbow.

"Sure you can, honey." Cara bent over so that her ear was close to Amanda's lips.

"Where's your little boy?"

"He's still back in the city," Cara said quietly. "He's staying with a friend of mine."

"Is he coming here?"

"Maybe. Would you like to play with him if he does?"

She nodded solemnly. "I think so, but only if he's not too noisy."

"I'll tell him to hold it down."

She seemed satisfied with this and plunged her fork into the banana cream pie Vera put in front of her. It had a mountain of real whipped cream on top.

"Mom, you're going to kill us all," Steve groaned when she set his down.

"Oh all right, I'll just take yours back to the kitchen then," she said and made a grab for his plate, but he snatched it back and held it away from her.

"No! You can't have it!"

"Well, stop complaining then," she laughed. "Kids! I don't know how I put up with you!"

" 'Cause I'm charming and good-looking, that's why," Steve said. "I'm the cream in your cream puff, aren't I ma?" Cara knew that look. Mickey often looked like that when he was trying to be deliberately winsome. It usually worked too.

"I'm the chocolate on your eclair," Amanda lisped beside her. This must be an old game, then.

"I'm the meringue on your pie," Marcie chimed in.

"I'm the icing on your cake," Vera added.

Cara thought quickly, "I'm the chip in your cookie?"

"Oh, good one Cara!" Steve said, and looked expectantly at his father.

Mac wrinkled his brow. "Oh, durn," he said, "I can't think of anything."

"That means you're the nut in the chocolate bar," Amanda said triumphantly. "Grandpa's a nutbar!" She giggled.

"I can never think of anything," Mac said to Cara, shrugging.

After dessert, Cara and Marcie helped Vera take the dishes into the kitchen, then carried mugs of coffee into the living room, where Mac and Steve were watching the final inning of the game.

"Oh, I see the Jays are snatching defeat from the jaws of victory again." She handed him a mug.

"Yup, up to their old tricks," he said, "Thanks Cara."

Amanda was nodding on the floor.

"Somebody's worn out," Marcie said.

"She's not the only one." Cara was yawning. She felt full and content and happy. When the Jays finally won in the tenth, she got to her feet. "I've got to go home and go to bed," she said. "I can't keep my eyes open. Thanks Vera, Mac. Good to see you Steve. Nice to meet you Marcie." She would have said good night to Amanda, but the little girl was fast asleep, her thumb in her mouth.

As she was getting her coat on, Marcie slipped to her side.

"We're here until Tuesday," she said. "Do you think it would be a help if I came and sorted your mother's clothes? I really wouldn't mind, but only if you want me to."

Cara was moved by the offer. "I'd like that very much," she said. "Thank you."

In retrospect, Cara knew she had been a real pill as a teenager; Steve's description of her had not been far off the mark - wherever there was trouble, she had been in the middle of it. It had started when she was around thirteen or fourteen, but what exactly the causative factor had been she had no idea. All she remembered was that when she was twelve her father had been the most wonderful man in the world. A year later, she was doing everything she could to annoy him. Her mother scarcely seemed to notice her antics; her father rose irresistibly to the bait.

She no longer drew elephants and giraffes and whales in the margins of her school notebooks. Now they were decorated with phantasmagorical and disturbing swirls of abstract images. Boxes disappeared within boxes, circles ended in confusing illusions, colours burst from one side of the page only to march into oblivion at the other.

"What are those things you're drawing, dear?" Bernice would ask, looking over her shoulder as she sat doodling at the kitchen table. She was prepared to like anything Cara produced, but she didn't know how she was supposed to respond to these.

"It's what's inside my head," Cara replied moodily.

"Oh." Bernice wrinkled her brow. " Never mind, dear, I made you a chocolate cake. You'll feel better after you have some."

Edna had always dressed her daughter like a doll, in pinafore dresses and shiny patent shoes. Cara was still fashionable as a teenager, but now fashion called for blue jeans, accessorised almost exclusively with plaid flannel jackets, ribald T-shirts, and Greb Kodiak work boots. Her long, wavy hair was parted severely down the middle and hung in a hank down her back.

She eschewed make-up of any sort, but then, Edna thought, she was the sort of girl who could afford to.

She was outrageously popular with a certain cadre of boys. Girls began wanting to hang out with her too, not because any of them were friends particularly, but because where Cara went, the boys were sure to go.

She was suspended from school for a week when she was caught smoking in the girls' washroom; for weeks she rode to school on the back of a motorcycle with Ricky Macdonald who wore nothing but black leather with lots of zippers; she was very nearly caught at a beach party in possession of an ounce of hash. Fortunately, a call of nature had placed her behind a sand dune at the very moment the police raided the party, and she was able to crawl away under a bush and hide until the coast was clear.

She harangued her father for being in "business" and part of the "corporate conspiracy" until he finally lost his temper and threatened to cut off her allowance.

She played Led Zeppelin and Black Sabbath full blast on her stereo until the old house shook and even Bernice complained.

She spent hours in her room, reading Herman Hesse and Thomas Wolfe and Rolling Stone, surfacing only for meals.

Len complained to Edna. "Can't you at least get her to be civil at the dinner table?"

"It's a stage", she said. "We all went through them too."

"I don't ever remember being like this. When I was fourteen, I thought my father was wonderful. We spent a lot of time together."

"That's right, you and your father spent time together dodging the truant officer."

"Well, yeah", he said, "but at least it was something we did together."

"She thinks I'm stupid", he said another time, "and an old fogey. Me, Len Collins! Sometime I should sit her down and tell her a little history. My God, I've done things that would curl her hair, if she knew."

"You'll do nothing of the sort", Edna replied. "You'll only give her ideas. Besides, did it ever occur to you that she's just like you?"

"She is not. She takes after her mother. I wasn't the one who ran away from home and had to be rescued."

"Just leave her alone", she advised. "Unless you want her standing out on the sidewalk with a suitcase, waiting for some juvenile delinquent with acne to come along and pick her up."

"You were picked up by a juvenile delinquent with acne?" Len said."You never told me that. Was this something that happened before I married you?"

"You were the one who picked me up," she pointed out.

"I never had acne."

"Look, Len, just shut up, and as the kids say, back off."

Len shrugged and from then on Edna could see that he really tried to let Cara find her own way. It hurt him, she knew, that this daughter for whom he had once been the centre of the universe was now spinning in an orbit that took her far, far away from him. She hoped he had the patience to wait until she spun back again, but she was afraid he didn't. Patience had never been Len's strong suit.

Neither of them said a word when she scraped through Grade 11 with a fifty-five average. They didn't say much when she was caught climbing back into the house at two in the morning via the basement window. They didn't even comment when Bernice complained about the strange smell in her room, an acrid, spicy aroma of smoke and burning herb.

That's why Cara was so surprised when they made such a fuss about Steve.

She'd been at a party with a group of kids she didn't normally hang out with. They were older, some of them were actually finished high school and working. There had been nothing much going on with her own crowd that night, so she'd tagged along with a friend who was going out with a nineteen year old apprentice mechanic named Mark.

She knew Steve, of course, but only to say hi to. Although their mothers were friends, Steve was too much older to have taken much notice of Cara. He was in the last year of high school, an honour student, a forward with the basketball team, Vice President of the Student's Council and head of the Yearbook Committee. All of the restless energy he had exhibited as a youngster was now channelled into a myriad of constructive outlets. Steve Dunlop was going places, everybody said. He had the drive and the focus for success and he would make the school proud.

Two boys who had dropped out of school shared a house and hosted a party every Saturday night, cramming their tiny living room full of people and booze and smoke. Shortly after they arrived, Cara's friend disappeared into the bedroom with someone, she wasn't sure who, and wasn't sure her friend knew either. She didn't know anyone at the party very well, and they were a drinking crowd. Someone passed a bottle of rye. She thought it was vile, but drank anyway. She was beginning to regret the half tab of acid she had dropped before she left home.

She wandered outside. Steve was sitting on the back stoop drinking a beer.

"Hey." She dropped down beside him, flopping flat on her back. It was a clear night and she was amused by the stars, which kept dancing away on the periphery of her vision.

"Hey. Want a swig?'

She considered for a moment, then shook her head."Nope, can't sit up."

"Have to drink it myself then." She realized he was very drunk. "You've grown up a lot since I last noticed," he said.

"Yeah. I'm a big girl now."

"I used to think you were a little snot."

"I used to think you were a stuck-up prig."

He finished his beer and threw the bottle over the back fence. "That's the last of that", he said. "I should've brought a two-four."

"I've still got a half a tab. You want it?" She pulled it out of her pocket.

"I don't think so. If I did that I might end up doing something I might regret later."

"What? You mean like puking all over the back yard?" It was the sort of remark that Cara used to separate the sheep from the goats. If a guy was put off by it, he probably wasn't worth bothering with.

But Steve laughed. "Well, maybe that too, but later. Wanna go sit in the car? We can listen to the radio."

Oh what the hell, she thought, it's Saturday night and the car is parked in front of a house. If he gets too pushy, I'll just get out.

They climbed into the back seat, Steve leaning forward to turn on the radio. Good stuff. Santana and Clapton. He settled back with his arm around her. He nuzzled her neck.

"You've really grown up a lot Cara", he said. "I can't believe I didn't notice until now."

She turned her head then and kissed him, her tongue reaching way inside his mouth, exploring.

"Hmmmmmm...."

"What?"

He pulled away and grinned. "Really grown up."

She kissed him again, but she was too stoned to focus on making it any good. She started to giggle.

"What?" he wanted to know.

"I can't feel my lips," she said. "Sorry."

"That's okay," he said. "I think I'm too drunk to find them anyway. You know, when you said you'd sit in the car with me, I figured it was my lucky night, but I don't think I'm in any position to press my advantage, so to speak."

"Aw go on," she said. "You must have lots of lucky nights. You can keep your pecker in your pants for once."

He sighed. "Actually, I'm real good at unhooking bras. But that's as far as nice girls usually let me go."

"Nice girls? So what does that make me. Nasty?"

"Aw, come on, Cara, I didn't mean it that way. It's just that...well... your reputation isn't exactly spotless, you know. A lot of guys talk."

"Well, they may talk, but they don't always tell the truth, do they?"

He smiled. "That's true", he admitted. "Anyway, here I was all ready to go in for the kill, but you know something? I keep thinking about what my mother would say."

Cara laughed then. "Yeah, I know what you mean."

"Why don't we just drive around for a while?" she said after a few minutes, when she finally got the words out of her brain and past her lips.

He considered. "Nope," he said. "Not a good idea. Don't think I can find the keys anyway."

So they sat in the car and listened to music until she decided it was time to go and haul her friend out of whatever bed she was in.

He called her the next day. Edna answered the phone and was puzzled when he identified himself.

"It's Steve Dunlop", she said to Cara. "He wants to talk to you."

"Hi" he said when she got on the line. "I had a really good time last night. Thanks."

"So did I. Thanks yourself."

"So, you want to go to a movie tonight?"

She took a moment to think about it. A movie? It had been along time since anyone had asked her on so innocent a date. What was next, the sock hop? No wonder he was never lucky.

"I don't know Steve....."

"Aw come on", he said. "I'd really like to see you again."

Oh what the heck, she thought. "Okay. Pick me up at seven."

"What did Steve want?" her mother asked when she hung up.

"He asked me for a date." She shrugged. "That's okay I guess."

She'd already turned to go back upstairs so she couldn't see from her mother's face that it was far from okay.

She stood at her closet door, looking at the rows of jeans and plaid shirts. Somehow none of it seemed like the right thing to wear on a movie date with a boy like Steve Dunlop. Jammed at the back, scrunched on its hanger was a green silk blouse, a Christmas present that she had worn once, on one of the occasions when her mother insisted she dress up. She hauled it out. It was sadly wrinkled, and the top button was hanging by a thread. She tried it on. She liked the way it made her eyes look, tawny and wild. She'd have to ask Bernice to sew the button on, she had no idea how, and maybe she'd iron it for her too.

She grabbed her hair brush and brushed out the tangles in her hair. Maybe she should pull it back in a pony tail. She was holding it up, turning this way and that in the mirror, when she realized her mother was standing in her doorway, watching her.

"Did you want something?" Her room was inviolate, and even though the door had been ajar, she was disturbed that her mother was there.

"No...... I was just going by and I noticed you had your silk shirt on. I just wondered why. I didn't think you liked it."

"I don't particularly. I just thought it might be nice to dress up a bit. I don't think Steve is into flannel."

"How come Steve is asking you out all of a sudden?"

"Because he is," Cara said shortly. "What's with the third degree?"

"Nothing." Edna tried to smile. "Just asking, that's all. Don't be too late, okay?"

He arrived at seven o'clock sharp. Cara was surprised when he climbed the front steps and knocked politely on the door. Most of her dates sat at the curb and honked the horn.

They drove to Belleville. The Regent Theatre in town was no longer showing movies or anything else for that matter, its neon marquee unlit and its frescoed foyer dark. The radio played as they sped through the April night, the insistent drum beat reverberating through the car's body, matching the thrumming of the wheels.

Cara was a little at a loss for words. "So, you're almost done, eh?" she finally said.

"Yeah. Goodbye high school, hello life."

"Do you like working at the garage?" Steve had a part-time job after school and on weekends pumping gas at Smith's Sunoco.

He shrugged. "It's okay. I'm trying to save up as much money as I can. I'd really like to go on, but it's going to be tough. Dad doesn't make much and he doesn't see the point anyway. Mum would love to have a university graduate in the family, but I'd have to score a whack of student loans to make it work. You've still got a couple of years don't you?"

"Yeah. But I already know what I want to do."

"What?"

"I really want to go to Art College. It's the only thing I'm good at."

"How do you make a living at that?"

Cara didn't know, but she didn't think it mattered anyway. Her father had lots of money. Besides, she didn't need much, just a roof over her head. She wasn't into the conspicuous consumption bag, not like her folks with their big cars and big house and cocktail parties.

"I don't suppose making a living matters to you much, does it?" he asked, reading her thoughts.

"No, but not for the reasons you might imagine."

She suddenly felt sorry for Steve, and very very lucky. Now that she thought about it, she knew Steve was right, his father didn't have much money. They still lived in the house Vera had inherited from her mother, just down the street from where Cara's grandmother had lived. Mac still worked for the County, a good enough job for around here, but he would never do better. He would never even make foreman, the paper work would have been beyond him. Where did Steve get his brains from? she suddenly wondered. Couldn't have been from Vera. Cara liked her mother's best friend, but even she realized that Vera was no intellectual giant, her world was bound by recipes and miracle cleaning products.

"I hope you make it," she said and smiled.

He reached across and took her hand and squeezed. "Thanks." He didn't let go, steering the car easily with his left hand, playing with her fingers with his right. Cara looked at the two hands, entwined in her lap.

"Look, our hands are the same shape," she said.

"Bizarre."

They went to the Belle. The Capitol was playing "The French Connection", but Cara had already seen it.

"The Last Picture Show?" Steve said dubiously. "I don't know anything about it. Sounds like they should have played it at the Regent just before they closed it down."

They sat in the back row and watched Cloris Leachman deliver an Oscar-winning performance. They held hands and necked a little during the slow parts, but there was an awkwardness between them that prevented anything further. Cara was used to boys who dispensed with preliminaries and got straight to the point. Anybody else would have had my jeans unzipped by now, she thought. Was there something wrong with her, or was Steve just shy? Finally, she decided she was overanalyzing and settled back to enjoy his diffident approach.

After the movie they got Cokes and a plate of chips at a greasy spoon down the street.

"So do you think Cybil Shepherd is sexy?" she asked him.

"Nah, too skinny," he said. "No tits."

"But she's a model," Cara pointed out.

"Yeah, but there's nothing to hang on to."

"You've hung on to a lot in your time have you?" she taunted.

"Yes, I've hung on to a lot," he said solemnly. "I can say without a shadow of a doubt that I'm incredibly well hung. I hang on every night."

He delivered the line just as she was taking a swig of her Coke, and she snorted it out through her nose when she laughed.

"You asshole," she laughed, mopping up the mess with a paper napkin.

He just looked at her and grinned. It was a lop-sided grin that she liked a lot. She wadded up the sodden napkin and threw it at him.

"Hey, do you like to fish?" he asked suddenly.

Cara hadn't gone fishing since she was thirteen, the last time she had gone out with her father on the boat. She thought for a moment. "Yeah, actually, I do," she allowed.

"You wanna go fishing Sunday?"

She shrugged. "Sure."

"You know, I couldn't ask that of most girls."

"I'm not most girls."

"I noticed."

He held her hand all the way home, and when they pulled up in front of her house, pulled her over to him and kissed her. When she got out of the car he waited until she was safely in the front door.

She was surprised to see a light on in her father's study and even more surprised when her father came to the door.

"Where have you been?"

"Out." She was puzzled. It wasn't much past midnight, her curfew, and she had told her mother where she was going.

"Who with?"

"Steve Dunlop."

"What were you doing?"

"We went to a movie."

"Are you going to see him again?"

"Yes. What's with the big inquisition?"

"I just wondered, that's all." He turned abruptly and went back into the den, closing the door.

Cara knew he was upset, but she couldn't understand why. It had been an innocent enough date, with a guy her parents should have approved of, for once. Steve was every mother's idea of the perfect boyfriend; clean, polite, well thought of by his elders. He was also the son of her mother's oldest friend. Unlike the boys she usually went out with, he didn't even drive a motorcycle. She shrugged. Parents. Who could figure them out?

He picked her up at six a.m. Sunday morning.

"We have to get an early start before the bay gets too crowded," he said. "The fish all disappear by eleven."

Bernice was astounded when she appeared in the kitchen at such an early hour. She hadn't seen Cara before noon on a weekend in at least two years. She was even more astounded when she disappeared into the basement and emerged with a fishing rod and tackle box.

"Have we got any worms?" she asked, looking in the refrigerator.

"Of course we don't have any worms. What on earth would we have worms for?"

But Steve had lots of bait and they piled it and their gear into a small aluminum motorboat that was tied up to a cottage dock on the high shore. Cara climbed down to the boat with the ease of long practice. Steve watched approvingly.

"You've been on a boat before."

"Well of course I have. You didn't figure I was a dock fisher did you?"

They headed for a small island at the head of the bay.

"I've had pretty good luck here," he said.

Cara took his word for it. She had never gone fishing for the sake of fishing before. It had always been something that was done as part of a larger excursion on her father's boat. She sat in the bow and inhaled the breeze deeply, suddenly content in the sunshine and wind. She had forgotten how much she enjoyed being out on the water.

Steve tucked the boat expertly behind the island and threw out the anchor. Cara got the bait can.

"Do you want me to put the worm on the hook?" he asked her.

"Of course not," she said.

"It doesn't make you squeamish?"

"No." She was genuinely puzzled by his concern.

He grinned. "Cool."

They cast out their lines and settled back on the cushions.

"You want a beer?" Steve asked.

"Cheap beer buzz in the morning? You betcha."

He opened a cooler and handed her a can. Just as she took it, there was a tug on her line. She reeled in. A small perch hung on the end.

"And Cara wins the fish sweepstakes," she announced, dangling the still-wriggling body in front of Steve's face.

"Do you want me to get it off the hook for you?" he asked.

"Listen, asshole," she said. "I can put the worm on the hook myself, I can take the fish off the hook myself, I can clean and fillet the goddam thing for you, if you like. The only thing I won't do is cook it for you and serve it up for dinner, 'cause I don't do that shit. Okay?"

"Yes ma'am."

"Oh fuck off, Dunlop."

"Yes, ma'am."

He had decided to try a jig in the hopes of catching a walleye and was crouched in a half-stance over the tackle box. Cara lifted her foot and planted it against his backside, giving him a shove that caught him off-balance. He flailed his arms in a futile attempt to regain his balance. She had thought he would fall forward against the seat, but his windmilling arms skewed his body around and he pivoted off the edge of the boat and slid gracefully into the water.

"Oh my God! I'm sorry!" She clambered to the edge and peered over, expecting to see a sputtering and furious Steve, but there was only a widening circlet of tiny waves where his body had disappeared.

"Steve?" She was a little alarmed. What if he had hit his head on the way over and was now spiralling down to the bottom of the bay? She wondered if she should dive in after him, to pull his body to the surface, but had no idea what she should do then. She didn't know CPR or artificial respiration. What if it was already too late and he had ceased to breathe? No, she decided, he must be lurking under the boat somewhere, hiding so she would be frightened and contrite.

In spite of the fact that she was half-expecting it, she was still taken by surprise when his arm shot up and grabbed hers, pulling her over the thwarts and into the icy water beside him. She went in headfirst, inhaling a lungful of water, and broke the surface coughing, choking and laughing.

"You bastard!"

He laughed and pulled himself up onto the side of the boat. She clung to the side looking up at him. The water was perishing, and she wasn't sure she could feel her legs anymore.

"C'mon, I'll pull you up," he said, holding out his hand.

"How do you know I won't pull you back in again?"

"Because if you're as cold as I am, all you want to do right now is get out of there. Oh God, I'm frozen."

She held up her hand and he pulled her into the boat. His arm looked blue. She was shivering and shaking, but couldn't suppress her giggles.

"Serves you right, you know."

"You too."

"Do you have a blanket or anything on board?"

"No. We're in for a long old cold ride home."

He hauled up the anchor and looked relieved when the engine started right away. "All we'd need right now is engine trouble."

She giggled again through her chattering teeth.

By the time they reached the dock, Cara was so cold she was sure she was in the end stages of hypothermia. Steve looked just as miserable as she felt. They grabbed their gear and ran for the car. He started the engine and turned the heater on full blast.

"These seats are going to get really wet," she pointed out.

"Oh, okay," he said. "I guess we better walk home then."

"You go first."

"Hey, don't hog the heat." She had been holding her hands up to the blast of warm air.

"Bugger off."

He shoved her with his shoulder to push her away and thrust his hands in ahead of hers.

"Hey!" She shoved back.

"Hey, that's how we got into this trouble in the first place. My God, I think my hands may actually be able to hold on to the steering wheel now."

Shaking from cold and laughter they sped back to town.

"Boy, that was some fishing trip," she said as she got out of the car. "All I caught was one lousy perch."

"All I caught was one lousy girl," he pointed out.

She stuck her tongue out at him and turned to go into the house when she realized her father was standing right behind her.

"What the hell happened to you?" he demanded.

Cara giggled, aware of her sodden clothes and dishevelled hair. "We had a small mishap. I accidently pushed Steve into the bay and then I had to jump in and rescue him." She put on her best contrite face, a ploy that usually worked quite well with her father.

But he was having none of it. "You moron!" he yelled at Steve. "Do you know how easy it is to drown in water that temperature? Why the hell weren't you looking after her?"

Steve refused to look at Len. He glared out the front window of the car, his hands gripping the steering wheel tightly. Cara could see that his face was flushed.

"Daddy! Stop! It was my fault, not his, okay? We were just horsing around."

"You've got no goddam business horsing around in a boat! You know better than that. Get into the house and get some dry clothes on for God's sake!"

Steve put the car into gear. "Sorry Mr. Collins," he said without looking at him.

"Sorry doesn't cut it buster! Don't come around here again do you hear me? Leave her alone!"

"Call me later," Cara yelled as Steve sped away. She had no idea whether or not he heard her. She was shaking again, as much from anger as from the cold. She turned and faced her father. "What is your fucking problem?" she shouted at him.

His face was twisted with anger, and something else Cara couldn't quite identify. Fear? Guilt? He didn't answer her, just slammed into the house, leaving her puzzled and bedraggled on the sidewalk.

Steve caught up with her in the hall at school the next morning.

"You okay?" he asked.

"Yeah." She smiled up at him. "I had a great time. Thanks."

"What was going on with your dad?"

She shrugged. "Who knows. He's always been funny about boats. My grandfather drowned out on the lake, I guess that has something to do with it."

"I didn't know whether to call you or not."

"Call. I don't care. I hang around with whoever I want."

He leaned up against the bank of lockers. "So do you want to hang around with me?"

She smiled. "Yeah."

Like wildfire, the news spread around the school that Steve and Cara were going out, but unlike the usual flames of adolescent passion, their relationship had a comfortableness to it that delighted and puzzled them both. They often held hands. They often kissed. But they both seemed hesitant to take it any further.

The problem is we have the same sense of humour, Cara thought. They would reach a certain intensity, only to have something strike them both as unutterably funny, and they would dissolve in paroxysms of laughter.

Cara was not inexperienced; she had had a few encounters, but she wasn't the easy mark that her reputation held her to be. For her, what she imagined to be love was a necessary prerequisite for physical intimacy. Was she in love with Steve? She thought maybe she was. She loved being with him, loved sharing her thoughts and feelings, loved talking about what was important to her. When she was away from him she would fantasize about what it would be like to take their relationship to its natural culmination, but when she was with him, camaraderie seemed more important.

Was this just a friendship then? Certainly friendship was a major component of their relationship, but she hadn't thought it was possible for men and women to be just friends, to share an intellectual intimacy without physical intimacy getting in the way. Cara had a great adolescent belief in Karma; perhaps they had been friends in a previous life, she thought, and in this one were merely trying to emulate their previous connection. David and Jonathan transfigured and transmuted into another existence. Or was this the real thing? She had never been able to imagine herself committing to one person for a lifetime, but she began to get a glimmer of insight into how it could happen. Did a good marriage start with a good friendship? She realized for the first time that her mother and her father were probably friends, in spite of the differences in their personalities. They often engaged in the same sort of banter that she and Steve did. They didn't do a lot of stuff together, but maybe that was the outcome of many years of familiarity. She thought her parents probably had a pretty good sex life, there was that smoky undercurrent to them, but she also had difficulty imagining her mother sweating and moaning under her father, calling out his name in abandoned passion.

Whatever it was she had with Steve, it was wonderful. For the first time in her life, Cara actively sought the company of someone her own age. Although she would never have admitted it, not even to herself, hanging around with Steve gave her the same emotional satisfaction and sense of completion she had derived from her previous closeness to her father, but there was an inherent equality in this relationship that delighted her.

They spent every weekend together. They scrambled over rocks at the shore, they drove in Steve's father's car for hours, they went to movies, they listened to music. They even went fishing again, after Cara promised, not to behave herself, but to at least be a little more circumspect.

They almost upped the stakes one Saturday afternoon not long before Steve went away.

They packed a picnic lunch consisting of a bag of potato chips, a box of flaky pastries and a six pack of beer and drove to Point Petre, a largely deserted rocky shore beloved of teenagers. The point was owned by the Ministry of Defence, who had used it as a bombing range during World

War II and had never relinquished ownership. There was a transmitter station at the end of the point, something to do with nearby Trenton Air Force Base, its towers and bland architecture contrasting oddly with the little white lighthouse just down the road. The rest of the point was bleak and windswept scrubland, colonized by low bushes and stunted trees.

They found a clearing by the shore about halfway down the point. Steve had brought a sleeping bag, which he spread on the clifftop grass overlooking the water, where they could watch the sparkling waves crash against the flat, cracked limestone slabs.

They sat in silence for a while, tugging intermittently at their beers.

"I'm going to miss you when I'm gone," he said finally.

It was a subject they had avoided, the fact that Steve would be leaving for university in the fall.

"You're really going?"

"Yeah. I think I've got just enough money. I'm okay for a student loan, too, I guess."

She didn't reply. She had known all along that he would be leaving, but she had preferred not to think about it. She knew she had no rights or claims, no basis upon which to demand inclusion in his plans. There was no way it could ever possibly work anyway. She still had at least a year of high school left, and was as determined as ever to be an artist.

He turned to her. "I'll be home a lot, for holidays and weekends sometimes."

She considered this while she watched a piece of driftwood bash itself against a rounded outcropping of rock a few feet from shore. There would be letters and phone calls at first, she supposed, and joyous reunions at Thanksgiving and Christmas. Soon, she was sure, an awkwardness would creep in, an inability to find common ground, conversations petering out as they both groped for things to say. His would be a very different world from hers; campus rallies and lectures and beery parties with engineers. She could feel him slipping away from her, even as she sat beside him. She was damned if she was going to let him see it, though.

She leaned over to him. "I'm going to miss you, too," she said, kissing him lightly, provocatively on the lips. "But don't make promises you can't keep, okay?"

"Aw, Cara, I feel bad. I really like you, but I just don't see how this is going to work."

She forced herself to smile then. "Don't worry, neither do I." She knew this wasn't true; she had been having ill-formed fantasies about spending the rest of her life with this boy who was such good company. She determined then that she was going to have something to remember him by.

She pushed him backwards onto the sleeping bag and kissed him again.

"Let's just worry about the here and now. After all, we've still got this summer."

Cara's previous encounters had been furtive and hurried affairs in the back seats of cars, with boys who were eager to get the business over with before they embarrassed themselves by demonstrating just how eager they were. She had let them because she thought that was what she was supposed to do, and because she, too had a need, but for her it had all been a little disappointing . She found herself wondering afterwards what all the fuss was about.

She and Steve moved slowly with each other, exploring and savouring, inhaling each other's essence and tenuating each moment into a long and tender caress. In the small part of her mind that wasn't drenched with arousal, Cara was glad they had waited for this sort of significance.

He was above her, poised, searching her eyes for assent when the khaki-clad figures came crashing through the bushes. Cara had been focused on Steve and he on her, or they might have heard the air cadets coming; if part of the troop's training exercises included instructions on how to move stealthily through the undergrowth, they were failing miserably. The first thing Cara did see was Bruce Jackson, a boy in her geography class, who, unaccountably, was dressed from head to toe in camouflage and brandishing a rifle. She screamed. Bruce yelled. Steve gave a grunt of surprise and quickly pulled the sleeping bag over them both. "What the hell?" he growled.

Bruce reddened. "Er...sorry. Didn't know anybody was here. Hi Cara."

"Go away."

"Uh... yeah sure. Sorry." Bruce turned to his gang of hopeful soldiers. "Move out men. Nothing for us here."

They obeyed quickly, embarrassed, although one or two of them peeked back over their shoulders in the hopes of catching one more glimpse of Cara's naked body.

Cara was shaking. Steve thought she was sobbing at first. She managed to remain silent until the last cadet disappeared into the bushes before she exploded in laughter.

"Oh My God.... did you see the look on his face? Poor Bruce."

"Poor Bruce? I was the one with my butt hanging in the breeze." He was beginning to laugh too.

"I've never seen anyone look so embarrassed."

"Me or him?"

"Both. Oh God, I thought we were being invaded."

"You were being invaded. Or about to be, anyway."

"Oh yeah, I bet that's not standing at attention any more."

"You got that right."

They tried again after that, but it was no good. As soon as one settled down, the other would start to giggle. Finally, they gave up. It didn't really matter, anyway. There was a whole summer left.

Edna was alarmed, but she had no idea what to do. She wasn't really sure whether Cara was sexually active or not, but she had a strong suspicion that she was. Steve was her first steady boyfriend. If it hadn't happened already, it was bound to sooner or later.

Vera was nearly beside herself. She knew they had to stop this, but how? She certainly couldn't tell the truth. Mac would find out, sure as shooting, and then all of her ghosts would come back to haunt her. She couldn't forbid Steve to see Cara. He was eighteen and perfectly capable of walking out the door and out of her life if he felt like it.

Edna agreed. "If I try and force Cara into anything, she'll just dig her heels in. That won't work."

"Well, we have to do something," Vera said snappishly. "What if they... well... you know."

Edna did know. What she also knew was that she could never broach the topic with Len, even though she knew he was upset as well. Vera swore that she had never told him, never so much as dropped a hint, but Edna was pretty sure that he at least suspected. When she thought about it, she was pretty sure that a lot of other people suspected as well. Steve was too like Len physically; the same lean height, the same hazel eyes. Sometimes when she saw Cara and Steve together they looked more like brother and sister than boyfriend and girlfriend. Well, I guess that's what they are, she thought with a pang. Sort of. She had nightmares about six-toed idiot children hidden away in attics.

She tried talking to Cara. "Aren't you seeing an awful lot of Steve Dunlop?" she asked.

"Yeah. So?" Edna could tell by the set of her shoulders that Cara was getting defensive.

"It's just unusual for you, that's all," she said. "Are you two going steady?"

"No. We're just good friends," Cara replied. "We like hanging out."

"I hate to see you monopolized, that's all. After all, you're only sixteen."

Cara looked at her coolly. "You used to complain that I went out with too many different guys. You wanna make up your mind?"

The sins of the fathers, Edna thought. Oh God, I'm starting to sound like my mother. In the end, circumstances rescued them, along with a little careful manipulation. Steve had applied to several universities and, with his stellar marks, was accepted at all of them.

"Which one does he want to go to?" Edna asked.

"He's really thinking about Queen's," Vera said. "He says their business program is top-notch."

Edna sighed. Queen's was in nearby Kingston, an hour's drive away. Too close. He'd be able to get home every weekend.

"Is there any way we can talk him into the University of Outer Siberia?" she asked, then immediately regretted it. If Steve was too far away, Vera would never get to see him.

"He's accepted at Western, too. That wouldn't be too bad."

Western was in London, off in the southwestern part of the province. It was a good five hour drive away.

"Let me see if I can't sweeten the Western pot a little," Edna said thoughtfully.

That night she knocked on the door of the den, something she rarely did when Len was in there working. He still conducted a great deal of business from the office at Charles Furniture, but there were certain papers he kept at home, away from the prying eyes of the store's gossipy staff. He would often spend his evenings with plans and contracts and agreements.

He looked startled when she came in, his face lit only by a spill of light from the lamp on his desk. She was struck suddenly by the fact that Len had finally started to look older. He was still trim, but his shoulders had grown heavier, and there were lines on his face that she hadn't noticed before. Why, he looks like a middle-aged man, she thought. Did she look middle-aged too? She guessed she must, although when she got up in the morning, the same old face always looked back at her from the other side of the mirror.

"Is something wrong?" he asked.

"I've come to ask a favour," she said. He looked surprised. Edna seldom asked for anything. She didn't need to.

"It's about Steve Dunlop." He looked wary then, as though she had presented a trap, and he was calculating the odds of escape. She knew for sure then that he understood the problem full well, but she had no intention of forcing the secret into the light of day. They had spent nearly twenty years ignoring things they didn't want to talk about. She wasn't going to change that now.

He pretended to think for a moment. "Steve Dunlop? Oh yeah. Vera's kid. The one Cara's seeing so much of."

"Yes. Vera's kid. He's a bright boy, you know. He's been accepted at every university he's applied to."

"Is that right? Where has he applied?" Len was quick enough to understand that she was presenting him with a solution, but he hadn't quite grasped what it was yet.

"I believe Queen's....." she almost laughed at his reaction, but held it in check. ".......U of T and Western. The only problem is, he's a little short of money. You know Vera and Mac don't have much. I know it's a lot to ask.....," she played it perfectly, the diffident wife beseeching her husband on behalf of an old friend,"..... but is there any way we could help them? He's really leaning towards Western, there's a good business course there, but it's so far away and housing is so expensive."

She thought he already had property in London, one of his companies had built a large nursing home there, but she had no idea if he owned anything like a house or apartment building. Tough bananas, she thought, if he doesn't own one now he can buy one.

He caught her drift immediately, as she knew he would.

"Hmmmm... London, eh? You know something, I've got a little building there... nothing special you know, it's really pretty modest, but I think there's a vacancy right now. And I do need somebody to look after it... just routine maintenance stuff, a little grass-mowing, keep the hallway clean, that kind of thing. Do you suppose Steve would be interested? I'd give him an apartment in lieu of wages. Come to think of it, it's pretty close to the university. Or on a bus route anyway. I'd need somebody right away, though. He'd have to leave as soon as he's finished school."

She smiled. "I'll run it past Vera and see what she thinks. Thanks, Len."

He smiled back. "It's the least I can do for your best friend," he said.

Vera had no real difficulty getting Steve to agree to the arrangement. Free rent meant that student loans could cover tuition and books, and his savings would keep him comfortably in food and beverage.

"How did all this come about?" Steve wanted to know when his mother told him.

"Cara's mother happened to mention it," Vera said vaguely. "It's awfully kind of them to offer it to you, you know. It'll be a real help."

Steve knew that for some reason Len Collins didn't like him. He also knew that he was being bought off, offered a dangling carrot that would take him far away and out of Cara's life. He genuinely debated with himself for a few days, wondering if he should do the noble thing and tell Mr. Collins he didn't need his help. The only trouble was, he did.

He tried to ask his mother about it.

"You're the first steady boyfriend she's had," Vera said. "He's always been over-protective. He probably just feels she's too young."

Steve knew that was a load of bull and knew that Len's dislike went far deeper than that, but in the end he decided to accept the offer. He would be a fool not to.

He broke the news to Cara while they lay baking in the sun at the beach. It was still only June, but the last part of May had been unseasonably hot, and the water in the little bay was already soupy. He waited until they had swum, splashing each other on the way in, diving into the green water and grabbing each other's legs, laughing as they chased each other back to the shore with gobs of seaweed. Cara collapsed on the blanket they had spread on the sand and cradled her head in her arms.

"I love summer," she said, and closed her eyes. "This is going to be the best one ever."

They flew open again when Steve began to speak.

"Next week? You're leaving next week? Why?"

"I've picked up a job down there that's going to set me up for the rest of the year. I can't afford to turn it down, Cara."

He could see that she was extremely upset, close to tears, something he had never seen before.

"Look, if you're that strapped, I'll give you the money. I'll get it from my dad. I'll make him give it to you."

Steve was embarrassed. "Um... it was sort of through your dad that I got this. Your mum mentioned it to my mum and it just sort of went from there."

Cara stiffened. "My Dad? My Dad offered you a job in London?"

"Yeah." Steve pushed at the sand with his foot, not looking at her.

Cara sat up. "You asshole, you're going to let yourself be bought off like that? You know what he's doing."

"Yeah, I know." He squinted, looking out at the lake, looking anywhere but at her.

"And you're just going to go ahead and let his money do the talking."

He was angry then. "It's all right for you, you don't ever have to worry about anything so sordid as money. The rest of us have to eat, you know." Then he softened his tone. "Look, just because I'm in London doesn't mean we can't see each other. I'll be back sometimes. I'll call. I'll write. I promise."

She knew that he meant it then. He was leaving her behind.

She stood up. "So go," she said.

"Aw, Cara don't be like that."

"Judas. Take your forty pieces of silver and go. You were going anyway, so go. I don't care." She gathered her things and walked away. She'd get a ride home with Ricky MacDonald.

Cara's relationship with her father had been strained before; now it was icy. When they passed in the hall, or sat at the dinner table or met coming in the back door she quite simply refused to acknowledge that he was there. When he spoke to her, she ignored him.

"She's just angry with you," Edna said to him. "She can't keep it up forever. Give her time and she'll come around."

But the summer went by without a word spoken between them.

"Wait until she gets back to school," Edna said. "She'll meet someone else and then everything will be all right."

But the school year started and everything wasn't all right. Edna had expected her daughter to resume a wild round of parties and pranks, but to her surprise she seemed to settle down. She would never be an exemplary student, she had never developed the study habits required for that, but she did put a push on and at Christmas had raised her marks to a B average.

"Well, it's an ill wind, I guess," Edna shrugged. Len looked glum. Cara was still ignoring him.

Although their family was small, Christmas had always been a riotous time in the Collins house. Edna insisted that Christmas Eve include Jack and Margaret, who were invited to drink eggnog while Len and Cara decorated the tree. Len always bought a tree that was far too large for their living room, and festooned it with at least eight strings of lights. After the lights came the decorations, each with a story.

"This little elf was left behind at the North Pole one Christmas night long ago," Len would tell Cara. "He was so lonely he cried all night, and that's when I found him and brought him here. Now, he's happy, because he has a tree and a family." He would hand the wooden elf to Cara who would place it carefully on a lower branch.

"These Christmas balls lived at the circus," he would say. "They got tired of being juggled by the seal, so they came here to live instead." And together they would place the glittery globes on the tree while Jack and Margaret and Edna watched. Mud watched too, his tail wagging because everyone was happy.

As more ornaments came out of the box, Len's stories got wilder, and Cara giggled more, until finally, all the decorations were up and they were ready for the tinsel. This was the part Mud loved best, for neither Cara nor Len had the patience to hang it strand by strand. They would take great hanks of the silvery stuff and dance around the tree, throwing it at random. Mud would dance with them, barking and trying to grab the tinsel as it fluttered towards the overloaded spruce. He always caught at least a few. Some years he would be as tinselled as the tree. He nearly always ate a few strands.

The only solemn moment of the evening would come when the blue and white painted angel took her place at the very top of the tree. The room would hush and everyone, for some reason, held their breath while Len climbed the stepladder and set her on the single upthrust branch. Only when they were certain she was secure would they begin to laugh and talk again.

Later Edna would re-arrange the tree, moving the ornaments so they were dispersed evenly and separating the tinsel. She would pick up the fallen strands and replace them and put the Christmas presents carefully underneath, making sure that anything breakable was at the back, away from passing traffic. As soon as the presents were brought out, Mud was banished to the back porch where he would spend the rest of the evening puking up the tinsel he had eaten.

Christmas morning was for the three of them. When Cara was little, the day had often started at six a.m. She would be warned not to go downstairs until everyone was up, and so, when she could no longer stand lying awake and alone in her own bed, she would creep in with her parents, pushing her cold feet against Len's back. He would groan and burrow deeper, away from her. She would begin to talk then, a soft whisper at first, right in his ear.

"Daddy, I heard Santa Claus. I'm sure he's been already. There were hoofbeats on the roof."

"Not yet, Cara," he would groan.

"Yes, I'm sure."

She would be silent for a few minutes, just long enough for them to drift back into sleep again.

"Daddy." This time her voice would be a little louder, a loud whisper.

"Umm-hmmm."

"I saw Rudolph's red nose."

"No, it was a car."

"Uh-uh."

Finally, when she would be on the point of exploding from impatience, Len would join in.

"Mummy," they would say. "Mummy, come on, it's Christmas! Wake up!"

They would rush down the stairs, Cara running straight to her Santa Claus present, the one that was always left unwrapped and sitting in front of the tree. Edna would start the coffee, and then the orgy of unwrapping would begin, Cara and Len tearing at the paper while Mud ran through the ribbons and barked.

Even later, when she thought she was too old for such sentimental nonsense, Cara would get caught up in the excitement of Christmas and the routine would be the same.

But not this year.

When Jack and Margaret arrived on Christmas Eve, they met Cara at the door. She had her coat on.

"Oh," said Margaret, who looked forward to the occasion all year. "Aren't you decorating the tree tonight?"

"Sorry, Aunt Margaret, I promised I'd help at the Christmas Eve Service." She hadn't, but it was the only excuse she could think of that would get her out of the house.

Jack and Margaret tried to make light of it, but neither were able to dispel the gloom that settled over the living room. Len refused to drink eggnog, instead pouring himself liberal amounts of rye. In the end it was Edna who climbed the ladder and placed the angel on top of the tree, where it sat dispirited and lopsided. Cara, who had found nowhere else to go, spent the evening at the donut shop.

It was nine o'clock when Edna awoke the next morning to the smell of coffee. Len was already downstairs. He was in the den, working.

"On Christmas?" Edna protested.

"Well, get Cara out of bed then so we can open the damn presents," he said grumpily.

Edna roused her daughter, who reluctantly got out of bed and came downstairs to the living room. She sat in one of the armchairs waiting passively while her mother passed present after present, which she opened without a word and set back underneath the tree. Edna put Christmas carols on the stereo and kept up a running chatter of bright inanity, hoping to strike a note that would animate her family. It didn't work. Cara and Len sat in a glowering silence.

Mud wasn't even let out of the back porch.

By the time the turkey and the plum pudding had been eaten in silence, Edna had a pounding headache and went to bed. Cara went out. So did Len.

Cara went for a long walk with Mud. Len went to Francine's.

Francine was astounded. He had already been around the day before with her Christmas present, a lovely diamond necklace, and she really hadn't expected to see him again until after New Year's. He didn't visit her nearly as often as he used to anyway, and when he did, he often just sat and talked. He would arrive out of the blue, always with news of some triumph or to discuss some strategy. Francine sometimes longed for the days when he would tumble her into bed like a whirlwind, and sometimes it still happened, but more and more he just talked, bouncing ideas off her, using her as a sounding board. Or a mother confessor, she would sometimes think ruefully.

This time she knew something was wrong. She poured him a drink and waited until he was ready to tell her.

"Worst damn Christmas I've ever had in my life," he said, glaring at her.

Still she waited. It took three drinks, but finally the story came tumbling out.

Steve and Cara. And Vera. Vera and Len.

Francine only vaguely recalled that Vera had once been at The Palace of the Moon with Len. She had been just one more addlebrained girl that had buzzed around him, unremarkable and unremembered. But she had seen Vera's boy at the gas station, without knowing who he was, and had wondered a bit, he looked so familiar, so when she heard the truth it came as no surprise.

"Edna says I should just leave her alone and she'll get over it, but I don't know what to think." His face was bleak, and she could see that he didn't believe it.

It did surprise her that Edna evidently knew the whole story; but then, she remembered, Vera and Edna had always been bosom buddies. The obvious depth of the friendship astonished her; at some point they must have discussed, evaluated, forgiven and, in the end, decided to remain friends in spite of everything. Francine had never had much use for the manipulations of women, she found men far more straightforward and infinitely more interesting, but she was impressed with the way Edna and Vera had handled this, for she had no doubt that they had taken stock of the situation and neatly manufactured the solution. It was a far from perfect solution, or Len wouldn't be pouring his woes out to her, but she was sure that in time it would all resolve itself.

"How do I put this right, Francine?" He looked up at her and she could see tears in his eyes. She wished she had some answer for him, that she could point out something obvious that he had missed, that she could take Cara and shake her, force her to make it up with her father, but in the end the only thing she could think to do was to offer him the comfort she always had.

Well, doesn't this beat all? she thought as she held him in her arms. Len Collins has finally met a woman who can break his heart.

Steve tried to call a few times after he left, but Cara had given Bernice instructions to say that she was out. He wrote regularly, at least for the first few months, but as time went on he found it harder and harder to find things to say, and the fact that he never received a letter in return made his efforts seem pointless. Eventually he stopped, caught up in a new and profoundly exciting life.

Cara left home a week after she graduated from high school, refusing even to say goodbye to her father.

She had expected to be thrilled by the city, by the neon flashing against the night, by the bustle, by the anonymity. Instead, she was homesick. She had never been good at making friends, but she realized now that the familiarity of a small town had made close friends unnecessary in a way. Now she was on her own. No one cared how she dressed, or how she acted. There were no tongues wagging about her every move. No one noticed any of her moves.

She found a small studio apartment, within walking distance of the College of Art, at the top of an old house owned by a couple with three small children. He was a stockbroker, she was something with one of the banks. They must have been appalled, she thought, when their first two children turned out to be girls, necessitating the production of a third child who proved to be obligingly male. The couple had a Filipino nanny, who also did the housework. Cara could hear her as her sandals clip-clopped around the second floor, and as her sharp tone quelled the rising voices of the children in some squabble over toys.

Over time she adjusted to the rhythm of the city, with its incessant wail of sirens and rumbling, honking traffic. Gradually she found her way around the College and the rows of classmates turned from a blur of faces to people with names. She concentrated on fine art courses and once or twice had coffee with a gang of other students after class, but volunteered little information about herself. She was intimidated by these students, with their airs of sophistication and world-weary exhibitions of knowledge. She knew that her speech sometimes betrayed her, some archaic expression or peculiar syntax contrasting with their carefully cultivated, unidentifiable drawls. Try as she might, she couldn't imitate this speech; there was always a native anomaly waiting to trip her up.

"You might better make that a shade darker," she said one time, commenting on a fellow student's work.

The student had erupted in laughter, and for a time "might better" was a much-bandied phrase amongst the other students.

"No, I don't like boughten cookies," she said another time, in response to the offer of an Oreo.

It was Derek who persuaded her to relax. Derek was a handsome boy who sat beside her in art history.

"A lot of them are from towns just as small as yours," he said. "They have to work really hard to sound citified. I must admit, though, " he laughed, "you do have a strange way of speaking."

She didn't know whether to be reassured or embarrassed, but then he asked if she wanted to go for a coffee after class, and she felt better. He took her to a different place, one where the other students didn't normally go. She was on the point of deciding that he didn't really want to be seen with her, when he explained.

"I get so tired of that rabble. I found this place a couple of weeks ago and decided it would be nice to get away from their constant drivel. Sometimes they make me tired, they know so little." He sipped his espresso elegantly, lit a cigarette and looked with weariness out the window, then turned to her. "So where are you from?"

She told him and he nodded knowingly. "Big sand dunes, lots of water, right? I went there once with my family for a holiday. Nice place, but a little odd."

She tensed. She really was odd, then, it wasn't just her imagination.

"We had a cottage for the summer and I played with some of the local kids. Half the time I didn't know what they were talking about." He chuckled. "I'd spent my whole life in the city. I didn't know you could just pick a tomato off a plant and eat it. It was a great summer, though. You must have had a wonderful childhood."

She wanted then to tell him about her childhood. About swimming off a rocky ledge and Mud and sailing out in the middle of the lake with her father, about Bernice's cookies and Rhonda who broke everything, but something held her back. She didn't quite trust the sheen from this polished person who sat across from her.

"It was fun," was all she said, and then she discovered it was all she needed to say. Derek was perfectly happy to keep the conversation going by talking about himself.

He took her out for coffee several times a week after that and then to his apartment, where she allowed him to take off her clothes and make urgent, hurried love to her. She wasn't sure she even liked him, but she thought, quite rightly, that sex was something she had to offer to keep his friendship. He was convenient, someone to hang out with, a way of keeping the other students and her loneliness at bay.

It was through Derek that she met Cass, who had just opened her first store.

"I have a friend who needs an illustrator," he said to her one day.

"An illustrator of what?"

"Drawings for a small Christmas catalogue. You know, bottles of lotion, crystal wind chimes. Just line drawings to go with the description."

"Why don't you do it, if she's your friend?"

"Because you have a better eye for proportion. And you're into realism."

That was true enough. Derek favoured massive canvasses with enigmatic blobs of colour.

"Besides," he went on. "You don't have the same sort of natural distaste for commercial work, not that she's paying all that much."

Cass was ecstatic with the drawings Cara produced, each item faithfully depicted, but with a panache that made them irresistible. Cakes of oatmeal soap were shown piled up and surrounded by bubbles of laughing, frothy lather. Giant sea sponges frolicked with starfish and turtles in reefs of coral. Exquisite glass paperweights held sheaves of paper firmly down while tornado-force winds blew by.

The two women hit it off on a personal level, too. Cass was short, "a midget" she would call herself, very pale and would have been very blonde except that she dyed her short hair a deep, midnight black. It made her look like a vampire. She made constant references to Cara's height.

"A midget and a giant," she would laugh. "A freak and a thoroughbred, walking down the street side by side."

It was Derek who pointed out the significance of their names. "Cass and Cara" he said, "Cascara. A bitter fluid extracted from the bark of the California buckthorn tree and used as a laxative. How appropriate."

They adored the description, referring to each other as "ExLax" and "Milk of Magnesia" and agreed that, whatever else they were, they certainly weren't full of shit.

Long after Derek departed, Cass continued to rely on Cara for the artwork in her quarterly catalogues, and to find other small commissions through her numerous connections. Because of this and a growing disenchantment with the rigidity of fine art classes, and the even more rigid attitude of her fellow students, Cara began picking up more graphic design and commercial art courses.

Here she was more at home. These students all had one eye firmly on the future; they couldn't afford attitude and they were a whole lot friendlier because of it. She began to feel almost at home, a part of a defined group, at one with the pulsing city, and her homesickness finally left her.

Her new-found sense of belonging exploded with one phone call.

CHAPTER EIGHTEEN

The ringing startled Edna out of a dream in which she stood on Vera's front porch pressing the doorbell. Even though she knew she was expected, no one came to answer. Again and again she rang, and even peered in through the front window, but all she could see was the empty hall where Vera's coat hung on the rack and a huge pair of rubber boots stood in the shoe tray. She awoke to realize that it was not a doorbell, but the telephone that was ringing so insistently. Len padded in from the bathroom and grabbed the receiver off the hook before she came to enough to answer it. She rolled over and looked at the clock on the bedside table. Six a.m. She groaned and rolled back again, burrowing into the blankets. Len's day always started early, but usually people were polite enough to wait until at least eight before they called.

Whoever it was on the other end was doing most of the talking. "Um-huh...um-huh..." was all she could hear, and then, "Okay Art, see you tonight then."

"I have to go to out of town," Len said, hanging up the phone. "Hello? Good Morning? Are you with us?"

"Mmm..mmm." Edna's head was buried under the blankets.

"That's what I love about you," he said, going to the closet. "You're so charming first thing in the morning." He threw his carryall on the bed and started rummaging for socks and shirts.

Edna pulled the covers down far enough to expose her face, so she could watch him as he packed. "You're not coming back tonight?"

"Don't know yet." He leaned over, pulled her tousled hair away from her face and gave her a wet, smooching kiss. "I'll tell Bernice to bring you some tea, okay? See ya."

Edna never knew how long Len would be away when he went on these trips, and he seldom gave her an itinerary, or even the name of the hotel he was staying at, if he stayed at a hotel at all. It didn't bother Edna much; that had been the way it was from the first. Sometimes she went with him, but not often. There was little for her to do, other than browse through dress shops and department stores where she occasionally picked up a new outfit or bought something for the house, something she couldn't find at home. Evenings would be spent with Len's associates or friends, sometimes with their wives. Complicated deals were finalized over drinks, financial transactions solidified at dinner, and Edna listened to them with half an ear as she discussed fashion and children with the other women.

She was more content to stay home with her garden and her house, to play the occasional rubber of bridge, to drink tea and gossip with Vera, and to wait until Len came home. This suited Len, too. He no longer really needed her along and he could move further and faster alone.

She liked the rhythm of her life; calm and ordered when she was by herself, exuberant and unpredictable when Len was there. They had drawn closer in the aftermath of the troubles with Cara. He by no means confided in her but there was now an unspoken pact between them, a feeling that after so many years together they could count on each other when they needed to.

Every once in a while, late at night when she couldn't sleep, Edna's mind would return to the episode with Sacha, for that was how she thought of it now, an episode, a brief disruption in the flow of her life. There was a faint embarrassment that lingered over these memories, but if she were truly wide awake, she could set that aside and recall their lovemaking with a fervent nostalgia. Len still aroused her, of course, and she enjoyed the fact that he still tumbled her into bed frequently, but the recollection of the afternoons spent with Sacha had now been cast in a golden retrospective light that, occasionally, she allowed herself to bask in.

She fell asleep again until Bernice arrived with a breakfast tray and the mail. There was a new book she had ordered about how to grow herbs and she idly flipped through the pages. An old-fashioned herb garden would look lovely over by the coach house, she thought. Sectioned, with gravelled paths leading to a small garden bench in the middle. Basil and sage and camomile; fenugreek and horehound and coriander; the words were redolent with mystery, speaking of a long-forgotten time when cures and tonics came not from vats and test tubes, but from the earth itself.

After she dressed, she rummaged in Len's study until she found a pad of graph paper and painstakingly drew a design. When she finished, she realized it was lop-sided, and that she had forgotten to put in oregano. She crumpled the paper up and threw it at the wastebasket, but missed, the paper bouncing away over the broadloom to fetch up in the corner. She moved to pick it up and then decided it didn't matter. Mud in his old age spent most of his time curled around his cushion in the warm kitchen, odd pieces of trash now remained undisturbed. His days were numbered, she knew, and she expected every morning to find him cold and lifeless in the corner, his cataract-clouded eyes no longer able to discern the metal buttons on a uniform or the temptation of an untended piece of paper.

Maybe we should get another dog when Mud goes, she thought, it would be nice to have one. This time it could be a purebred, like Len had wanted in the first place. She made a mental note to talk to him about it when he got back.

Bernice appeared in the doorway. "Bill Braxton's at the door, Mrs. Len. He wants a word with you."

The handyman was waiting on the back stoop. It had started to snow and the man's head and shoulders were covered with the fine, white powder.

"Come in, come in, you must be frozen," she said. "Bernice, is there any tea left for Bill?"

"No, no, she already offered," Bill said. "I've got to go on this morning. I haven't put Mrs. Jackson's storm windows on yet. I just thought I'd let you know that some shingles have blown off the back of the carriage house. Must have been that big wind we had a couple of nights ago."

"Can you fix them?" she asked.

"Well, I'll patch it up for the winter," he said. "But you really ought to consider putting a whole new roof on in the spring. Some of them shingles are getting worn pretty thin. The thing is, if you just want a patch job, I'll put good shingles back up, but if you're going to put a new roof on anyway, I'll just tar down the old ones."

Edna wasn't sure what to do. "Mr. Collins is away right now Bill. But I'll get him to call you as soon as he gets back and let you know which. Okay?"

"That's fine, ma'am. Just wanted to make sure you knew about it." He glanced up at the sky. "Wind's coming out of the east, we're going to get another blow tonight." The snow had intensified just while they had been talking.

"Thanks Bill." He tipped his hat and went on his way.

The storm built over the afternoon, and by four o'clock the grey November afternoon had turned icy, with hard white pellets pummelling the house. This was the kind of weather that bothered Bernice's arthritis, Edna knew, so she went into the kitchen to make them a pot of tea.

"Do you think Mr. Len will be back tonight?" Bernice asked. It was not curiosity, but rather a practical question about what to make for dinner.

"No, I don't think so. Why don't you and I just have bacon and eggs or something easy? I'll make it," she added, for she had noted that Bernice was moving gingerly, all the old injuries she had suffered at the hands of her no-good husband rising up in protest at the dampness in the air. Bernice let herself down into a kitchen chair gratefully.

"My I hate this sort of weather. Makes you glad you don't have anyplace to go."

Edna agreed, for by now the back step was covered with a layer of slick ice. "It's nasty out there, all right. I think you should stay over here tonight." She couldn't see letting Bernice hobble across the driveway in the snow, and what was the point anyway, if Len wasn't coming home? When she was alone in the house, she often preferred it that way, and the housekeeper would sleep in one of the back bedrooms, making the house feel a little less empty.

Bernice nodded. "Don't mind if I do."

They took their time over tea, chatting companionably about Cara and Rhonda and little bits of household business that needed tending to. It was late, nearly eight o'clock, by the time Edna started their casual dinner. She enjoyed these kitchen conferences; it was a restful part of her other life, the Len's-not-home life, and it never seemed as comforting when he was around.

By the time they had finished eating, Edna couldn't even see across the driveway. Isabel Jackson called, to see if she was all right.

"Bill told me Len was out of town," she said. "Thank God he finally came and put the storms on. You okay for everything?"

"Snug as a bug. I thought you two would be at Hannah's." There was a pre-Christmas party at Rick and Hannah Fletcher's. She and Len had been invited, but they hardly ever went to those things anymore.

"I thought I'd be there too," Isabel said. "Fred refuses to get the car out, it's that bad. When was the last time you found me sitting at home on a Friday night?"

She could tell that Isabel was bored and warming up for a long gossipy conversation, that was the real reason she had called.

"Isabel, I'm getting a lot of static on the line," she lied, "I can hardly hear you. I better call you back tomorrow."

Bernice grinned.

"Okay, but if you need anything you call and I'll send Fred right over, okay?"

Poor Fred, Edna thought. "Okay, Isabel, thanks."

"Well, I'm about all in," Bernice said when she had hung up. "If you don't mind Mrs. Len, I'll just do the dishes, then go on up." She hoisted herself painfully out of the chair.

"Oh, don't bother about them," Edna said. "I'll rinse them and put them in the dishwasher. You go to bed."

"Don't mind if I do," she said. "Lordy, I'm glad I'm inside safe and sound," she muttered as she climbed the back stairs.

Edna pottered around the kitchen, rinsing their plates, wiping down the counter, pouring herself another cup of tea before she shut the house down for the night. The wind was howling in earnest now, slamming into the windows on the east side of the house. The temperature was dropping too, she could feel it as she walked around turning off lights.

She had been about to flick the back porch light off when she saw them, bent against the wind, their heads down as they concentrated on their footing along the icy path. They seemed to be moving in slow motion, but whether it was the wind pushing them back or just her imagination, she didn't know. She waited until they were at the door before she opened it. The wind tore it out of her hands, but one of them, one she knew, George Franklin, grabbed it before it could slam against the side of the house. They pushed their way in.

"What are you boys doing out on a night like this, George?" she asked, to let him know that she already knew who he was.

George's face was grim. "Can we come in, Mrs. Collins?"

"Of course." Her heart was racing as she led them through to the kitchen and invited them to sit, but they remained standing, shifting uncomfortably from one foot to the other. Suddenly a low growl issued from the corner.

"Be quiet," she said, but Mud was not to be denied. It had been a long time since he'd had the pleasure of growling at a uniform. The snarl intensified, and the hair on the back of his neck stood straight up. He got his feet under him and staggered across the kitchen floor to confront the enemy. She waylaid him and steered him into the dining room, shutting the door firmly behind him. He whined and began scratching at it. "Sorry," she said, "he thinks he's fierce." She forced her mouth into a smile. "I'm afraid I don't know you," she said to the second policeman. "Are you new?"

"This is Don McBride. Uhhh... maybe you'd like to sit down yourself, Mrs. Collins?" She shook her head. George cleared his throat, and looked at her sadly. "I'm afraid there's been an accident."

In Edna's world, accidents were trivial things, shingles that blew off roofs and pieces of china that Rhonda dropped. But these didn't require the presence of the police. She waited for George to go on.

He spoke gently, watching her face. "There's been a car accident. Your husband's car went out of control on Highway #15, just north of Kingston. I'm terribly sorry, Mrs. Collins, I'm afraid he didn't survive."

Even though she had been expecting it, had known as soon as she saw them coming up the path, the words made no sense to her. How could Len not survive? Len always survived. It had to be a mistake, a gruesome misunderstanding. And yet she knew that road, it twisted and turned, held sudden hills and blind corners. She decided to sit after all.

"What happened?" She had trouble finding the words, and they came out in a whisper, but it was important that she heard the exact circumstances, the unforeseen chain of events, the malignant combination of forces that had resulted in his car going off the road. If she knew this, she could find the flaw in their reasoning and then Len could come back to her, laughing at so silly an assumption.

"He must not have realized he was driving into a storm," the other policeman said. "This is a pretty localized blow, mostly lake effect stuff, but the temperature dropped real fast north of here. As near as we can figure right now, he hit a patch of black ice and spun out of control."

She tried to imagine Len out of control, not able to make the big, solid Buick do what he wanted it to. Len was used to driving everywhere, in every kind of weather. He was never out of control. Still, she began to picture it. The big car would have started to slide and he would have steered with the skid, hoping to correct his course as soon as the wheels found solid pavement. He would have turned in an arc, the landscape spinning by crazily, only to leave the road and strike.... what? A tree? A stone wall? Another car? She fiddled with the tablecloth. There were still toast crumbs on it from supper. She should get a cloth and wipe it down, she thought, so Bernice won't have to do it in the morning. Then she realized that the two men were waiting for her reaction to their words.

"Was anyone else hurt?" she asked finally.

"No, ma'am. Just the single vehicle involved in the incident." George cleared his throat. "Unfortunately, he wasn't wearing a seatbelt. He was propelled through the windshield and suffered extensive head injuries on impact."

Incident. What an odd word to describe an event that was so cataclysmic but she knew that George was relying on the formal language of the police report to soften the words. In a way they did, and it was far harder for her to imagine this part. Len flying up over the steering wheel and through the glass, over the hood of the car, his head striking the ground. Was his fate illuminated by the car's headlights or did their beams shoot up into the sky at some crazy angle? Was the radio still playing or had the car completely died when it settled into the ditch? She didn't have enough of the details to make it real to her, but she couldn't ask those questions. Not now, when the news was so fresh.

"There's no mistake?"

George shook his head wearily. "I'm afraid not, ma'am. The license plates match and his identification was in his wallet."

Mud had stopped whining and was starting to bark now. She knew he would soon start to howl.

"Mrs. Len, what is it? Do you need me?" Bernice was on the stairs, hovering on the landing, unsure if she should come all the way down or not.

"Yes." But it wasn't loud enough for Bernice to hear, so one of the policemen, the one she didn't know, what was his name? Don. Don walked to the bottom and called up to her.

"I think you'd better come here, ma'am."

Bernice was wearing a flannelette nightgown and had thrown an old terry cloth robe over it. In her haste she hadn't bothered about slippers, and Edna noticed that her toes were gnarled and cold-looking.

"Which one?" she demanded of the policemen standing in her kitchen, for there was only one reason for them to be there. "Cara or Mr. Len?"

“It’s Len,” Edna said. She found she was wringing her hands, something that heroines always did in the novels she read. She had never dreamed that she would ever wring her hands, but she couldn’t stop herself. "What happens now?" she asked.

"Ummm.. we’ll need you to make a formal identification,” George said. She was grateful that he didn’t say “identify the body” the way they always did on T.V. “Then if you can let us know, um..., who you would like to deal with, they can arrange to have him transferred directly."

It took her a moment to understand what he meant. Of course. A funeral home. Undertakers. Coffins to be picked out and services to be arranged.

"Jones." She only barely managed to croak the word out before the tears, which had been pricking at the corners of her eyes, bubbled over the top and down her face. This was no error, no case of mistaken identity. This was real. He was gone. Bernice held her while she cried.

“Are you staying with her?” the policeman, the strange one asked. What a silly question, Edna thought bleakly. What else would the woman be doing here in her nightgown?

“Don’t you worry,” Bernice said in an unsteady voice. “I’ll look after her. I know what to do.”

George left a card on the kitchen table. “If you need to get hold of me, my number’s there,” he said. “We’ll see ourselves out.” He gave Edna a final nod of the head, and they left.

Bernice knew only too well what to do. She, too had sat in a kitchen, not as nice a one as this, mind you, but she’d sat there while two policemen informed her that a car had left a road, a husband wasn’t coming home again. She hadn’t even particularly liked Chester all that much, but that hadn’t made the whole thing any easier when it came right down to it. “Do you want me to call Mrs. Dunlop?” she asked. Edna nodded.

Vera arrived in a cab, still in her nightdress. Bernice had made more tea and poured them each a mugful, and Vera laced it with generous slugs of Len’s brandy.

“Oh, Edna,” she said, as she handed the mugs around. “I’m so sorry. I’m still in shock, I can’t believe it. Were they absolutely sure?” She didn’t wait for an answer. “Well, of course they are, aren’t they? That was a stupid thing to say, forgive me, it’s just that I can’t quite seem to come to grips with the whole thing...”

Neither could Edna, and she sat in grateful silence while Vera prattled on. She found it soothing, as she had known she would. Vera only echoed the thoughts going through her own head, and it was nice not to have to search for the actual words to express them.

“Did you want me to try and get Cara on the phone?” Bernice asked after a while.

Edna shook her head. "No, we'll call in the morning. Let her have one good night's sleep anyway." She noticed then the fatigue on the housekeeper's face. "Why don't you go up to bed now? I'm going to need a lot of help in the morning."

Bernice nodded and shuffled off, already considering what foods needed to be ordered, prepared, cooked. Edna felt a clumsy exhaustion numbing her body, but she knew it was useless to try to sleep. Her stomach was upset and she had a headache and the picture of Len flying through the windshield kept going through her mind, especially when she closed her eyes. She wanted an aspirin, but she couldn't remember where they were kept.

Vera began making a list of things they needed to do; who should be notified, who they would ask to be pallbearers, was there to be any visitation? She found comfort in the discussion of details.

Edna participated only half-heartedly, almost annoyed at the intrusion of such practical concerns, though she knew these were all things that needed to be dealt with. She was trying to get used to the idea of Len not being there. She wondered what her life would be like without him. Like it was when he was away, she supposed, only permanent. Odd, she had always cherished her solitude. Now she was sure she would miss the commotion.

"I suppose we'd better call Len's lawyer," Vera was saying. "Someone should be taking care of business, shouldn't they? It probably can't just be left to go on all by itself." She marked "lawyer" down on her piece of paper.

"What?"

Vera hesitated, unsure which part needed repeating. "Well, I was just saying that we'd better call your lawyer in the morning, what with all of Len's doings."

Edna stared at her, wide-eyed, while the ramifications of what Vera had said filtered through to her. She had never been taken into Len's confidence and she had never known exactly how he made his money, but all those dinners where she had listened with only half an ear were enough. She didn't know whether or not there was any outright illegality involved, but she did know that he had never quite trusted his lawyer, never quite trusted anyone for that matter, not even her. He kept his business to himself and his books in the study.

She jumped up, spilling tea on the kitchen table. Vera moved to mop it up with a serviette.

"Leave it. Bernice can see to it later. We've got more important things to do." And she strode off towards the den.

"What is it?" Vera still had no idea what she had said, or why her friend had looked at her so strangely. She followed along behind.

Edna was pulling desk drawers out, spilling their contents on the floor. They all looked like legal documents to Vera. That stood to reason, Len must have dealt with lawyers all the time. She wondered if Edna were having some sort of breakdown, a delayed reaction to grief. She looked wild-eyed enough.

"We've got to clear all this stuff out of here tonight, and we've got to do it so nobody can tell that we've done it," she said, shuffling through papers. Ah." She had found an account book, a ledger, bound in brown leather. "See if there's another one here somewhere."

Vera shuffled through the papers. "Here," she said, handing her a green volume.

Edna flipped it open, reading the date on the inside. "Okay," she said slowly. "They're for the same year. So which is the real one?" She hefted both of them in her hands, as if she could tell by their weight. She turned to Vera, who was still kneeling on the floor. "Go find some cardboard boxes. Look in the cellarway. And for God's sake, don't wake Bernice up doing it."

"I don't understand," Vera wailed when she returned. "Why do we have to sort this stuff out tonight?"

"No time to sort, we'll just have to move it all." She started throwing papers into one of the boxes. "I need to make it plausible," she muttered. "They have to believe the lawyer handled everything."

"Who's they?"

Edna shrugged. "I'm not sure, but whoever it is won't find anything. Grab whatever you think looks like it should be locked away. Besides me," she added.

Together they cleaned out the desk drawers, and replaced what they had removed with anything they could find; Bernice's household account book, photograph albums, Cara's old report cards. They stuffed the filing cabinet full of Edna's gardening books and several wads of Christmas paper. They stacked magazines and catalogues randomly, until Edna was satisfied that it looked like it they had always been there.

"What are you going to do with the boxes?" Vera asked when they had finished.

"I'm going to put them in the car in the morning," Edna said. "And then I'm going to give you a ride home."

Vera finally twigged. "Oh," she said, "and then I'm going to clean out my attic tomorrow, so I can find some storage space at the back, right?"

Edna smiled. It would be the last time she would do so for quite some time.

Cara was still muzzy-headed from too much beer when the phone jangled. She groaned. Who would call her at ...what time was it?...eight o'clock on a Saturday morning? She reached for the receiver only to bump up against a humped obstruction in the narrow bed beside her. She pulled back the blankets. Brad? Brad spent the night? She groaned. She would have to smuggle him out later, past the stockbroker and his wife and the Filipino nanny. She reached the phone on the eighth ring.

"Hullo?" It was her mother. What could she want? Her mother called her once a month, on Sunday nights, when she was most apt to be in.

"Oh, Cara!" She sounded funny. Had she been crying? Her mother never cried.

"What is it?" But she knew. There could be only one reason for this call, and she knew it before she heard the words, a wrenching sickness forming in the pit of her stomach.

"There's been a terrible accident. Oh God, Cara, there's no way to tell you this gently. Your father's dead. Last night. I'm so, so sorry....."

Like Edna, Cara needed the details to make it real. She needed to know the when and the how and the why. What could have happened, what force could possibly be strong enough to erase such exuberance? He couldn't be dead, she thought, there must be some mistake. But, like Edna, when she heard the details, she could finally let herself believe it was true. The tears were streaming down her face as she hung up the phone.

She kicked at the body beside her. "Get out."

Brad only moaned.

She pulled the covers off him in one rude, abrupt motion. "Get out."

"What's wrong?" he asked when he saw her face.

"My father died. Get out. Just get dressed and get out."

He struggled into his jeans, found his shoes and socks and coat.

"Look", he said awkwardly at the door. "You probably shouldn't be alone right now. I know you don't want me here, but is there somebody else I can call?"

"No, just get out."

He left, puzzled and slightly relieved, and offered no explanation to the disapproving glares of the family downstairs.

The island had an efficient, if somewhat macabre, method of disseminating the news of death in the community. There were two funeral homes in town, Jones and Carruther's. At one time, the century old businesses had had premises on the main street, one at each end of town. They had long since moved to more dignified quarters, but the practice of taping small white death notices in the front windows of their former buildings had continued. Every day, passersby clustered around these notices on their way to other errands, to see who had passed on in the night. A death was never truly official until one of these small cards had been posted, noticed and commented on.

Francine O'Brien still worked behind the soda fountain at Fletcher's Drug Store, but she had been an employee for so long that Rick Fletcher took her reliability for granted, often entrusting her with tasks that by rights, he should have done himself. She was just tackling dishes from the morning coffee crowd when he stuck his head out of the office.

"Francine, do you have time to run up to the bank and make a deposit?" he asked.

Her back hurt from bending over the sink anyway, and a breath of fresh air would do her good after the rush and chatter of the early morning customers. She threw on her coat and grabbed the deposit bag full of cash. The bank was two blocks away and as usual, she glanced at the Jones' Funeral Home notices on her way by. There was a crowd clustered in front of it today.

"I can't believe it," one man said with a shake of his head.

"He was only forty-seven. Jeez, it kind of brings you up short and sharp, don't it?" said another.

"What the hell was he doing driving around in that storm?"

"Don't look like he had anybody with him, if you know what I mean. Now there's a mercy."

She pushed her way through, to take a closer look.

"COLLINS, LEONARD HAROLD" the card read. *"Suddenly, near Kingston, Friday November 13, 1976 as the result of an accident. Beloved husband of Edna Elizabeth (Charles), sadly missed by daughter Caroline. Predeceased by parents Harold and Naomi Collins. Visitation at Jones' Funeral Home, Monday evening, November 16 from 7 p.m. to 9 p.m. Services at Main Street United Church, Tuesday November 17 at 2 p.m. "*

The man next to her noticed her then, and moved away.

"Jeez," he said to his wife that night. "She was standing right beside me, reading the notice. I don't think she'd heard until then."

"Who would have told her?" his wife pointed out. "Everybody but Edna knew about her, but who would ever have thought to call?"

Francine made it to the bank, and looked after the deposit. She made it back to the drug store and finished the breakfast dishes. She made it down the aisle to the office, where she told Rick Fletcher she wasn't feeling well, and wanted to go home. Rick had heard the news in the meantime.

"Why don't you take a few days off, Francine?" he said tactfully. "Don't worry about coming back until you feel better." He looked at her worriedly. "And if you need anything, you let me know, okay?"

Oddly, when she got home, she had trouble recognizing it as a place that belonged to her in any way. She felt detached and strange, as if she were floating in some sort of viscous liquid that supported her and cushioned her against the outside world. She crawled into bed and huddled into herself. If I can just shut it out for a little longer, she thought to herself, then I'll be all right, but suddenly the numbness evaporated and she started to cry. He's finally left me, she thought. All those times I thought I'd lost him, and now he's really gone. Who would have thought that it would feel so cold?

It was one of the biggest funerals ever held at Main Street United Church. The rearmost pews, which were always taken first, were filled by one-thirty and after that the crowd kept growing. There were many faces that were familiar to Edna; people she had grown up with, gone to school with, conducted the business of everyday living with. There were others she had never seen before. Grizzled, grey-haired men in sombre well-cut suits, some alone, some with elegantly dressed women by their sides. Business people, she supposed, drawn from the mob of developers, investors, bankers and contractors that had filled Len's world, come to pay their last respects to one of their own. There were women who arrived alone, clutching lace-edged hankies, hoping their grief went unnoticed. Edna noticed them all.

Len lay in a mahogany casket at the front of the church, surrounded by masses of flowers. Everyone, it seemed had sent an arrangement; the Town Council, the Rotary Club, the Chamber of Commerce, there was even one from the Premier of Ontario. One by one the mourners picked their way through the masses of cloying bloom for one final look.

Ralph Jones had done a good job. There were no signs of the disfigurement that had been so evident when she had gone to identify the body, no evidence of that smashing fatal blow to the skull, no shards of glass left in his face. Ralph had made him look peaceful, but there had been no way to make him look natural. Without constant, restless energetic motion, Len could never look natural. The grey in his hair was noticeable now, as were the lines that had started to gather around his eyes and mouth. Cara had been upset, Edna knew, by her decision to leave the coffin lid open, but unless the body was in full view it was too easy to believe that it was someone else lying there. She couldn't let him go so anonymously. Again and again she replayed their last morning together, wishing she had said more before she let him go. It had seemed to be just another of his flying trips out of town. How could she have known that this one would be his last, that this time he wouldn't fly home, but through the windshield?

I never told him I loved him, she realized. And now that it was too late, she realized that she did, and that she had for a long, long time. He had filled her life with laughter and warmth and incident, the catalyst by which she had journeyed from a drab, grey world to a resplendent universe of brilliant colour. He had been a friend, a lover, a companion. She would retreat to grey again, she guessed, and only once in a while would some small thing blush into a pale shadow of his blazing light.

Vera sat beside Edna in the church. She had been a constant companion, returning home only to change her clothes, leaving Mac to clumsily grumble around the kitchen on his own. She had had one last look at Len before the crowds arrived. It all seemed so long ago now, that night at the Palace of the Moon. It had occupied such a central place in her heart for so long, each moment and detail marked and remembered and treasured. She had thought, once, that she loved this man, who had not loved her. He had been an ideal gone astray, a lost horizon, a remembrance she could warm herself with late at night when the stars shone in through her window and Mac lay slumbering beside her. She reached over and took Edna's hand, holding it tightly through the service.

Cara would not look at her father. She didn't want her last memory of him to be this hollow shell lying so inertly amid ceremony and flowers. She wanted to remember his strong arms holding her, the smell of him, the way he moved so effortlessly and gracefully as he scooped her up to sit on his shoulders. She wanted to be his Cara Mia again. They had groped towards a reconciliation in recent months, their encounters less hostile, their conversations warmer. There had been indications that someday the old easiness would return. Now he was gone, before she had a chance to meet him on level ground, as an adult, and to let him know that the old Cara, the one who had adored him, was still there.

Francine waited until just before the service started to slip into the church and stand at the back. She had no need to see him one last time, no need to burn the look of him into her memory. She was merely paying her respects to this man who had brought her so much unexpected happiness, and for so long. She had never believed that Len would make old bones; he had been profligate with life, using it too fully, too enthusiastically. It would have been unbearable for him to grow grey and stooped, stiff in the joints and slow of thought, careful and conservative. Better for him to go this way, so that he would remain always in their minds the same laughing boy who had enchanted them all.

She wondered what his pretty wife would do now. She would have plenty of money, Francine guessed, and she was still very beautiful. Was she the sort of woman who might marry again? She couldn't imagine wanting anyone after Len, she wouldn't, but some women couldn't cope with being alone. Was Edna the sort of woman who needed a man? The friend was sitting beside her, she noted, and she guessed that was a comfort. They had both loved him and that would be enough to see them through, for a while, anyway.

It broke Francine's heart to look at the girl. Her face was a mask of bewildered grief, but she would survive, she was young, she would find a man of her own, one who would eclipse her father in her affections, be the sun and the moon and the stars, the way Len had been for her. Maybe.

There was no graveside ceremony, no interment; the unyielding, frozen earth would not permit it just yet. The body would remain stored and vaulted until the spring, when the ceremony of saying goodbye must be reenacted, the mourning revisited.

The custom was that grief must be fed and the United Church Women had assembled vast amounts of small sandwiches and cakes to buttress the mourners afterwards. They were like a swarm of voracious grasshoppers, denuding the trays and draining the teapots amid a cacophony of chatter and condolence. Edna moved through the crowd, shaking hands, embracing, thanking them for coming and acknowledging their comfort. It was a morbid parody of the performances she had given on many a social occasion; setting everyone at their ease and making them feel welcome.

Cara stood apart and wondered how her mother managed it. She herself was incapable of speaking with anyone. It was tempting to think that her mother didn't care, had no emotion, but she knew this wasn't true. She had seen her ravaged look, had noticed the slumping of her shoulders, and the faltering of her step. Cara had never been sure of the dynamics of her parents' relationship. They had seemed so opposite, so opposed in temperament, at times so remote from each other, but now she knew one thing for sure; her mother had loved her father, deeply, but in her own way, without losing herself in the torrent. She felt a sneaking admiration for this woman who could steel herself to meet the world so graciously when her own lay in smoking ruin.

It was no surprise to either of them to return home and discover that Mud, too, had passed on, but peacefully, in his sleep, the way Edna had expected him to. It was a fitting denouement to a day of mourning.

CHAPTER NINETEEN

Just as Edna expected, there were enormous complications in the wake of Len's death. His lawyer, Thomas Radford, kept asking her to find this document or that, ownerships and agreements and licenses and deeds. Just like Len, she didn't trust him, and claimed an innocent ignorance of anything he asked about. She was afraid of making a wrong move, of revealing too much information, of inadvertently saying something that would cause everything to come tumbling down.

Polite at first, the lawyer soon became exasperated. "For crying out loud, Mrs. Collins, the tax boys are all over me like a piranha on a pork chop. Are you sure you don't have any of this documentation?"

She denied all knowledge of everything.

She was called to a meeting with the lawyer and some auditors from Revenue Canada. Although they were polite, she sensed their suspicion that she was hiding something, that she possessed some information they could prise out and use against her. She began to be grateful that she knew so little. She possessed no information they could twist, no words that could betray her; she was genuinely uninformed.

Len's various partners and shareholders were in an uproar. There were discrepancies, shortfalls that needed to be explained, monies to be accounted for. Questions were being asked, hard questions about the flow of funds from company to company, project to project. There was a frenzy of accusations and allegations. They were like a pack of hyenas, she thought, descending on what was left of the carcass.

On one very frightening day, men with badges descended on her house, search warrant in hand, and went through every drawer, every cupboard, every box in the basement and every corner of the attic. These men weren't local constables like George Franklin and Don McBride, who had so gently broken the news to her on the night of Len's accident. These were hard-faced men in suits, who said little to her other than to ask that she accompany them as they moved from room to room. She protested that she had no idea what they were looking for, and held her hands helplessly aloft while they rummaged through the drawers, the kitchen cupboards, even Cara's dresser. She thought the photograph albums in the desk were a nice touch and had to smother a smirk when they found the Christmas paper in the filing cabinet. At the end of their search, Bernice urged them to stay, so she could make them "a nice cup of tea." They declined, and shortly afterwards left, empty-handed.

Radford became distraught. "I'm going to take the fall for this," he howled. "You can't let them do this to me. I was only following your husband's instructions."

And making a great deal of money in the process, she thought, but she did have a few qualms then about what she was doing. At this point she judged that her part was over, that she wouldn't be interrogated again. She had played her role perfectly, as far as she could tell. She had been a vapid and unproductive lead, charmingly helpful, of course, but obviously uninformed and perhaps a little dim. No, she was safe for the moment, but now it was time to find out what had really happened, so she could decide what to do next.

She went to Vera's and together they sorted everything into chronological order, laying the papers out on the living room floor. It was like a giant jigsaw puzzle, she decided. She had always been good at puzzles; the trick was to look carefully at the pieces, at the colours and the pattern and the shape and decide which ones matched precisely. Even so, even with the mound of paper she had cleared out of the den, there were many elements missing. She struggled through agreement after agreement, company after company, partnerships and options and investments. It took weeks. Each morning after Mac left for work, she and Vera would drag the heavy boxes out of the attic to take up where they had left off the day before. Each afternoon before he came home again, they would drag them back up the stairs to their hiding place.

Vera brought books home from the library that helped as they puzzled through the papers. They didn't dare ask for help from any other quarter. Gradually, the pieces fell into place and it all started to make sense to them. They were still forced to make a number of large assumptions, hazard some hazy guesses, and surmise some tenuous connections, but in the end, they had a pretty good idea of what he had done.

Where he had come by his initial stake was undocumented, but Edna was sure it had something to do with the old fishing rig and the many trips he and his father had made across the lake when he was in his teens. After Harold's death, Len had invested in the stock market; penny stocks, fledgling companies, never the safe, blue chip stocks that produced small but steady dividends. He liked the wild fling, the hunches, companies with new technology, mining stocks floated on the basis of someone's intuition that gold or silver or bauxite might be found in some remote, geologically promising valley. He was remarkably lucky. In many cases, she realized, he had sold his stock just before the rest of the world realized that it was worthless. He had made some money this way, not a lot, but some.

In October, 1953, he made his first land purchase, the fields behind Charles Furniture, for $2,000 cash. It seemed, in retrospect, a ludicrously small amount for what had turned out to be a valuable piece of property, but at the time the owners must have congratulated themselves on getting anything for what they thought was worthless land. It was only because of the access across Charles land, Edna realized, that the property had any value at all.

Using the useless, wooded piece of land as a foundation, he had formed a company to build the houses behind the store; using the subdivision as collateral, he had bought more property, with minimal downpayments, and easy terms, and then enticed builders, developers and investors into doing something with it. That, in turn, provided the wherewithal for the next scheme. And with every deal, with each new company, he would take a finder's fee, a management contract, a stock option. Seldom would his name appear amongst the officers of any of these companies; he had worked through dummy corporations, numbered accounts, willing third parties. Edna recognized many of the names involved; they were men she had entertained at her dinner table. George Almont, for instance, as well as Thomas Radford on a number of occasions.

It was a shaky structure of breathtaking audacity, insubstantially built on a constant but fluctuating cash flow. A paper empire. It was only bad luck, one error of judgement on a slippery curve, that brought his kingdom crashing down.

Len had been the lynchpin. He was the one with the vision and the energy that had drawn others like moths to the flame; with his death, investors in the latest scheme became nervous. This set up a chain reaction, Edna could see, that caused the rest of it to implode. Like dominoes, each company failed. Without the latest infusion of cash, there simply was not enough money in the system to cover all the debts.

She knew now why the lawyer was so hysterical. There was blame to be assigned here, sharp practice to be called into question. The investors who had lost money were howling for blood. They didn't care whose.

There was still property that Edna judged to be beyond the reach of mere creditors: their house, which he had put in both their names; their personal bank accounts; and Charles Furniture, which, unaccountably, seemed to belong to her alone. These she could salvage, but only if no finger were pointed directly at Len.

She found the agreement, the granting of right-of-way across company property, made out to Len and dated September 20, 1953. This, then, was the dowry he had referred to so laughingly that day on the ferry. This, not her father's blessing, was the permission he sought when he went, alone, to talk to her parents the day after she had found refuge with him. Access down a roadway. The true measure of her worth. Her bride-price.

This was the key, the one thing Len needed to open the lock on his dreams. He hadn't needed Charles Fine Furniture, didn't want it, in fact. He would have had no interest in being a shopkeeper, whatever money came from the store was only a bonus granted with her father's heart attack. He must have seemed like a saviour to Hetty, though, an angel sent from heaven, when he not only offered to run the store for her, but insisted that he take nothing but a salary. He must have been at his most charming when he refused to accept any stake in the ownership. The business should have gone to Jack and Bill, they were the rightful sons, but Hetty would have been unwilling to trust them, knowing that it was Len who had turned her fortunes around so dramatically. They had compromised, or so Len would have termed it, and agreed that Edna would inherit the store, on the understanding that Jack would be the permanent manager and that a place be found for Bill if he wanted it. It was the perfect solution for both of them; Hetty would continue to collect her profits and Len would be in a position to make sure that there were no questions, no hitches in his agreement regarding the strip of land that ran by the side of the building. They both must have been smugly satisfied with this arrangement.

This strip of land was the reason he had played her so carefully in the beginning, she realized, why their courtship had been such a slow dance. She was never just another conquest, another pretty girl to lure into bed, but a prize to be coaxed along, so that she would waltz willingly into step. God, he must have been amused when Hetty so obligingly delivered her straight into his arms. They had both manipulated and manoeuvred her, each to their own ends. She had no doubt that her mother had manufactured some complicated moral reasoning that justified her actions. Len was a different matter; he would have done what he did simply because it was to his advantage. In a sense, Hetty had been quite correct in her initial assessment of him; he was a crook.

Was this what her marriage boiled down to then: an arrangement between her mother and her husband, with herself as a convenient bargaining chip?

Vera disagreed. “After he sold all those houses it didn’t matter, did it? He didn’t need the right-of-way any more. If it was nothing more than that, you can bet your bottom dollar he would have dumped you. He dumped everybody else fast enough, didn’t he?”

It was rather an inelegant way of putting it, but Edna realized that she was right. He hadn’t needed her after that. Of course, after that, there was Cara to consider. He would never have left Cara. She pointed this out.

“Oh for crying out loud, Edna!” Vera was getting a little exasperated with her. “It may have started out as a cold-blooded business deal, but you can’t tell me that’s all it was by the end of it. Why do you think he never said anything to you about Sacha?”

“Do you think he knew?”

Vera rolled her eyes. “Well, of course he knew. Everybody else knew, why wouldn't he?"

"Then why didn't he say anything?"

"What was he supposed to say? You never said anything to him. He didn't have a leg to stand on in that department, and he didn't want to lose you. I don't know what he thought he was up to in the beginning, but if you ask me, somewhere along the way he fell in love with you." As soon as she said it, Vera knew it was true, and momentarily felt the old hurt, but she went on anyway. "Anybody who ever saw the two of you together figured it was the perfect match. The only two people who wouldn't ever admit were you and Len."

Well isn't that ironic? Edna thought. Neither of us willing to budge, to let our guard down, until it was too late. "Love ya, Eddie," he would say, always casual, always playful, so his words could be easily dismissed. His flippancy had hurt her, but she had been too proud to press for more. Had he, in his turn, been too proud to risk rebuff, to ask for the words in return? Had she hurt him as well?

He had been quite honest with her, she realized now, he had laid his cards on the table the night her mother had thrown her out of the house. He had admitted that he liked women, he had told her that she was the kind of woman he needed as a wife, he had said that he had plans and that they could make a nice life together. He had promised her fun. He had been striking a bargain with her, and she had willingly agreed to the price.

But Vera was right, at some point it had all changed, become something far more, but they had been stuck with the original contract, neither of them willing to renegotiate the terms. They had both needlessly lived up to their agreement. If only he had asked, she thought. If only I had offered.

She wondered what bargain he had struck with Francine. She always thought that the house on the outskirts of town had been a mere rental, but she discovered that he had made Francine a joint owner. She would own it outright now.

Vera was outraged. "You should see a lawyer about that," she said. "You could probably contest that."

But Edna had had enough of lawyers and they of her. Besides, she felt no ill-will towards Francine. She would never understand the dynamics of her relationship with Len, never know what he had promised her, what negotiations had taken place, but she would live up to whatever pact they had made. She could have the house.

But in order for Francine to keep the Collins house, in order for Edna to hang on to her own home, in order to protect Cara and Jack and the family store, she was going to have to let the lawyer take the fall. Without the papers she had squirreled away in Vera's attic, she was sure no one could make a coherent case against Len. If they dug hard enough they could probably find it all eventually, there had to be more of it somewhere. She suspected a lot of it might be at Francine's, and that was probably a pretty good place to leave it, if it hadn't already been burned, but no one would ever go looking for it there. No, it would be easier to blame the others, especially Thomas Radford, who after all, was not entirely innocent in the matter. Lawyers were supposed to know the law, weren't they, and this one had obviously gone along with everything Len wanted to do, whether it was against his better judgment or not.

She was surprised when she didn't feel the least bit guilty about her decision.

CHAPTER TWENTY

Thomas Radford did not take the fall. In the end, it was poor George Almont who was indicted on several charges of fraud. It didn't surprise Edna that Radford slithered away, he was, after all, a lawyer and could bend the law to his own bidding. She might have felt sorry for George if he hadn't had such execrable taste in women.

When after what seemed like forever the dust finally settled, the taxes were paid and the will cleared probate, she realized that in spite of her efforts, she was going to be desperately short of money, at least short by the standards she was used to. Cara still had to finish college, and the money for that would have to be found somewhere. Steve was only in his third year at Western and Edna was determined to uphold the arrangement she and Vera had made. She wouldn't see him short if she could help it. And there was the house to run, and herself to keep. Somehow.

Her only income would be whatever profits came in from the store and they were dwindling. It wasn't Jack's fault, it was changing times. Canadiana was suddenly in vogue, and the newly prosperous, who once would have bought the solid mahogany and cherrywood pieces Charles Furniture was famous for now scoured antique stores and flea markets for old pine tables and chairs. They stripped the paint off and proudly put kitchen furniture in their living rooms.

She knew that the store could ill-afford to keep her, but she had no option. It would have been nice, everyone said, if she had been able to turn the business over lock, stock and barrel to Jack, after all it was a family business and hadn't he managed Charles and Sons on salary all these years? Edna agreed with them, but she simply couldn't afford to do it.

It was about what everyone expected. They had watched as Len shot through their midst like a blazing meteor and they had been waiting for him to crash to earth for years. They hadn't expected the explosion to be quite such a spectacular one, but then, it had been a long time coming, hadn't it? Poor Edna, caught in the shockwave, left with the smoking debris. Well, what was she thinking to marry him in the first place, he was, after all, only the son of that shiftless Harold Collins, and the apple doesn't fall far from the tree, now does it?

She considered selling the house, and consulted Fred Jackson.

He advised against it. "Nobody wants a house this big any more," he said. "Oil prices are shooting up, it's too hard to heat and too hard to maintain. All the women are out there working and they don't have time to keep a house like this. You won't get anywhere near what it's worth and the way rentals are right now, it'll probably cost you as much or more to live somewhere else."

She realized he was right and was relieved to hear it. She would take what was left of their money and pay off the mortgage. She might freeze, she might starve, but at least she would have a roof over her head.

"Tell you what, though," Fred went on. "You could sell the coach house. This is a double lot and I think they're registered separately. I don't know if you want neighbours that close to you, though."

"But what about Bernice?" she asked, although she knew that she couldn't go on providing free housing. She couldn't go on providing anything at all, if it came to that, not even Bernice's salary.

"Well, take a look at the rental value" Fred said. "If Bernice can pay you more in rent than you'd get from investing the sale proceeds, then let her stay. If not, then you're going to have to take a good, hard look at the arrangement."

Edna knew Fred was right, but she dreaded telling the faithful housekeeper that her services were no longer required and that she might have to move out. Bernice saved her the trouble.

The two women had continued the habit of sitting together over a pot of tea in the kitchen in the late afternoon and it was during one these cosy conversations that Bernice sidestepped into the topic.

"You know, Mrs. Len," she said, "it's awful lonesome over at my place now that Rhonda is gone."

"I know what you mean. It's real lonesome here, too," Edna said ruefully.

"I was thinking you know, it's silly, two women living a stone's throw from each other and both lonely. I never would have suggested this when Mr. Len was here," her voice choked a little as she said this, "but why don't I just move across the driveway? You could rent out my place. Give you a nice little income, and this place seems like home anyhow."

"I would love that, Bernice." Edna looked at her sadly. "But I don't know if even that much is possible. I know most people would find this hard to believe, but Len didn't leave a lot of money."

Bernice had heard the scuttlebutt. It wasn't hard to believe at all.

"I've been trying to find a way to break it to you for weeks," Edna went on. "I don't know if I can pay your salary much longer. I'm sorry, as far as I'm concerned you're family, but I just don't see any way around it."

To her amazement, Bernice broke into a broad grin. "Well, don't that beat all," she said. "I've been racking my brains trying to figure out how to tell you I'm past all this housekeeping nonsense. I turned sixty-five last month and now I've got the pension, that and what I saved over the years. It's quite a lot too. Mr. Len always paid for nearly everything, and no rent neither, so I never had much to spend it on."

"Are you telling me you don't want to work for me anymore?'

"That's exactly what I'm tellin' you. I don't want to work for you no more, but I wouldn't mind sharing a house with you. I can afford my half of the expenses, don't you worry. I was just so disinclined to leave my home after all these years, I wasn't sure what I should do for the longest time."

Edna's hands were shaking as she put down her teacup. Rent from the coach house apartment, maybe a small amount from the store, plus whatever Bernice could afford to kick in, and there should be enough to cover taxes and heat and food, with a little left over.

Bernice watched the play of emotions across Edna's face with satisfaction. She had spent many a sleepless night working out the details of this plan, plotting how to present it so it looked like Mrs. Len was doing her a favour, not the other way around. It was a proposal that appealed to her greatly. She liked the idea of sharing quarters, after all they had been doing essentially just that for over twenty years now and they were both real comfortable with it, but the plan had one overriding, and for Bernice, supremely satisfying point in its favour. It would allow her, after all these years, to repay all the kindnesses shown to her and Rhonda.

Edna finally finished her mental calculations and smiled at her now former housekeeper. "Deal," she said.

Bernice's eyes twinkled. "Mind you," she said, "it'll take some getting used to. I may forget once in while and clean something."

The transition was nearly seamless. Bernice simply packed up her personal belongings and carried them across the driveway. She insisted on taking one of the back bedrooms as her own, rather than the sunny front room that had been Cara's, although it was larger and nicer and Edna offered it.

"I don't want her to feel like she doesn't have a home anymore," she said. "If she comes back and can't stay in her own room, it'll be just like she's a visitor."

Privately, Edna thought that was exactly what Cara was. She returned only on occasion, usually for major holidays, and only for a few days at a time. Then she wafted through the house like a spectre, unbalanced, unbuoyant and bereft.

Bernice would try and entice her with old favourites like chocolate chip cookies. Cara would smile and thank her, but leave them half-eaten on her plate.

"I just don't know what to do with the girl," Bernice said. "She's like a ghost in the house."

"Just leave her be," Edna advised. "Whenever she comes home, she's reminded all over again about her father. It'll take time, but she'll come to terms with it sooner or later."

Edna assessment was correct. Cara found that every corner of the old house was filled with memories. Her father waiting on the bottom step to catch her when she slid down the front staircase bannister; the wooden swing he hung from the maple tree in the back yard; the electric train set he brought home one evening and set up in the attic. Her mother had objected to this at the time because she was sure that he had really bought it for himself. She had been right, but Cara ultimately became fascinated by the miniature world constructed on a sheet of plywood.

Even more distressing were the reminders that had disappeared. She came home for Christmas, and her mother tried to make it as festive as possible, but they were all depressed by the puny little Scotch pine in the corner of the living room. They hadn't even needed a stepladder to put the blue and white angel on the top of the tree. Jack and Margaret had come as usual on Christmas Eve, but there was no one to tell stories about the Christmas ornaments and no Mud to go romping through the tinsel.

It was on this visit that she first noticed the pale patches on the walls.

"What happened to the painting that used to hang in the dining room?" she asked.

Edna was vague. "Oh, I moved it. I'm thinking of redoing the wallpaper." But the paper was never replaced, and on each visit Cara noticed a new absence, a new telltale square of unfaded wall. She knew that her father had left things in a mess, but she hadn't realized how bad things were. She was certain her mother was selling the paintings so that she could stay in school.

She began to accept every commission Cass could find her. At first it was because she didn't want to be a burden, was determined to pay her own way, but after a time she began to find the work soothing. She could lose herself in it, and for long stretches of time forget her grief. It became her excuse not to come home, not to confront the ghosts that haunted her.

By the time she was in her final month at college, she had eight clients, all wanting the little black and white line drawings like the ones she did for Cass. She would place each article on a pedestal in the middle of her room, smoke a joint and stare at the object until inspiration came. She realized that some of her earlier efforts were just a little too off the wall, like the screaming garlic bulb ensnared in the jaws of a plastic garlic press but eventually she was able to gauge just how far she could go with each customer, achieving the necessary balance between realism and whimsicality.

She considered this work a sideline to the real art she intended to produce any day now, but to her surprise, her tiny illustrations were enormously popular and she started selling the original pen and inks, matted and framed on their own. Cass advised her on how to market them.

"Give me five or six of your best to hang in the shop," she said. "You may sell some to walk-in, but most of your customers will have a specific illustration in mind. Charge them an arm and a leg and don't ever make prints. They'll all be bragging that they own a Collins original. You might think about producing some more detailed eight by tens along with the thumbnails too."

Cass was right. Two of the drawings sold in the shop. Orders came in for the originals of eight others, all purchased on the basis of tiny reproductions in small Christmas booklets.

One of the walk-in buyers turned out to be the publisher of a home improvement magazine. Would C. Collins be interested in freelancing the occasional illustration for his section on how not to renovate houses? C. Collins would, thank you very much, and her work attracted the attention of several more publishers of magazines with limited circulations. None of them could afford much in the way of an art department; they relied mostly on photographs. The work was sporadic but lucrative and Cara moved seamlessly from full-time student to full-time artist. She was amazed at the amount of money she made. It was nothing in comparison to the amount of money her parents had always thrown around, of course, but it was more than adequate for her needs, and relieved her mother of the necessity of supporting her. It even allowed her to move out of the attic apartment into a small loft in a renovated industrial building.

The light in the loft was perfect, and the atmosphere inspired her drawings. It did little for her oils or watercolours, though. No matter how carefully she painted, they were dead and lifeless next to the comical little black and white sketches.

She consoled herself with the fact that, compared to most of her classmates, she lived a wildly free and creative existence. Four of her fellow pupils had found entry-level employment in the art departments of major magazines. Here they were expected to practice their craft, not with brushes or pencils, but with computers, learning to marshall balky bits and bytes into glossy graphic layouts. Later, if they were successful, or lucky, they could return to canvas and paper, but as the lowest of the low in the production room, they laboured at rows of computer terminals under the unforgiving glare of fluorescent overheads. Most of the others were unemployed, or working as waiters.

She spent most of her time alone, even when she wasn't working, a fact that annoyed the gregarious Cass who was always trying to find her more friends, male or female, it didn't matter which.

"The encounter group's meeting at my house Thursday night," she said one time. "Why don't you come along?"

Cara groaned. "I don't have anything I'd particularly like to encounter," she said. "I don't have any men I need to bash this week."

"So sit in a corner and shut up," Cass returned. "Maybe you'll learn something. Besides, I'm doing the snack." Cass always had her food catered. Cara shrugged. At least she'd be fed well.

She was late, as usual. When she arrived, eight women were sitting cross-legged in the living room of the untidy apartment. Most of them were in their late twenties or early thirties. One woman was feeding a baby, its small greedy mouth latched onto her breast, while its mother recounted how difficult it was to get its father to change its diapers. The other women murmured in sympathy.

Cass introduced her. "This is Cara. She has some unresolved issues around her father."

Cara glared. "I do not."

"See?" said Cass to the others.

Cara considered leaving right then and there, but she really didn't want to offend Cass, who set such store by these emotion-fests.

"Fathers," snorted one of the women, "Nothing unresolved about my issues. If I ever meet the bastard again, I'll kill him."

"Margaret was abused as a child," Cass murmured to Cara. "Her father used to beat her with a belt."

Cara could think of no adequate response to this.

"We're not doing fathers again, are we?" asked a woman with short brown hair who was holding the hand of another woman with short blonde hair. "As far as I'm concerned, they should all be lined up against a wall and shot for what they've done to us."

"Absolutely," agreed the woman with the baby. "It's taken me years to get over being sexually abused by my stepfather. But the person I really blame is my mother, for letting him get away with it."

The others all nodded knowingly. Cara was confused. She knew that many women had suffered horrifically at the hands of their parents. More and more cases of physical and sexual abuse were coming to light after years of dark secrecy, dredged up from hidden places in damaged psyches. She could feel sympathy for these women, who had been turned into sexual objects by the very people who were supposed to protect them. Sympathy, but not empathy. Try as she might, her memories of her father yielded no instance of violation, no case for mistreatment, nothing but an overprotective parent who had only been doing what he thought best for her. How terribly unfashionable, she thought, I'll be drummed out of the sisterhood if I can’t do better than that.

"We're being awfully rude," Margaret pointed out. "We've all had a chance to speak except our guest." She turned to Cara. "Would you like to share any experiences with the group, Cara? Cass said you'd like to talk about your father."

"No actually, I wouldn't," Cara said. "There's nothing to share."

They gave each other knowing glances.

"It's all right," Margaret said. "We all know how hard it is to face these things for the first time. You repress and repress and repress and sometimes its difficult to get the floodgates to open up. But we've all been through it too, you can trust us."

"I haven't repressed anything," Cara said. "Basically my father was pretty great. He died and I really miss him."

"I think you'll find," said the woman with the baby, "that in order to deal with your grief, you're going to have to face the trauma of your childhood. Otherwise, your emotional state will just remain unresolved."

Cara gave up.

"You know what?" she said to Cass. "I think I'll pass on the snack. I'll call you tomorrow."

Just as she was leaving, Margaret gave it one more try. "If you ever reach the point where you'd like to talk about all this, we'll be here for you, you know."

When pigs fly, she thought, as she went out the door.

Cass was a little more successful in fixing Cara up with men friends. Oh, there were lots of one-daters, and a couple of one-night stands, but over the years Cass grew adept at picking out the kind of man who might interest her, at least for a little while.

There was Todd, the accountant who did Cass's books.

"I'd go after him myself," she said, "but I don't like to mix business with pleasure."

Cara didn't mind at all, and got Todd to file her last three years' income tax returns before she stopped returning his calls.

There was Mark, who worked in public relations. He had more flamboyance than Todd, but it was still coupled with an orderly and organized mind. Their relationship finally faltered when he realized that no matter how many messages he left, or how many watches he bought her, Cara would always be late, and furthermore didn't understand why anyone else had a problem with this.

"I can't believe it," he said just before he left. "If you were in the middle of something, you'd keep the Queen of England waiting."

"And why shouldn't I?" she wanted to know. "I've got work to do. All she has to do is wave at the crowd."

By the time Cara was thirty, Cass had given up.

"You're going to die an old maid," she said.

"So what?"

"Don't you want a family?" Cass had finally married a potter who made a line of earthenware she carried in her store. Together they had produced two dimpled, tow-headed children who pottered happily around their father's kiln until he ran off one day with a glassblower. Now they pottered happily around Cass's store.

"Someday," she allowed. But someday was approaching fast, and Cara was aware of her ticking biological clock. Oh, there was plenty of time still, but she didn't want to be pushing a baby carriage at forty-five. Besides, she hadn't found anyone she could imagine settling down with.

And then there was Randy.

After ducking out of Cass's party that first night, they had stayed at the bar where his friends were playing until closing time, then they went back to Cara's loft. He was still there the next morning. And the next evening. When she finally asked him to leave on the third day, he confessed that he didn't really have anywhere to go.

"I dumped my stuff at a friend's house," he explained, "but I don't think his old lady wants me hanging around. Bad influence." And he grinned his lop-sided grin at her.

"I can see why she would think that."

"So... is it okay if I just sort of crash here for a while?" he asked.

"Okay," she said against her better judgment, "but only for a while. And you'll have to get out of the way when I'm working."

It wasn't a bad arrangement, at least at first. Cara's best working time was first thing in the morning, before the sun was too strong and before she was distracted by hunger or the telephone. She would huddle in her dressing gown with a cup of coffee and a cigarette, focusing on what it was, exactly that defined the unique character of the object she wanted to draw. At some point, she knew, it would make its personality known and work could commence. Her dressing gown was a disaster of ink stains, coffee spots and burn holes as a result of this routine, but she reasoned that dressing gowns were easily replaceable, while creative urges were hard to come by.

Randy always slept until noon, at least, leaving her undisturbed. He would have been out on a gig the night before, or sitting in a bar listening to another band out on a gig. He seldom arrived back at the loft before two a.m. Sometimes Cara went with him, but not often. She didn't know many of Randy's' friends and it was too hard to make conversation over the noise of the music. If she went, she would sit in a corner by herself, nursing a beer, until Randy had time to talk to her. Most of the friends assumed she was his girlfriend, or a groupie, and treated her with the disdain that female appendages engendered in these circles.

Cass called her. "Are you and Randy living together?" she asked.

"Yes and no," Cara said. "Yes he's staying here, but we aren't exactly living together. He just doesn't have anywhere else to go right now."

"Uh huh." Cass was skeptical. "This is a platonic thing is it?"

"Well, no. Anything but, actually." In spite of their wildly different schedules, they spent what seemed like an enormous amount of time in Cara's bed. Or rather, on Cara's mattress on the floor.

"I like it," Randy said. "I don't have to worry about falling out."

"Or fall out either. In case of nuclear attack we can hide underneath."

"Huh?" He didn't follow her twisted logic.

"Never mind." Damn, she thought, nobody ever gets it.

"This is disastrous," Cass said. "I'd never have invited Randy to the party if I'd known it would turn out like this."

Cara was nettled by her high-handedness. "What do you mean by that?"

"Randy is a Goat and you're a Monkey. It'll never work." Cass had recently discovered the Chinese horoscope, and made vast assumptions on the basis of her sketchy knowledge of the subject.

"It doesn't have to work," Cara pointed out. "It's a temporary arrangement. He's just staying here until he finds somewhere else to go."

"Sure."

"Honest. He'll be gone any day now."

But he wasn't. Weeks turned into months and Randy was still very much present in the loft. Pieces of band equipment mysteriously gathered themselves up and moved in too. With them came Randy friends, acquaintances and recently encountered fans, who crowded in after the bars closed and the equipment was torn down, littering the loft with beer bottles, cigarette smoke and articles of clothing. They would burst in the door, laughing and chatting, often waking her up. A heavy sleeper, she would struggle to come to, disoriented and annoyed. They would leave just at the time when she would normally start working.

She couldn't let it go on. She finally said something after one of them had knocked over and broken a bottle of India ink, which had spilled over a half-completed drawing. "You've got to stop bringing your friends here so late," she said one afternoon.

"Why?"

"Because I can't work when they're here all night. And they make a mess of my place."

"You're still pissed off about the drawing aren't you?"

"Why wouldn't I be?" she asked. "It's hours of work down the drain."

"Well, if my friends aren't welcome here, don't worry, I won't bring them," he said nastily.

"It's not that they're unwelcome, it's just that I need a little consideration." She kicked herself after she said it. After all, it was her home, her space. And Randy didn't even chip in towards the rent. What was it about this man? She would have shown anyone else the door long ago.

He must have known what she was thinking, because he suddenly turned sweet. "I'm sorry," he said. "I just wasn't thinking. Of course you have to work. I'll make sure you're not disturbed. Why didn't you say something before?"

Cass wasn't buying it. "What else is he going to say?" she asked. "He knows if he pushes you too far, you'll throw him out."

"God you're a cynic."

"Yup. And I'm usually right, too."

Cara knew in her heart of hearts that what Cass said was true, but she wasn't quite ready to give up on Randy yet. She didn't become ready until she was positive that he was seeing someone else.

Little things had started turning up in her loft, odd things, things that she was sure he would never have bought himself. A new shirt, with the Eaton's label still attached. A mug with his name on it. A charm bracelet that he claimed was for his sister's birthday. And final irrefutable proof, a tape of the latest Depeche Mode release, whose music Randy had once dismissingly called "Euro-Trash Techno-crap."

"Where did this come from?" she asked when she found it.

He was vague. "Oh, somebody gave it to me. Thought I should listen to it. Pile of crap. I'll throw it out."

But he didn't. He kept the tape and the shirt and the mug, and the charm bracelet disappeared, although Cara knew that he hadn't seen his sister in months.

He began staying out every other night or so. She was extremely ambivalent about this. On the one hand, she had been wishing that he would leave. On the other, she would miss those sweet afternoons in bed. She wondered if she were jealous, and decided that she wasn't, it wasn't that sort of relationship, but she also wasn't about to provide free room and board if he didn't even have the decency to keep it at home.

She had finally braced herself to insist that he move out when he announced that his band had picked up a tour. They would be opening for Slide Blues Boogie, a group that had recently achieved moderate success with their latest CD release and had booked gigs across the prairies and into B.C. He would be gone for three months.

She helped him pack and wished him well, and resolved to discuss their living arrangements when he returned. Within three days of his departure, she had settled into her old routine, shuffling around the loft in her dressing gown in the early hours of the morning, producing a month's worth of work in the space of a week.

He really has to go, she thought to herself after three weeks of blissful solitude. I'm just not geared to living with another body in the house.

He had been gone for a month and a half when she realized something was wrong with her. The first cup of coffee each morning, something she had always relished and savoured, began to sicken her and refused to stay down. She was overwhelmingly tired by two o'clock in the afternoon, and began taking long naps, interrupted only by her insistent bladder.

Cass, who hadn't heard from her for two weeks, arrived unannounced at the door late one afternoon. Cara had been asleep, and was muzzy and dishevelled. She hadn't managed to get dressed yet that day.

Cass was alarmed. "My God, you've got circles under your eyes that go all the way down to your chin. What have you been doing?"

"I don't know. I think I've got the flu or something. Do you want a cup of tea?" She shuffled around the kitchen while Cass watched with concern.

The tea betrayed her. One sip was enough to send her scuttling to the little walled-off bathroom, where the sounds of her retching were audible throughout the loft.

When she returned, shaken and pale, Cass took charge.

"When was your last period?" she asked.

Cara didn't know. "It can't be that," she said. "I'm on the pill."

Cass went into the bathroom and got the little pink packet out of the medicine cabinet. "Cara! This prescription was filled like three months ago. And you only took half of them as it is!"

"Oh." She thought back over the last few months and realized that the confusion of having Randy and his friends in the loft had made her absent-minded and unfocussed, but even she found it hard to believe that she had forgotten to use birth control all that time. She must be losing her mind.

Cass went out to a drugstore and got a home pregnancy test, and they huddled anxiously over the little dipstick until it turned, unmistakeably, the colour of gestation.

"Shit." Cara sat on the edge of the bathtub. "What do I do now?"

"What do you want to do?"

She knew what her options were. She could get rid of it easily enough, after all women did that every day when the circumstances suited them. It would be the sensible thing to do. She was single, with an unreliable source of income and a bohemian lifestyle. How would a baby ever fit into that?

But she was in her thirties. How many more chances would she get? And with whom? Certainly not with Randy, she didn't want him anywhere near her. Just for a moment she tried to picture him in the role of father, breadwinner, protector. It just didn't scan.

She looked at Cass. "I think I want this baby," she said.

"Okay. I can understand that. So how are you going to work it?"

"I don't know."

"What about Randy? It is Randy's isn't it?"

Cara nodded.

"Does he fit into the equation?"

"No." She was emphatic.

Cass shrugged. "Just as well. Apparently his little chickie went on tour with him."

"I figured as much. Guess that's over."

"You're still going to have to deal with him." She folded her arms and leaned against the sink.

"What do you mean?" Cara looked at her friend with alarm.

"Well," she said. "I'm not saying you should marry him or anything, but he is the baby's father. He may want to have some input into what goes on here."

Cara laughed. "Randy? The original Peter Pan? My guess is he'll be running for the hills as soon as he hears."

It was a long time before Randy heard, and when he did, he didn't care. He had come back from his tour in a sour mood. It hadn't gone well. The crowds hadn't been bad, but most of the fans were there to hear Slide Blues Boogie's big hit and they barely hid their impatience with the opening act. For Randy there had been too many mind- and bum-numbing drives along flat highways between cities, too many exhausting load-ins and too many even more exhausting load outs. Too much beer and, Cara suspected, too many fresh-faced prairie girls anxious to make it with an honest to gosh musician, even though none of them had ever actually heard of him. The grapevine had it that Randy's girlfriend had departed after a nasty and extremely destructive argument in a restaurant in Brandon, Manitoba.

Cara had packed his remnant belongings in cardboard boxes. There were pathetically few of them. The first box she filled with articles of dirty clothing, which she didn't bother to wash first. She kept some of his CD's, the ones she liked, reasoning that since he hadn't been paying any rent, she was entitled to the discs in lieu of. The rest went into a second box. A third contained reams of paper, used envelopes, serviettes and cigarette packages, all of them scribbled with set lists and tablatures. She piled the boxes on top of someone's old amplifier and set them all by the front door.

"Well I'm home. I hope to Christ we've got some beer." He banged into the loft, threw down his suitcase and headed straight for the refrigerator, bypassing the pile by the door.

"No."

Startled by her tone, he turned to look at her and finally noticed his belongings.

"What's this?"

"Your stuff."

"What's it doing there?"

"Leaving."

He looked confused for a moment, then made the mistake of getting angry. "For Christ's sake, I just got back from driving a thousand miles through every hick town in Saskatchewan, and I've still got to go unload the truck. Can't you even say hello before you throw me out?"

"Hello. Goodbye. Find someplace else for your stuff. And yourself too while you're at it."

He slammed the refrigerator door shut.

"This is great. This is just bloody great. Where am I supposed to go?"

"Go rent a place. You just did a tour. Surely you can come up with first and last."

She could tell by his face that he couldn't, that the money he'd made was gone already. Probably blew it all 'cause he figured he could just scuttle back here, she thought. Think again, bozo.

"Look," she said finally. "I like you, Randy, but I don't want to live with you. You were supposed to find someplace else months ago. I can't cope with you being here."

"Oh, so that's it," he sneered. "The great artist can't possibly function if she has to put anyone's needs ahead of her own. I've got news for you, baby, you ain't no great artist. All you produce are glorified cartoons."

That hurt, but she refused to let it show. "Nevertheless," she said coolly, "my 'cartoons' as you call them, pay my rent, which is more than you do. Now, please get out and take your things with you."

He threw his arms up in the air. "What am I supposed to do, take all this stuff on the streetcar?"

"Not my problem." She knew if she relented on even one small point, he would wheedle his way back in. She pulled the amplifier, with the boxes on top of it out into the hall.

"Hey, don't do that! Somebody'll take it!"

"That's right. You'll take it. Now. And can I have my key back, please?"

He threw it at her, the corner catching her forehead and ripping open a small piece of skin.

"Thanks for nothing, bitch!"

She let the key lay where it had fallen and ignored the blood running down her face.

"You're no big prize, you know," he jeered. "I don't know where the hell you figure you're going to get another man. You're well on the way to over the hill, honey, you should've grabbed me while you could."

He slammed the door as he left. "You're nothing but a washed-up old broad." He was still shouting at her from the hall. "Frigid bitch." She heard a box go bump, bump, bumping down the stairs and knew that he had kicked it off the landing. She turned the lock behind him.

Her mother seemed unsurprised when Cara announced over the telephone that a baby was on its way.

"Is there a father?" she asked.

"Yeah, but he's not in the picture. Not any more."

It was as much as Edna had always expected, only she had expected it to happen when Cara was sixteen or seventeen, not now. I suppose she knows what she's doing, she thought, she always has, but I wonder if she realizes what she's in for?

"You're not upset, are you?" Cara asked.

"Why would I be upset? You're a grown woman. Besides you always did whatever you wanted to anyway."

"I just didn't know if it would make things awkward with your friends, you know the neighbours and all."

Edna laughed. "If I'd ever worried much about what the neighbours thought, I'd never have married your father."

After she got off the phone, she had a fit of giggles over the idea of Len as a grandfather. That would have been something to see, she thought. And then it struck her that she would soon be a grandmother, and somehow that wasn't so funny. When did that happen? she thought. It seems like just yesterday that Cara was a baby. She wondered if she would get to see much of the new child. She and Cara touched base often, by telephone, but their worlds had so few overlapping edges that conversation tended to be awkward and they confined themselves to pragmatic discussions of work and money and schedules. She found herself thinking that it would be nice to have a baby in the house again.

I must tell Cara she's welcome to come home if she wants to have it here, she thought. I could help, and we could all pretend that Bernice was helping too.

Abetted by years of scrubbing floors and washing windows, Bernice's arthritis had finally conquered her. She now hobbled painfully between the easy chair in the living room and her chair at the kitchen table where they ate most of their meals. Their positions had now been reversed. It was Edna who did the housework and cooked dinner, although she was careful to maintain the pretense that Bernice was being useful, often giving her small mending jobs to do, or letting her polish the silver, things she could do sitting down.

"Was that Cara on the phone?," Bernice asked.

"Yes. She has some big news. She's finally going to have a baby."

"Let me guess, she's having it all by herself."

"You got it."

"Don't surprise me. That's probably the only way she's ever going to get one."

Edna was astonished. "What do you mean?"

Bernice snorted. "That girl has always used her father as a yardstick when it comes to men. And who could ever measure up to Mr. Len?"

Who indeed? Edna had certainly never found anyone.

The first months after his death had been a confusing welter of detail, made fraught by the tangle he had left behind. She had been too worried and exhausted and stressed to do anything but fall into a dreamless sleep each night, hauling herself reluctantly out of bed each morning to face the next crisis.

After that came desolation, arriving in waves like physical blows, when she least expected it. She would be dusting furniture or washing dishes and some small object or random thought would make her realize all over again that he was truly gone. This would leave her in a maelstrom of emotion, souring her stomach and making her head pound. She had allowed herself the luxury of wallowing in grief when Sacha left. It had seemed like the end of the world then, but it was nothing to what she felt now. This time it was not a lover who was gone but a husband, a companion of years, a beloved, and there was no hope of his ever returning. She fought for some kind of equilibrium. She stood her ground, and as the months passed the waves receded, each one a little less intense.

Then loneliness was her companion. She had been only forty-two when Len died, in her prime, still eager and hungry. It was torment to lie alone in the big four-poster bed, longing for the scent of car leather and cigarettes and rye whiskey. In the night, half-asleep, she would throw her arm across to the other side, only to discover that no body was there, only empty sheets. Further sleep impossible, she would go over and over the events of that last morning. Why hadn't she gone with him? He wouldn't have been in such a hurry to return then, he wouldn't have driven so fast, they could have stayed, safe and snug together in a hotel room, cuddling away the stormy night. Why hadn't she thrown her body across him and demanded that he stay with her? Why hadn't she made love to him one last time? Thus she arrived at the core of her loneliness, the physical craving that wouldn't go away.

She knew that everyone expected her to marry again sooner or later, after all, she was still attractive, but she was wary of involvement. Not that there was a great deal of choice for her anyway. She supposed she could have had affairs with any number of men in town if she had been so inclined, but she knew them, and their foibles, too well. They held no interest for her, and the complications would have been too intricate for her to cope with.

Instead, she filled up her days with the house and the things in it. She tried to sort Len's clothes, with the intention of giving them to the Salvation Army, but his scent still clung to them. Unwilling to see it dissipated, she packed his things in boxes or hung them on racks in the attic.

Everyday items turned into souvenirs. His shaving mug still sat in the cabinet in the bathroom; she left it there, even after the soap shrivelled away to nothing.

The end table in the living room had a wobbly leg; he had set his drink there on many an evening; she put it in the basement.

Her orange lilies were a poignant reminder. She had been planting the first bulbs when he had demanded to know who had made such a mess. He had cautioned her to wear gloves, she recalled, and to put on a hat.

She was loathe to throw anything away. The paintings were all gone now, as was some of her jewellery, the finer pieces that had a resale value, but she was determined to keep everything else. There were so many memories, how could she be expected to keep track of them all without the appropriate tokens?

In the old days, Bernice might have gone ahead and cleared the whole mess out in a fit of zealous housecleaning, but that was beyond her now, and she let the things accumulate without comment, content to sit in the kitchen with Edna drinking tea. We're turning into those two old spinster ladies who used to live here, she thought. What were their names? The Lambert sisters. What is it about this house, that it wants old ladies living in it?

Edna spent more time with Vera, too. The two would lunch together often, and once, when Susan was home to look after Mac and Rhonda could stay with Bernice, they had gone on a bus trip to New York City. They had had fun, visiting museums and art galleries and had gone to several Broadway shows, but it had been expensive, and something they knew they probably would never do again.

As time went on, she grew used to her circumscribed life and the loneliness eased, but, she never quite got around to throwing any of Len's things away.

She gave up on the notion of another relationship. That was a part of her life that was evidently over, and she surmised that she was only the first of the widows, the first of her friends to be husbandless, manless, without a gentleman escort. From now on she would keep the company of women, or so she thought until she met William.

William had been transferred from Owen Sound to the local bank after its previous manager had a heart attack. He had introduced himself to her one day when the bank had telephoned to say that she was overdrawn, but if she could deposit twenty-five dollars right away they wouldn't bounce the cheque she had written to the local utility company. She had been flustered and embarrassed, and had dropped her purse at his feet just as he was coming out of his office, coins scattering across the floor and papers flying everywhere. He had helped her chase the errant quarters that rolled under chairs and behind the potted plants.

He seemed to realize that she was upset and insisted that she sit in his office for a moment to catch her breath. He had a calming way about him, unhurried and unflappable.

"I haven't met you before," he said. "But then I've only been here a week and I haven't met anybody yet."

She sat in the customer chair in his office, at a loss for something to say to this stranger. He was a big man, sandy haired, with worry lines that creased when he smiled. She guessed he was in his late fifties. Finally, she pulled herself together, thanked him for his help and didn't give him another thought until he called the next day.

"The cleaners found a lipstick under my desk," he chuckled. "I expect they've jumped to all sorts of conclusions, but I'm sure it must be yours. I guess it rolled there when you dropped your purse."

She didn't get upstreet for two days after that and was surprised that it hadn't just been left with one of the tellers for her to pick up. Instead, she was again ushered into the manager's office and prevailed upon to take a chair. He didn't give her the lipstick right away either. He smiled at her and fiddled with the tube.

"I know this may seem presumptuous," he said finally, "but would you care to join me for a cup of coffee?"

She was taken aback, it had been so long since anyone had suggested such a thing, and then she decided that yes, she would like to have a cup of coffee with this nice-looking man.

Later she realized that the circumstances were eerily like her first encounter with Len, only this time it was a tube of lipstick and a cup of coffee instead of a speeding car and a chocolate malted. She wondered if, subconsciously, that was why she agreed to it so readily.

"You must forgive me for being an old snoop," he said when they settled into the booth at the cafe across the street. "I asked one of the tellers who you were, and she told me. My wife passed away a couple of years ago, so I figure we're more or less in the same lonely boat."

"Oh. I'm sorry. What did she die of?"

"Breast cancer. Fortunately for her, it was quick. Unfortunately for me, it was quick. How did you lose your husband?"

"Car accident." She found she didn't object to the euphemistic way he had phrased the question. That was exactly what had happened. She had lost him, never to find him again.

"Children?" he asked.

"One. In Toronto. You?"

"Two. A boy and a girl. Well-launched. Heard from occasionally, usually at Christmas time and on my birthday."

"So how do you like our little town?" It had been so long since Edna had had a conversation with someone who didn't know her that she found she had to struggle through the opening ceremonies. Who are you, how did you get here, where do you fit in? These were all questions she hadn't had to ask for a long time.

He sensed her discomfort. "I'll be honest with you. It's damn lonely. I thought by transferring I could get away from all the memories, but I'm discovering that all I've done is cut off my support system. This is the first real conversation I've had since I got here."

She smiled. "Well then I'm glad you're having it with me. So tell me, what do you like to do, and I'll tell you how to go about doing it now that you're here."

He thought for a moment. "You know something," he said slowly. "One thing I always enjoyed, and I haven't done it since before Millie got sick, is to go dancing. Real dancing." He stared at her. "Could I invite you to have dinner with me Saturday night? Someplace where they have a dance floor?"

She was surprised. He was such a big man, he gave the impression of shambling when he moved. Dancing was the last thing she had expected him to say. Then she realized what he had, in fact, said. She was being asked for a date.

Bernice was dubious. "How do you know he's not one of them Texas chainsaw massacrers?" she asked, as Edna twirled around the kitchen in one of the cocktail dresses she had dug out from the back of her closet.

"Oh for goodness sake, Bernice. He's a bank manager. They don't often put homicidal maniacs in charge of banks."

"But you don't know," she pointed out. "After all, he's from away. You don't know one single thing about him or his family either. For all you know, he could still have a wife somewhere."

"For all he knows, I could still have a husband somewhere," she pointed out. "It cuts both ways, you know."

"Just don't be too late, okay? I'm too old to worry that much."

"I feel like I'm sixteen again."

"I know," Bernice said. "I'm being a fussbudget, ain't I?"

"You and Vera both."

She had called Vera as soon as she got home.

"A date?" she had squealed. "Aren't you too old for dates?"

"It's just dancing. And dinner."

"That's what they all say. Are you going to go to bed with him?"

"Vera!"

"Well, that's what it's all about, isn't it? It always was, we were just too young to realize it the last time around."

"No, I am not going to go to bed with him."

And she didn't, at least not right away.

The nearest restaurant with a live dance band was in Belleville, at the big hotel. He had reserved a table at the edge of the dancefloor, but he needn't have bothered. There were only four or five other couples in the room.

"My idea of a good time seems to have gone the way of the dodo," he said ruefully, looking around the room.

The four-piece band was doing its best with songs written for a much larger orchestra. William ordered drinks, then stood and led her to the dancefloor. He moved surprisingly well for so large a man, and she was able to close her eyes and relax into the music. She couldn't identify the after-shave he wore, but she decided she liked it as she moved closer and laid her head on his shoulder.

Over dinner they chatted about books, which he liked, and gardening, about which he knew nothing. When he dropped her off at her house well before midnight, she was surprised when he didn't attempt to kiss her goodnight. It's been so long, she thought, I've forgotten what the rules are. It was just as well he hadn't tried anything. Bernice was still up and had hobbled to the window as soon as she heard the car.

Vera called her the next day. "Well?" she asked.

"Well, what? We had dinner, we went dancing."

"Did he kiss you goodnight?"

"Of course not." She wasn't going to admit, not even to Vera, that she had been expecting him to.

"Did he ask you out again?"

"Yes, you nosy thing. I don't know what Bernice is going to think."

"Oh to hell with Bernice," Vera said. "You're a grown woman and she's not your mother."

"I know," Edna said. "It just feels like it."

He took her dancing three more times before he summoned up enough courage to kiss her. She had been about to open the car door and get out when he put his hand on her shoulder. She turned towards him, knowing what was coming, but when it did, it was tentative, an "is-this-all-right?" sort of kiss. She answered him by cupping his face between her hands and kissing him back with authority. She found it an odd sensation to be in control. She had always been off-balance with Len, and too needy with Sacha.

"Would you like to come in for a drink?" she asked after a time.

"What about Bernice?" Edna had filled him in on Bernice's faintly scandalized reaction.

"She went off to visit her daughter and said she was staying all night. I think she's given up on me in disgust."

He looked odd in her living room, too big somehow, and obviously at a loss. She mixed two martinis without asking him what he'd like and brought them to the chesterfield, where she sat down beside him.

"Good drink," he said, sipping at the martini.

"I learned from a master," she said.

"Len?" She nodded. He set his drink on the coffee table and took her hand. "I know how much he meant to you," he said. "Millie meant the same to me, but it's been too long." He shifted uncomfortably and laughed a little. "I don't really know what I'm supposed to do now."

Until that moment, Edna hadn't been sure either, but it had been too long for her too and she quite liked this kindly, lonely man.

"You know, I haven't given you a tour of the house," she said. "Bring your drink."

She hadn't known what to expect. He was shy about removing his clothing and when she finally got them off him, she understood why. He had an old man's body, with its wrinkles and sags and the beginnings of a paunch.

"I'm no prize," he said apologetically. "I'm afraid the old bod has seen better days."

"Oh good," Edna replied, "I won't have to be so embarrassed about mine then."

He had laughed, and then it was all right. He was gentle, almost too gentle, and there were no fireworks for her, but she enjoyed being held again, the feel of his skin, the male scent in the bed. He seemed grateful afterwards and quick to reassure her. She enjoyed lying in his arms in the dark while he stroked her hair. They woke at dawn.

"Oh my God," he said, leaping out of the bed. "It's morning."

"It can't be that late," Edna said, not moving. "The sun's only just up."

"It's late enough that your neighbours are going to notice my car parked out in front of your house."

"So what?"

"That doesn't bother you?" He was puzzled by her lack of concern.

She propped herself up on one elbow. "Does it bother you?" He was standing with one leg in his trousers.

"I don't want to put you in an awkward position."

She smiled. "I'd say you're the one in an awkward position right now." He realized that he had frozen in mid-dress and quickly pulled his trousers the rest of the way on.

"You know," she went on, "if there was one thing I learned from Len it was not to worry about what other people might think."

He sat on the edge of the bed and stroked her shoulder. "Len sounds like he was a law unto himself," he said slowly. "I'm different. I know we're not doing anything wrong here, we're neither of us married and there's no reason we shouldn't be seeing each other, but I don't particularly want everybody talking about it either."

Edna laughed. "It doesn't matter how discreet we are. They'll know anyway."

He looked puzzled. "What do you mean?"

"They just know. They always do."

He didn't understand. He hadn't ever lived in a small town where the real news never appeared in the newspaper or on television, but made its way simply by flying through the air. "I'd better get going then," he said finally.

He finished dressing, then hesitated in the doorway. "Can I call you again?"

She smiled. "Of course. Can you let yourself out?" He nodded and left.

She was disappointed, then decided she was being unfair. It was only the first time, they didn't know each other that well, how could he know how she would react? In time, she was sure, they would establish the ground-rules, move beyond his old-fashioned notions of chivalry. And it really was different for him, she realized. He had to meet people every day, establish his credibility, represent himself as an upright member of the community, so that no one would ever hesitate to entrust their money with him. It was just that discretion had never been one of her strong suits. "You have a wild streak," Len had said to her once. She had denied it at the time, but he had probably been right.

She laughed at herself then, categorizing one night with a man as "wild". I really must be getting old, she thought, I'm starting to think like my mother.

She and William had seen each other on a regular basis for the next year and a half. It was nice to have a squire again, and they occasionally went to William's apartment or to Edna's when Bernice wasn't there, but for her, at least, it was an arrangement of convenience, the fulfilling of a physical need. When William left to trouble-shoot an out-of-province branch eighteen months later, she was surprised when he asked her to go with him.

"Thank you, I'm very flattered," she said. "But I don't think I can do that."

He was a little hurt. "I thought we liked each other," he said. "I had visions of us growing old together. I could provide you with a pretty nice life, you know. You wouldn't have to worry about money again."

He had always been concerned about her financial straits, and there was no question that he was offering her a security she hadn't had in a long time. But what would she do about Bernice? Or Vera, for that matter, how could she leave Vera behind? Or her garden? What would it be like to walk down a street and have no one say hello or ask some question about her life that was really none of their business, but asked in such a concerned and compassionate way that you couldn't take offence? Who would she turn to when things went wrong? She had lived here all her life, with too many entanglements, too many obligations, and besides, she realized, she just plain liked it here, where she was still Mrs. Len Collins, still Bert Charles' daughter, Cara Collins' mother. There was an enormous freedom in having such a fixed place in the community. There was never any need for reasons or explanations or apologies, she could just be herself, the same way she had always been. How could she trade such riches for the life of a banker's wife in a strange town?

She missed William when he left, of course, at least for a little while, but she never regretted her decision. It just hadn't been a good enough deal.

Cara found pregnancy exhausting. Beginning in the eighth week, her ankles had swelled alarmingly. She gained twenty pounds in the first four months. Her eyes were puffy. Her breasts were sore. Her fingers were like sausages, making her drawing pen awkward to hold. She was too tired to work anyway. Instead, she would lie on her mattress on the floor while the light poured in through the loft windows, bathing her naked, suddenly ill-proportioned body in a yellow glow that only emphasized the greenish tinge of her complexion.

"You should have seen me with the twins," Cass said when she complained. "I was huge by the third month. And I didn't have the height to carry it like you do."

Cara was waiting for the bloom she had read about, the madonnic aura that supposedly surrounded all expectant mothers. Surely any day now she would develop the incandescent blush of gestation in progress. Instead, she gained more weight and continued to spend every morning with her head hanging in the toilet. By the sixth month she had started to waddle alarmingly as her hip joints loosened to accommodate the growth within her. By the eighth month, she longed only to complete this impossible task she had set herself, so she could return to being Cara, the artist, the woman, the person, instead of the walking incubator, who was awakened in the night by the insistent kick, kick, kick of tiny feet and hands and head against her bladder.

In the end she decided to go home. Home, where her mother and Bernice and Vera and Rhonda could fuss over her and cosset her and wait on her hand and foot, where she no longer had to worry about whether or not she had enough energy to walk to the corner store for milk, or remember to buy toilet paper.

Her mother was quietly supportive, exactly, as Cara now realized, as she had always been. It was Bernice who fussed, who hauled herself up from her kitchen chair to fetch cups of tea and glasses of milk. Cara protested.

"You don't have to do that, Bernice," she said. "I don't feel real well, but I'm not an invalid."

"I'm happy to do it for you. It's just like the old days, when your mum was expecting you. I had to do this for her too, you know."

Finally, her mother had taken her aside, and told her to let Bernice do whatever she wanted. "You wouldn't believe the difference in her since you came home," she said. "She pretty much spent all her time sitting in the kitchen drinking tea. Now she has someone to look after again, she's got a new lease on life."

"But I feel so awful when it takes her fifteen minutes to get out of the chair," Cara said.

"I know, but you aren't doing her any favours by stopping her."

So she let Bernice wait on her, and secretly she quite liked it. She quite liked her mother's quiet way of being there when she needed her and disappearing when she didn't. She quite liked the tiny sweaters and caps that Rhonda knit prodigiously in blue, pink and yellow. "One colour for each," she joked.

But most surprisingly of all, she liked to just sit with her feet up and chat with Vera. There was really no need to contribute to the conversation at all when Vera was talking, she was quite capable of carrying it all by herself. Cara found this curiously relaxing. Her mind could wander at will while Vera filled the silence. When she did listen to her, her advice was reassuring.

"Of course you feel awful," she said. "In my opinion, the woman who blossoms during pregnancy is a rare bird. After all, your body is going through hell, it's no wonder it protests a little."

She was quite emphatic about the delivery. "Of course it hurts," she said. "How could it not? But it isn't anything you can't handle. And don't expect to feel wonderful all of a sudden right after you have the baby, either. It doesn't work that way. You'll be exhausted and sore and probably depressed too. Don't let it worry you. You'll get over it."

It was Vera who persuaded her that it would be a good idea to live at home for the first month or so after the birth.

"I don't care how independent you think you are, you can't handle a newborn baby all by yourself, especially these days when they kick you out of hospital as soon as you've had the last contraction. Let your mother and Bernice help you out. You'll be glad enough to hand it over to them when you've been walking the floor for hours, believe you me."

Cara's labour started in the middle of the night. When the pains were five minutes apart, she padded down the hall to her mother's room and knocked softly on the door, hoping she wouldn't disturb Bernice. She might just as well have shot off a cannon.

"Is that you Cara?" Bernice called. "Is it time, dear?"

Her mother came to the bedroom door, took one look at her, and dressed quickly. She made her wait in the kitchen while she got the car out and then she drove her rapidly, but not recklessly, the few blocks to the hospital, where she commandeered a wheelchair and completed the checking-in process with a minimum of fuss.

Cara was uncomfortable at first, and near the end of the delivery in actual pain, but Vera was right, it wasn't anything she couldn't handle. Afterwards she did feel exhausted and sore and a little depressed, but Vera had said she would get over that. She also knew that she wouldn't be running back to the city anytime soon, because she realized, just as the baby was being born, that she didn't know a damn thing about looking after it.

It was a boy, and Edna gasped when she saw him. In spite of the obvious difference, it could have been Cara lying there swaddled in a swatch of flannelette.

Vera also gasped when she saw him. I hope Mac doesn't remember what Stevie looked like when he was a baby, she thought. And then she realized that he wouldn't. Men didn't pay any attention to details like that.

Edna and Rhonda loaded Bernice into the car and brought her to the hospital as soon as visitors were allowed. She cried and then she laughed when she saw the little boy. "My word, what a little angel," she said. "What are you going to call him?"

It was a problem Cara had been struggling with for some time. She wanted her father's name in the middle, she knew that for sure, but she couldn't decide what to put first. Had she been married she would probably have called him Colin as a gesture towards her own maiden name, but his last name was to be Collins too. Colin Collins was just too cute, and too much of a mouthful.

The problem is, she thought, we have such awful names in this family. She refused to load him down with anything as plain as her uncles' names. Her father's father had been Harold and her mother's father Albert, middle-aged men's names that she wouldn't even consider. She was at a loss, but she had to come up with something soon, the hospital was pressing her to fill in the papers. And then, the afternoon of the second day, a couple of hours before she was discharged, the teenaged mother in the next room turned her portable radio on. “You can’t always get what you want,” the Stones sang, and Cara made her decision. Michael Leonard Collins. Mick. Mickey for now. “But if you try sometimes,” she sang along as she cuddled the tiny baby close to her, “you just might find you get what you need.”

CHAPTER TWENTY-ONE

Marcie was as good as her word and arrived at noon on Sunday.

"Still need some help?" she asked when Cara answered the door.

"Yes please." Her method of starting at the top of the house and working her way down had stood her in good stead; almost all of the bits and pieces that needed to be removed had at least been sorted and packed in boxes or garbage bags, but on the way down she had again bypassed her mother's room. Now it was the only one that hadn't been touched.

Marcie attacked the chore briskly and efficiently. "I suggest we just start going through things drawer by drawer and if we find anything that looks either good or interesting, we'll set it aside. Otherwise let's just put everything usable in boxes and we'll get Mac to take it to the rummage sale at their church. Everything else gets thrown out. Is that okay?"

It was very okay. Cara doubted she would keep any of her mother's clothing. The idea of wearing the dead woman's clothes gave her the willies, besides, she was so much taller, none of it would fit anyway.

"I had to do this for my parents," Marcie explained as she started on the dresser drawers. "Best thing to do is just get rid of most of it. You always think you may use the stuff but it ends up just hanging around in the closet."

They worked away in silence after that, Marcie folding slips and sweaters while Cara sorted through her mother's jewellery box. There were a few nice pieces, presents she supposed, from her father, but not nearly as many as she expected. There were a couple of pairs of earrings that she might someday wear, but the costume jewellery was out of style or too fussy for her tastes. She picked out a rather nice sterling silver bracelet but it was far too small; her mother's hands and wrists had been tiny. On impulse she showed it to Marcie.

"Would Amanda like this, do you think?" Amanda was petite, like her mother.

"I'm sure she'd love it," Marcie said. "but are you sure you want to give it away?"

She demonstrated how small it was, and shrugged.

"But what if you have a daughter someday?"

Cara laughed. "No thanks. Mickey is all I've planned for."

She set the costume jewellery to one side, to go to the rummage sale along with her mother's clothes. She tucked the rest in her pocket and left the box itself where it was. She scooped the cosmetics and creams that littered the table top into a garbage bag that Marcie had already filled with bras and pantyhose, items destined for the town dump.

The dressing table had small drawers on each side of the kneehole. When Cara opened them there were more bottles of lotion and jars of wrinkle cream. She hadn't realized her mother spent so much time fussing in front of the mirror. Too impatient to sort them individually, she pulled the drawers out and dumped their contents straight into the garbage bag. The drawers had been lined with a scented paper, the pattern still fresh, but the fragrance long faded. Underneath the liner in the bottom drawer was a carefully folded piece of paper. It didn't look as though it had slipped under by accident and then been forgotten, it looked like it had been hidden. It was a poem, of sorts, she discovered when she smoothed it out. She scanned through it quickly, then went back again to read more slowly.

STOLEN TIME
We sliced through the bay,
White wings swelling
Like the breast of a seagull.
Early summer sunshine
Smiling on us,
Waves slapping the hull.
I looked up.
The sun caught the light in your eyes,
Your hair tossed in a wild wind dance.
You smiled.
And I knew that someday when I was old and cold
I would warm myself in the memory of that glance.

It was signed, E.E. Collins, July 1964. Like e.e. cummings only with capitals, Cara thought incongruously. It wasn't bad as that sort of poetry went, but she hadn't known that her mother wrote poetry. She hadn't known that her mother wrote anything. She fished through the mess she had just dumped into the garbage, in case there were more pieces of paper that had been hidden, but there were none. Just that one. She tucked it into her pocket, too, to take out and read again later.

She suddenly realized that she was hungry. It was one-thirty already and she hadn't had any breakfast. Marcie had finished with both the dresser and the closet anyway.

"You have to go back to Vera's for lunch or anything?" she asked.

"No, I didn't know how long this was going to take, so they're not expecting me."

"Great." She grinned. "I have a suspicion that down in the basement there may be a great bottle of wine with our names on it."

"I have no idea what this is going to be like," she said as she climbed the basement stairs wiping the cobwebs from the dusty bottle. "It's probably from the stock my father put down, so it'll either be very, very good or very, very bad."

It was very, very good and they lingered over their meal of salad and leftover funeral pastries, chatting about children and houses. The more she talked with Marcie, the more Cara liked her. She seemed level headed and straightforward without being too earnest about it.

She had grown up in a small town in the interior of British Columbia, the only child of elderly parents. They had both passed away by the time she graduated from high school. She had used their insurance policies and small savings to finance her education, opting to leave lotusland for the adventure of central Canada. She had never been back.

"I would love to get Amanda down here more often," she said. "There's nobody left on my side so Vera and Mac are the only grandparents she'll ever know." Her brow wrinkled. "Besides, they're getting on, and I keep telling Steve he needs to pay more attention to them."

"So where's Susan?" Cara had never been particularly interested in Susan, and had not paid attention when Vera chattered about her.

Marcie grimaced. "She and her husband are in Halifax now and on their way to God knows where." Susan's husband was in the Armed Forces and they moved around a lot. "What with postings and five kids, they never get home." She shook her head. "Susan is such a pudding. I guess she's just like Mac. You know, I love them both dearly, but I don't understand how those two ever produced Steve."

Cara had often wondered the same thing herself. "How did you and Steve meet anyway?"

"Oh, it was silly," she said. "I was working part-time at one of the student pubs. I had this killer psych final coming up and had my books spread out all over the bar trying to study and wait on tables at the same time. He was horsing around with his friends and knocked a whole mug of beer all over me and all over my notes too. He felt so bad about it, he insisted on buying me a drink when I got off. It just sort of went on from there." She laughed. "Stupid, huh? Just goes to show you never know." She raised an eyebrow and looked at Cara speculatively. "Steve sort of filled me in, you know."

Cara had been pretty sure all along that this was the reason Marcie had offered her help. A reconnaissance mission. She didn't blame her. Who could resist the temptation to size up an old girlfriend? She wondered what, exactly Steve had told her. "I won't pretend, Marcie," she said finally. "It took me a long time to pull myself together after Steve left."

"He knew it was a sell-out, you know" she said softly. "He still feels bad about it, what it did to you. He just didn't have a whole lot of options at the time."

"Yeah? He seemed to be able to walk away from me easily enough." Funny, some of the old hurt was still there. She hesitated. "No, I'm sorry," she said slowly, "I guess that's not true. I pretty much shut him out after he left. It all happened in such a hurry."

"He couldn't turn it down, Cara. He'd never have made it through if it hadn't been for the help he got. His savings went a lot faster than he figured, and tuition gobbled up the student loans. As it was, he thought he was going to have to drop out after third year, but your mother wouldn't hear of it."

"What?" Cara stared at Marcie with astonishment.

"Oh God, have I said something I shouldn't? You knew, didn't you? You knew your mother kept sending Steve money after your father died?"

She hadn't known, but she should have been able to guess. In spite of the fact that the house was piled high with things her mother would never throw away, there had still been too many things missing. The paintings, the expensive rings and necklaces that should have been in the jewellery box. Her mother must have sold them, one by one, not only to keep Cara in school, but to see Steve through as well. But why? It was one thing to help the son of an old friend when you were rolling in dough anyway; it was quite another when you were having trouble making ends meet yourself.

"Steve is going to kill me," Marcie moaned. "I thought you knew."

"Did he ever say anything to you about my father?" Cara asked, trying to puzzle it all out. "I never could figure out what the problem was."

"Neither could he. He just knew that your father didn't like him."

Cara shook her head. "It was just weird, you know. Steve wasn't far off the mark last night, I was nothing but trouble. I used to hang around with these awful guys who rode motorcycles and smoked dope all the time, but as soon as I found a nice guy, my dad hustled him out of town as fast as he could. And now it seems my mother did her damnedest to keep him out. And Steve was such a nice guy, you know, he really was. He still is I expect."

Marcie didn't hesitate a moment. "The best," she said.

"I give up. I don't know what was going on." She started to giggle. "So, tell me," she said, with a leer. "Now that we're on the subject, how is he in the sack?"

"What do you mean? You know."

So Steve hadn't told her quite everything. Time to reassure her a little. Cara shook her head. "Nope. Never did. Every time we tried, something happened and then he was gone before we got there. So?"

She blushed. "Also the best."

"Aw, damn. I knew it. Oh well, water under the bridge. So are you taking some of these clothes with you, or what?"

"Oh, shoot," Marcie said, "I almost forgot. There's another four boxes of stuff in the car we'll have to move first. Vera says they're a bunch of old papers your mother had stored in the attic, but that you should have them now."

Cara groaned. "Great. Just what I need. More old papers. What were they doing in Vera's attic?"

"I don't know, she didn't say. It's something to do with your father's estate, I think. She figures they should probably just be burnt, but she says that's up to you."

"I'll never finish." She grabbed her throat melodramatically. "This house has me in its clutches. Every time I think I'm finally done, something grabs me in its tentacles, holding me here. I'll never leave."

Marcie laughed. "I'm not entirely sure why you want to," she said.

Cara phoned Mickey that night. She missed him terribly, and knew that he missed her. Cass's girls were miniature copies of Cass, energetic extroverts and he sometimes had difficulty coping with their exuberance. They bowled him over, not because they were deliberately inconsiderate, but because they were too enthusiastic.

"How much longer is it going to take you to clear out The Little House on the Island?" Cass wanted to know.

"I don't know. It's not that simple. There's so much more of it than I expected."

"Well, hurry back, will you? You've got three catalogues waiting."

"Listen, Cass, can you send them down with Mickey? I honestly don't know how much longer I'm going to be."

Cass sighed. "Oh, all right. Why do I have the feeling I've lost you forever to Hillbilly Heaven?"

Cara chuckled. "Don't worry I haven't bought a banjo yet. And none of the pickup trucks parked in front of the house are mine."

"Is that Mummy?" Mickey was hovering near the phone. Cass put him on.

"How ya doing, honey?"

"I miss you. The twins broke my Lego castle."

"Never mind," she said. "You'll be here tomorrow. Have you got your clothes packed?"

"Yup."

"And what about your toothbrush?"

"Yup."

"And what about Mr. Muggs?" Mr. Muggs was a tattered stuffed terrier that had been his sleeping companion since he was a toddler. Whenever

Mickey was anxious or upset, Mr. Muggs was dragged out of the toybox again.

"Yup. Can I ask something?"

"Yup." She waited while he worked to formulate the words. "How do I know when I'm at the right place?" he asked finally.

"You mean the right place to get off the train?"

"Yeah. What if I get off in the wrong place? I won't know what to do."

"Don't worry about it, honey. Auntie Cass will tell the conductor that you're travelling all by yourself, and that he's supposed to tell you when it's the right time, okay?"

"Ummmm....okay."

"And you talk to the conductor, but nobody else, okay?"

"Okay." He sounded more confident now.

"Okay, now tell me what you're supposed to do." Cara had found that it always paid to have Mickey repeat her instructions. That way she could be sure that he had heard her correctly and she could clear up any of his misapprehensions right away if he hadn't.

"I pack my toothbrush and Mr. Muggs and Auntie Cass puts me on the train and I don't talk to anybody but the conductor and you'll be there when I get off. Oh... and the conductor tells me when it's the right time."

"Cool," said Cara. "See ya later alligator."

"In a while, crocodile."

The island no longer had train service, the tracks that once ran through its heart ripped up and sold for scrap. The nearest station now was across the bay, in Belleville. The next morning Cara attempted to start her mother's car well before it was time to leave, but it refused to turn over, sputtering twice before it gave a gasp and subsided into silence. In a panic, she phoned Vera's looking for Mac, but he had taken one of his refurbished cars out on a test run, and she didn't know when he would be back.

"I'll take her," Cara heard in the background.

"Steve says he can take you, dear," Vera said.

"Are you sure?" she said, as a matter of politeness.

"He'll be there in five minutes."

But it wasn't Steve who came for her, it was Marcie. Well, well Cara thought, who doesn't she trust, me or him? Marcie gave no sign that anything was amiss.

"Steve promised to take Mandy to the beach," she said by way of explanation. "I got too much sun yesterday, so I didn't want to go. Hope you don't mind."

Cara didn't care who drove as long as they got to the station on time. As they sped along the highway, she was aware of the occasional appraising glance in her direction, but she was too concerned about Mickey to worry much about it.

"So, does Mickey see much of his father?" Marcie asked after they had turned on to the main highway.

"No, thank goodness. Randy was a jerk. Still is a jerk. At least I don't have to deal with him jerking Mickey around." No, there is no man in my life right now, Marcie, she answered silently. She was a little amused by the oblique line of questioning, and wondered if anything she'd said the day before had been the cause of it. Had Marcie reported their conversation to Steve, asked questions? Had they discussed it, or was she simply running on instinct, scenting a potential threat the way Mud had always been able to scent the mailman long before he came down the street? Funny, she hadn't thought about Mud in a long time. Someday it would be nice if Mickey had a dog like Mud, but it was out of the question in a loft in the middle of the city. A small dog, maybe, but not a great galumphing idiot like Mud had been.

Marcie had asked her another question, but she had missed it. Speaking of idiots. "I'm sorry," she said, "I was off in another world." Here she was thinking about dogs, while this poor woman was trying to ascertain whether or not Cara still wanted to sleep with her husband. It was something Cara had yet to ascertain herself.

She had changed the subject. "I just wondered if you were happy with Mickey's school. Amanda's is really getting hit with all the cutbacks. This year there were forty kids in her class."

"Yeah, the city's bad, too. A lot of the programs are being cut. Like art. Apparently it's a considered a frill."

Marcie laughed. "Well, you know that artsy-fartsy stuff, what good does it do?"

"Well, you certainly can't make a living at it, can you?" Cara returned.

"No, what we need are more people with business degrees. They're the ones who make a real contribution to society, you know. When they can find jobs, that is."

The little tickle of an idea that had crossed Cara's mind at Vera's returned. "Steve went on to get his M.A., didn't he?" she asked.

"Yeah, Business admin. Thought it was a sure-fire thing at the time."

"Where was he working when he got laid off?"

"A place called DiPlex. He was comptroller until they were bought out."

"What exactly is DiPlex? What do they do?"

"All sorts of things, but mostly they make plastic bits and pieces for other things. That's not very specific is it?" Marcie laughed. "Okay, let's say you needed a certain kind of plastic drawer stop. You'd go to DiPlex and they'd design and manufacture it for you. But Steve didn't have anything to do with the process, he just looked after the money part."

"Must have been a bummer when he was let go."

Marcie looked depressed. "I don't mind telling you, it's getting a little scary. He got a small buy-out package, but he needs to find something to do soon. We're pretty much at the end of our tether, but there just doesn't seem to be anything out there for surplussed business grads. Thank you, Mr. Mulroney," she added bitterly.

They were almost at the station. Cara resolved to give her idea more thought later, when she had time to think it through. They had arrived in good time. The train wasn't due for another half hour. Anxiously, she paced up and down beside the tracks. I must be insane to send a seven year old on the train by himself, she thought. What if he's abducted? What if, even though he had seemed clear about the instructions, he got off too soon and was even now wandering around a strange town, prey for monsters of all kinds. What if the conductor was a drunken sot and forgot about the little boy with the stuffed dog. What if he was a homicidal maniac or a pedophile or just plain incompetent? Oh calm down, she said to herself. Children travel alone every day of the week. Your father would never have coddled you like this. She wasn't really sure that was true, but before she could continue the argument with herself, she heard, off in the distance, the rumble of the approaching train. The conductor, who seemed like quite a nice man after all, tipped his hat at her as he helped the little boy down the step.

"Is that your Mum?" he asked, before he let go of Mickey's hand.

"Yeah."

"Are you sure?"

Mickey was outraged. "Of course, I'm sure."

The conductor smiled. "Just checking, sir. You come on my train again sometime soon, okay? You and Mr. Muggs."

Mickey was full of his adventure. "They brought me a pop and some cookies," he said, "and the man kept calling me 'Sir'. Can we go back on the train, Mummy?"

"You betcha," she said. "What have got around your neck?"

"Auntie Cass gave it to me. It's a owl."

"I can see that." The stylized pewter owl hung from a slender chain. Cara recognized it as part of Cass's stock at the store. "Why'd she give it to you?"

"She says it's a good luck charm for travellers. Owls can see in the dark, you know."

"Oh! So you can't get lost at night, right?"

He grinned and nodded.

Marcie had hovered tactfully in the background. Now she stepped forward.

"Mickey, this is Marcie. Marcie has a little girl just about your age."

Mickey was suspicious. "What's her name?" he asked.

"Amanda. But she doesn't like boys," Marcie shrugged.

He considered this for a moment. "She'll like me," he said. "I like girls."

"You do?" This was news to Cara. Marcie looked at her and winked.

"Are we staying with them?" he wanted to know.

"No, we're staying at grandma's house."

"I thought grandma was dead."

"Well, she is. But her house is still there."

He wrinkled his brow. "Did she die there?"

"No, honey, she died in the hospital."

He seemed relieved. "Okay. Can I sleep in my old room?"

Cara marvelled at the resilience of children. As soon as his fears about ghosts were laid, Mickey's mind turned to the practical. Where are we staying? Where will I sleep? Is there peanut butter toast for breakfast? Sometimes children have more of a handle on things than we ever give them credit for, she thought.

Marcie's casual tactic worked, and Mickey and Amanda hit it off right away. Vera insisted that they stay for dinner and the children chattered in front of the T.V. while the smell of frying chicken wafted out of the kitchen. They sat together at the table, where they discovered they had a hatred of green beans in common.

Although Mickey was almost a year younger, he was already a little taller than Amanda and Steve good-naturedly teased him about it.

"Why, we can't call you Mickey the Mouse," he said. "We'll have to call you Mickey the Giant. If you don't watch out you're going to grow right up to the ceiling."

"I'm going to grow right through the ceiling," Mickey crowed, flushed and pleased at the attention. "Right up through!"

"You'll hurt your head on the rafters."

"Nope, 'cause I'm too tough. That won't hurt me a bit! And then I'm going to keep growing and growing and growing until I reach the moon!"

"Gee, you're going to have a hard time finding a pair of pants that fit," Steve pointed out, and laughed.

The little boy laughed with him, and Cara was suddenly struck by how alike they seemed. Mickey's eyes were blue, like Randy's and he had inherited her dark, wavy hair, but there was a similarity in the way he and Steve held themselves, the way they grinned, and most of all the way they laughed. She was about to comment on her observation when she happened to notice Vera watching them too. Her face was white.

"Are you all right?" she asked.

Vera fanned herself with her serviette. "Oh, yes, it's hot in here, that's all. That and all the excitement of having you both here." She looked back with an expression Cara couldn't read. A plea? A warning? Whatever it was, no one else seemed to notice.

Steve broke in. "Hey, Cara, while you and Marcie were picking up the baggage at the train station, Amanda and I went to the beach, didn't we honey?"

Amanda nodded. "We went swimming and made a sand castle."

"And," Steve continued. "We went looking for the Palace of the Moon. You know, the place you were asking about the other day."

"But there's nothing there any more, is there?" Vera asked.

"Well, we couldn't find anything. So we stopped at the visitor's centre and asked about it."

"What's the Place on the Moon?" Mickey wanted to know.

"Palace of the Moon," Cara said. "It's a place where people used to go to dance."

"Apparently it closed in the early fifties and then just sat there," Steve went on. "Eventually the roof caved in and the whole thing got covered over with shifting sand, but what's left of it is still there, buried underneath a dune."

"Oh my goodness," said Vera. "That's so sad. That lovely dance floor."

Cara thought it was sad too, a place that had once been full of light and music and laughter abandoned, lying forever empty under the sand. But no, she thought, it's not really empty, not when you think about it. It must be full of ghosts and memories.

Vera obviously thought so too. She had a dreamy expression on her face, lost in some reminiscence of days gone by.

"Oh, oh Dad." Steve said. "Mum's got that goofy expression on her face. She's thinking about some old boyfriend I bet."

Vera snapped out of her reverie and blushed.

"Watch out Mum, Dad'll get jealous if you're not careful. Why there must be a million men out there just waiting to snap up a purty young thing like her, isn't that right Dad."

"That's right," Mac said. "I always thought she was just about the prettiest thing I'd ever seen."

Amanda giggled. "Grandpa's got a crush on grandma," she announced.

Mac nodded. "That's right, honey, and I always did."

"Oh, go on," Vera protested. "You old fool." But everyone could see that she was pleased. Mac just smiled at her. Cara ducked her head, pretending to fuss with her mashed potatoes, so no one could see the tears that had suddenly gathered at the corners of her eyes.

Peter Melbourne called two days later with the surprising news that he had a couple in his office who wanted to look at the house. "I'll be honest," he said. "I thought it would sit on the market for months." He chuckled. "I guess I shouldn't have told you that, eh?"

Cara laughed too. "No, you should have sold me a line about your superior abilities as a salesman. You're never going to cut it as a big-league conman, Peter."

"That's okay," he said. "I'm just glad I have some good news for you. We'll be there in about half an hour, if that's all right."

As soon as she hung up the phone, she looked around the house with dismay. There were boxes and piles of garbage bags everywhere, along with clusters of rolled up dust that had fetched up in the corners. There was nothing she could do about much of it at this point, but she did send Mickey up the stairs to pull up the covers on his bed.

She had a chance to get a good look at them before they came in the house. Peter walked them around the outside first, and she could see them pointing at the peeling trim and the worn shingles. Peter had used the term "couple" on the phone and it surprised her that the pair were in fact two middle-aged men, both quite handsome and very well-dressed.

"This is Edward Parton," Peter introduced them when he brought them inside, "and this is Neil Havel."

"This is a fabulous house," Neil said. "Classic Georgian. It's unusual that it's been left alone. So often people brick in a front porch or put stucco on or do something that ruins it."

"My father had a real eye for stuff like that," Cara said. "He wouldn't allow many alterations."

"Peter here tells us you're an artist," Edward said. "What kind of art?"

"Actually, artist is a pretty high-falutin' term for it. I do sketches for magazines and mail-order catalogues."

Edward looked puzzled for a moment and then his face lit up. "C. Collins. You're not the one who does the illustrations for "A Place in the Sun" are you?" This was one of the small catalogues whose Christmas issue was even now waiting for her on the kitchen counter.

"Yeah, that's me," she admitted.

"My God! I love those! We bought two of the originals, the colander one with all the eyes peering through the holes and the mountain-climber plate hanger. Neil, this is the artist!"

She was a little embarrassed by their enthusiasm, but the look on Peter's face was priceless.

"I didn't realize you were famous," he said, slightly awed.

She laughed. "Neither did I."

Edward and Neil oohed and aahed their way through the house, exclaiming over the intact mouldings and the oak floors. Their faces fell a little when they saw the kitchen.

"Oh, this needs some work," Edward said, and Cara agreed.

They tut-tutted over the furnace and grimaced at the bathrooms, but waxed rhapsodic in the attic.

"What a wonderful space!" Edward said. "Why on earth aren't you using this as a studio?"

"This was all my mother's. I have a place in the city." Cara explained. "I don't actually live here."

They stared at her. "Whyever not?

"I grew up here. Couldn't wait to get out."

"But this place is paradise, Neil said. "My God, if I owned a house here, I'd never sell it. I'd just live here until I died."

"Shut up will you?" Edward said. "Don't give her second thoughts. We're trying to buy this place, remember?"

They were interested, it turned out, in turning the house into a bed and breakfast, just as Peter had predicted. Cara could hear their huddled conversation as they discussed the details.

"There's some work to be done, but you know it won't take much. The house is sound, except for the roof. What do you think?" Neil shrugged. "I wonder if she'd sell it with the furniture?" he asked.

It didn't surprise her that Peter came back with an offer later that afternoon. It was on the low side but, as Peter pointed out, at least it was an offer. "They'll come up a bit, but it's early days, you know. You could wait and see if you get a better deal later in the season."

But Cara didn't have any quarrel with the price they eventually settled on. It was fair, and it would take her off the hook for the bills that had piled up during her mother's illness, with quite a lot left over besides. She didn't have a problem with the buyers, either. They obviously appreciated the house and would do a wonderful job of fixing it up. What did bother her was Neil's chance remark about paradise.

She had been enjoying her stay on the island, in spite of the reason for her presence. She realized that she had always thought of it as home as long as she had the option of returning. With this sale, she would no longer be able to pretend that home was here.

"Who were those men?" Mickey wanted to know.

"They're thinking of buying this house."

"To live in?"

"Yes."

"But where will we live?"

"In the loft."

"No." Mickey's face was screwed up in concentration as he searched for the words that would say what he meant. "Where will we live *here*?"

"When we come to visit, you mean?"

"Yeah. We're still going to come here, aren't we?" His face was twisted with concern. "I like to visit. When it's here."

She hadn't considered Mickey. She had assumed that she would dispose of whatever property there was and go back to the city, take up her old life, hunker down in the loft and draw whenever they weren't doing something together. Except for Cass, she seldom spent time with anyone else except when she was nagged into it. It always seemed like so much trouble. But for some reason it wasn't any trouble here. It was natural and easy and required no effort on her part. She hadn't realized that it was probably the same way for her son.

She studied the small boy in front of her. He was like her, or so she had always thought, self-contained and self-possessed and not in need of a lot of company. Maybe that was unfair to him, though. Maybe he was like that because that was the way she had organized his life for him. She doubted he would ever be a social butterfly, not by a long shot, he was too shy, but in retrospect she realized that she had always had the comfort and support not only of her mother and father, but of Bernice and Rhonda and Vera and yes, of her grandmother, and Uncle Jack and Aunt Margaret and any number of people who could be counted on to assist, to bolster, to meddle, or at the very least, to say hello when she walked down the street. The essential fact of belonging here, as irksome as it had sometimes been, had always been a part of her. And in some way for Mickey too, she guessed. Now they wouldn't have that any more.

"You like it here, don't you Mick," she said.

"Yeah."

"What do you like about it?"

Again, he struggled to find the phrasing. "I like the beach... and the water.... and all the trees."

"Uh huh."

"It's not so noisy here........um..." His face brightened. "I like it when we go into a store and they talk to me. The lady at the grocery store always asks me if I'm going to eat all the food by myself." He rolled his eyes at her and giggled. "This part is a secret," he warned.

"Okay."

He stood on tiptoe and cupped his hand around her ear. "I like Amanda," he whispered, and then he giggled again.

Neil and Edward wanted a quick closing date, hoping that renovations could be completed in time for them to catch at least the tail end of the tourist season. The lawyer advised that the legalities were in order, and Peter promised to push everything through as fast as he could. He called Cara in a panic a few days later.

"There's supposed to be a survey on file, but the registry office can't find it," he said. "I know it's got to be there, and so do they, but they're in the middle of renovations themselves and everything's a mess. They said they'd have it by next week, but it would really simplify things if you could just find your copy."

Cara hadn't seen anything that looked like a survey in the papers she had already packed up, but she promised Peter she would have a look, so reluctantly she started going through the boxes that Vera had cleaned out of her attic. She found the flat, folded survey in the second box, under a sheaf of papers that had been bound together with an elastic. She gave them a cursory glance. They seemed to be legal agreements and deeds and letters of intent, things in which she had no interest, really, except that one with a London address caught her attention.

It was the deed to the apartment building that Steve had looked after when he went to university. What caught her attention even more than the address was the date of purchase, a mere two weeks before he left. With her new-found knowledge of real estate transactions, she could see that the purchase had been made in a hurry, with a very short closing date. Typical of her father to go to such great lengths, she thought, all opposition swept away by his money and determination. Money talks, they say. Surprising how often it does, if it's wrapped in the right packaging.

She couldn't fault Steve. She had been naive and sheltered and she realized now that if she had been in the same position she probably would have done the same thing. After all, theirs had been an adolescent romance, destined to sputter out in time, as they all did. No, it wasn't Steve she had been angry with, it was her father.

She knew that in the years since he'd died, she had invested his memory with a kind of golden glow, recalling him as loving, fascinating, exciting and mesmerizing, the father he had been to her when she was little. Until recently, until she saw Steve again, she had seldom thought about her turbulent teenage years, her outrage. She had shoved these memories to the back of her mind, and when they did pop to the surface, she dismissed them as mere teenage angst, laughable in retrospect. Anything else would have been speaking ill of the dead, tempting fate, disturbing the picture she treasured of a happy, perfect childhood. She knew that this picture was skewed, but it had never seemed to matter. He was dead, after all, and this idealized version of him gave her comfort.

But he hadn't been perfect, had he? She had thought he was hopelessly old-fashioned when she was fifteen. She had been scornful of him when she was seventeen. She had just started getting over it all when he was whisked away. Would they have been friends again, if he had lived? Would they have resumed their old, easy adoration of each other? Or would she have been like her mother, wary, unable to overcome her suspicions that everything was not as it seemed?

When she had first gone away, and new acquaintances asked what her father did for a living, she had always answered vaguely, "developer" or "businessman". In uncharitable moments, she now remembered, "wheeler-dealer" had seemed more apt. There was all that money he threw around, using it to make circumstances bow to his bidding. She never knew where it came from or why it had disappeared so quickly after his death. She knew that he had left his affairs in a mess, although her mother had never told her as much. She knew that the police had been involved, that there were questions of illegalities or at the very least, improprieties. She knew that her mother had somehow tapdanced through the difficulties and saved what she could.

"Making another run, Len?" That was what the American, the one she hadn't liked, had asked on that first trip to Main Duck Island so long ago. "Did you know your old man is a pirate, Cara?"

"I'm not in the business anymore," had been her father's reply. What business had he been talking about?

"I thought she was a little younger than your usual type." Unbidden, the rest of the conversation returned to her.

He must have had a lot of them, she thought. A lot of women.

There was the house on the edge of town, tangled with the enigmatic Francis O'Brien, who thought enough of him to leave her worldly belongings to his only child. How many others had there been? How many other women had lifted their hands to his face in a loving caress?

She was appalled at the thought that slipped into her head then, and tried to shove it away, but it was too late. It explained too many things too neatly; her father's dislike of Steve and his outrageous manoeuvrings to get him out of her life; the odd ways in which Steve and Mickey were so similar; Vera's reaction that night at dinner when they had been like mirror images laughing together; the companionable rapport she and Steve had always had. They had often joked about their similarities. "Identical twins separated at birth" Steve once said. Not nearly so melodramatic an explanation, but the only one that made any kind of sense.

She tried to picture it, Vera and her father. Not the rolypoly chatterer of later life, of course, but the Vera in the photograph albums. The Vera who had been pretty and vivacious and petite. The Vera that Mac Dunlop had a crush on.

My God, she thought, if it's true, they must have been having fits. The old taboo. She and Steve had been so close so many times, but events had always conspired to interrupt or distract them. Had they somehow known? Was there some innate awareness that they shouldn't do what they both had so evidently wanted? This aspect of their relationship had puzzled her for years.

And where did her mother fit in, what had been her reaction? Did she even know? She must have, why else would she have sent Steve money when she had so little, unless she saw it as a debt, an obligation?

"At one time we were at odds," Vera had said in the hospital. "But we got over it." Was this the quarrel she had been referring to? How could a friendship survive such a revelation? But no, she realized, Steve was older than she was. Before. Before her mother had been standing on the sidewalk with her suitcase. Before her father had scooped her up and taken her away. Still, it must have caused a strain, not only between Vera and her mother, but between her parents as well.

So who had her mother written a poem for? Certainly not for her father, she had called it "Stolen Time". Who had the time been stolen for? What had happened in 1963, the date written on the bottom of the paper? Cara had been only seven years old, too young to pick up on any tensions in her parent's marriage. Had her mother somehow become aware of her father's proclivities and retaliated in kind? Maybe she was reading too much into it, it was only a poem after all, and she herself was often annoyed when someone assumed a linear correlation between art and the artist. But why, then, had it been hidden away so carefully?

She pulled it out of her pocket and read it again. No, she decided, this was not a description of a real lover. The words were too full of longing, the picture too pretty. "Old and cold" were the words she used. How had her mother known so long ago that moments of joy must be snatched out of time and hoarded, that they were too easily wasted, that there were far too few of them to squander?

She knew so little about these women. Her mother, Vera, Francine. Even Bernice, whose mind was now as crippled as her body. Did she, too, have moments of happiness that nourished her as she lay wasting? Cara had always had the arrogance to believe that life for these women was simple and straightforward, but now she realized that there were layers of incident and innuendo that she would never be able to pry apart and understand, that she could never truly know what their lives had been like, what actions and accidents had defined them. The only thing she knew for certain was that they had taken what life handed them and played it out with grace and dignity and aplomb and that in the end, they had achieved friendships that had lasted all of their lives.

She suddenly didn't want to know the answers to the questions that had been plaguing her. She didn't need to know. It was enough that her parents had loved each other, in spite of imperfections and infidelities. It was enough that they had loved her. It was enough that Vera and Bernice and Rhonda and Francine and, in fact almost everybody she knew in this peculiar, gossip-ridden little place cared about her, in ways that few could understand unless they too were a part of it. She had tried to wall herself off from it, she had tried to run away, but in the end, she had been lured back by its jacklight, not to ruin on the rocks, but to a warm and comfortable place by the fire.

She was surprised to find tears rolling down her face then, tears that should have been shed at her mother's funeral, but that hadn't come until now. When I die, she thought, I hope someone discovers that my life has been as rich and as filled with such joy, such pain, and most of all, with such great and constant friendship.

She set the survey aside, to take to Peter Melbourne later, but the rest of the papers she left in the boxes. With Mickey's help, she lugged them out to the back yard and piled brush around them, tucking pieces of newspaper carefully into the spaces. She found a box of wooden matches in the back porch, and after she had lit one, handed it to Mickey to hold against the paper. The fire caught on an edge and swelled into flame.

"What are we burning, Mummy?" Mickey asked.

"Just some old papers."

'Were they grandma's?"

"Yeah. She should have got rid of them a long time ago."

They watched as the fire gained hold, spreading through the newspaper, then catching on the cardboard and twigs, turning it first into a bright orange pyre, then a blackened pile, before subsiding into grey and anonymous ash.

"When the fire burns out, we can dig the ashes into the garden," she told Mickey. "It'll make the flowers grow."

When she finally settled on the details, she could have kicked herself, it was all so obvious. It was so obvious she didn't even bother to marshal her arguments before she picked up the phone to call Peter Melbourne.

"The coach house?" he said doubtfully. "Sure, it's registered separately. I don't know how that's going to impact on the offer you have, though."

"Tell them I'll throw in whatever furniture they want."

"Some of that stuff is pretty valuable," he protested. "Are you sure you want to do that?"

"Look," she said. "Just sit down and come up with something that will work."

She walked out and inspected the coach house as soon as she hung up. It was rather a grand term for what she would have called a garage. The last tenant had left a bit of a mess, too. There were holes in the living room wall where the plaster had come away, thanks to two large nails that had been pounded into the wall, garbage lay in a corner and the whole place needed a paint job, but there really wasn't anything that couldn't be brought up to snuff fairly easily. A living room, a kitchen, two bedrooms; Mickey would finally have his own room, something that she suspected he would appreciate in the not so distant future. The only other thing she needed was someplace to work.

The shed on the back was just that, a shed, but it had a good foundation, as far as she could see, and one side of it faced north. She visualized it opened to the peak, with windows and skylights. Surely she could draw here as well as anywhere. She didn't have to be in the city to do what she did, after all, and maybe, just maybe, a change of scene would do her good. Maybe, just maybe, she could start producing some serious work. If not, it didn't matter. She had nothing to lose. Now, if Edward and Neil will just co-operate, she thought.

She ran it past Mickey that night.

His face lit up confirming her suspicions. "My own room? Neat. Will I go to school here?"

"Yes, you'd go to school here."

"With Amanda?"

That remained to be seen. "Maybe," she said.

Mickey's eyes narrowed. "Will I get to play with the twins?"

She was surprised at that. "Sure, we can visit or they can come down here sometimes."

"But not too much, okay?"

"Okay," Cara said. "But it has to be sometimes."

"Why," he wanted to know.

"Because your Auntie Cass is my best friend, that's why."

The next conversation wasn't quite so easy. Cara considered for a long time before she finally picked up the phone and called Steve's number. Please be Marcie who answers, she prayed as the phone rang. Her prayers were answered. Marcie seemed surprised to hear from her.

"Are you alone?" Cara asked.

"Yes." She sounded wary. "Amanda's at a friend's. Steve took the car in to get the brakes fixed."

Cara took a deep breath. "Look, Marcie, I have an idea, but I need your help and I need to make sure that you and I are absolutely straight before I ask for it, okay?" Her heart was hammering, and it took a moment for her to collect herself. "Oh boy... I don't know how to say this, so I'm just going to say it. You don't have anything to worry about with me and Steve. There are a whole lot of reasons for that and I'll tell you about it someday, but for now can you just trust me?"

Marcie didn't insult her by pretending she didn't know what she was talking about. "Okay. I guess that's the best guarantee I can get right now."

Cara exhaled.

"So," she asked. "Does Steve know anything about the furniture business?"

Cara waited until the children had taken Amanda's Lego up to Mickey's room and Vera had plunked the teapot in the middle of the table. She had conferred with Marcie on her approach, but she was still nervous and cleared her throat several times before she spoke.

"You're probably all wondering why I called you here today." They laughed, but she could tell they had been waiting for this.

Steve had been puzzled when Marcie insisted that they visit his parents again so soon.

"We were just there," he said. "We're going to wear out our welcome."

"I doubt that. Your mother adores it. It'll be nice for Amanda, she hardly ever gets to spend time with her grandparents. You can take her fishing."

He had grumbled, but there was no good reason not to go. It wasn't as if he were busy or anything.

Vera had been surprised when Cara invited them all to dinner.

"Are you sure you wouldn't rather come here," she asked. "It's so much trouble for you."

"Well, I'm not guaranteeing that it'll be as good as yours, Vera, but it's time I returned your hospitality."

She and Mickey had picked up a frozen lasagna and some eclairs. With bread and salad, it would do. It's times like this I miss Bernice the most, Cara thought. She had been careful to have everything ready ahead of time, so that Vera would have nothing to do but sit and make conversation for once. Nevertheless, she had jumped up from the table to set the kettle boiling as soon as her meal was finished. Now she poured, passing the cups around the table, while everyone waited expectantly for Cara to continue.

"I have a proposition for you Steve," she said.

Steve grinned at her. "I always like propositions from beautiful women," he said.

"Back off, will you? I'm serious."

"Well at least your language has improved over the years," he pointed out. "You used to positively assault my delicate ears whenever you were ticked off."

"Just shut up and listen." He waited for her to go on. "I'm in a bit of a bind with the store, you know."

"In what way?" He was listening seriously now.

"It isn't doing so great and Uncle Jack wants to retire anyway. My choices are to sell the place for next to nothing, or try and run it myself." She looked at him with what she hoped was a helpless look. "As you probably remember, I can barely make change."

He chuckled. "I do seem to recall a certain disability in that direction."

"Well, damn artists, you know, notorious for being impractical." She shrugged. "What do you think about having a go at it?"

"What? At running the store or making change?"

"Idiot. Running the store of course. You're one of those nasty business types aren't you?"

He looked dubious. "But I've never run a store. I haven't had much experience in any kind of retail."

"Uncle Jack is willing to stay on for a while. He'd help you learn the ropes. It was the way he started, after all, with my Dad."

Steve looked at Marcie. "Jeez, Cara, I don't know...." There had been a discussion after all, she thought. And Steve was making it clear where he stood. She liked him even better for it.

Unexpectedly, Mac spoke up. "For crying out loud, Steve," he rumbled, "the lady's offering you a job. Besides, you got all that fancy education, you might better be using it." Cara could see that he was pleased by the idea.

"What do you think Marcie?" Steve asked. It was all up to her.

"It's your call Steve," she said. "But I wouldn't mind."

He looked surprised. "Okay, what's the deal?"

"I start you out as assistant manager," Cara said in a rush. "After a year, if everybody's still happy, Jack retires and you take over. I probably can't pay you as much as you're used to getting, but I have an idea that could help with that, too."

"You're just full of ideas aren't you?"

"Listen, I've given this a lot of thought and done a lot of footwork already. As part of your salary, I can throw in the house out on the edge of town. It needs some work, and it's kind of small, but you could probably fix over the basement to give you more room. Free rent. All I'll ask you to do is cover the running expenses and the taxes."

"What's the salary range?"

She could almost see the numbers being added up in his head when she named a figure that Jack had told her would be fair.

"Jeez, Cara, that's one hell of a deal." He looked at Marcie. "If we sold our house for anything close to what it's worth, we'd be pretty much out from under."

Cara decided then to play her trump card. She put her hand over Steve's. "You'd really be helping me out, Steve. I can't begin to cover the expenses on all this property and the agent tells me it could take years to sell. This is a good deal for me, too."

He frowned. "I'll need a couple of days to talk it over with Marcie. When do you need an answer?"

"Take your time," she said with a wave of the hand. "Make sure it's what you really want." But she could see that he wanted to say yes. She didn't dare look at Marcie, so she looked across the table instead, right into Vera's ecstatic face. Cara hadn't even factored her into the equation, and she could see now that it had been an oversight. If Vera had anything to say about it, and Vera usually had a great deal to say about everything, Steve would be installed at Charles Furniture before the month was out.

Cara and Marcie cleared the table, while Steve and his father added and subtracted figures on the back of an envelope. Vera was bent over the kitchen sink, rinsing dinner plates.

"Well, you two certainly sorted that one out," she said without looking up.

"What do you mean?" Marcie busied herself with putting food in the refrigerator, while Cara tried to keep her expression as neutral as possible.

Vera chuckled and patted her arm with a damp, chubby hand. "Never mind, dear," she said. "That's the way your mother and I always managed things too."

Cara and Steve met with Jack the next day to discuss the impending changes. She knew that Jack approved of her plan, he had said as much when she'd discussed it with him over the phone, but approving in principle and making it work in practice were two different things.

She relaxed as soon as she realized that the two men hit it off right away. Steve had an easy way with him that offered the older man deference without being over-polite.

"What's your take on the business, Jack?" he asked. "What do you think needs to be done?"

Jack chuckled. "If I could figure that out, I probably wouldn't be retiring." He considered the question for a moment. "More than anything, we need to find some way to compete with the big chains. They buy in volume and they sell in volume. We just can't match their prices."

Steve nodded. "You're not alone. Almost every small business has the same problem. Why don't you show me around the store so I can get a feel for the stock?"

Jack was happy to oblige and they left Cara sitting in the office with Lori, the young woman who had replaced the ancient Mabel.

Lori grinned at her. Cara's plans to keep the store open were apparently common knowledge, although, as far as she knew, nobody had breathed a word about it.

"Are you going to be living here too, Mrs. Collins?" Lori asked.

"Please, call me Cara."

Lori rolled her eyes. "It just doesn't seem right," she said. "After all, you're the boss."

"In name only."

"So, are you moving back here?"

Cara was saved from having to answer by the telephone. It's bad enough they know my business, she thought, they can damn well wait to find out about my personal life. And then she realized that Lori had only been looking for confirmation of the rumours that must be flying. How do they always know? she wondered.

Jack took her aside after Steve left.

"He's a good fellow," he said. "You chose well, and I'm sure it will all work out just fine, but I think you should consider spending more time down here, especially after I leave." She hadn't told Jack about her other plans yet.

"Why?" She was puzzled. The whole point in having Steve take over the store was so that she wouldn't have to bother with it.

"He's a capable man," Jack said, "but it never pays to leave a manager to his own devices. If you're the owner, you have the ultimate responsibility to keep the company healthy." He smiled. "Take it from me. If your mother had paid more attention to what I was doing, the place might be in a little better shape right now."

"I'll never believe that one as long as I live."

"Seriously, though. I want you to think about what I've said. Stick your nose in once in a while, just to keep everybody honest."

Neil and Edward came through, and agreed to exclude the coach house from the sale.

Vera beamed when Cara announced the news. "I'm so glad, dear. We worry about you, all alone in the city, you know."

But that wasn't the real reason, as far as Vera was concerned, although she didn't say it to Cara. She missed Edna terribly, and she was afraid that she would start forgetting her, the same way that Len had started to fade out of her mind after he died. She didn't know how two people who had meant so much to her could disappear so rapidly, but they had. It was as if they were frozen into some impossible posture in time, like in a washed-out snapshot where the form was captured, but the essence remained hidden, bleached away by the sun.

Cara reminded her so much of them both. In looks, just like her father, except for her hair, which was curly and luxuriant like her mother's. At times she had Len's exuberance, expressed in quick and quixotic action. At other times, she showed Edna's stillness, the wariness of a wild animal unsure of a stranger's intentions.

There was Mickey, too. Who he would turn out to be like, Vera couldn't tell right now, but when she looked at him he was so much like Steve she was astounded and grateful that everyone else didn't see it too.

It was almost as if everything had worked out after all, with a few detours along the way, of course, but it gave her comfort to see their children, hers and Len's and Edna's, walking along in lock-step, not quite the way she and Edna had thought it would be those years ago when they played in the woods, but at this point in her life, it was close enough for Vera.

CHAPTER TWENTY-TWO

May had been cold and rainy, but the Sunday of Victoria Day weekend dawned clear and sunny. Mickey had been pestering her to go on a picnic and on impulse, Cara called to see if Steve and Marcie and Amanda would like to go too. They would, and Marcie offered to pack a lunch.

They frequently did things like this together, taking the children to a movie or skating on the bay. Marcie was still a little wary of her at times, still not quite sure of her motivations, but as time went on, Cara was certain they could become friends. Someday I'll tell her, she thought, someday when Mac and Vera are gone and it won't matter any more. She wouldn't ever tell Steve. That was a task best left to Marcie. She'd know how to handle it, as soon as she understood that whether it was true or not, there was no possibility that Cara could ever view Steve in the same light again.

They drove to Little Bluff, a spectacular outcropping of eroded limestone that dropped dramatically to a stony beach. Behind the beach lay a marsh, before it was a tiny cove. It was one of Cara's favourite places, and Mickey's too.

They parked their cars at the top and made their way down the steep path to the beach. The children ran on ahead, scampering down with ease.

They spread their blankets on the small round stones about halfway down the beach, Amanda and Mickey busily collecting driftwood for the fire, Marcie fussing with coolers and bags of food. The beach was littered with the debris of winter, thrown up onto the stones by howling gales and fierce, pounding spring waves. Later, after the tourists came, the beach would be scoured clean of its winter gifts.

"Can we go swimming, Mummy?" Mickey asked.

"No, it's too cold. It's only May."

"Can we go wading then?" Without waiting for an answer, the children tore off their shoes and socks and set off along the shore, picking their way carefully through the loose stone. They headed towards the bluff, where the shingle gave way to slabs of limestone, layered up the cliff. It was easier there in bare feet, and Cara knew that further on they would be unable to get past an outcropping of undercut rock unless they waded in the water. Around the rock was a tiny cove, secluded and cut off from the rest of the shoreline. It was completely private there, easy to imagine it as a desert island or a wrecker's cove. Cara always imagined herself stranded there, living in delightful barbaric comfort in a shack constructed from driftwood, catching fish and picking berries from the bushes that grew grudgingly on the cliff face.

"Want a beer?" Steve had opened a can and was holding it towards her. "Can't start a fire without a beer."

"Nope, just like you can't paint without a hat."

"I'll never get all the rules straight," Marcie laughed. "It's like being in a foreign country."

"It is a foreign country, "Cara said. "But that's okay, you've got a passport."

"Who, him?" She pointed at Steve. "He can't even get a fire started."

"The wood's wet. What do you expect?"

Cara watched him struggling with the matches for a moment, then rose and walked over to the marshy growth behind the beach. The tops of the grasses were brown and fairly dry, old growth from last year, and it took only a handful of it to feed the feeble flame and make it catch the driftwood.

"Smartass."

"Learned that from my Dad."

"That's okay," he laughed. "I learned this from my Dad." He threw his head back and chugged his beer.

Cara leaned back on her blanket, basking in the warm sun, content with the afternoon. She had been working all week on a fall catalogue and felt she had earned a rest, something she would never have allowed herself before. It was surprising how her priorities had changed, how she had mellowed since she and Mickey had gone to pack up their belongings and arrange a sublet on the loft.

Cass had been there to help, dubious and slightly amused.

"I wondered how long it was going to take you to run back to Hicksville, " she said. "You can take the girl out of the country, but you can't take the country out of the yokel."

"What's a yokel, Mummy?" Mickey had wanted to know.

"Somebody who has sense enough not to live in a city," Cara replied. "Seriously, Cass, do you think I've lost my mind?"

"Hell, no," she said. "After all, you've got a business to run. Your Uncle Jack is a wise man - never leave a stranger in charge of your affairs. Although I take it that this Steve isn't that much of a stranger...."

"Not a chance." Cara looked at her sternly. "Nothing left. Sorry. Besides, I like his wife too much." Cass had always accused her of having a father fixation. She wondered what her reaction would be if she found out that it had been, in fact, a brother fixation. Maybe she should join that encounter group after all.

Cass sighed. "I don't know how you think you're ever going to find anybody way out in the sticks."

"Back off. Look what happened the last time you introduced me to somebody."

"I know, but he's beautiful, isn't he?" she said, tousling Mickey's hair. "Oh well, at least now we have someplace to go for holidays."

"That's right, there's a bed and breakfast right next door," she said pointedly.

Neil and Edward had painted and papered and reroofed and gutted and rebuilt, until the house was a shining and exquisite example of sensitive renovation, one that promised to be featured soon in a decorating magazine, if they had anything to say about it. They had taken a great deal of the furniture, exclaiming on how appropriate it was, and the fine quality of it, and were delighted when they learned that a lot of it had come from Charles and Sons.

"Just look at the detail on this chair leg, Eddie." Neil was admiring one of the occasional chairs in the living room. The diminutive took Cara aback for a moment.

"How ya doin' Eddie?" her father would say to her mother, grabbing her in a bear hug and giving her a smack on the cheek. It was odd to have another, and very different, Eddie in the house.

They had turned their attention to the overgrown garden too. She had expected them to tear everything out and start over again, but Neil had exclaimed over the mature shrubs and the naturalized plantings and was carefully nurturing it back to health. They had built a cobbled courtyard around the birdbath and often hosted outdoor parties to which they invited not only Cara and Mickey, but all of the Dunlops as well.

She had not been sure what Mac and Vera's reaction would be, but they seemed to notice nothing amiss, and soon "the boys" as Vera called them, were consulting her on the proper procedure for making jam, and the best way to cook a turkey. She hadn't been sure what the town's reaction would be either, and was pleasantly surprised when there were few comments. It was old hat to them, she realized. There were so many new people now. The island would absorb them, chip off the edges, make them fit, no matter how odd the shape.

What they did comment on were the changes at Charles Furniture. Fletcher's Drug Store was long gone and the corner stores had been superceded by a supermarket, but people still gathered around the post office steps to exchange the day's gossip.

"Nice to see she's going to keep it open." Neil and Edward had overheard and reported the conversation to her.

"She may be an artist, but she has a head on her shoulders, that one..."

"Takes after her father, I guess. My but he was a character..."

"Why I could tell you stories..."

She had furnished the coach house with furniture Neil and Edward hadn't wanted, and when the sale was finalized had arranged with a local contractor for her own, less ambitious renovations. The rebuilt shed had turned out almost exactly as she had imagined it, airy and open and filled with light. When they moved in, she and Mickey ceremoniously hung her grandmother's little watercolour painting in a place of honour by the door. Mickey was delighted with this tangible evidence of his great grandmother's existence. "Nomi's picture", he called it, just as the exquisite blue and white painted decoration they hung at the top of their first real Christmas tree became "Gramma's Angel."

He was happy, she knew, and she thought maybe she was too, although at times she found the small town almost as claustrophobic as she remembered. Time would tell, she thought. Who knew what small accidents would collide into the circumstance of her life? She would take it as it came, and treasure her contentment.

Her pleasant reverie was interrupted by the scrabble of rock. Steve and Marcie were standing at the shoreline, picking rocks off the beach and skipping them across the water.

"Why is you can't be near the water without throwing rocks into it?" Marcie called.

"It's another rule," Steve said.

"Anthropologists have an explanation for that, you know," Cara said without sitting up. "It goes back to the days when we were monkeys living in the trees."

"Speaking of monkeys, I can hear our two coming back. Should we start the hot dogs?"

"Daddy, daddy look what I found." Amanda ran up the beach with a large black and white feather. "Is it an albatross?"

Steve ran the feather through his hand, smoothing it back into its tightly woven pattern. "No, I think its a cormorant feather."

"What's a cormorant?"

"It's a big bird that lives near the shore. It eats fish."

"Can I keep it?"

"Sure." But his answer was drowned out by a small boat with a big motor that came out of nowhere and buzzed into the little bay.

"Oh God, don't they know this is our beach?" Cara muttered. "Go away!" She picked up a rock and threw it in the general direction of the boat. The rock plunked harmlessly into the water a couple of feet from shore.

"What was that about anthropologists and monkeys?" Steve asked.

The driver of the boat seemed oblivious to the disruption he was causing and buzzed back and forth across the bay a dozen times before he finally tired of it and drove off around the point and out of sight and sound.

Mickey and Amanda scorned the grill Marcie had brought and opted to cook their hot dogs the traditional way, surveying each scrubby tree until they found the green branches they wanted. Along the way, they found several gull feathers, a long-lost float from a fisherman's net, and a wine bottle, empty but with the cork still in it.

"You could put a note in that bottle and send it out to sea," Steve pointed out.

Mickey's brow furrowed. "But what should we write?"

"That's up to you," Steve said. "You could say hi to all your friends."

"But how would they know?"

"You could put their names and addresses on the note and ask whoever found it to mail it to them. That's what they used to do in the old days."

"Really, Daddy?" Amanda's eyes were wide.

"That's right," Cara said, and told her the old story of The Schooner Picton, about how it disappeared except for a note in a bottle, found by a little boy in Sackett's Harbour, far across the lake.

Marcie had a notepad and a pen in her bag and tore off a sheet so they could write their note. After they dropped two hotdogs in the fire and burnt half a bag of marshmallows, they went down the beach to confer. Cara could hear the edges of their earnest conversation as she lay back on the warm stones.

"... can't write that!"

"Yeah, put that in..."

"No, we can't..."

Finally, they agreed and returned with the note wadded up tightly inside the green bottle.

"Can we put it in the water now, Mummy?" Mickey asked.

"No, not here. You need to throw it off the bluff so the current will carry it out into the lake. We'll do it when we leave."

They were exploring the marsh when the boater returned, once again roaring crazily across the bay. This time they all ran to the edge of the water and threw rocks. The boater must have seen them and divined their displeasure, because he turned abruptly and sped back around the end of the point.

As the sunny afternoon ebbed away, the wind turned cold, although Cara could detect that delicious balminess in the air that signalled the imminent arrival of summer. Reluctantly, they gathered up their bags and blankets and doused the fire. Mickey held her hand as they climbed the steep path, Cara pulling both of them up along the iron rail that ran along the side.

"We should go right to the top of the bluff," she said. "If we throw your bottle off there, the current will be sure to catch it."

'Do you think anyone will find it?" Amanda asked.

"I'm sure of it. It will probably go all the way to New York."

The edge of the bluff was crumbly rock, held together by sparse grass and the roots of scrubby bushes. They stood back a few feet, not trusting the undercut rock, which looked as if it could go plummeting into the water below at any moment. Across the horizon they could see banks of cloud forming out over the lake.

"Throw it really far out, so it won't wash back into the bay," Cara instructed. Amanda and Mickey each held an end of the bottle and on the count of three, heaved it over the cliff. It turned end over end, the low-lying afternoon sunlight glinting off it as it spun. It hit the water and sank, then bobbed up and floated slowly out in the direction of open water. They all cheered.

Mickey tugged at Cara's arm. "Mummy?" he whispered. "Do you want to know what I put in the bottle?"

"I thought it was a secret?"

"It is, but not from you!"

"Why thank you."

"I put my owl in it."

"The owl that Aunt Cass gave you?" He had worn it constantly, taking it off only in the bathtub. "I thought that was your good luck charm?"

"I told in the note that whoever found it could use it to see in the dark, so they wouldn't get lost," he said earnestly. "I don't need it anymore."

He slipped his hand into hers, and they turned to walk back along the path to the car when Steve called to them. "Look!" he said, and pointed at the clouds over the lake. For a moment, Cara couldn't see what he was pointing at, but then she realized. It was the boat that had buzzed them in the bay, or at least an image of it, riding high in the sky and upside down. It seemed to travel across the cloud bank, eerily noiseless, its transposed image charting a course through the heavens.

"What is it?" Marcie whispered.

"It's something I've heard about all my life," Cara said, "but this is the first time I've ever seen it. It's an inversion."

"How does it happen?"

"It's a mirage," Cara said, "A magical mirage."

They stood in wonder as the image traced a long arc across the sky, caught in the last rays of the setting sun. For what seemed forever, it travelled its silent and uncanny course until, at last, it reached the low horizon and in a duplicitous instant, disappeared around the edge of cloud.

THE END

66431146R00186

Made in the USA
Charleston, SC
21 January 2017